A Touch of DESTINY

A Touch of Destiny

To request permissions contact the publisher at
authornicolevelazquez@gmail.com

Cover Design: Kristin Barrett
Interior Illustrations: Clara Hernando Lavín
Developmental Editing: Danielle Harrington
Copy Editing, Line Editing and Proofreading: Shay Miranda

ISBN: 979-8-9880163-1-1 *(Paperback)*
ISBN: 979-8-9880163-2-8 *(Hardcover)*
ISBN: B0C4167NFQ *(E-Book)*

Published by Nicole Velazquez
www.authornicolevelazquez.com

TRIGGER WARNINGS

I have done my best to cover much of the potentially triggering content in this book as possible, but may have missed some. If you believe I have not listed a trigger that is worth being added, please contact me at authornicolevelazquez@gmail.com with your concern and the information so that I can consider adding it.

A Touch of Destiny will feature the following sensitive subjects:

General Content Warnings: murder, guns, constant alcohol use, attempted suicide, torture, ratphobia, claustrophobia, panic attacks, language, implied neglect, implied child trafficking, discussions of sexual assault, discussions of suicide, explosions, gore, explosions, weapons, stabbings, attempted sexual assault (off-screen), fade to black kidnapping, beheadings, hangings, forced captivity, and death.

Social Content Warnings: colorism, prejudice, racism, discussions of historical genocide, discussions of body shaming, fatphobia, mentions of slavery and colonization, and sexism.

AUTHOR'S NOTE

While A Touch of Destiny is a historical fantasy, I have depicted real aspects of Caribbean history that have affected my people, especially the indigenous cultures. I spent a long time doing the appropriate research to ensure the roots, myths, and language of my ancestors were accurately represented to you all.

A Touch of Destiny mainly takes place in Jamaica and Haiti, but it presents homage to Puerto Rico (my home) and other Caribbean islands, cultures and languages. That being said, my story mentions atrocities not only inflicted by generations past but also current ones. Genocide, racism, oppression, ignorance. They're all discussed here, and you'll see my anger surrounding those topics present as you read.

For years, Puerto Ricans have been lied to by our education system and higher-ups. We were told that we were *discovered*; savages in desperate need of saving. But that couldn't be farther from the truth and the outrageous thing is that those lies are still being taught *today*. Reaping and sowing more ignorance and thoughts of inferiority, which then get passed down.

All I have to say is that we were not discovered, we were *stolen*. We were conquered and *colonized*. Our voices were silenced, our culture was ripped from us, our language replaced. For decades, we've been told our ancestors, the Taínos, were exterminated. But they're *not*. They live on our island and within us. They are present en la gente de campo, in our food, in our stories, en nuestros *viejitos*, and music. So, it pains me to see mi gente being evicted from my homeland to make way for others who have treated us as less than. It pains me that the Puerto Rico that once existed is being destroyed piece by piece simply for money. Our culture, our language, our elders... disregarded and disrespected.

Nonetheless, money doesn't buy knowledge, it buys *ignorance* and *silence*. Money has purchased a way that forbids us from reclaiming our home, our language, our culture, further separating us from our resources and fauna. All because of greed.

Puerto Rico cannot be bought. It belongs to *our* people. Always has, always will.

A Touch of Destiny (and the series) is a love letter to Puerto Rico, my ancestors, and those who have lost their identity trying to fit into spaces where they are not welcome. May you reclaim your power... the world needs your culture and individuality.

AToD PLAYLIST

When you scan the QR code, you'll find the official A Touch of Destiny playlist. There are a total of 55 songs and they correspond with each chapter. Enjoy!

To the fearless firstborn daughters who have walked the forsaken path of darkness.

May your journey to reclaim your power inspire others to break their own chains and forge their own path.

CHAPTER
ONE

There is nothing I enjoy more than seeing a man on his knees, begging me to be merciful as his soul slowly drains from his eyes.

I examine William Pettigrew, savoring as he grows more and more unsettled. It's nice to see the damsel in distress role reversed every once in a while. Especially when the damsel is a white man. His doe-like gray eyes tear up, and I smile at his palpable fear.

I can't lie when I say I love how they squirm under my gaze, knowing they've wronged me. Knowing they've messed up beyond repair. That nothing they could say or do will change my mind.

The palm trees outside sway to the rhythm of the Caribbean breeze, the sweet aroma of mangoes lingers in the atmosphere. I grab his pointed chin, tilting his angular face toward me and kiss the tip of his freckled nose. I release him, taking out my pistol and aiming it right at his head.

His breath shudders. With his hands tied behind his back, there's no way he can fight me. He might overpower me out there, but in here? I'm the one in charge.

And as the person in charge, I want the last thing he sees to be me. My dark brown eyes, freckled, golden round-shaped face, and the smirk creeping on my lips.

"Please, Catalina, give me a second chance to make this right," he pleads, choking on his tears. *Pathetic.* His whole body quivers, letting his strong man's demeanor fade away for once.

Not so tough when there's a gun pointed at your head, huh?

"As you know, *William*, I don't give second chances, much less to men who plunder and murder *my* people. Men who steal what belongs to *me*, to *my* land. Just like *you* did," I state rigidly. I charge the weapon, not once taking it away from his forehead. He whimpers ever so slightly. Is this what true power feels like? "Today, you'll finally meet your maker."

"Catalina, don't do this. The clues will lead Edmund to you."

I laugh. Does he think I'm a neophyte?

"That's where *you* are wrong, my kind sir." I smile, caressing his face with the barrel of the pistol. He squirms, shivering. Sweat beads on his forehead. "You may have power where you come from, pero esto es el Caribe, mi vida. You're in my kingdom now." I stand up straight, pointing the pistol at his forehead once more. "Which means your naïve little brother Edmund will never know."

I shoot him, and his thick body drops to the side, his blond curls plastered to his forehead. His irrelevant Pettigrew blood oozes from his forehead onto my expensive carpets. I put away the pistol, tapping William with my foot. His lifeless gray eyes stare back at my proud, brown ones, his pale skin turning whiter by the second.

I don't look away. I don't feel remorse.

Only satisfaction.

"Cut!" the director exclaims, clapping. "That's exactly what I was looking for! Luz, baby, that was perfect! Samuel! Love it!"

Sam laughs, wiping away the red, syrupy substance from his forehead. I stay a foot away to ensure the concoction doesn't cover my powder blue 18th-century-era dress, or else my costume designer will have my head. Quickly, the crew changes the antique set for tomorrow's scenes. They'll mostly be outdoors, in the constructed village, but a few will be inside the building, saving us from the relentless Kingston, Jamaica heat and humidity.

What we film is a historical drama set in the Caribbean, showcasing the lives of aristocratic families and society scandals during the eighteenth century. They adorned the set inside with lush, tropical elements to evoke the Caribbean feel inside my home. A golden chandelier hangs above me, a wooden, ornate table with velvet covered chairs sits a few feet away from us. The curtain resembles a colorful sarong, swaying with the breeze that comes from the outside. One assistant removes the basket of mangoes, quenepas, starfruit, and papayas. Sam takes a mango from the basket before it's too late.

"You never cease to amaze me, newbie," Sam says in his standard Southern accent. A heartbeat later, his costume designer runs toward us with some rags. "Bennett needs to look out. You're comin' for his throne, aren't you?"

"I would never do that, Jones," I tease. "Oliver can keep his Broadway throne and you can keep the annoying side character throne."

"Careful, Narváez, or I'm going to report you for a hostile work environment."

I snort and he laughs, wiping all the blood away with the rags. It even got in his hair, staining it a light pink.

"You did beautifully, my love!" A cheerful voice chirps.

Oliver, the British protagonist of the show—and my boyfriend of five years—strides toward me, a boyish grin on his face. He places a gentle kiss on my lips, my heels making me nearly the same height as him. His emerald eyes land on mine, and the smell of sour candy comes from his mouth. His simple outfit of jeans and a t-shirt let me know he must've not had scenes to film today.

Lucky him.

"Ugh, romance. That, my friends, is my cue to leave," Sam states, flicking the damp rag at Oliver. "See y'all at Pierre's later tonight. Please keep the PDA to yourselves. Some of us prefer being miserable."

"How can I? Have you seen her?" Oliver asks, gesticulating.

Sam makes a train noise. "Y'all hear that? The awkward express is leavin' and I do not want to be left behind." He bows to us, holding back a laugh.

I laugh as Sam struts away with his mango. Oliver hugs me, burying his head in my brown curly hair that's tied delicately in a fancy updo. I wince, tension rising from my scalp. He releases me, apologizing quickly. A sigh of relief escapes my lips.

"We should go to the beach tomorrow. Just you and I," Oliver murmurs in my ear.

I walk over to a nearby vanity, and Oliver follows. "Trying to see me in a swimsuit?"

I watch myself in the mirror as I yank the pins out with slight tugs. My broad shoulders shift after every hastened movement. Oliver helps me, my tight dark curls falling down my back.

"Maybe. Maybe not," he jokes, winking.

"You just want to show yourself to the fans," I say, rolling my eyes. More curls rest against my back, the pressure releasing in my head. "Unfortunately, the same can't be said about me."

"Babe, I don't care about them. I care about you."

"No. You always do this." I whirl around to face him. "You're a very fit, white guy. I'm a fat, tall Puerto Rican woman. We are not the same in the eyes of the public."

He smiles, caressing my cheek. "Well, *mi amor*, that's why I don't read those articles about us. You shouldn't worry about them."

I pull back, scoffing. Here we go, again. "Easy for you to say. You're the amazing British heartthrob."

He raises his eyebrow, studying me. "And what's so wrong about being a heartthrob?"

"Nothing, Oliver. They make you the golden child of the relationship, while I'm la oveja negra. Every article about me surrounds my weight, my messy ethnic hair, or the rumors about me using you to rise to fame."

He waves my words away as if I was speaking blasphemy. "None of that is true."

Anger bubbles in me, so I turn away from him. I stare at myself in the mirror, comparing my broader frame with his. My rounded belly—reminding me of the ancient goddesses and unyielding women that were worshiped during the

Renaissance—tucked into a corset, giving the illusion of a much thinner woman. While Oliver may resemble himself, I'm hidden under fabric, made perfect for society.

"Nevermind, Oliver."

Oliver sighs. "Listen, don't let them win. I love how you look, okay?" I scoff, and he holds my face, forcing me to gaze into his emerald eyes. "Maybe I could show you how much I love that gorgeous body later." I smile and he takes this as an invitation to kiss me.

"Please stop this pervy shit before I end it all," my best friend Octavia demands as she struts toward us. She takes off her sunglasses, her smooth ebony skin glistening under the fluorescent set lights. Urging an assistant to bring us towels, her slender, blonde waist-length box braids sway behind her. Her hand grips a plastic cup, surely filled with sorrel.

"No, don't end it all before you help take this off me," I beg, turning around for her.

She places her cup on the vanity. "Just don't make any babies in front of me. I don't get paid enough for that, m'kay?" Her Haitian accent is prominent. "And I don't want to be a teenage auntie at twenty-five."

"You *don't* get paid for this, teenage godmother," Oliver reminds, stifling a laugh. He takes out the last of the hairpins, scrunching up my curls.

"Exactly. Which means I get to see your sappy love for free." She grimaces, rolling her upturned brown eyes. Huh, she chose brown contacts today. "And you love me whenever it's convenient for you, sè." *Sister.*

"You, shut up," I tease, laughing. "You." I point at Oliver. "Get me my phone. I need to check my emails."

"Wait, I need to answer this text," Oliver replies, taking out his phone instead. "Seriously? I said beige!"

As Octavia hums a song I've never heard before and releases the strings to my corset, my mind drifts to the email I'm expecting from Jessica, who works with the Smithsonian National Museum of American History. I've interned with them, worked part time, and taught courses as a volunteer in the past seven years, all while hoping for an opportunity to work full time. Plus, they promised me the role.

I enjoy acting, but I think these last six years of being an actress have been way too stressful for my liking. Tabloids, rumors, hate mail, endless jetlag and get-togethers with predatory celebrities. Even having to use my parkour skills to get away from the press. So, when they opened up a position and encouraged me to apply, I didn't hesitate to put in the application to continue working in the place I love most. I want to continue my research, and get my doctorate in history. By doing this, I can also have a more stable life away from the spotlight.

I hate that my destiny is in their hands.

I fidget with my ruby necklace—a delicate thing, sharp around the edges—as Octavia helps undress me. It was my inheritance after my grandmother died when I was sixteen.

When I was younger, Mami Julia would tell me how the strong women in our lineage held onto the intricate jewel for over two centuries. No one in the family is sure if her words were true, but we never believed otherwise. Another curious detail about my heirloom... they have only passed it down to every woman in the family. *Not* the men.

Mami Julia had two sons, my uncle and my father, who also had boys as firstborns. I was the first daughter and granddaughter born, so the necklace passed to me. While it's hard to trace our gut-wrenching history on paper because of slavery, separation of families, colonization, and genocide, this necklace is proof my female ancestors persevered and overcame every challenge life and our oppressors threw at them.

It's my hope to be as strong as them someday.

"Why would they put a million layers on you?" Octavia complains behind me, unzipping my dress. She groans loudly. "This is taking *forever.*"

"Why didn't you let the actual costume designer take over then?" I ask, rolling my eyes.

She brings her head next to mine. "And let them ruin this beauty of a dress? No, no. This is silk. Adhira is rough. This needs to be treated with *respect.*" She runs a hand through my sleeve. "Plus, Oliver was busy with three ominous phone calls. He wasn't willing to entertain me."

Oliver fidgets with the charm hanging from his phone, avoiding eye contact with me and Octavia.

"Mysterious?" I ask. "Don't tell me you're sneaking off again. We had a talk about how this makes me feel."

"Luz..." His phone goes off again, and he steps away, reluctantly taking it.

I give Octavia a look, unconvinced, and she glances back.

Octavia continues helping me out of this monstrosity of a dress, while Oliver speaks in a hushed tone. Layers upon layers of blue fabric engulf me, making me feel like an antique doll at a window display. I watch myself in the vanity mirror, studying the body I consider my sacred temple. The fabric hugs my curves and hides my plush form, making me more socially acceptable to society. The corsets push up on my chest, bringing the illusion of fuller, rounder breasts that are the object of desire for many men. My strong, thick legs and calves hide underneath the soft linen.

While most hate my appearance, I love it. It's mine. It's a reminder of the strong women that came before me. Women who survived famine, genocide, slavery, oppression, and sickness.

"And I specifically told you to text me. What part of no calls did you not understand?" Oliver demands, hanging up. He goes back to texting, his thumbs racing each other in an imaginary marathon. He's as attached to that phone as Octavia is to her crystals and tarot cards.

"We're almost done, okay?" Octavia reassures.

My phone goes off nearby, the instrumental pirate music filling the air. Oliver goes to it and informs me it's *Museum Jessica*. My heart drops. No. *Not right now.* Out of all the times she could've possibly called. I shift my weight from leg to leg, knowing I can't do anything until they help me take off my clothing. This process can't be rushed to avoid the fabrics getting stained, ripped or crumpled.

Once Octavia pulls it off of me, I run toward Oliver in my undergarments but it's too late. The call has finished.

"Why didn't you answer it?" I shriek, yanking the phone from his rough fingers. I call her back, getting an answering machine instead. I leave a voicemail, my nerves eating at me from the inside.

"I'm sorry," he apologizes. "What was I—"

"¡Cómo no es tu otra novia!"

"Luz, what other girlfriend? What are you—"

"You know exactly what I'm talking abo—"

"Maybe they'll leave a voicemail," Octavia intervenes, rubbing my shoulders. Oliver averts his eyes, fidgeting with his fingers. "Relax, okay? You'll know soon enough, I'm sure of it. Maybe I can consult the cards for you tonight."

I chuckle, rolling my eyes. I ignore Oliver. "I respect what you do as an astrologer, but I don't think the cards will tell me anything." She side-eyes me, pursing her lips. I sigh. I'm saying the wrong things right now. "I've simply got so much riding on this job. Everything has to be *perfect.*"

She raises her eyebrow, tilting her head ever-so-slightly. "Why? Are you trying to prove something to others?"

Obviously this job is for me. Not because I have something to prove to my family. Especially not my brother, *Dr. Narváez.*

They wouldn't think he's so perfect if they knew he had to sleep his way through his bachelor's degree. The irony of the situation is not lost on me.

Without answering her, I head off to wash my face, my heart pounding inside my chest. Octavia and Oliver follow, the cold water waking me up.

"You know what you need?" Octavia asks as I dry my face with a towel, the rough cotton scratching my skin. "Food, those weird pirate movies you like, and a card reading."

I fling the towel onto my shoulder. "I can't go out dressed like this."

"Oliver, get the woman her clothes, don't just stand there."

His watch goes off and he laughs nervously, his eyes darting everywhere. A few strands of his blond hair fall on his blushing forehead.

"I... I actually have an appointment. I completely forgot about it," he stammers, pushing his hair back. "I'll see you guys at Pierre's later."

I raise an eyebrow, gripping his wrist. "First the calls, then the texts, and now this? Where could you possibly be going *this time?*" He takes a deep breath, and my anger from earlier rises.

"He's going to get his hair done, Narváez, haven't ya heard?" Sam says, approaching us with a soda in hand. "Those golden locks don't maintain themselves."

I release his wrist, crossing my arms and scoffing. *Unbelievable.*

"I'm sorry. I have to go," Oliver apologizes, kissing my cheek.

An appointment. At five pm. On a Friday. He never mentioned any appointments for today. Yet here he is saying he has one. I've never been the jealous type, however, my nerves have been on an uptick with all the secret escapades he's been having alone. I try to not think too much about it, but I'm Puerto Rican, and my Latina senses are tingling.

"Sam!" Oliver calls out.

"Sorry ladies, His Royal Highness calls," Sam curtsies and jogs to Oliver.

Octavia places her hands on her hips. "Whatever. Who needs men anyway? It's Oliver. If he's doing something he's not supposed to, we'll know soon enough thanks to the press," she says. "Let's have a girls' night. No men allowed."

I laugh. "You're certain?" She smirks, resting her head on my shoulder. Her citrus, floral fragrance travels upward to my sinuses.

"If the man was cheating on you, we'd know. For someone who acts for a living, he's a horrible liar." She laughs. "Let's go. We can watch that movie with your favorite real life pirates that only weird history geeks love."

"Listen. Not all history geeks love pirates. That's just me."

"You only love them because they're portrayed by hot actors, don't you?" I shake my head, grabbing my bag. "What were the pirates' names in real life? Lucas something? Sullivan Edwardson?" She releases me, grabbing her sunglasses.

"Lucas Córdova, the Spanish pirate captain, and the other was Sullivan Edwards, a Creole pirate captain. Put some respect on their names."

"My apologies. But, let's forget that the boys exist for the rest of the evening, okay?" she suggests, toasting with her remaining sorrel. "Men ain't shit."

"Fine, let's just leave."

Taking a few wrapped sandwiches from a basket, we head toward her hotel room, where she insists on cleansing my energy with incense before giving me a thorough card reading, like the one she gives to her clients.

I just let her do as she pleases. Whatever comes out, I'm the holder of my own destiny. The cards don't tell me what to do and even if they did, they'd tell me I'm destined for the job.

I'm sure of it.

Luz

CHAPTER
TWO

I've always believed fate is our number one enemy. Growing up, Mami Julia would tell me everyone's fate is predetermined at birth. Barely one minute old and there's a path already carved for you. Signed, sealed, and decided. In Mami Julia's case, it looks like it was her fate to die of cancer. To have her life cut abruptly short by the illness invading her body. That's why I prefer the term destiny instead. It is not written, not signed, but uncertain, waiting to be shaped into the reality one wishes.

That's what I like about history. While our interpretation of history fluctuates, past events can't be undone. They're set in stone, and while atrocious, they can't be twisted into what anyone wishes them to be.

They simply are.

"Please leave a message..."

I am sent straight to voicemail for the fifth time in less than twenty-four hours. Of course I do. It's Saturday. There's no one in the office. I throw my phone onto the table, groaning.

It's no help that I've been feeling nauseous all day. It's either the stress from the call or Oliver's behavior. I take deep breaths as I study my pallid face in the mirror in front of me. With trembling fingers, I remove two Adderall pills from their container, place them in my mouth and swallow with water. I have to confront Oliver about how I no longer feel safe with him, and this time, he better listen to me.

"The call will come when it comes, Luz," I tell myself, sighing.

My phone rings, and I run back to it. It's Abel Narváez, my older brother.

"Sea la madre del diablo..."

I let the call go straight to voicemail. The last thing I need to do is listen to the taunting voice of el niño de oro in real time. *Ding!* I play his message. His tense, deep voice sounds as if he was reading from a building manual.

Mira, te estoy llamando to let you know I can't take care of Sole for the next two weeks. I have a... work convention. Um... yeah. Anyway, well, since my layover is in Kingston tomorrow and you're there, I'm sending Soledad your way 'til I get back from my important things. M'kay, thanks, bye.

Of course. He needs his built-in babysitter.

Grabbing my bag with my items and phone, I leave my trailer, seeing a reddened Oliver waiting for me, phone in hand once again. He leans against a palm tree, hiding from the harsh Jamaican sun and heat. The clacking of my shoes against the concrete announces my arrival, instead of becoming a hermit. Just like one card that came out yesterday for me. The hermit, the devil, the chariot, the strength, the lovers, and the death cards. Octavia informed me that change and transformation are coming. I hope it means I get the job.

"Hey, beautiful, hiding again?" Oliver asks, smiling.

His bright emerald eyes twinkle in the sunlight, his short wavy hair sweeps over his forehead. His British militia outfit—red, black and ironed—complements my ensemble of a scarlet 18th-century-dress and ruby necklace.

I approach him, my stomach churning. He couldn't have been waiting for me for longer than ten minutes. Knowing him, he probably snuck off.

He puts his phone away and joins my side, his heavy arm draped around my waist. I tense up, discreetly inching away from his touch. *He better not be cheating on me...* He studies my face, his gaze refusing to leave mine. He's never been the best at guessing what I'm feeling. He's not very good at listening... or understanding my emotions.

We pass a variety of people. Production designers making sure everything is perfect, set decorators putting the finishing touches on the outside structures, and members of the craft service passing out food and water to some of the set builders. A few locals take pictures and videos as Sam hangs out with them, conversing as if he were at a family function. Two white women throw themselves at him, but he pushes them off, loyal to Octavia.

The gentle breeze causes the palm leaves to dance with the wind, the ocean waves crashing from a distance. Being here reminds me of home. Not Pennsylvania, but Puerto Rico, where I was born and raised.

"Oliver," I say, my mind made up. "We have to talk and I don't want to keep—"

"Mwen sèmante mwen pral touye ou!" *I will kill you,* Octavia shrieks, an espresso in her hand. Her waist-length braids sway from side to side as she approaches. "Where have you been and why have you been ignoring my texts? I thought you left Jamaica without me."

"I was in my dressing room, Miss Guillebeaux, not on a plane headed to Iceland." I put my arm around her waist, separating myself completely from Oliver. Her contacts are gray today. "And maybe not Iceland. I was thinking more of Paris."

"Aren't your grandparents French, Oliver?" She asks, changing the topic.

"Ah, Paris, ville lumière, et amour," he sighs romantically with a mock French accent. All these lessons and he still can't get words right. "But yes. Don't tell them my French sucks, please. They'd be so disgraced by me."

"Oh no, we wouldn't want our golden boy in trouble with those who love him, would we?" I taunt, an edge on my voice.

He raises an eyebrow, his nose scrunching up. "What's that supposed to mean?"

I stop walking, glaring at him. "You know *exactly* what that's supposed to mean, Oliver."

"Hey! The set!" Octavia interjects laughing awkwardly. "How pretty."

Oliver sighs, crossing his arms. "Well, I can't read minds, Luz."

I scoff, grimacing. "Or emotions, by the looks of it. But let it be a text from—"

"So, that new scene today, huh?" Octavia intervenes once more.

I storm off ahead, into the constructed village where our outdoor scenes will be filmed today.

Octavia asks Oliver about the upcoming scenes, trying to diffuse the tension between us, but my mind keeps drifting to the call the Smithsonian gave yesterday. They said my being an actress wouldn't interfere with their decision, and I've repeatedly reassured them that filming for Sins of Montenegro around late December. What if they think this won't work out because of my lack of availability? Because I failed to cater to them for five minutes?

I can't botch this job. It's my way out.

Without it, I'm stuck in this life.

Forever drowning by the current of hate and never-ending rumors that surround my livelihood.

Loud voices jar me out of my thoughts. Some of the press has snuck through the security barriers and bombard us with questions, especially Oliver. Questions regarding the filming of the show, our five-year relationship, and even a pregnancy rumor that was started by a random Hollywood magazine. Because of my weight.

Lately, dealing with the press has become tedious to the point of me avoiding outings altogether. Especially family outings. When I first began acting at a small scale, I wasn't cornered like this nor did I have to run away from them. I wasn't very well known yet, so I didn't have a need for bodyguards—I could simply parkour elsewhere. I miss the anonymity that came with having a normal life. Which is why I need that job. It won't give me anonymity, but I'll have a less stressful career... away from everyone. Including my overbearing mother and stuck-up brother.

Oliver's security detail finally appears—took them long enough—and chases away the press so I relax, letting Oliver's hand guide me through the set. I'll deal with him later.

Shabby exteriors of wood and clay are lined up down the village. The extras await at their places, some using the scripts and paper fans to brush off the unbearable heat. The smell of freshly brewed coffee and fried fish fill my senses, making me crave the traditional Jamaican food instead of the endless sandwiches provided for us.

"Looking forward to your slap, I'll cherish it forever," Oliver fangirls, pulling me into a hug. Octavia gags and walks off to the costume design section.

"If you have no more *appointments*, let's talk after we finish, okay?" I suggest. He nods, pushing his hair back, and we split up to our specific areas.

The assistant director pulls me aside for a last look. Veronica, the director, arrives, brushing everyone off.

"She's perfect. Leave her be before I lose my patience," Veronica yells, exasperated. The assistant director yells for everyone to be quiet on set. Crew and actors all scramble to their spots. Veronica sighs and collects herself. "Action!"

As the scene progresses and I slap Oliver's character, Edmund, for stepping out of line, I wonder what the call from yesterday encompassed.

I have all the things they asked for.

Experience in the history field, references from the senior staff, and research papers I've made for them. I don't believe in all that superstitious stuff, but it's my destiny to go there.

I have to make my family proud of me. This will definitely do that.

After a few takes, we're officially done for the weekend. Dusk is showing, signaling the end of a long and tedious day. I remove my shoes and change into my white sneakers, my feet feeling as if I was standing on a cloud after hours of wearing heels. I grab my smart watch and check for messages. Thankfully, none from my family, and unfortunately none from the Smithsonian. I take my dark brown curls out of their delicate yet infernal updo and my head aches from the pins.

Finally, I've somewhat morphed back into myself. Into Luz Narváez. Kind of, considering that I'm still wearing the red dress. I'm too hungry to take it off.

Oliver approaches me with a disheveled appearance, and hugs me. My body recoils under his embrace automatically. Octavia joins us with an overly eager Sam, both of whom are giggling.

"What a magnificent scene. I felt your anger," she says, pulling me into a hug. "I wanted to slap Oliver, too. Actually I should, considering he's been acting—"

"Come on, babe, give the man some slack," Sam interrupts, a boyish grin on his lips. "If he was hiding something, we'd know, right?"

Oliver chuckles, pushing the strands of his hair back. Something he does to show he's nervous. "I was told I'm not a great liar," Oliver replies, putting his arm around my waist while shooting a look at Octavia. "So, yes, you'd know."

"Guys. Let's just go eat. Please?" I beg, holding my stomach. "If I wait any longer, I'm resorting to cannibalism, and I'm eating whoever is closest to me."

"Let's go, y'all. I'm too attractive to be eaten," Octavia teases, interlacing her fingers with Sam's. She whips out a paper fan with her right hand from her purse, fanning herself.

Laughing, we walk toward whatever food place is closest.

"Wait, Oliver, where's Tony?" I ask, halting. At six-foot-four with a body that looks like they made it in a laboratory, no one would dare mess with Oliver's bodyguard Tony.

"We should be fine. It won't take longer than thirty minutes," Oliver replies. "He said he was on his way. But if you're worried, Sam and I are here, and we won't let anything happen." He takes my hand in his, caressing it reassuringly.

"Ah yes, my heroes against evil."

"You know it, baby!" Sam whoops.

We leave the set, the cool night breeze calming down our hot flashes. Lamp posts turn on automatically, and the

Kingston nightlife has begun. Reggae blasts from the bars and restaurants filled to the brim with tourists. The smell of fried fish, jerk chicken, and plantain fills my sinuses, making me salivate.

"There they are!" A voice yells from one restaurant. *Great.* Just what I needed. "Mr. Bennett! Miss Narváez! Mr. Jones!"

The press corners us in front of a small pub. I glance away, preventing them from getting a clear shot of me. Oliver shields me with his body, using his phone's flashlight to ruin their photos. Octavia curses at them in Creole, bringing up her fan to her face, and Sam tries to make a path for us, yelling at them.

On his way, my ass.

What kind of bodyguard are you if you're not going to guard this man?

"Oliver! Oliver! Sources say they saw you on a secret excursion with a red-haired woman yesterday in a jewelry store. Is she your mistress?" a woman asks and the rest call his name. *Mistress?*

"Luz! Can you confirm the pregnancy rumors?" a man asks, shoving his phone in my face. I push it away, exasperation rising in me. Not only because of the repetitive pregnancy rumor, but because of what they revealed about Oliver, whose face is the shade of my dress. He shuts off the flashlight, his mouth wide open.

Oliver, I swear to God...

My watch vibrates, distracting me. It's an email. From Jessica, the hiring manager at the Smithsonian. As I try to click on it, Oliver grabs my hand and smiles, drawing my attention to him. I raise my eyebrow, my anger declining while my suspicion rises. I try to catch what my email says. So far I can only see *Dear Luisa Narváez García.*

"What are you doing?" I ask and skimmed the first few sentences on my watch's screen. The nausea from earlier makes a reappearance.

> Unfortunately, we have decided to move forward in choosing a more qualified and reliable candidate for this role. While we had guaranteed a spot for you, ultimately we decided that the latest rumors surrounding your public presence wouldn't be appropriate for our family and what we stand for. We understand this may come as a disappointment to you and encourage you to continue your volunteer work with us.

Forget the woman he was with. Who cares about her?

"I have to talk to you. It's important," I plead.

They rejected me.

My world shatters, and my chest physically aches. My knees weaken by the second, the environment turning hotter. The wind picks up, thunder rumbling above us. Rejected. Never in a thousand years did I see this coming. Not once. Especially since it was a role specifically opened for *me*.

"Oliver, can we please go? I got an em—"

"I have to tell you something important as well," Oliver says, grinning.

Tears threaten to escape my eyes, but he doesn't notice my inner turmoil. He's too wrapped up in his own head. The flash of the cameras and scattered voices take away his focus from me. I'm being pulled out to sea. Drowning. Engulfed by waves and sea foam.

Please, for once, listen to me.

"Luz, my whole life has been full of theatrics. I've never had the chance to be myself. Not truly. Until I met you," he confesses, and everyone quiets down. You can hear a pin drop.

Or my racing heart. "With you, I'm whole. I can be myself. I love the way you are, the way you think. Your love for history. I love you. I've always loved you and will always love you."

Getting down on one knee, he pulls out a red velvet box from his pocket. More thunder above us. The wind stops, creating an eerily still environment.

No.

Gasps. Camera flashes going off. My eyes dart around, overwhelmed. Sam covers his mouth and Octavia grips his shoulder, her acrylic nails digging into his skin.

It can't be.

We haven't spoken much about this, but he knows enough to know that I hate people in my private business.

My heart rate increases and my hands get clammy. The air thins around me and a tear trails down my cheek.

This is *not* how I imagined a marriage proposal.

"Luisa Karina Narváez García. Will you marry me?" he asks, looking through his lashes at me.

As Oliver holds one of my hands, the email from the hiring manager flashes on my watch. A heart-wrenching rejection. A public proposal.

Will you marry me? Frankly... I don't know if I can.

Rain pours over us at once. Scattering the press away like rats.

Confused, angry, and frustrated at those who promised me this role, at Oliver, at my future that has gone down the drain, at the fact that I *failed,* I pull away from the man who is supposed to know me best and run to the darkened bay. The thunderous reactions drown out his call for me.

CHAPTER

THREE

My heart feels exactly like the weather. Gloomy. Ravenous.

I reach the beach, away from the press, from Oliver, from everyone.

Lightheaded, I cling to a nearby lamppost, sobbing and screaming. My throat burns and I cough viciously to moisten it. *This is all his fault*, I think, *Oliver did this.*

The sun slowly sets on the horizon. The slanting rays create swirls of pink and dark orange in the gray sky, making the flowing water glisten. If it wasn't for the beautiful beige string lights and lampposts, I wouldn't be able to see much. It looks like an event happened, as there was an abandoned table with a ruined hibiscus centerpiece.

I can hear the commotion through the scattered sound of rain and cicadas. I wander away from the pole, my hands shaking, and I want nothing more than to disappear. I pass a small dock with three stationed yachts; the waves hit against their hollow hulls.

A loud whistle goes off and a gunshot, along with screams.

Oliver's bodyguard probably arrived at the scene.

I plop myself down on the wet sand, bring my knees to my chest, and cry. I cry for my botched future. Oliver's proposal. About the fact I tried so hard to gain control of my life but once again failed.

Without that job, who will I be? Will I continue being a pawn in my own life?

I read the email carefully from my phone and apparently, my spot on the program will be given to a more *reliable* candidate who has worked with them as well. Someone who is there on-call and able to bring a positive, calm environment to the workplace. I shove my phone in my pocket and continue crying. Thunder cracks over me as my heart breaks more.

This is all my fault. I shouldn't have become so obsessed with a future at the museum and away from the hate. I should have lowered my expectations. I should have known I would not get the job. Instead, I held on to a bit of hope, and that optimism hurt me. This is why I don't do things like this and stay in my lane.

It's safe in my comfort zone.

I've become so consumed with the job that now I don't know how I'll tell my family, especially my mother. I can already see the disappointment in her eyes, and hear the comparisons between me and Abel. My perfectly perfect older brother who can do no wrong.

"At your age, Abel was balancing being a father and being in a PhD program!"

The impending comparison with Abel Narváez García makes my chest hurt so I watch the tempestuous ocean to calm my nerves down. While I've always hated being on the ocean, there's something entrancing about it that reminds me of my deceased grandmother.

It's all because of her urban legends regarding the Aycayias, the mythical sirens of the Taínos in the Caribbean, especially Puerto Rico. She'd exaggerate their stories, their myth, scaring even herself, claiming they would roam the seas, waiting for their next victim. Apparently, they would only kill men, but I'm not willing to prove the theory.

The rain calms all around me. My inhales shiver, lessening the air in my lungs. I can't let anyone see me like this.

Sloshing footsteps wake me out of my negative thoughts. Oliver approaches me, and I stand up. His flushed beige complexion takes the shade of my dress, and his eyes scan our surroundings. His blond hair is plastered to his forehead, his clothes see-through.

"Luz," Oliver says, but I step back, putting an obvious distance between us.

"I have nothing to say to you, Bennett," I snarl and face the ocean. My anger returns, replacing my harmful and self-critical thoughts. Thunder cracks in sky above us, startling us both.

"Then please just listen, I never meant to hurt you. I—"

"I didn't get the job, Oliver. I got the email as you publicly proposed to me." I cross my arms, my tone getting harsher. Wind picks up around us once more, threatening to throw me off balance. "What the hell was that? A publicity stunt? An ego boost?"

Oliver's face registers my pain, and his entire demeanor changes. He kicks some sand away and pushes his hair back. He holds his hands behind his neck, muttering to himself. His eyebrows are so creased together it could be a unibrow.

"Oh Luz, I'm so sorry. No, it wasn't like that. I was going to propose tonight," he admits, pointing at the table that sits abandoned. "That was for us but the filming ran behind, and everyone had to leave, so I hesitated and I didn't know what to do… I should've thought this through. I really am sorry." He looks at his fingers, interlacing them together. "My next idea was to propose publicly so they could leave us alone, but I didn't realize it would only mess everything up."

"Well, no SHIT! Now they'll be talking about me declining your proposal. Don't you understand? I'm always the target of rumors and hate in our relationship. It's always me. *Oh, Oliver is dating Luz Narváez? Must be for pity! Who knew Oliver Bennett wanted some of that spicy Latina magic! Too bad it's from HER!*"

My knees give out and I sob out of rage on the sand. The rain ceases, its remnants falling dripping from the palm trees. Oliver sits next to me and tries to hold me, but I push him away. I've had enough of him and his ignorance.

"I'm so sorry. I wish I could make this up to you. I should've listened to you. I shoul—"

"No. I've had enough Oliver. This isn't the first time you've ignored my feelings, and you know what? I'm done."

He gasps, the color washing away from his face. "What are you saying?"

I stifle a sob. The salted gale returns, my wet hair thrashing violently behind me. "I'm saying that we are done. I can't do this anymore. I can't continue being with someone so careless, so ignorant! Someone so blinded by the lights that they care more about their image than me!" I wipe my tears, more trailing down in their place.

His lip trembles, his eyes watery. "Luz. You can't mean that. You're—"

I stand, my throat tightening. "Stop telling me how I feel! I know what I'm saying and I want you to leave! It's over!"

A sharp pain shoots upward from my abdomen, and I wince, holding my stomach. The pain is so intense that I fall, Oliver grabbing me.

"Are you okay?" he asks, his eyes bloodshot.

"It doesn't matter," I wince. "Take your hands off of me."

He gets to his knees, grabbing my hands. My entire abdomen throbs, the pain dispersing. "Please. Let me make this up to you. I'll give you everything you deserve and more. I love you, Luz."

I glare at him, disgust in my body. Just like the scene I filmed with Sam yesterday. I pull my arms away, ignoring the stabbing sensation. "Perhaps I loved you once, but that love I felt is gone. I've given you plenty of chances, Oliver, but you've disappointed me in the way I disappoint my family. I don't need you to be there for me. Leave."

He sucks in his breath and stands, hurt registering in his eyes. He's going to break. My heart aches for him, and longs for me to be in his arms. Am I making a mistake? *No.* I'm better off alone.

"You are not a failure or disappointment, Luisa Narváez García. I admire you and I will never stop loving you. I'm proud of you," he whimpers, his down-turned green eyes gazing into mine. "Whenever you are ready to talk, my door is always open. I'm really sorry about everything."

With that, he caresses my cheek and heads off, his shoulders slumped forward, his feet dragging in the wet sand.

Rain prickles my skin as faraway thunder weakly roars in the darkening skies.

The night sky has finally settled on the horizon, darkness devouring my surroundings and my heart. The cicadas begin their synchronized song, competing with the crashing waves and sprinkling rain on the bahia.

My phone goes off. It's Abel. Surely to call and confirm I'm still taking care of my niece tomorrow while he goes and parties for two weeks. Various missed calls and texts from my family pop up on the screen, all regarding the engagement news from the press. First, I check out the ones from my cousins, and even my niece.

Nico: Al blanquito le gusto nuestro sazón parece, LMAOOtellhimtopayoffmystudentloansbefo reyouofficiallybreakupOOO

Gabbie: Acho, no me digas que dijiste que no!

Fernando: Mira nena, is it true?

Sole: **Tití! You said no? OMG! Also, can I have jerk chicken tomorrow? Thanks! :)**

I ignore those to tackle the two most out-of-pocket messages from the people I stand the least...

Mom: **This is the perfect age for marriage. Say yes to him. It's rare for a woman with your appearance to receive love. Think of the family. Think of me.**

Luz: **thanks, Mom.**

Abel: **Can you pay for Sole's taxi tomorrow? I'm low on cash.**

Luz: **sure, whatever, mister neurofuckingscientist. Next time, te vendes en la esquina.**

More calls. More texts. I ignore them. I don't want to deal with their crap right now. I even see a notification with the headline *Luz Bennett? I think NOT!* With a video of me running off and Oliver being left with the ring in hand. Frustrated, I shove my phone deep into my pocket and remove my watch from my wrist, throwing it on the sand. I don't care if someone finds it. Let them have it.

I drag myself to the dock, the rain a soft caress against my skin. The air has turned cool; the wind turned to a gentle breeze. Everything that could've gone wrong, went wrong. And no one seems to give a damn.

Defeated, I sit on the edge of the pier, next to an old, rusty ladder. I face the ocean and the darkened sky, feeling ashamed, alone, and betrayed. Not knowing what else to do, I cry for this sudden twist my life has taken. For Mami Julia, whom I wish was here with me to help me cope with everything. While I have a love-hate relationship with my mother, only my grandmother truly understood me. My goals, my desires, my struggles. I was *enough* for her.

It's been around eight years since her death, but it still feels as if it was yesterday. I bring my hand to my necklace, my fingers tightening around it. I think of her and only her.

"Mami Julia, I miss you. Ayúdame. Guide me. What's next for me?" I sob. "I hope you're not disappointed in me like the rest of the family must be."

There's a hole in my chest. I don't want to fail my family. I want them to be proud of me, but how can they be proud of the girl who never does enough despite trying her hardest?

With the darkness matching my mood, I sniffle, feeling more alone than I've ever felt. My feet dangle above the water, the waves softly crashing against the wood, their soothing rhythm calling to me. Part of me wants to walk into the ocean and never resurface. The only person who would miss me is dead. The other part of me wants to go scream at everyone I encounter, releasing my anger on them.

This can't be my life.

I let my necklace fall to my collarbone, distraught. I need to head back before the drama gets too out of bounds. Out of the corner of my eye, the jewel in the necklace—usually a dark scarlet—faintly shines.

What the...

Taking it into my hands once more, the fiery red light pulsates, as if it were a beating heart instead of a lifeless antique rock. With each beat, the glow increases, but my adrenaline diminishes.

Faint, beautiful voices surround me. The hairs on the back of my neck stand, goosebumps filling my arms. I glance around, seeing if there's someone nearby speaking to me. There's no one. More murmurs in a language I can't understand consume me, along with a sense of desire and longing. My eyelids grow heavy, the sounds of nature vanish. Nothing else matters. Just the ethereal lullaby being carried by the Jamaican breeze.

The throbbing light grows stronger by the second, and I'm drawn to it, like a moth to a flame. The more it shines, the more I lose focus of reality. Of who I am. The haunting melody grows and I lose in this never-ending sea of mesmerizing whispers. My heart beats along with it, yearning to find this ominous call.

I want nothing more than to go to it.

A slithering touch on my ankle startles me, waking me from my trance.

The next thing I know, I'm pulled by my ankles into the gloomy seawater. I scream and try to place my feet on the bottom of the ocean, assuming it's shallow, but it's much deeper than I expected. With my dress absorbing the water like a sponge, I attempt to pull myself up with the rotting rails, but they disintegrate in my hands.

The sea suffocates me, the tide and waves crashing with such force that they push me under every time I bring my head up. I thrash while gasping for air, water entering my lungs viciously. A red, fiery substance spills into the ocean, the same color as my necklace and dress. One thought comes to mind. I'm dying. This is my blood reflected by the moonlight. This is it. This is the end for me. All those swimming lessons for naught.

Nothing helps to keep me afloat. I struggle ferociously, fighting off invisible demons. The coldness of it enters my throat and lungs, gagging me. I descend deeper and deeper, darkness engulfing me in its menacing shadows.

Even through all this tenebrosity, my blood encompasses me, bringing a subtle warmth to my entire body. I'm losing this fight. I can feel it. So I give up, allowing the depths to swallow me whole and make me another piece of their ecosystem.

CHAPTER
FOUR

I cough up water, its violent escape burning my throat. I'm on the edge of the shore, the waves crashing on my feet. I don't know how I got here or how long I've been knocked out, but I'm grateful to be alive. Laughing and physically exhausted, I slowly stand, the weight of my drenched dress pulling me downward. My curls cling to my face and neck. My mouth tastes of salt and sand. My sneakers are utterly soaked and uncomfortable.

It's like there's wet concrete all over my body.

I take out my phone, thankful it's waterproof and... Three hours have passed. Oh my God, three hours? And no one came looking for me? Not even Octavia? Something's up. I use my phone's flashlight to guide my way, squinting through the darkness toward the shining lights ahead. Testing my balance, the set-up from earlier is no longer there. The beach is solitary. My shoes make noise with every step I take, absorbing sand through the laces' opening.

The hair on the back of my neck spikes up. Something's changed.

The air feels different now. Less polluted. The environment feels more genuine, and antique. The set has been transformed. Probably the designers setting up for tomorrow's scenes. The buildings are a mixture of genuine brick and wood, their structures resembling churches and inns. Very unlike the clay, plaster, and drywall previously used.

"El collar," I gasp, stopping dead in the middle of the lantern-lit road. I throw my phone into my pocket, grabbing my necklace instead.

I check the jewel, expecting to see it glowing, but its color has gone back to the common dark red. Damn it, I missed my chance to investigate. It was probably the moonlight reflecting down on it.

But what explains the mysterious, ethereal whispers that enchanted me? Those beautiful voices that made me forget my worries, my problems, even my name. It must've been the same thing that grabbed me by my ankles and pulled me into the sea.

Or was I simply imagining everything?

I reach the set, my sneakers slosh as they're pressed against the ground, announcing to everyone that I've arrived. The heat is unbearable, but it's drying my dress. My hair is a worry. The clinging humidity is doing its job. A few people stare at me, their expressions ranging from wonder to fear to even disgust. An older white man spits my way unprovoked. I keep my emotions in check because if I were to call him out, I'd be the villain in this situation.

Ignoring him, I pass a small corral, full of pigs, mud, and hay. Previously not there before. A horse-drawn carriage with a footman rushes by me, and the white couple inside throw bones at me. I look down, not touching the trash as their echoing laughter roars behind me.

"Move, girl, before yer killed," a second white man barks at me, pushing me with his horse. He, too, laughs as I land on a pile of mud, my dress ruined.

My costume designer is *not* letting me see my twenty-fourth winter for ruining her dress. Where did all of this come from? This harshness? Are they filming a new scene and I got in the way?

None of that merits all this negativity.

I stand, wiping the mud off of me. I try to call Oliver, but I have no service. *Of course.* I put the useless thing away, beginning to feel like I'm getting lost in this set.

Where's the press trying to eat me alive?

Where are the others?

I keep wandering across the village. I pass a pub bursting with laughter, drunken accusations, and the sour smell of liquor. Standing near a window, Oliver cackles with a bottle in hand. He's now wearing a black long coat, a beige shirt, and pants. I grimace. Who wears a coat in *Jamaica*?

He's surrounded by men dressed similarly to him, their coats a Navy blue with gold embellishments. He's laughing with the boys and enjoying life as if I haven't been gone for three hours. As if I didn't break up with him.

A sense of longing overpowers me, and I want to take back everything I ever said.

"We need to talk about what happened earlier," I say as I approach him.

"I beg your pardon?" Oliver asks, turning his head to face me. His voice sounds different. Deeper. More menacing. No matter. I reach out and hug him and he tenses up with my touch. The men quiet down.

I release him. "I'm sorry about the break-up. I didn't mean to. I was angry and took it out on you."

His brows scrunch together, and his hair is a tad longer, enough to be in a ponytail, just like the wig and extensions he wears for the show. The three men that accompany him eye me curiously, eager to see what happens next. They don't look familiar. Where's Sam? Where's Octavia? Tony?

"Lads, who knew we'd stumble upon a whore tonight." *Whore?* He grabs my waist and pulls me closer, a devilish grin on his face. "Tell me, my dear, can you take all of us at once?"

The three men laugh at the comment. Oliver licks his lips, lust in his eyes. I get loose from his grip, anger bubbling in me. Not once has he spoken to me like this. It must be whatever he's drinking. He drinks from his cup, eyeing my entire body. Chills run through me. Something's off.

"What in the hell is wrong with you? How many drinks did you have?" I exclaim.

Oliver laughs at me, dismissing my concerns, and tries to plant a kiss on my lips, but I shove him with force. He stumbles but doesn't lose his balance. I step back, my mouth wide open. I've never used physical aggression with anyone, especially not *him.*

Dear God... I'm turning into my brother.

Oliver raises his hand and slaps me. My cheek stings as blood rushes to it. I bring my hand up to my face, protectively, as a fight-or-flight response. Under no circumstance has he hit me, not even while under the influence of alcohol.

His expression turns dark. No longer does he tease me. He's like a completely different person.

He grips my plush arms, shaking me as if I was a rag doll. "I don't know who you believe you are, but you best not lay another finger on me," he growls.

He pushes me on the ground, and a choked sound escapes my lips. Pain spasms up my arms as I gape at him, a cold sweat running down my lower back.

"What's gotten into you?" I find his eyes so he can face me, and for the first time, I look at them clearly. The light from the lantern above us allows me to see that they're a light shade of azure.

Oliver's eyes are not blue.

He squats in front of me, smirking. "No, my dear, the question is, who are *you* to speak like that to an Admiral of the Royal Navy. Mixed breeds like you, especially the bitches, need to be dealt with accordingly."

Mixed breeds? Bitches? Royal Navy?

The environment inside the pub continues its lively course, while the outside with the four of us has turned as cold as ice. The men with Oliver encourage him to do with me what he pleases, to enjoy the fact they're stationed here.

"Perhaps, we could even sell her, she looks like she comes from a good family," one man purrs, kneeling down next to me.

Oliver squats in front of me and his hand comes towards my neck, but stops when my necklace catches his eye. He touches it gently with two fingers and his entire demeanor changes in less than two seconds. His eyes soften, his mouth parts, and his breath staggers. I stay quiet, watching him, my heart in my throat. He twists the jewel, mumbling the words *la sirène perdue*, in a near perfect French accent, something he hasn't managed to achieve.

La sirène perdue? Sirène sounds like the word siren in both Spanish and English. Did he just call me a *mermaid?* Yep, this man is probably having alcohol poisoning by now.

"Wh- who are you?" he asks, his eyebrows scrunched. His blue eyes glare into mine, desperation arising in them. Unlike what I expected, his eyes don't look bloodshot. Then why is he acting this way?

He releases my necklace and grabs my shoulders, his fingertips pressing into my skin. "I asked you a question. Who are you? Where did you get this?"

"You know damn well who I am, Oliver Bennett. Let go of me right now," I demand.

Oliver yanks me upward. He tells the men something, again, in perfect French.

They grab me. Their grips are stronger than Oliver's. I yell obscenities in both English and Spanish, trying to get someone's attention. This has gone on long enough.

A few strangers stop dead in their tracks. Customers from the pub run out to see what's happening, but no one moves a finger to come help me. Instead, they ogle at the spectacle. Chuckling. Whispering. Watching me as if I was something that needed to be eliminated from this world.

A light-skinned man in rags asks what the problem is. *Finally.* Someone who intervenes. Oliver takes out a gun. Rather, a pistol—like the ones we use on the set—and aims it at him. Terror stabs my heart, and I try to regulate my breathing. He can't shoot anyone with these pistols. They're props. They're empt—

Bang! Oliver shoots down the man in cold blood.

The blood in my vein freezes, a scream lodged in my throat. The man grabs his side, falling to the ground with a loud thud.

I thought those weren't loaded. *How are they loaded?*

"What will you do with her, Admiral Nau?" one man asks, his voice slurred. Did I hear correctly? Did he say Admiral Nau? As in... no it can't be. They have to be playing tricks on me.

"Oliver, did you just kill—"

"Silence! It's Admiral Johann Nau of the Royal Navy and East India Company to you, scarlet wench," Oliver interrupts. "Gents, we shall take her aboard The Glory. She is valuable. Worth more than what the Royal Navy can offer me." *Excuse me?* "It's a miracle you encountered us, my dear. Wouldn't want you falling into the wrong hands, would we?"

What is he even talking about? Is this about me declining his proposal and breaking up with him? Seems a bit melodramatic. Terrifying and unnecessary. He's just trying to scare me. The nameless dead man bleeding out on the ground is an actor. He has to be.

Thunder stirs in the sky above, flashing us with its lightning.

Johann Nau. The name bounces around in my mind. Nau. *Nau.* It sounds like a French name. He spoke in French perfectly. Who is Oliver even pretending to be?

It hits me. Johann-Laurent Nau de Vernay. He used to be one of the most infamous and ruthless French pirates the Caribbean ever saw before The East India Company forced him to pledge his allegiance to them in exchange for his life. For that, he was mocked by pirates everywhere, who called him The Shadow of the Flail. Especially pirates of color. I remember mentioning Johann in my Master's thesis, which spoke about colonization, the effects of the trade in the Caribbean and how some people moved to the "New World" to exterminate the indigenous people and enslaved Africans.

Is Oliver mocking me not getting the job I wanted? Is this what this is? He's gone too far. If he's mad at me for declining his proposal, he can simply communicate.

Noticing that they're rather distracted discussing whether I'm worth more dead or alive, I decide to do what I'm best at:

parkouring away from people. I catch them off guard, get loose from their grips and run away from Oliver. Or the person he's pretending to be. The person he's convinced he is. Johann Nau. The Shadow of the Flail.

"Stop her!" Oliver, Johann, whoever he is, calls out, chasing me.

Rain pours, the cold pricks stabbing my exposed skin as I run down unfamiliar roads and alleys. Everything moves too quickly around me, swirling together. My breaths catch in my throat as I run, but I can't let it stop me. I silently scream for someone to help me, but all that comes out is whimpering.

I'm thankful for the countless lanterns that hang from the buildings, illuminating my way as I escape.

I do the one thing I'm not supposed to do when running away from someone: look back. I've got a fair lead on Oliver, giving me an advantage. Maybe I should–

I crash into someone, knocking the wind out of me. It's a man, hissing at me in an unfamiliar language. With thick long straight hair as dark as night and skin the color of bronze, he's dressed in what looks to be pirate attire. His narrowed eyes study me, his expression unreadable. I'm not much taller than him, possibly around two inches. He doesn't seem familiar. He must be new, or someone who works behind the scenes. Normally I'd refuse to approach a man for help, but this is an extreme situation.

"Please, help me," I beg. Oliver screams behind me in French, getting closer by the second. Shallow gasps come from my lips.

Rain drenches the both of us.

The man eyes my necklace, my mud-covered dress, my hair, and raises an eyebrow, amused. He seriously can't be judging me for being dressed like this when he's dressed like a pirate. If he's supposed to be a pirate, where are his tattoos or nose rings? The gold teeth? The wooden leg or hand hook? Is everyone having a costume party, and I wasn't aware?

"That jewel. Where did you find that?" he asks sternly, his eyes darkening and slicing to mine. His voice is deep and rich, demanding respect.

"What? I'm about to be fucking killed—" I shriek. The wind picks up, and thunder booms above. Behind me, Oliver yells some more. Threats of what's to come are taunted from nearby, and this man is worried about my *necklace*?

"There she is!" one man yells.

Oliver glares at me, his blond hair plastered to his face, but then looks at the man, who's taken a defensive stance next to me. The man's hand rests on a black handle of some sort, but I can't tell what it is from here. Oliver takes out his pistol, breathing deeply.

"Ah, Héctor, didn't know the scarlet whore belonged to you. Figures," Oliver scoffs. He tilts his head, smiling. "Unfortunately, she will come with me."

Oliver turns the pistol towards the man's direction—this Héctor—and shoots. My fight instinct overtakes me, and I push the black-haired man out of the way.

CHAPTER
FIVE

An eruption of gunfire shatters the silence, piercing the air with danger and deadly intent.

Héctor stumbles, but doesn't fall. He grabs my arm, pulling me behind a stack of barrels. I clutch my chest, my heart threatening to escape, next to me, Héctor closes his eyes, mumbling to himself. This reminds me of whenever Octavia, my cousin Nico, Oliver, and I went paintballing to clear our stress. Only this isn't a game, and our lives are on the line.

We have no way to escape Oliver's spine-chilling behavior.

"When I release the barrels, get ready to run," Héctor informs, taking out his pistol with his left hand. He adjusts to the right, closer to me, as the bullets create a rain of wood chips.

"What? *Run*? They're shooting at us," I yell, controlling my breathing. "Besides, who are you?"

Héctor glares at me sideways, rolling his eyes. His gaze lands on my necklace. Putting his pistol in his waist belt, he reaches for the rope beside me. His illuminated dark brown eyes gaze into mine. He leans in, his lips stopping short of my ear.

My breath catches. My hands grow clammy as my heart threatens to burst forth from my ribcage. I've never had a man who isn't Oliver this close to me. I pray he doesn't do anything to me.

The rain turns to a deluge, with winds reminiscent of a tropical storm.

"I am the one you should not have encountered," he purrs in my ear, pulling the necklace from my neck with such force, it comes off. *No.* The little fucker. I reach for him, but he moves away, taking out a knife and pointing it at me. "Wrong place, wrong time, eh, princesa?"

"Give it back!" I yell over the rain. The bullets have stopped. Oliver curses loudly behind the barrels.

Héctor throws the necklace inside a satchel that hangs across his upper body and grabs his pistol from the ground. Anger fills my body. I want nothing more than to kill this man. As I lunge at him to take what belongs to me, he shoots the rope next to me, a deafening boom ringing in my ears.

Héctor pushes the barrels with his foot toward Oliver and the other men.

"Come with me. Now," Héctor orders. The four of them grunt and complain, cursing this man out loud.

"NO! Give back my necklace, you thief!" I demand, reaching for his satchel, but he aims the pistol at me. I glance at Oliver as he avoids the barrels, stomping to us.

"Princess, I am at the top of Nau's execution list. You already got me involved in his hunt for you. You either come with me, or stay and die at his hand." He pats the satchel, smirking. "Your decision. I got what I wanted either way. You cannot cause trouble without it."

I stand there, bewildered.

"Villanueva, don't you dare move!" Oliver orders, approaching us. Oliver takes out a sword from his scabbard, his pace quickening. Hail plummets from the sky, crashing against the wooden structures.

"Enjoy being killed then, lass," Héctor states, and turns to leave. I can't let him go with Mami Julia's necklace.

"Fine! I'll go with you!" I protest, running to Héctor. The rain gets stronger, blinding us.

He nods, takes my hand—interlacing his soft fingers with mine—and we run away from a furious Oliver amid a monsoon. Oliver and his entourage run after us, yelling in English and French. Calling us colored bastards, undesirable, half-blooded children.

Taunts I haven't heard in a good while. Taunts that feel out of place.

Their hurtful words circle through my mind as we run, everything else drowning out. Oliver racially discriminating against me? This can't be possible. My Oliver wouldn't do this. He wouldn't dare.

More insults spew from their mouths, and while they're taking a huge toll on me emotionally, Héctor seems unbothered. How much has he heard in his lifetime? He keeps leading me away, maneuvering through congregated bodies, oncoming carriages, and loose barn animals roaming the streets at this hour.

"Héctor, I order you and the wench to stop! You shan't escape justice forever!" Oliver yells from behind us.

The way he's ordering Héctor to stop feels dark. Like there's something personal lurking underneath. Something horrible.

"He's getting closer!" I shriek, running out of breath. Héctor briefly looks back at Oliver and his crew.

"I am aware, thanks!" He replies, his voice harsh. "This way, come along."

He yanks me to the right into an unlit alley, my neck hurting from the whiplash. Instead of stopping at the edge, he pulls me deeper. There are no more lanterns in this area. An intense darkness surrounds us until it's all we can see and feel. My chest tightens, not knowing where this man is taking me. This is dangerous. Potentially even more dangerous than Oliver trying to kill me.

Why didn't I think this through?

My heart beats viciously inside my ears, the hairs on the back of my neck creeping up. We come to a sudden stop, and I catch my breath. I put my hands over my head to avoid being hit by hail.

"We are not stopping here. Climb, I need you to climb," he says in a whisper, grabbing both of my hands in his and placing them on some damp wood in front of me.

"Where'd they go, Admiral?" A voice asks outside of the alley.

Héctor chuckles under his breath. "Little Shadow. Never the first. Always the last," he says in a singsong voice.

Adrenaline kicks in. I raise my leg and climb. It's a ladder. Leading to God knows where. I either face a murderous, scorned Oliver or I climb this creaking ladder with this unfamiliar man who has stolen my necklace. I choose the latter.

I ascend the wooden ladder until I can't anymore. Héctor climbs after me, his steps quiet unlike mine. It's as if he's taken this hidden route before. Oliver's cursing voice fades in the night, distressed at having lost both of us.

I reach the top and scramble through a window into another darkened area. Héctor urges me to move. *We aren't safe until we're inside*, he insists. He enters after me. This is by far one of the worst nights of my twenty-four years of life.

The floor is steady underneath, my steps echoing. I take a minute to catch my breath while he mumbles to himself in the language from earlier, the clanking of metal utensils filling the room. The tongue isn't Spanish or English. It's a quick-spoken language, fluid and intricate. Like a melody.

I've heard this language before, but with a thousand thoughts running through my mind, I can't pinpoint from where or from whom.

Suddenly, there's light. I take in my surroundings, feeling as if I just stepped into another area of the set. The room is lit by antique oil lamps, their flames growing stronger by the second. A wooden desk sits in the middle of the room, as if this was an office. One wall is covered in yellow wallpaper with a map of the Caribbean and Atlantic sea, showcasing the islands of Puerto Rico, Haiti, Jamaica, Cuba, and the Dominican Republic, along with the U.S. Virgin Islands. The window has a blue velvet curtain drawn to the side, making it an easier escape for those coming in or out.

Items catch my eye as I pace around. Antique relics. Perfumes in glass bottles that resemble blown sugar, a dainty hair brush, a small, cracked mirror. These are authentic, unlike the plastic props we use during filming.

But if these are the real deal, why do we have the real thing tucked away in a room we have not filmed in yet?

"I cannot place your accent," Héctor comments, startling me out of my pensive cloud. He's leaning against the wall, watching me. Studying me. His body is visibly tense, letting me know he mistrusts me just as much as I mistrust him. "You are not English, French, Portuguese, nor Spanish." He covers his mouth, his eyes unfocused. "You also have Little Shadow desperate to find you, so I have concluded you must be bad fortune." *Little Shadow.* What he called Oliver.

"It doesn't matter who I am. I demand you give me back what is mine," I state, crossing my arms. "You had no right—"

He raises an eyebrow. "I am going to stop you right there. You cannot demand anything from me. I saved you because ultimately, you were a lady in need of assistance. I could have left you there, but unfortunately I cared, so I did not." He eyes me up and down. "Therefore, I had every right to take it. I shall consider it my payment."

I scoff, looking away from him. "Fuck you."

"Only if you join me in doing so, princesa."

I take a deep breath, trying everything in my power to not slap this son of a bitch. My dress drips onto the wooden floor, creating a puddle at my feet. Both of us are drenched. Our hair and clothes adhered to our skin.

"You're unbelievable," I remark, placing my hands on my hips. "And you can't actually believe that he's Johann Nau."

He chuckles. Dry and insulting. "What world are you living in?" He asks, his brows furrowing together as he straightens and walks towards me. "You have Admiral Johann Nau, of the British Royal Navy, the Little Shadow, chasing you, and you refuse to believe that was him?" I stay quiet, not knowing how to take this. "While you might be dangerous, you do not want to be in his path. Especially with how you look."

"Why do you keep saying I'm dangerous? Was I the one who shot at you? No, I wasn't."

He gestures to me, side-eyeing me. "Look at you. Everything about you screams danger. Your voice is odd, Nau did not murder you on sight, you carry the jewel of ruin,"

Héctor says. "Well, you *carried.* I did the intelligent thing and took it off before you unleashed hell."

I shake my head, facing the window. I grip the wooded frame, calming my laughing fit down. *Intelligent thing? Jewel of ruin? Unleash hell?* I want some of whatever he's on.

"That... that can't be Johann Nau."

"I refuse to keep entertaining this delusion." He paces back and forth behind me. "Do you want the Flail of the Spaniards, Johann's *father*, to rise from beyond the grave and confirm it for you?"

The Flail of the Spaniards. Sir Jean-David Nau, also known as François l'Olonnais, one of the most ruthless, deadliest pirates of the Caribbean. Oliver is pretending to be the son of a deadly French pirate. I laugh, not caring that Héctor is watching me. How much is Oliver paying these people just to get back at me for breaking up with him?

"Why do you keep saying I'm dangerous? Was I the one who shot at you? No, I wasn't," I say, rubbing my temples. My laughter continues, my heart races.

"Es que esto no me puede estar pasando," I whisper.

"What cannot be happening?" Héctor asks. Now that it's just us, his voice sounds a tad different. Still stern and melodic, but somewhat relaxed. As if his other voice was a facade.

I turn back to him, my body shaking. "Listen, I need my necklace back. That's not a request. I want it back now. Whatever joke you're all playing at can fucking rot."

He sighs. "Before that, I want to—"

"No. You don't get to ask *me* questions, thief. I ask the questions here. Who are you?"

He rolls his eyes, bowing mockingly. "I am Héctor Villanueva, second mate to Captain Sullivan Edwards aboard *The Devil's Fury* and who might you be, *princesa*?"

Second mate to Sullivan Edwards? He can't be serious. No, thank you. This joke has gone too far.

"A woman who's running out of patience. How much is Oliver paying you for this?" He looks at me bewildered. "Tell him, or Nau, whoever he's pretending to be, that it's not funny."

Instead of answering, he turns away from me, sighing and rubbing his temples, making no sign of wanting to answer my question.

"Lass, just how drunk are you?" he asks, standing in front of me. "Or did Nau hit your head really hard before you trampled me alive?"

"Neither," I say, glaring at him. "Tell me how much he's paying you."

"The day that Nau pays me is the day fire rains down to earth from the heavens." He laughs, crossing his arms.

"Listen, Héctor, second mate of the *Devil's Fury*, I can't continue this. This farce. So, if you're a gentleman, you'll give it back."

He shrugs, his calculated narrow eyes tired and indifferent. "I never said I was a gentleman."

I groan loudly, rubbing my temples. I curse him in Spanish, but he ignores me, walking to the window. He takes out my necklace from his satchel, bringing it up to the window. I shut my mouth.

The moonlight reflects on the jewel, and it's as if it was calling out to me. Twirling it around his fingers, he stops abruptly when he reaches the back. I know what he's reading; the non-legible scripture on the back, written in some variation of different languages. Mami Julia always gave different answers when asked about it. Some days it was Latin. Others it was Arawak, the language of my ancestors. Another was Ancient Greek. But what was written never changed.

Family first, she said it meant. And reiterated it.

Héctor's eyes turn to mine, his lips parted, the necklace dangling from his left hand. "It is you…" he says hoarsely. "Why have you come?"

My brows furrow together. "Excuse me?" I ask, flabbergasted.

"Why have you come? What are you after? Why *here*? Why *now*?"

I scoff. "I don't have time for this." I reach for my necklace and he pulls it away. "I'm after a way home. I'm after whoever is behind all of this."

He glares at me, his eyes darkening. "You are lying, I am certain."

"Why would I be lying?" I grasp for it, and he holds his hand out of the window, as if to drop it down below. The storm outside has turned to gentle sprinkling. "Ni te atrevas a tirarlo por la ventana." He smirks.

Whatever I expected, it definitely wasn't this. I stare at him, dumbfounded. Unable to form any tangible words. Why would I be lying about my necklace? Who is he to tell me I'm lying? No one. That's who he is. He's simply trying to con me. But then again, if he's a conman, why was Oliver suddenly so interested in it too?

Nothing here adds up. Nothing.

"There is more to you than meets the eye and until you tell me the truth, you are not going anywhere," Héctor says, still holding the necklace over the darkened alleyway.

"Bullshit, you can't keep me here."

He chuckles. "Want to join Nau instead? Be my honored guest." He pockets my necklace, moving away from the window. How am I going to take it away from him now? "Make no mistake, *princesa*, it is clear neither of us wants to help each other, but if you know what is good for you, you will come with me."

I place my hands on my waist, clicking my tongue. "You're resorting to kidnapping me?" *He can't possibly be serious.*

"I prefer the term *accompanying without struggle*."

"In your dreams, pirate boy."

I walk by him, toward the door at the opposite side of the room, but he grabs my arm and spins me around so my body is tightly pressed against his. He stares into my eyes, his breath smelling faintly of alcohol. I recoil, for the alcohol reminds me of a drunken Oliver who's trying to kill me.

"Let me go, you worthless—" I demand, outraged and trying to get loose from his hands. While he's shorter, he's stronger than me, making it difficult to escape his grip.

With one hand, he retrieves a piece of rope from his satchel and ties it around my wrists in front of me, the rough material scratching my skin. I hate this man so fucking much.

"Pirate, *mi vida*, it is what I am and what I will always be," he says, releasing me. Did he say he's an actual pirate?

He's messing with me.

He struts toward the door and makes a bowing gesture, indicating I should go with him. And saying no is *not* an option. "If you want your precious jewel back, you will come with me."

Sighing, I stomp toward the door. I can't believe this guy. The audacity.

"We are about to embark on a rather interesting journey, princesa," he teases, leading me out. "Maybe we will even get to have a bit of *fun*."

I curse Héctor Villanueva, the second mate of Captain Sullivan Edwards in every language I know.

Héctor

CHAPTER
SIX

Have you ever been so furious that you wished looks could kill? But not just any type of death. A slow, painful, unbearable death reserved for your worst enemy.

That's exactly how I feel as I walk behind Héctor.

"Come, princesa, I will not bite, unless you ask me to," Héctor teases, gesturing for me to move in front.

His wet chest-length hair falls to the side, his smile playful, as if he didn't just admit he's kidnapping me. I hate him. Still, I catch up to him, not wanting to be left alone in this dimly lit hallway. It smells of liquor and dampness; the humidity makes the ambiance worse. The only light comes from two oil lamps hung above us.

Héctor offers his arm to me, but I pretend he's not even there. He scoffs, adjusting his damp brown vest. The walls in the hallway hold intricate portraits. Miguel de Cervantes, Shakespeare, Mona Lisa, The Vitruvian Man, The Last Supper. I've seen these before in museums. The last few are DaVinci pieces. I run my rope bound hands across the rough canvases, wondering how they made these replicas so realistic.

As we descend a creaky staircase, I can't help but wonder what is truly happening. Did I survive that fall in the ocean? For all I know, I'm still passed out on the beach with a bump on my head. This is a dream. A very vivid dream. A hallucination. Who knew I'd dream of being in a time where heavy sexism, racism, homophobia, and even xenophobia are prevalent?

Is there a chance I died? It's a huge possibility. I could feel the water in my lungs and my life source draining away. And was the water glowing? Or was that just my eyes playing tricks on me?

It's official. I'm in some type of peculiar afterlife. Trapped in a hell with an evil Oliver, a gorgeous yet irritating thief, and no phone service. Perfect.

A hearty faraway laugh brings me back to the present. I'm at the very bottom of the staircase.

"Mi vida, stop staring at me with those eyes," Héctor taunts. "I do not know whether you want to kill me or court me. Frankly, I would enjoy both." I scoff at his insinuation.

"You wish I was staring at you, thief," I snap, passing him. "And I bet you won't enjoy it when I'm choking the life out of you."

"Who knows? Perhaps I am attracted to that sort of thing." Another laugh.

My eyes follow the sound of laughter toward a group of men congregated around a wooden table, their voices falling and rising as they speak. Some of them carry drinks, their faces range from beige to brown to black. I can't tell what they're saying no matter how hard I try. One man, an older Black man who has an aura of authority, is gesturing for emphasis on the tabletop, tapping different sections. The air is thick with anticipation.

Five wooden doors stand to my left—three opened, two shut. Giggles and groans of pleasure emit from the shut ones. I ignore that for my sanity. Oil lamps hang from the ceiling, illuminating the room. The intertwined odor of sweat and liquor makes me gag. A couple of wooden chairs sit untouched. The walls are bare, and undecorated, the curtains drawn shut.

"Come on," Héctor says, pulling me away from the staircase.

The wooden floor is unsteady under my feet, making me extra conscious about keeping my balance. While my footsteps make every possible sound, Héctor's make no noise at all. The heel of his boots barely touch the ground, his tread light and sneaky.

"Aye, we must strike whenever possible," the Black man orders.

With worn and filthy button-down shirts in neutral colors, brown vests, and black pants, they're the epitome of the Golden Age of Piracy. Some have opted to add coats to their ensemble, either in earthy or dark colors, like navy or burgundy.

A Black boy that looks no older than sixteen skips to us with a huge smile on his face. His posture is that of someone who is confident in himself yet knows how to cause mischief. With a thin build, black cornrows, and welcoming light brown eyes, he kisses my hand but immediately turns to Héctor. Héctor's demeanor softens, and he takes out a glass bottle with a brown liquid that doesn't look appetizing. The boy takes the bottle and looks like he wants to say more, but Héctor shakes his head, as if preventing him from speaking to me.

"Why didn't you let him talk to me?" I ask as the boy leaves.

"The child does not need to be influenced by the likes of *you*," Héctor explains, pulling a wooden chair. He motions for me to sit in it and once I do, exhaustion kicks in.

I laugh. "Influenced by me? I'm not the one who lied, stole, and kidnapped someone. You also tied me up." I shove my tied hands in front of his face, the skin of my wrists burning against the rope. "Don't think I forgot about that."

He raises his eyebrow, pulling a second chair and sitting on it. "Unlike you, *princesa*, I have not lied to you. I may lack the qualities of an honorable gentleman, but a liar? Never."

I stay quiet, rubbing my temples from the oncoming headache. My brain refuses to process a reasonable solution, and the fact that my Adderall wore off is not helping. Oliver is pretending to be a man who killed hundreds—no, thousands—of my people. The last gift I had of my grandmother was taken by this man who's fully convinced he's a part of Captain Sullivan Edwards' pirate crew. As if.

I've died, and these are my seven minutes of hell. Or, I've truly been kidnapped and Oliver is conspiring with them. He's not the brightest person out there, but he is full of people skills. Why would he work with them? Why shoot at me?

"Do me a favor, princesa. Tell me your name," Héctor demands, elbows on his knees. He leans forward, his eyes looking up at me through his lashes. "Where did you come from? What are you truly after? Or whom?"

I sigh, leaning back, staring him down. My frizzy, damp curls cling to my exposed skin. My legs ache from running. My head hurts from all this mess. Not to sound entitled, but we've been parading around the streets of Kingston for the past few months, filming our show. It's impossible to not see or hear about us.

"First. Stop calling me princesa before I start calling you *thief.* Second, my name is Luz. How about you do *me* a favor and give me the jewel that belongs to me?" I bargain.

"Let me think about it," Héctor says. "No."

I scoff and look away, wondering if there's any way I could outsmart him. I'm taller than him, but he's well-built with broad shoulders. He's quick too, as proven when we were upstairs. I would need to take my necklace from his bag and run... while my hands are tied. Already I'm at a disadvantage.

What if I manage to steal my necklace back and encounter Oliver once more? Héctor isn't letting me go soon by the looks of it, but Oliver actively tried to shoot me down like I'm a deer.

This feels like a very lose-lose situation.

I turn my focus on the men around the table. Why are they dressed like pirates? Héctor insisted he is a pirate. Could... could he be right?

Are these people as obsessed with pirates and history as I am?

"Now, brother, ye know I ain't able to stay away from beautiful women for long, so I had to come back for more." The boy from earlier stands right in front of me, grinning. There's a small scar on his top lip. "Who is she? Does she bite? If she does, she can *absolutely* bite me."

Héctor laughs and the dumbest thought enters my mind: I like his laugh. No, I'm not supposed to like his laugh. I'm supposed to dislike everything about this man who has officially tattooed the word *liar* on my forehead.

"She is no one, James. Run along," Héctor discloses, making it clear that he doesn't want to talk about this. James, however, seems like he's not one to back down easily.

"If she's no one, then why is she here? She for me?" James asks, taking a sip of his 'hard cider.'

I grimace. Do I also have the word *easy* on my forehead too? "*You?* You look like you're *twelve.*"

"Ah, she speaks."

"Almost constantly," Héctor snaps, standing. "The problem is getting her to speak the truth."

I stand too. I refuse to look up at any man. "You're the one that—"

"I hate to intervene," James interjects, "but I'm rather lost."

"This should be self-explanatory," Héctor remarks, taking out my necklace. It dangles from his fingers, the jewel shining with the light from the oil lamps.

James' mouth hangs open, taking it from Héctor. He mumbles *Aycayia* as he studies the jewel. My grandmother told me that Aycayias are a Taíno myth, their version of a siren. All caribeños have their own version of sirens or mermaids. We're told about them when we're kids, to scare us into not going too deep in the ocean or approaching water streams at night. It certainly did the job for me.

James studies me, his eyes widened. "Is ye sure?" he asks, and Héctor nods.

The boy admires my necklace, his breath slightly trembling. This is it. This is my chance to take it and run. James doesn't seem as physically strong as Héctor so I push him with my hip, startling him. I rip the necklace from his hands and run up the stairs of this strange building.

"Get back here!" Héctor orders, scrambling to grab me.

They run after me, and while they're fast, I got a head start. As I run, I throw things in the way. A table. A hanging portrait. Shit, I even swing open a door. All with my hands bound. They bark out orders. I ignore them. They can't stop me.

I body slam the last door, which leads me to the room from earlier. I'm almost free. Reality here I come. Therapy here I come. Oliver, prepare to be strangled.

I swing over the rail, placing my feet on this very unsteady ladder. The dark causes my chest to tighten, giving me vertigo. Chills run through my entire body and as I'm getting ready to climb down, I'm yanked backwards by waist, picked up and carried across the room.

"Put me down!" I demand, thrashing my legs around, but they ignore me. My throat is on fire, threatening to give out. I continue my rambling in both English and Spanish. Héctor carries me down, while James hurries to open the door. I scream obscenities at both of them as I'm being taken out of the room.

"She spirited, ain't she?" James comments out loud, chuckling. I cuss him out too. You're never too young to be cussed out.

Even as I'm thrashing and yelling, part of me is stunned at Héctor's ability to carry me, a fat, squirming five-foot-nine woman, down some stairs. I underestimated his strength. Appearances *can* be deceiving.

Héctor says something to James in an unfamiliar language, and he complies, opening one of the closed doors on the first floor. I quiet down. What's behind that door? A torture chamber? My worst nightmare? Only God knows.

They take me inside and it's a plain bedroom with no windows.

"Take the jewel from her, d'atiao," Héctor commands.

"Take it and I'll kill you," I hiss, my throat on fire.

"I'd love to see ye try, Red," James teases and rips it from my fingers.

Then he disappears into the living room, shutting the door behind him. My necklace can't be farther than what it was before. Héctor throws me on the bed and I sit up, furious. I could kill him with my bare hands right now.

"Are you out of your mind? I did not risk my own well-being for you to throw yourself back out there and make things worse," Héctor scolds. He takes a deep breath, running his left hand through his hair. "This is for your own good. For *our* own good. I do not want to help you, I want nothing to do with you, but—"

"You're a monster! You can't keep me caged in here like I'm some sort of animal," I retort, my voice struggling to sustain my outbursts. I get up, staring his deceitful, cold dark eyes down.

He moves in close to me, his jaw tense. "You think I am a monster? Princesa, I have killed dozens of men with my bare hands. I could kill you in the blink of an eye if I wished to do so. I can truly be the nightmare you speak of, believe me." He stands tall, his voice loud but not raised. As if he's refusing to yell at me. "But Nau is the real monster and if he is after you, he will be after *me*. So, I suggest you cooperate with me, savvy?" *Savvy*? That means understood. Understand? No, I don't *savvy*. He storms out, slamming the door behind him. "No one goes in and she does not come out."

Whoever is nearby agrees with him.

His footsteps retreat. I cry tears of anger, my whole body shaking. I march to the door and bang on it with my fists. Demanding I be let out, demanding I speak with whoever is in charge. It's difficult to pound on the door, but I do it either way, not caring that my wrists are yearning for freedom. I scream until my voice goes hoarse. It's clear my demands won't be met. I'm nothing to these people. And this is only the beginning.

I slump to the floor, crying. The lack of windows makes the room like an eerie basement, the only light comes from a candle on a small wooden nightstand. Two buckets, one with water, one without, sit a few feet away from me. The smell of alcohol, tobacco, and sweat surround me, reminding me of Abel. Just what I needed.

I bring my knees to my chest, struggling to take out my phone. After a few minutes, I succeed. Still no service. I try to call 911, but the call doesn't go through. I give up on trying to get help. There's nothing more I can do. Except look at the photos in my phone. Photos of Oliver. The real Oliver that isn't trying to kill me. Of Octavia. Of my grandmother. Of my niece Soledad. My other friends. My family. Will I ever see them again?

I lean my head against the door, shuddering. I want my life back. My life before I was forced to play this role by these men. Even if it had gone down the drain, it was in my comfort zone. Even if the press is having a field day. I want to wake up from this hallucination, from this hell where I'm told to cooperate to avoid being murdered. I want to go back to being miserable in peace.

Wait a fucking minute.

I sit up, gasping.

If the only way out of this situation is to play along with everyone—with Oliver, with Héctor, with James—then you best believe I'll play my part to perfection. I smile to myself. *This is my way out.* Become so agreeable and intolerably nice that they won't have any other chance than to feel guilty of making me go through this.

I stand and lay down on the flimsy mattress, my body is sore and tired. My eyelids grow heavy from the strenuous effects of running for my life, all the adrenaline I felt in the last few hours spent. My hazy gaze lands on the lit candle, its appearance becoming fainter by the second.

But I don't care.

I have it figured out.

Shutting my eyes, I relax for the first time tonight.

You boys want to play games? *Let them begin.*

CHAPTER
SEVEN

I wake up, not knowing if it's morning or nighttime. With my body full of hope, I open my eyes praying I'm safe in my own bed, the smell of eucalyptus and chamomile eroding from my humidifier. Instead, my vision adjusts to the subtle darkness, letting me know I'm still in the cursed, wooden, windowless room that reeks of liquor and the sweat of fifty men. I groan.

"Lo único que me faltaba," I curse, sitting up. My throat clenches with every word, feeling like sawdust.

Water. I need water.

I know there's a water bucket, but I'm not drinking from it. What if it has poison in it? No, thank you. I rub my eyes, seeing if doing so can wake me from this never-ending nightmare. Alas, I'm where I woke up. In the dungeon. With my wrists bound thanks to Héctor.

I stand, exasperated. Not only am I going to have to carry out my plan of pretending to be amenable, I'm still in this dress that squeezes me as I move around. I always needed help with my clothing for the show, and now, I'm stuck with it. Great, just great.

I walk toward the door.

Someone has to be nearby.

I bring my fists up and bang on the door, twice. "I need water. I'll die of dehydration right here and now without it," I threaten, my voice cracking. Even this small effort bothers me to the point of feeling pins and needles.

Footsteps depart from the door. It worked. I quickly sit back down on the cotton mattress, showing them—whoever they are—I've calmed down enough to cooperate with them. It feels as if I was about to deal with my family. Sometimes they say I'm too outspoken, too rebellious so I keep my mouth shut to avoid the "*you're such an ungrateful daughter*" speeches.

This situation feels eerily similar.

The door unlocks and in walks James with an antique double handle silver cup. He smiles tightly, the hazy sunlight shining behind him. He's wearing the same thing from last night. A run down brown coat with gold buttons, with a worn purple poet blouse and black pants. Only today, he wears a brown tricorn hat that matches his coat. While his expression tries to be playful, his eyes show exhaustion.

Was he the one keeping watch?

"Hello, lass, I bring water," James says, and I basically rip the chalice from his fingers. I gulp down the room temperature water, not caring that it's getting everywhere. I drink down to the last drop. It's not enough. "Does her majesty require anything else?" The sarcasm is not lost on me.

"More water, please and thank you," I state, handing him the cup. My thirst isn't quenched yet. "And I need to speak to the embodiment of bitterness, so please bring me Héctor."

James snorts, breaking character. So he agrees Héctor is a bitter little sh— "I'll be back, yer majesty." He smiles. "And for yer information, I'm *fifteen*, not *twelve*." The way he corrected me reminds me of Sole, and it makes me want to protect him with all my soul.

He leaves, locking the door behind him once more. As if I couldn't be trusted. They're the ones keeping me here. I'm the one that should be skeptical of them.

I lean back on the wall, interlacing my fingers. What awaits me today? Where's Oliver? Is he sober now? Is he looking for me? Is Octavia okay? I wonder this as the candle runs out of wax to burn. The flame blows out in the airless room, making me feel like this is an omen of what's to come.

The door is suddenly unlocked once more, and in comes Héctor with two brown satchels, one in each of his strong, bronze-colored hands. His brushed hair is in a half-up, half-down style today. He has a defined jaw, high cheekbones, and a hooked nose. The outfit is the same as when I first met him, yet somehow, now that I'm not running for my life, I find that it flatters him.

I've never seen someone so classically beautiful before.

"You sent for me, *princesa*?" Héctor asks. James comes in behind him and hands me the chalice. As I drink James whispers something in Héctor's ear, eyes me one last time and heads out, his mouth slightly upturned. He shuts the door, leaving me and Héctor alone, but I smile. I've begun winning the kid over. I can tell.

I take one last gulp of water, my thirst subdued. "I've decided I'll cooperate with you," I assure him. *I won't,* but he doesn't need to know that.

His eyes open wide, his eyebrows raised. I think he expected yet another fight from me. "Why the sudden change? Were you not trying to claw my eyes out last night?"

I sigh nonchalantly. "I felt bad that you almost died because of me. So, I'll listen... *for now.*"

He smirks, pleased. "Well, I am glad to know you will not make this difficult for both of us." He takes out a knife and cuts my hands free. I stretch my fingers, rubbing my sore wrists.

My eyes are drawn to the wooden ring on his left index finger. It reminds me a lot of the one Mami Julia had given my grandpa, Papi Gustavo, for his birthday five years before he passed. She enjoyed woodcarving, and was always picking up peculiar hobbies, so she carved a wooden ring for him, with the words *forever and always* engraved on it. The ring Héctor wears is similar in color and texture, but it has symbols around it instead of words.

Héctor clears his throat to get my attention, and hands me both satchels, taking the empty cup from me.

I take the bags suspiciously, but my curiosity takes over. The first bag holds an assortment of fruits. One red apple, two ripe guavas, three mangoes, and even a cluster of quenepas—Spanish limes. A clean silk handkerchief and a large waterskin, which feels full, have also been included. The other holds fabrics. It's a change of clothes. A poet blouse like the one he has on, but off-white, worn black pants and a brown cotton vest. My eyes meet his, and I'm rendered speechless.

"It is not much, but it should sustain you as it has sustained my people for centuries," he states, crossing his arms. *My people?*

"Thank you," I say, genuinely grateful.

"You are welcome." He rubs his hands together. "You had mentioned you would cooperate. Tell me what you are after."

Here we go again. "Héctor, I've told you the truth. I'm after a way home. I don't want to be here any more than *you* want me here."

He takes the necklace out from his pocket, gripping it with his slender fingers. "The inscription on the back. What does it mean to you?"

My breath catches. "*Family first.* That's what my grandmother said it meant. There, happy?"

His jaw clenches, unconvinced. "I suggest you change. Now. We are leaving."

Another knock. The door opens and someone drops boots on the ground before it's shut once more. Héctor throws the necklace back in his pocket.

"But—"

"Change. Knock on the door when you are finished. We are burning daylight." He turns, placing his hand on the knob, but I stop him. "Yes?"

My face goes hot. I can't believe I have to ask him this. "My, um, I need help with the gown. It's stuck."

He sighs, approaching me. "Turn around." I grab my hair to the side and face the wall. Fabric rips, the pressure I felt in my torso and back diminishing. Thank God he did it quickly because this feels wrong. "Done. Change. Now."

He leaves before I can thank him, slamming the door. I quickly take off the six layers composed of the linen smock, sleeveless kirtle, open-fronted gown laced up the front, corset and two petticoats. Héctor didn't even try untying the top part, he cut straight through the layers. Barely missing my skin.

I leave on my undergarments and put on the clothes they brought me, surprised they fit loosely on my body. I assume the boots are for me so I go for them, seeing that they're bigger than my sneakers, so they'll be a tad loose. I take off my sneakers, placing my foot inside the cool, firm black leather boots. These are made for running, and they fit me well enough to not injure my ankles. I don't have a mirror, but I bet I look like a true pirate.

It's as if I'm eight years old again, dressing up with my cousin Dominico to play pirates in the river near Papi Gustavo's finca. We'd get lost in our world for hours, pretending to be searching for treasure, and any adult or older brother who came to get us was the Kraken ready to take us to the depths.

I ball everything up and place it under the bed, hopefully for evidence that I was there. Whoever finds it will know it belonged to me. I also rip out some hair from the root and spread it around. On the bed, on the ground, in the empty bucket. I press the softened wax with my thumb as well. My excessive sweat should count as bodily fluids. This should be enough for the authorities to confirm I was here.

Taking a deep breath, I put on the satchel with the food across my body, the weight of the bag noticeable, and throw my phone inside. Hopefully, I'll find some service out there so I can reach someone. I grab the empty bag and head toward the door, lightly tapping it with my fist.

I can't believe I have to go as far as playing dress up. If I wasn't so confused and desperate to get out of this situation, I'd actually be enjoying this.

The door opens and Héctor stops dead in his tracks, studying me. His jaw clenches, his eyes turn dark. He clears his throat, motioning for me to leave the room.

I walk out, throw him the empty satchel and ravage the apple they gave me. I'm so hungry that I finish it in a couple of bites, its juices flowing down my hand. I may be ravenous for food, but I'm more starved for freedom.

I glance at Héctor, who's folding the satchel, then at the front door behind us.

While I want my grandmother's necklace back, it isn't worth my life. This is my opportunity to escape, and the longer I wait, the more it slips from my fingers. With a pang in my chest, I take off, swinging the front door open and bolting the hell out of there.

"Hey!" He calls out, his voice growing fainter by the second.

I run, my muscular legs carrying me through the maze of buildings and structures. Fog and watery sunlight reign over the village engulfing the various buildings, the morning silence so tense you could slice it with a knife. My footsteps are anything but quiet, making it their mission to step on every branch, leaf and rock I encounter. The heat and humidity from last night are subdued, making it much bearable to breathe the air reeks of excrement and uncleanliness.

"Come back here!" Héctor shouts.

A shot is fired, hitting a horse trough. Is he *shooting* at me?

"LEAVE ME ALONE!" I yell, a wooden pole catching my eye. It's no more than seven feet tall, standing next to the roof of a building.

Perfect. Time to parkour away from this man.

I climb the pole with such quickness I land on the wooden roof before he even catches me. I may be thick, but that doesn't mean I'm not fit. Parkour requires stamina, agility, and strength. He looks up, aiming his pistol at me. I run on the roof, creating the momentum I need to leap over to the next building. I land upright, my knees taking most of the impact as I concentrate on my balance.

He's shouting at me in his language, probably cursing me. Good. I'm not someone he'll take easily.

Another shot brings me out of my thoughts and just in time too because there's nothing next to this building. I'm stuck. Catching my breath, I whirl my head around, finding a way out. My heart threatens to rip out of my chest, my legs sting from the climb.

I look down. There's a horse cart, with hay inside. I have no other choice. I jump down, and land on the rough grass, the air filling with dust. I wipe off the hay, climbing down from the cart. I don't see him anywhere. I've lost—

"You deceitful little—" Héctor yells, grabbing me from behind.

I gasp, elbowing him right on his chin. He stumbles backward, but recovers quickly, covering my mouth. He lightly pushes me against a wall with his left hand, standing right in front of me. We both take shallow breaths as his eyes darken, his shoulders and jaw tense up. Blood trickles down his lip from my hit, but he doesn't wipe it away.

"What is wrong with you?" he growls. "I did not risk my life for you to be parading yourself around the streets of Port Royal!"

I push his soft hand away from my mouth, breathing deeply. A couple of my unruly curls fall over my forehead, blocking some of my eyesight. He's way too close to me again, so I grab his shoulders and pin him to the wall instead. With a grunt, he glances at me, his hair loosely tousled and unkempt. I take the pistol from his waistbelt, and point it at his neck.

He smirks, a drop of blood dripping onto his shirt. "Go ahead. See how long you last without me. I expect I shall find you dead within the hour, which would not be as horrible as it sounds," he taunts, smiling. He looks at my face, my eyes, my lips. My heart flutters.

"Bold of you to assume I need you, Villanueva," I state, pressing the barrel deeper into his neck. While I mean business, I try to ignore how it feels to have him this close. "Give me back my necklace, or I'll shoot you right here and pry it from your cold dead fingers."

He chuckles dryly, tilting his head. Not once does he take his playful eyes off mine. Is he... *enjoying this*? "If you were going to kill me, princesa, you would have already done it."

Fuck. He's right. I can't just murder someone.

Not even this thief.

Especially because I want answers too.

Héctor's left hand comes up to the pistol, his fingers tightening around mine. His eyes harden and narrow into slits, the mischief that was sparkling in them nowhere to be found. His forehead creases as he takes slow, deep breaths. He places his free hand on the crevice between my neck and chin, his fingers pressing lightly against my skin. My muscles tense and I'm unable to move, butterflies warning me of the imminent danger I've toyed with.

"If you value your life, you will do as told," he seethes, taking his pistol back.

Héctor releases me, pushing his hair back. He wipes the blood away with his hand, without flinching at the cut. Not once do his eyes leave mine. I shrink away, my body trembling ever so slightly.

"We are going. *Now.*" Héctor grabs my arm and pulls me roughly toward him.

I pull away, trying to get loose from his grip. "Why can't you just leave me alone?" I ask, as he leads me across the village. His fingers tighten around my skin.

"Answers. An explanation as to what you want." He yanks me into an alley on the left. "Nau will be after me too. I was out of his sights. Now, he found me once more, thanks to you. So, if I die, you are dying with me." I scoff. He's unbelievable.

We continue walking. More like he walks, and I'm dragged. A string of insults escape my mouth, a harsh melody meant to infuriate him. He doesn't budge, instead he leads me to a familiar area.

It's the pier.

Where it all began.

The fog has somewhat cleared here, the cries of seagulls soar above the ocean. A few people venture into the area, readying themselves for the day. Older men untangle a net, undoubtedly fishermen. A gasp escapes my mouth when my eyes catch the majestic vessels standing tall around me. Ranging from all sizes, the ships sway to the rhythm of the waves crashing against their wooden hull. All my life, I've longed to see something like this.

Some of these fantastical vessels have names written, such as the H.M.S. acronym, "Her Majesty's Ship." Ships like these were used by the British Royal Navy in the 17th, 18th and 19th centuries. The attention to detail in the reconstruction of these is impeccable. These replicas are truly awe-inspiring. Especially the one towering over me. The H.M.S. Glory. Johann-Laurent Nau's historical ship that hunted hundreds of others. The ship that hunted runaway slaves and indigenous people.

The documents and sketches I've seen do no justice to the enormous, yet murderous ship in front of me.

While it bears obvious signs of wear, the rest of it glistens under the sun as if it was gold. The ship flies both the East India Company and British Royal Navy flags, making it known that this is the ship. This uncanny replica makes me step back, a dark feeling growing in the pit of my stomach. If this is just a scheme, how did they build this so quickly? Down to the very details.

"Nau's Royal Navy ship, no match for *The Fury*, of course," Héctor remarks, not releasing me. "*The Glory* is no stranger, at least to me."

He sounds so genuine. So *honest*. I decide to feign indifference when my whole body reeks of shock. "As a prisoner or willingly?" I ask.

His eyes slice to mine as his jaw clenches. My body goes stiff. His entire demeanor changes in such a way that makes me fear him just like I feared Oliver last night. What horrific memories lie beneath those dark eyes?

Amidst his silence, he guides me towards the end of the pier, where a small group of men are loading another ship with barrels and provisions. The sea breeze hits my face, bringing a faint sense of foreboding. They better not make me get on that boat.

The men call him and Héctor finally releases my arm. He joins them, grabbing a bundle of ropes. His menacing eyes never leave my body, my face. If looks killed, he would slice me in half with that glare.

Good.

I bolt again, turning on my heel. I take off the same way we came, laughing. I glance back at him, and he watches with a smirk. He's not coming after me. I did it. I'm free. I'm—

I bump into something with such force, it knocks the wind out of me. My nose stings, and I stumble backward, falling. Whatever I collided with was the density of rock.

"Goin' somewhere, lass?"

Raising my head, the older Black man from last night towers above me. Burly with a height of at least six-foot-five, it's no wonder he's got an air of authority on him. He holds a polished cane in his left hand, but even then, he looks formidable. From up close, he has a salt-and-pepper beard, and gray locs underneath his black, feathered tricorn hat. A lavish outfit rests on his large body, comprising a worn gray vest, a pearly-white poet blouse, and a cerulean velvet thigh-length coat adorned with gold embellishments. His pants are brown, bordering the edge of pantaloons, and on his feet a pair of shiny black leather boots.

"Get out of my way," I declare, rising quickly. I brush my hands on my thighs, fixing my posture after.

He approaches me, glaring in a menacing manner. His footsteps are loud as he walks with his cane. His right hand rests on a pistol he has tucked into his waist belt, just like Héctor.

"Ye best speak to me with respect, lass. That's no way to address a Cap'n," he threatens, his voice low. His accent sounds Jamaican, but it's slightly different.

Captain. This has to be no other than Mr. Sullivan Edwards himself. The infamous Captain of *The Devil's Fury* that has defeated countless East India Company ships with the flick of the wrist. The man who Héctor answers to. He must be the one in charge of this scheme. I want to hate him so bad, but he's currently pretending to be one of my idols. Edwards was a founder of the Marauders, an underground movement that made it their mission to defeat the East India Company, the British Royal Navy, and the Spanish Armada. All organizations and governments that sought to colonize the Caribbean.

"You're Sullivan Edwards," I acknowledge. I wouldn't have imagined him to be portrayed by a Black man. Especially since the time they're trying to convey involves colonization and heavy oppression. In one portrait I remember seeing him drawn as a scruffy white man who looked like he was the product of incest.

"Aye, lass. *Captain* Sullivan Edwards," he informs. "Yer voice. It's different."

"*My* voice? How about *yours*? While the accent and articulation of a pirate is immaculate, I can't believe a man who looks like he has enough common sense sold himself to this crap."

He circles me, studying me. The wheels in his head are visibly turning. His right hand never leaves his pistol. My heart quickens. What if this man kills me and I'm playing with fire? "I've got enough common sense to know ye shouldn't be loose on the streets. I've heard tales of ye, of what happened last night and how ye nearly got one of my men murdered."

"Excuse me? *Dangerous?* I'm not the one who kidnapped a random woman! Yeah that's right, kidnapped! I guess you guys got the part of filthy pirates down to fucking perfection!"

He moves so that our bodies are pressed against each other. His darkened glare is hostile, his teeth bared, his jaw clenched. My breath catches. He's definitely more threatening than Héctor. "Don't ye ever call us filthy pirates again, ye hear me? I know who ye are and what ye stand for."

I step back, my body shaking but my gaze unwavering. "What I stand for? I stand for honesty! For freedom! Two things you're all keeping from me! So, my kind sir, I bid you goodbye. Hope the necklace brings you riches."

"Ye is not going anywhere," he growls. "Nau is on our tails. Chaos will rain upon us. Hell will be unleashed. I'd rather keep ye close than have ye running rampant."

"I dare—"

He picks me up, throwing me over his shoulder. His cane falls, rolling away from him. I kick and thrash my legs around, hitting his shoulders with my fists. Screams. Obscenities. That's all one could hear as he carries me toward the ship. Me in a boat with the son of a bitch who stole my necklace? It'll be a miracle if I don't throw him overboard in the next thirty minutes.

"Shut yer carcass before I throw ye to the depths," Sullivan hisses, his grip on my body relentless.

Te vienes a las buenas o a las malas, is what I'm taking from his behavior. The easy way or the hard way, this being the easy way. I quiet down, holding back my tears. We pass the group of men on the gangway, all of them watching the spectacle.

"Move, lads. We're leaving," Sullivan orders. Frantic footsteps finish hauling whatever they're taking onto the ship. "Zhào, get my walkin' stick."

Sullivan's heavy yet paused footsteps echo on the wooden gangway. I don't want to be on a boat. I don't want to be surrounded by open water with no escape. I want to be home. Where the ground doesn't sway underneath me to the rhythm of the waves.

I want this all to be over.

When Sullivan takes his last step aboard, he doesn't release me. Instead, I'm still over his shoulder, watching as some men finish bringing up barrels. Then, two men bring up the walkway, enclosing us here. This is it. I can't leave. I'm trapped.

Sullivan places me on the deck, shrugging me off, and grabbing his cane from an East-Asian looking man. Eyes land on me, studying me. Inspecting me. A couple avert their eyes, the color drained from their faces.

I push my thoughts aside. I need to be vigilant. There's around thirty to forty people here, their skin ranging from alabaster to the darkest ebony. They're all dressed in pirate gear, their bodies overcome with exhaustion, malnutrition, and vengeance.

"We have a new member aboard *The Fury*, lads," Sullivan asserts, motioning at me with his cane. "Remember the girl The Seer had mentioned?" A few crew members nod, others mumble amongst themselves, terror in their eyes. *The Seer? Who is The Seer?* "I believe this lass to be her. The air has changed. Hell has been unleashed. Chaos will follow us. It is imperative we take her to The Seer in Tortuga."

Whispers and grumbles erupt from the crowd. He turns to me, brows furrowed. His figure is menacing, demanding respect.

"The Seer will pay us a big reward if she's unharmed. Gold. Jewels. Unimaginable treasure. Therefore, she's to be untouched, for I fear the trouble we might encounter, savvy?" Sullivan finishes.

The crew mumbles in disagreement, but eventually agree with their captain. I swallow my anxiety. What have I been dragged into?

Sullivan turns to Héctor, pointing a finger at his dear second mate. "Ye watch her. Watch that she does not do anything that merits danger. I want her within yer arm's length. Ye will be punished if I see her or anyone in my crew injured," Sullivan commands.

No.

Anyone but *him*.

Héctor's eyebrows raise in shock. "Me? She nearly had me killed! I have duties, my captain! Watching her is *not* one of them!" Héctor protests, but Sullivan raises his hand.

"As my second mate, ye have sworn loyalty to me. Ye will do as told or ye will be marooned on Illusion Cove." His voice is stern, as if a father speaking to his child. "Did ye expect *me* to do yer work for ye? Huh? Answer me, boy!"

Héctor sighs, his whole body tense and radiating anger, but never does he lower his gaze. "No, I did not."

"Good. The lass is yer problem now, Villanueva. Keep her alive, and maybe, ye will be paid a glorious reward in ten days."

CHAPTER
EIGHT

The ship has begun its course for Tortuga, the pirate haven and sanctuary during the Golden Age of Piracy. Full of prostitution, thievery and ruthless pirates, Tortuga was one of the safe zones for those running from the law and more importantly, from Admiral Johann Nau. I knew Johann had absolutely no dominion over Tortuga, therefore, if he and the H.M.S. Glory got close, his leniency treaty would end and they would hang him for the piracy crimes of his youth. Unless the pirates themselves took matters into their own hands first.

This has gone way too far. I can't believe they're actually taking me to Haiti. Farther and farther away from reality.

For the next ten days, I've no protection out here on the sea. I'm stuck here until hopefully another ship passes and I can scream for help.

I sit on the wooden staircase that connects the main deck of *The Fury* up to the quarterdeck where Captain Sullivan is. The ocean breeze hits my face, spritzing my entire body with the salted sea. The air feels clearer, cleaner, with less pollution. While it smells of unwashed bodies and rum, my sinuses are at ease. My stomach, however, is churning cement. Threatening to make me vomit everything I ate after the ship left the pier. The nausea hits every part of my body and I softly hum to keep myself from losing every content inside me.

I don't know what to believe anymore. There has to be a lot of money on the line for these people. Are they acting against their will? Could Oliver be the mastermind behind everything?

His pranks are usually *harmless*, not *harmful*.

Pushing my thoughts aside, I run my hand through the damp wooden rails, the material rough—and very real—under my fingers. Lively chatter and activity on the deck fill my ears. Some men haul lines, others sweep, another climbs the towering mast. I've gotten glares, but no one has approached me. There's this one man who keeps glancing over at me as if he wanted me dead. With lightly tanned skin, a scruffy black beard and black waves that sweep over his forehead, he's the epitome of a biker. All he's missing is the leather jacket. I roll my eyes at him. *Get in line bud, I want to be dead too.*

"Ye too beautiful to be cryin', lass," a familiar voice says.

James leans against the wooden rail next to me, a huge smile on his lips. I shake my head, ignoring the first half of what he said. His outfit has changed. He now wears a soiled beige poet shirt with a lavender coat and mustard yellow loose pants. His brown boots show aging, but still look as steady as the ones I wear. A wooden rosary hangs from his neck down to his bare chest.

"I'm not crying. I'm trying to not lose my bearings," I clarify, staring straight ahead. I've also heard that not moving your head so much helps nausea.

He smirks and crosses his arms. "Ain't never been on a ship?"

"I prefer land over water, my dear James. I think it's visibly obvious."

He chuckles and sits next to me, offering me a small bottle with light brown liquid—his hard cider from last night. I respectfully decline and he shrugs, taking a couple of sips. He's so young, what's in it for him? How much is Oliver paying this boy?

I look straight ahead, focusing on the horizon in order to calm my seasickness, but it's getting worse by the second. My fruity breakfast is threatening to make a vicious reappearance, so I close my eyes and hold my head in my hands. The deep sea always unsteadied me, but that's partly my grandmother's fault. With her urban legends about the half-fish, half-women that live near Puerto Rico who sing you to your death.

"Here, take this," James says. I open my eyes and he holds a beige handkerchief in his hands. Hesitantly, I take it, unwrap it, and see freshly cut ginger pieces. "It ain't old, picked it up this mornin' before headin' out. Helps with seasickness."

"No, I couldn't. It's yours," I say.

"Red, if you ain't take it, I'll be the one having to clean the deck."

I give a weak smile and take the smallest piece he offers. I place it on my tongue and suck on it, the slight peppery taste making me forget about my seasickness.

"Thank you, you didn't have to do that," I admit, my stomach slowly steadying itself.

"Like I mentioned, I ain't want to clean the deck, savvy?" he says, playfully pushing me with his body.

He re-wraps the rest, putting it in his pocket. I smile at him, genuinely this time, and look back at the ocean, concentrating on calming my nausea with the ginger.

"So, Red, who are ye?"

"I'm just someone who's trying to find a way home, my dear James. And my name is Luz Narváez, not Red."

"Luz. It fits you, Red. Spanish for light?" I nod. He smiles, pleased with himself. "But ye can't be an insignificant someone with that jewel. Is it truly yours or did ye steal it?"

"I didn't steal it. It's mine. Always has been, always will be."

He raises an eyebrow. "Inheritance?"

"That's right."

A man with smooth sun-kissed skin around Abel's age approaches us, a cigar in his mouth. It's the man that gave Sullivan his cane. There's bags under his slanted brown eyes, a trimmed black beard rests on his face. His black straight hair reaches his neck. He eyes me, his expression quizzical, the bitter smell of tobacco making me cough. He wears a beige poet blouse, a stained navy blue thigh-length coat, gray worn pants, and black leather boots.

"James, don't ye have duties?" the man barks, raising his eyebrow at me. "Art Zhào, third mate." He stretches his arm, and I shake it. "Come along, Edwards. Ye can seduce her later." James Edwards. "Although, if ye've spent time with Villanueva, then ye probably lack seduction skills like him."

"Ain't no one able to resist my charm." James bows to me and leaves with Art.

Edwards. Just like the Captain.

In all the historical documents, I didn't know Sullivan had a son. He had a daughter, so did these actors get that detail wrong?

I am once again, alone. As much as I hate to admit it, his company wasn't too bad to have. Now that he wasn't around the sourpuss, James is rather chill. Maybe if I continue speaking to him, he'll provide me with more information.

I bite down on the ginger, dissolving it as much as I can before swallowing. The bitter spiciness makes me cough, so I take a quick sip of water from the waterskin inside my satchel. While not all of my nausea is gone, most is under control. I must remember to give James a thanks for sharing his ginger pieces with me.

"Ay, Mami Julia. Dime que hago. ¿Qué me está pasando?" I whisper, looking up at the sky. I wish I could hold my necklace.

My grandmother always assured me that if I ever had a rough time, I should hold on to her necklace and look up at the heavens.

I will always watch over you, from above, from the shadows. Siempre estaré allí, she had said to me, her wrinkled fingers wrapped around mine.

"Are you finished talking to yourself?" a harsh voice asks. I turn my head and see the devil himself. Héctor Villanueva. How does he always make zero noise?

"Stop sneaking up on me," I exclaim, standing, and pushing all thoughts about my grandmother away. "Come to make my life hell? Cause if you are, you've succeeded."

"The way you have made mine? No. Unfortunately, I came to show you your new quarters. If I am to be stuck with you, I want you as far away from me as possible, savvy?"

"Likewise, you're not the most likable person out there."

He brings his hand to his chest, clicking his tongue. "I am *very* likable. Have I stabbed you yet? No. I have not, princesa." He motions for me to walk, and I do so, rolling my eyes at him. He hasn't stabbed me, but stole my necklace, kidnapped me, and shot at me this morning. "Consider yourself lucky."

"Luckiest woman in the world right here," I say under my breath and follow him.

What if I were to just throw myself overboard instead of doing what they're asking of me? I can run off and jump into the ocean, ending my misery once and for all. Show Oliver that he won whatever game he's playing.

We walk toward the section underneath the quarterdeck. Héctor explains the quarters here belong to him, Sullivan, Art, and the first mate. The rest of the quarters are below deck, where they sleep in hammocks instead of having their own rooms. The quartermaster and boatswain have their room below decks, with all the weapons. Héctor grabs any chance he gets to mention that he's the second mate, flaunting his high status. Frankly, I don't care. Whatever it is, I assume being rancorous is in the job description.

"You shall stay with the first mate. She has unlocked her room so you can settle in, but do not touch anything that is not for you if you value your life," Héctor warns, opening the door. *She?* The first mate is a *woman?*

A tidy room is revealed, with tall wooden bookshelves filled with antique volumes. The details in this room leave me in awe. Starting with the wall of swords, cutlasses, knives and daggers. Each clean and impeccable, shown as if they were prizes the first mate has won. The room smells of incense, a nice change to the odors of uncleanliness. A desk with golden embellishments sits off to the side, holding a few yellowed scrolls and two wooden chests.

A small window with a rich green velvet curtain allows light to pass through, and a small table underneath holds an arrangement of pistols and even hand grenades. On the far left corner rests a twin-sized bed with lush olive pillows, a thin blanket of the same color, and a dresser the color of sand.

"She wanted me to tell you that you shall sleep there," he says, pointing at the other side of the room. A hammock. I'm going to sleep in a *hammock*.

When I was growing up and would fall asleep in the hammocks outside, Mami Julia would always tell me I shouldn't do that because los duendes, gnomes who live in deep vegetation and forests, would keep watch. Waiting until I was in a deep sleep to finally cut off not only my toenails, but my hair and my literal toes. I know that's a tale told to children to obey, but it worked in my case. Nevertheless, I'm nowhere near a forest, so I shouldn't worry.

Right?

"So what's the first mate's name?" I ask, eyeing the hammock out the corner of my eye.

"She will introduce herself to you. That is not my job," he says, pushing some hair behind his ear. His lip has stopped bleeding from my punch earlier, revealing a small cut. He's got a small diamond earring, and a small black tattoo pokes out from the nape of his neck. "That is all. If I find out you injured someone, I will not hesitate to throw you overboard myself."

"Ugh, please do. I'd rather be dead than anywhere near you."

He chuckles. "What a surprise. I feel the same." He crosses his arms, his mouth slightly upturned. "Unfortunately, your practice begins later tonight. Led by yours truly."

"Practice?"

"If you are to be under my supervision, you are to learn to defend yourself. You lacked skill earlier. Meet me at the first sight of nightfall."

He walks off, leaving me where I stand.

James

CHAPTER
NINE

Dusk is here.

I clench my hands into fists, determined to learn as much as I can in as little time as possible. Then, and only then, can I steal my necklace and run.

I've spent the entire day secluded, and contemplating my relationship with Oliver. Someway, somehow, I don't feel anything. No tears came. No guilt. Just emptiness.

The cloth hammock sways underneath me, my phone sitting on my lap. The no-service message at the top shines back up at me. Sighing, I mull over my choice of learning to fight. All I want to do is leave. But not without my necklace or an explanation. Learning what this man is about to teach me could work to my advantage.

"Ah, she lives," a feminine voice says, startling me.

A tall, thin silhouette stands at the door, highlighted by the candlelight in the hall. The room is dark, as no lamps or candles have been lit. The figure marches into the room, a match in their hands. After the clanking of a couple of objects, I come face to face with *her*.

The first mate.

A sharp breath exits my lips. She moves like someone who calls the shots. I know whatever she says goes. Her left eye is scarred, the pupil made white by an old cut. She's wearing a black loose poet blouse with the sleeves rolled up to her elbows, her arms bearing countless tattoos and scars. A brown corset holds a scabbard with the longest sword I've ever seen. Her black pants look worn but not ripped, as do her brown leather boots.

I stand awkwardly and she stops right in front of me. She's easily Oliver's height, maybe taller, at least six feet. From up close, her arms look muscular even under her sleeves, her face well-sculpted and defined. Her right eye has bags underneath and it shows an olive shade, like the blankets and pillows in the room. Still, she looks amazing. Her face is covered in freckles that suit her... Badass, yet feminine.

My breath falters. This woman is *breathtaking*.

"Ye must be the one that James can't stop speaking of," she assumes, her accent Irish. "What might ye be called, landlubber?" *Landlubber*. She may as well call me earthling.

I smooth my shirt down, shyness overcoming my body. "My name's Luz Narváez," I respond, clearing my throat. "Who might you be, ma'am?"

She smiles, taking off her black hat. It reveals her messy, ginger, pixie bob. I didn't know she could look better. "Lydia Brennan, first mate, at yer service."

I stumble backward.

How much do these people know about me and my hyper-fixations? First someone pretending to be Sullivan Edwards. Now her, pretending to be Lydia Brennan, one of the most powerful pirate women in the Golden Age of Piracy before Mary Read and Anne Bonny, who was Lydia's niece. I was obsessed with her growing up, as she was one of the first female pirates that took names and kicked ass without hesitation.

It was said Lydia and her crew of the Royal Nightmare came close to killing Johann Nau in early 1692, but ultimately the earthquake of Port Royal on June 7th 1692 got him first. Nevertheless, she was caught in 1701, but disappeared and was never heard from again.

Just like her niece, Anne.

Based on this information, it feels like the timeframe is before June 1692, since Johann is still alive.

She eyes me with confusion, her brows close together. "Ye look like ye've seen a ghost. 'Tis my eye, ain't it?" she asks, lighting an incense stick.

"No, no. I'm just honored to meet you," I lie. She scoffs at me, lighting a candle.

"Mhm, if ye insist." She turns back to me, taking out a knife. She directs the point at me, threatening to gut me. "Listen, I ain't care if we get along or not. I ain't care what ye've done. I ain't care that ye speak oddly. But don't mock me. We are to share my quarters, and I could kill ye in yer sleep, beautiful."

"Please do," escapes my mouth before I can stop myself. Her eyes open as wide as saucers. "I mean, I understand. I wouldn't mock you, I promise."

"Hm." She squints. "The second mate awaits for ye at the quarterdeck. Don't be late, savvy? He's a rather impatient man."

I groan. Maybe I should see what this irritating man offers. What if I can use it against him? Against the captain? What if what he teaches me ultimately helps me escape?

My thoughts recede as I leave her room, making sure I shut the door behind me. The deck is illuminated by hung oil lamps;

the ambiance contrasts the bustling activity from earlier. Compared to this morning, there are only five people roaming around in the decreasing sunlight. I spot James fixing a bundle of ropes, a knife placed between his lips. Immediately, my heart goes to my stomach.

It's as if I'm seeing my niece Sole with the knife instead.

A sudden thud with a grunt nearby makes me jump. I whirl my head around and see the threatening black-haired man from earlier. Fixing his stance and posture, he's not much taller than me, perhaps two or three inches. He wears no shirt, showing his muscular tattooed arms and upper body. Various chains and necklaces hit his chest, clinking together as he walks toward me. I clear my throat, refusing to show he intimidates me. He glares at me, spitting on the deck, and leaves.

I make a mental note to stay as far away as possible. Between him and Héctor, I don't know who might be worse.

I ascend the steps to the quarterdeck, where mister bitterness will be. Sure enough, there he is, his hands holding onto the wooden helm. The wind is blowing his hair backward, his posture like someone at attention. He shifts his gaze toward me, rolling his eyes.

Well, good evening to you too sir, the fuck?

I'm getting tired of this man's attitude. He's nothing but a spoiled, deceitful brat. I don't want to see him, talk to him, *or* be in his proximity. Words cannot explain how much I dislike this man.

With an internal sigh, I walk up to him.

"Took you long enough. The quicker I teach you, the quicker you can leave my personal space," he says, not bothering to look at me.

"I didn't want to come, but I was told that besides being a little shit, you're also impatient, so alas, here I am, kind sir. Be grateful I even graced you with my presence," I say, bowing a bit, and he glares at me, his eyes daggers that wish to penetrate my skin. I shoot a defiant look in response. Two can play this game.

Teach me everything you can, mister Villanueva, so I can use it against you in the most painful way imaginable.

He breaks eye contact and whistles, as if signaling someone to come over. Sure enough, a thin Middle Eastern man with golden skin, wavy brown hair, and a jolly smile arrives. His brown beard is trimmed, his unsteady brown eyes signaling that he's drunk or on his way to be. Regardless, he gives off the vibes of someone who knows how to have fun, just like my cousin Dominico. Actually, Nico somewhat resembles him, both in aura and appearance.

Héctor tells him to not steer off the course he's set; the man nods, grabbing the helm. Satisfied, Héctor guides me down the staircase.

"That was Cyrus Khan, our bo'sun," Héctor explains. Bo'sun. I believe it's the abbreviation for boatswain, and that they work with the quartermaster.

"How about the one with the black hair? With tattoos all over? Had plenty of jewelry?" I ask, wanting to know the name of the man who looks like he could kill me in a heartbeat. We arrive at the deck, a feeling of foreboding refusing to leave my body.

Héctor takes off his satchel and hat. "Pedro Córdova. The quartermaster."

Quartermaster.

The second most important rank. He's the one in charge of the punishments and weapons aboard the ship.

Córdova. Could Pedro's character be related to Lucas Córdova? The Spanish Captain who attempted to abolish slavery in Jamaica before they executed him in his mid-forties?

"Ah," is all I say.

"Steer clear of him," Héctor warns. "I may not want anything to do with you, but I do not want the Captain killing *me* if something occurs to you."

I bring my hand up to my chest, feigning surprise. "Are you... worried? Just for that, I may entangle myself with him."

He lets loose a dry chuckle. "By all means, approach him then. Let us see how long you live afterward."

I roll my eyes. "So what are we doing? Glaring at each other until we grow bored?"

"No, princesa. Tonight, you learn to face your problems head on."

He strides toward a nearby barrel, withdrawing a sword, its blade shining against the candlelight. I linger uncomfortably. Is he expecting me to learn how to sword fight?

A lively wood string tune plays with ease and precision. I cast my eyes about, catching a group of five men sitting on an elevated deck, which I believe is the bowsprit. James sits against a barrel, fiddle in hand. He's playing this instrument with such delicacy, it's entrancing. The other four men are arguing about a bet, insisting that the dice be drawn once more. One man is Art, cigar in his mouth, his black hair in a bun. There's laughter, drinking, and music, and I'd rather do that than stay here with the second mate.

"I want you to grab this and show me how much you know," Héctor says, handing me the sword.

He takes out his own, both weapons similar. The blade is slightly curved and sharp, reminding me of a cutlass. Never have I grabbed an actual blade. They've all been props for the show and for the shortest amount of time. But I do what I do best: improvise. Fake it 'til I make it.

I grip the handle and bring the blade up, taking an accidental swipe at Héctor with it. He jumps back, hissing at me in his language.

"I said *show me*, not *kill me*!" he exclaims. "Have you never held—"

"No. Never. Cut the theatrics and just show me if you're so perfect at it," I declare.

He raises his eyebrows, amused. "Hold it like it is your most precious item. The cutlass is a beautiful murder tool and should be treated as such."

"So you want me to treat this oversized butter knife like the necklace you stole from me?"

"Yes, exactly." *He's so aggravating.* "Let me show you how to grab it. I do not want you damaging my baby."

He sheathes his own cutlass and moves to stand near me, his hand grabbing my own.

He tells me to mirror him. Front foot facing forward, my dominant foot back parallel to the front. I turned my body to the side defensively. His fingers tighten around my fist, telling me my weapon should feel like a natural extension of my hand.

I try to take in what he's saying, but I can't concentrate. I don't know if my fluttering heart is screaming for me to get away from him. It must be. Here I am overthinking instead of paying attention to his methods so I can use them against him.

Concéntrate, Luz. He's not even that gorgeous.

Stop lying to yourself. He is.

"That should be enough," I say, stepping away from him. I shouldn't even be thinking about how good he looks.

"Enough? Okay, *princesa*, if it is enough for your intelligent self, let us begin," he insists, unsheathing his cutlass once more.

"Did you just compliment me?"

"Do not flatter yourself." He takes the stance he taught me and I mirror him.

"I don't have to; you're the one that's flattering me."

He lunges at me, ignoring my comment. I move out of the way, barely missing his hit. This man didn't warn me we were starting now. I may not be good at using the cutlass, but I'm good at evading things. Gripping the handle with two hands, I hit his sword with mine, making a weak hit. The clanking of iron carries across the deck. The hit, however, is enough to surprise him. He charges at me, making my cutlass vibrate in my hands.

We continue hitting each other's swords, with him guiding me and giving me countless instructions on how to move, what to do and how to hold it so that it doesn't escape my grip. All of these tips at the same time confuse me, muddling together in my ADHD mind, giving him the perfect opportunity to disarm me.

My cutlass falls on the deck with a loud thud.

He smirks and charges at me again, calculating my next move. I spin out of the way. What he doesn't know is that while I may suck at sword fighting, I'm not afraid of heights and parkour, as proven before. Disarmed and with no cutlass in hand, I run to the very edge of the deck, taunting him.

"You call yourself an expert?" I yell. "I was expecting more!"

His hastened footsteps come after me. Yes. This is just what I wanted. I need him to follow me. Before he can catch me, I do a wall run, up to the area where James is sitting. He's no longer playing the fiddle; he's watching us.

"I've outrun you three times now, second mate. I thought you'd be quicker," I provoke, sitting down to the right of James. Art sits to his left, grumbling and placing something in James' outstretched hand. *Did they bet on us?*

Héctor scoffs, crossing his arms. He's dropping his guard. Exactly what I need. "You run but will not fight. That will not save you." He says from the deck.

"It saved her now, didn't it?" James interjects, holding back a laugh.

"No one asked you."

"Come on now, Villanueva, ye makin' us look mediocre," Art taunts.

Héctor pivots on his heels and retraces his steps to the quarterdeck, mumbling. This is my chance. I jump down, doing a body roll when I land on the deck. His footsteps stop, turning to me, but I stay low like a hunter attacking prey. I do a quick foot sweep underneath him, causing him to fall forward. The element of surprise makes him drop his cutlass, which slides away from him. I grab it and when he lies on his back, I point it at his neck. He looks up at me, defeated.

After catching his breath from the impact, his intense brown eyes remain locked with mine. Unexpectedly, I find myself unable to glance away from his gaze either. I sense a glimmer in his eyes. Astonishment? Admiration? Jealousy, perhaps? Whatever the emotion, it reassures me he no longer sees me as the weakling he believed me to be.

I throw his cutlass aside and offer him a hand. Hesitantly, he takes it and stands, smoothing down his shirt and hair.

"Well, I'll be damned," Art remarks, whistling.

"Yes, lass!" Cyrus whoops from the quarterdeck. James cackles, pointing at Art. "Do it again!"

"Who's the damsel now?" I ask, pushing my frizzy hair back. I'm just thankful it didn't get in the way.

"Okay, okay. You are not as helpless as I imagined, princesa," he admits, chuckling awkwardly. "You still need to learn to fight and not evade."

"I'll stick with running for my life, thanks."

Rolling his eyes, he puts away his cutlass. "That is not running. That is knowing how to calculate when and how to avoid people. That involves thinking and precision. Balance and skill. You are rather good at that. Seems like there is more to you than meets the eye and I shall like to do the same."

"You want to learn to parkour?"

He tilts his head to the side and slowly nods. "Yes. I shall like to learn, what did you call it? *Parkour*. Teach me."

Maybe this is it.

Maybe by getting close to him, I can find a way out. I swallow my pride. "How about this? I teach you how to do what I did and you teach me how to fight, but not just the basics. I want to know it all."

"Ah, you are proposing an exchange of knowledge?"

"Yes. I don't like you. You don't like me. But damn it; I'll admit you have great skills."

"Likewise. I was not aware the fire in you was so... lit. I admire how you fooled me, not only now but earlier as well. Remind me, who is the deceitful one now?"

I laugh, holding out my hand reluctantly. *This is for my own good.* "Partners?"

He eyes my hand skeptically, but reaches out, shaking it. "Partners."

CHAPTER
TEN

I wake up, my whole body screaming for an ice bath. My arm feels like a thousand tons were dropped on it. Héctor kept me awake all night, teaching me how to hold the cutlass and strike him without fail. Afterward, I kept my part of the bargain and taught him how to do a wall run. He seemed more relaxed with me by dawn.

That doesn't take away that I'm still a *prisoner* aboard this ship.

When I entered the room, Lydia was waking up, laughing at my disheveled self. Embarrassed, I threw myself on my hammock and passed out, exhaustion taking over. I don't even know what time it is currently. How many days has it been? Three? I've been in this nightmare for three days.

Maybe I time traveled?

No. I couldn't have. But the thought is bouncing at the back of my mind, refusing to leave.

It's official. I need therapy.

I sit up, rubbing my eyes. My shirt is plastered on my skin from the sweat, the heat making the odor emitting from my body creep into my nose. I used to be someone who showered twice a day. Now I'm going three days without showering, surrounded by others who haven't either. Not the best-smelling environment there is.

Frustrated at my frizzy curls, I part my hair and make double French braids, tying the ends with some twine I found. I don't even care if they look unkempt. I'm just glad I can finally feel some breeze on the back of my neck.

I steady my footing underneath the swaying ship that's headed for Tortuga. What awaits me there? A torture chamber? Cameras with everyone saying *surprise*? So far, I know they think I'm dangerous and that some person called The Seer warned them about me, making them whisper in fear. The Seer, whom I will meet in seven days. Seconds tick away in the back of my mind like a time bomb.

The Captain repeatedly stated chaos will rain upon us and hell will be unleashed, simply because I encountered them. Who's hell will be unleashed? Mine when I strangle Oliver?

I just know that I need to escape as soon as possible.

My stomach rumbles, distracting me from my thoughts.

I'm starving and I know exactly where to get food. James. I grab my satchel with the dagger and waterskin, leaving Lydia's room, determined to find him. The sun is not quite high but not quite ready to set, so it must be some time after noon. It's temporarily blinding, disorienting me. I didn't exactly take a few minutes to stretch and relax on the hammock. I sat right up.

"Move, or I will move you," a voice hisses at me in a strong and defined Spanish accent. In a flurry of blinks, the biker man appears. Pedro Córdova. His menacing blue eyes highlighted by black eyeliner threaten to hurt me.

"I'm sorry," I say, stepping aside. He hits my shoulder as he passes by, mumbling in Spanish. His character has to be related to Lucas Córdova's character. This is exactly how I imagined Lucas. Threatening. Strong. Somewhat of a looker.

"Red!" a joyous, boyish tone greets me. "Yer alive!" James approaches, a broom in hand. He smiles big, genuinely happy Héctor didn't end me last night. He wears yesterday's outfit, complete with a brown tricorn hat.

"Alive and hungry, where could I find food?" I ask, smiling.

He giggles, shushing me. "Come." He drops the broom on the deck and leads me back to the hallway, toward the rooms. He takes out a rusty iron key and turns to me, his stance defensive. "We have to be silent. His Majesty's asleep and will probably maroon me if we wake him."

I nod. James unlocks the door and leads me in, putting a finger on his lip. We enter the room, and it's drastically different from Lydia's quarters.

You can tell it's a man's room.

Héctor doesn't seem like the most organized person out there.

A wooden desk with yellowed scrolls, journals, and compasses sprawled on top. A shelf holds antique volumes and even more scrolls. A barrel next to me secures swords and cutlasses, ready to be taken out at any point. As I stroll around the room, I encounter a sketch of Oliver with shoulder-length hair on a piece of parchment. A dagger stabs Oliver's angry yet realistic face, and I take a minute to realize it's supposed to be Johann Nau.

In the corner of the room lies a small bed with a shirtless Héctor thrown on top. A rag is thrown over his eyes, one arm flung across his forehead. Last night's training session drained him too.

By the end, he was holding his side, about to keel over dead.

While James rummages through a drawer near Héctor's bed, I study him. A scar on his forearm catches my curiosity. From where I'm standing, it looks like the letter Y. He's got a couple more scars on his upper body too.

I cast my gaze elsewhere, wondering what his story truly is. Before I can think any more about it, James turns back, a small potato sack in his hands. Yes. We can finally leave.

"What did I say about taking things without my permission, James?" Héctor groggily asks. He doesn't move to take off the rag, instead, he stays lying down. Did we wake him?

"I'm hungry, brother. So is Red. And I know ye have the good food," James replies, and I wince. The last thing I needed was for Héctor to know I was in here.

My nickname causes him to take the rag from his eyes. He sits up, glaring at me. I don't blame him. We barged in while he was resting.

"Why would you bring *her* into *my* quarters? Besides, I thought you already ate." He places his elbows on his knees, his hair falling halfway across his defined chest. I avert my eyes, glancing at the messy hammock on the corner of the room. Anywhere but *him*. "Just take what you need and leave. *Now.*"

James holds onto the sack, and pulls me out, shutting the door behind him. He leads me towards the staircase, where he sits and lets my arm go. He takes out salted dried fish, something similar to pita bread, and two mangoes from the potato sack. A decent meal.

James divides everything for the two of us, and I ravage my meal of cassava bread, saltfish, and mango, thankful for some carbs and protein for the first time in three days.

This cassava bread doesn't feel artificial or factory-made. It has the taste of simple and earthy ingredients. Like the kind Taínos used to eat. The texture is soft and pillowy, making me close my eyes as I savor this amazing thing Héctor was hiding away. The saltfish taste reminds me a lot of the bacalao Mami Julia used to make.

"I liked how ye tricked Héctor last night," James says, taking a bite of his fish. "He ain't easy to deceit and ye threw him off. Plus, ye won me a wager against Art."

I take a sip of water, taking in James' words. "I figured, if I can't fight, why not use the art of misdirection to get out of that situation?" I admit, slurping my mango.

"Ye need to teach me." This is my chance for a bargain.

"Okay, I will. But tell me this first, where would Héctor keep my jewel?"

He chokes, clearly thrown off guard by this question. "Er, I ain't know." *He's lying.*

"James. You and I both know you're lying." I wipe my mouth and lean against the rail. I have to get some information out of this boy. He looks away, taking a bite of bread. "Okay then, tell me this. Sullivan mentioned taking me to The Seer. Who's The Seer?"

"The Seer's a powerful voodoo worker. She can See things no one else ain't able to see. She also Sees the past, present, and future."

"Why does he want to take me to her then?"

"Because they believe yer dangerous and will unleash hell."

"Do *you* believe I'm dangerous?" I take another bite of the mango. "I haven't hurt you." I smirk, pulling down his hat. "*Yet.*"

He smiles, adjusting his headwear. "I enjoy seeing the good in people no matter who they may be." He drinks a sip of his water. "But, ye don't seem dangerous. However, ye carry the pendant of who we believe ye is."

"Who do you all believe I am then? You all owe me at least *that* since your second mate tried killing me... twice." Maybe he'll snap to reality and say my actress name.

He sighs. "Basically, they think yer the omen of ruin and chaos."

This time it's *me* who's choking on my food. "Now, what in the hell does that mean?"

James chuckles. "'Tis said that the omen of catastrophe would wear a pearl with the color of blood. That pendant, *yer* pendant, belongs to the Aycayia of Destruction. A chaos bringer. The legend says that everywhere she goes, ruin will follow. She's said to be just as bad as Johann Nau, if not more." A cold chill runs throughout my body. "That's why we're takin' ye to The Seer, to see if anythin' can be done."

I glare at him, trying to decipher if what he says is real. He raises an eyebrow. The Aycayia of Destruction? A *siren*? Oliv— sorry, *Johann*, called me sirène. I'm not a siren. Much less a siren of *catastrophe*. I can barely run away from these people. Sirens aren't real. They're the stuff from my grandmother's urban legends.

I throw the remaining food inside my satchel and walk away, bumping into the rope ladder leading up to the crow's nest. I climb, wanting to be alone.

The words replay in my mind. A taunt letting me know I will never escape this nightmare.

Who do you believe I am?

The omen of ruin and chaos.

CHAPTER
ELEVEN

The Aycayias' voices enchanted men to their deaths in such a violent manner that nothing remained of them. Aycayias were ethereal creatures, with skin the color of bronze, hair so dark it could be confused with midnight itself, and voices so soothing they could be lullabies.

I was told they thirsted for souls so dark, so wicked, they could be confused for Maketaori Guayaba's—the Taínos' zemí of shadows—underworld. The darker the soul, the more appetizing it would be. And they would take them without remorse.

That is who James said my necklace belonged to. To bloodthirsty mythical creatures.

Beautiful, but lethal.

A bringer of chaos and destruction.

The kid needs therapy too. This has definitely gone off the rails. They're immersed in their roles way too much.

Unless they're not acting.

Unless... they're actually the people they claim to be.

I should've had my Adderall with me...

I take out my phone, but still no service. Its battery is at forty-five percent because I've kept it turned off. I don't want to be here. I don't care about the mishaps that occurred before I fell into the ocean. I just want my normal miserable routine. It was monotonous, and I wasn't too happy, but hey, I was comfortable. I was used to it.

The sun has clocked out for the day, and the days are thankfully passing by pretty quickly. I'm assuming I'll have to sleep during the day and train overnight.

I shove my phone inside the satchel and climb down the rope ladder, wanting to put my things away in my shared room before I get to business. I have to get more information. Maybe Héctor will divulge a bit. If James knows where the necklace is, and the reason behind me being taken to Tortuga, Héctor must've been the one who told him. Legends are passed down by word of mouth, no?

"Ay sea la madre…"

I have no idea where to look for clues.

I could try Héctor's room, but my gut tells me he's not going to be ignorant and keep my necklace and clues with him, especially now since I've been inside his room thanks to James. I'm pretty sure Lydia doesn't have anything on her as we sleep in the same room as well. Should I attempt going into Sullivan's? Probably. He's the one with the authority. It's logical that he's the one keeping everything.

"Okay, Luz. In and out in five minutes. You got this," I tell myself, reaching the deck. I grip my satchel as I head down the hall. The wind picks up.

Surveying the scene, praying that no one is paying attention to me. They aren't.

Perfect.

Sullivan's closed door is straight ahead. The closer I get, the more my stomach churns. If it was Héctor's room, I wouldn't care if I got caught. What's he going to do to me? Nothing, that's what. Captain Sullivan though?

Gently, I push on the door. It swings open with a hush. Luck is on my side. I open it cautiously, peeking to see if Sullivan is inside. I don't see him.

"Voy a estar bien," I whisper, shutting the door behind me.

My beating heart echoes inside my ear. Sullivan's room is… how can I explain? Manly. A silver chandelier hangs above a wooden desk. Yellowed papers and scrolls sit atop his desk, and the space reeks of rum. The bed is made with lush velvet pillows.

With sweaty hands, I rummage through the Captain's room. I open all the drawers and pull everything out. The first drawer holds a stack of yellowed handwritten notes. Some addressed to him from "his one and only Casiguaya", others addressed to Casiguaya from "yours forever, Sully." Who knew Sullivan was such a hopeless romantic?

I grab one of the shorter letters, reading it.

My loving Sully,

I fear we shan't be able to continue being with each other, as they have given an ultimatum to me: your beating heart so I can keep my rightful crown. I refuse to sacrifice you for our cause, as you have proven worthy of an Aycayia's heart. You are not like those men who murdered our people. Who murder my children. For this reason, I must let you go. We shall encounter each other soon, I am sure of it. And when we do, I shall explain everything. To all of you. Especially my dear cnona nana. I love you, my dear Sullivan.

Forever yours,

Casiguaya
July 31st, 1675

Lowering the letter, I process what I just read. *1675?* No. There's no way. But, there's that name again. *Aycayia.* The name James mentioned. Did Sullivan fall in love with a siren? Do mermaids actually exist? No. This whole thing is fake. Props to liven up the ambiance. They have to be.

And that handwriting...

It's an enchanting dance of curlicues and loops, exuding an air of timeless elegance. It is written with meticulous precision, capturing my heart in a strangely familiar way.

Es la imaginación tuya, Luz...

I move onto another letter, my hands trembling. This one is more recent, I can tell from the texture of the parchment. The handwriting doesn't seem recognizable to me, yet, it still feels familiar.

Captain Edwards,

I write to you in regards to my recent visions involving your crew and her. The girl we spoke about. The bringer of ruin. You will know when you see her, as will he. She shall speak differently. Bring her to us. Do not stop on the way. Do not steer from the course. It is imperative you bring her straight to me before it is too late.

Many will try killing her. She herself will rise through pain and gloom, yearning for freedom, and power. Danger surrounds this girl with the red pearl and out-of-place curls.

November 4th is prevalent, as is The Wheel of Fortune. Fire. Ashes. Rain. Vengeance. Lavender. I see James. Héctor. A shadow. Death.

Where she goes, chaos shall follow.

Nadège, The Seer
September 6th, 1689

November 4th. The day it all went down the drains for me.

My chest tightens, my body suppresses a shiver even amidst the humid-filled air. The Seer—Nadège—is the one who wrote this, but who is she speaking about? Visions? Danger? *Death*? This can't be me. This absolutely cannot be about *me*.

I throw the other letters back in the drawer, shutting it hard. Hard enough that a piece of parchment falls out. On it, a date. Written repeatedly, like a mantra or spell. *November 4th, 1689*. A year after the Nine Years' War, but a year before it began in the Caribbean. *November 4th*. My stomach clenches and anxiety waves through my mind. *November 4th*. The day I received my rejection. The day Oliver proposed. The day I nearly drowned. But the year... the year is *off*.

The room spins all around me, nausea overtaking me. No. This can't be real.

November 4th, 1689.

They have to be fucking with me at this point.

I toss the parchment inside my satchel, along with the two letters, and run out of Sullivan's room, tripping over the desk. I'm pretty sure I've scraped my knee, but I don't care. I can't continue being in Sullivan's room. I don't care about the necklace. I can't spend another minute, another *second*, in there.

With trembling hands, I shut the door and rush toward the deck, not wanting to lose my bearings. I need air. This is what happens when I'm running around without my Adderall. I start overthinking.

Amidst my panic, I bump into someone. A scorned Pedro Córdova stares me down like I'm filth. He wears a beige shirt, black vest, and black pants. His breath stinks of liquor, his damp black waves cling to his forehead. I try to move around him, but he steps in the way, cracking his knuckles, threatening me with his gaze. It's like he was waiting for me.

My eyes scramble to find a way out, but there's a few more men behind him, watching me.

"I don't want any trouble," I admit, my palms growing sweaty.

"Not so tough without Villanueva around, ain't we?" he asks, his bloodshot eyes darkening. "If Sullivan refuses to get rid of ye, I shall take matters into my own hands, querida. We've already got yer power source. I'd rather kill ye now that yer defenseless."

"Please. I just want to be left alone."

He gets close, and I step back, my breath staggering. His aura turns menacing, like a murderer's. "Querida, ye are the trouble." He nods at the men, and they surround me. "Tie her up. I don't want her escaping. And cover her mouth, too."

I try to run, but two of the men grab me, picking me up. My fleeing instincts activate. I want to run away from them. I don't want them near me. I scream, surely someone can hear me above the men's mutters. I thrash around, trying to get loose, but Pedro ties my wrists together in front of me with rope, the material chafing against my skin. He covers my mouth with his right hand, his blue eyes show no emotion toward what he's doing to me.

Everything around me feels like a blur, my movements slow down against my will. The liminality of death floods my body like the ocean did days ago, the realization that this man might hurt me in any way quickens my breaths.

"Women bring bad luck on the sea, especially ye. It's begun, I can feel it. Nau after us once more, the weather outta sorts, that infernal pearl glowin' like there's no tomorrow, clearly calling out for its owner," Pedro informs, and I thrash around once more, trying to get loose from his grip. "Go to the depths where ye belong, *siren*."

He removes his hands from my mouth. "There's a place in hell for people like you!" I shriek, my voice cracking. No one is moving a finger to help me. His goonies laugh at my outburst.

Pedro smirks. "And I shall meet ye in it. Good night."

He nods to the men, and three pairs of hands raise me up, carrying me across the deck. I scream as much as I can, but they're laughing at me, covering my screams with their horrible cackling. My heart thumps painfully, a tidal wave churns in my stomach. I try to move, but I'm paralyzed in their hands that hold a tightening grip on my body. They're enjoying this. I feel it in their voices.

The ocean gets closer. This is it.

But maybe this is my means of escape. Death will bring relief.

"Give my regards to The Collector of Souls, eh, querida?" Pedro's voice taunts over the roaring laughter.

I'm swung a bit by the two men holding me as if they were getting the momentum to throw me into the water when a deafening gunshot goes off. The noise rings in my ears, echoing in my mind. The men's laughter dies off, turned to harsh whispers. I'm dropped on the deck, landing on my hip. Pain shoots up throughout my entire body, a warm tingly sensation coming from the area that broke my fall.

Pedro stands me up, his grip aggressive, and my muscles tense at his touch. Pointing a gun at my neck, he brings me forward, parading me. My pulse beats inside my ears, blocking out all other sound. My knees buckle a bit and I'm afraid they'll give out underneath me, making me look like a weakling.

Amidst my tears, I glimpse Lydia, Cyrus, James, Sullivan, and Art encircling around the group of men who attempted to end my life. In the center stands Héctor, his arm lowering; he's the one who pulled the trigger.

"Este no es problema de vos, Villanueva," Pedro spits, pressing the barrel of the pistol deeper into my neck. "I have more rank than ye."

Sullivan approaches us, rage in his eyes. His wooden cane thuds loudly with each step he takes. "But I have more rank than both of ye, quartermaster. She was not to be harmed. Ye disobeyed yer captain," Sullivan says, his voice stern but not raised. "Who knows what hell she could've unleashed! The time of prophecy is upon us and ye caused more trouble?"

"She already unleashed it when she led Nau straight to us!" He cocks the pistol. I choke on a sob. "I refuse to die protecting her. She's nothing to me!"

"We ain't protecting her, Córdova; we're delivering her to The Seer. Remember, she promised to pay us a big reward of over fifty pieces of gold per man if the girl is unharmed. Many are out for her. We're the only ones who will reap the rewards."

Pedro seems unconvinced, digging the pistol deeper into my skin.

"Córdova, believe me when I say that there is no one that wants her dead more than I do," Héctor interjects, taking two steps forward. "But think of the gold we shall receive."

The money. Héctor needs me alive to get a payment. I draw in a deep, trembling breath, watching Héctor's face through the tears welling in my eyes. He shows no emotion. At least James looks like he could choke Pedro with his bare hands. Art must know this, because he places his hands on James' shoulders, holding him back.

Pedro mumbles in Spanish and pulls the pistol away from my neck, but doesn't release me. He turns me around, eyeing my face with his darkened eyes. I flinch at his proximity, wanting nothing more than to be as far away from him as possible. He smells my hair, and shoves me away from him. I whimper, my legs collapsing underneath me. Steady hands hold me up. It's Sullivan.

"Everyone is under curfew!" Sullivan commands, his arm still around me.

The crowd behind Pedro disperses, muttering, but he stays, glaring at me. When he knows this is a fight he won't win, he spits on the deck and walks away, his footsteps heavy. I sigh. I'm no longer in his grip. He can't hurt me if Sullivan has me. Still, fear cripples me, freezing every muscle of my adrenaline filled body. Tears stream down my face as my knees give out, but Sullivan holds me up with his free hand.

"I'm sorry," I sob, wishing to become invisible. "I'm sorry." Lydia comes to me, knife in hand. She cuts the rope at my wrists and smiles reassuringly.

"Sorry for what, lass?" Sullivan asks, rubbing my shoulders like my father Yuri does whenever I'm upset. "Córdova has... anger problems. Ye probably encountered him at the wrong time. Just be glad he ain't snap yer neck. He's my quartermaster for a reason. He's damn good at what he does."

"Damn good, yeah sure," Héctor says under his breath, but loud enough for us to hear.

Sullivan turns to him and Héctor stands up straight, a flash of fear running through his eyes. "Cut the dramatics, boy. She was yer responsibility, but because ye were probably occupied yanking yerself, Córdova almost sent her to the depths knowing damn well that could've made our situation worse!" Sullivan rubs his temple and sighs. "We shall discuss these matters tomorrow. Make sure she makes it to dawn in one piece, eh, second mate?"

Sullivan releases me, leaving the deck. He calls Lydia, Cyrus, and Art to follow him, and they leave me with Héctor and James. James comes up to me, and I disintegrate into his comforting embrace, thankful for his presence. Even in his arms, a bitter taste clings in the back of my mouth.

"Are ye hurt?" he asks, releasing me. I wipe my tears with trembling hands, my eyes stinging from the flood of tears.

"No," I say. I turn to Héctor, who's putting away his pistol. "Thank you for firing that shot, by the way."

"Could not let the one who is to bring me riches die." Héctor shrugs, indifferent.

"But ye heard her first. Ye urged us to come. Are ye sure—"

"Yes, James. I am sure about wanting the gold. We are already on our way to The Seer. Her payment to us will be infinite."

I sniff, wiping my nose. "Got it. I'm nothing more than a reward to you. Glad we established that."

"Rewards tend to not give any problems, and you nearly got me killed by Nau."

I scoff. "Oh, you little—"

"I shall retire myself," James says. He makes to leave, but Héctor and I yell *no* at the same time. He raises his hands defensively, chuckling at us. "I shall stay then, my dear married couple."

Héctor rolls his eyes. "We are not married."

"I'd rather hang myself than marry him," I state, crossing my arms.

"Likewise."

"How about this? Since ye are both at each other's necks, I'll teach Red to tie knots tonight. I ain't want to deal with the bickering. Watch the helm, Héctor. Leave us."

"No. He will not leave us," I state. "What did Pedro mean by my necklace is still glowing?"

"That does not concern you!" Héctor hisses, pointing a finger at me.

"Yes it does! It's my property!"

Thunder rumbles above us, the sky cracking in half with a lightning bolt. James and Héctor jump, startled. They glance at each other, then at me. I click my tongue, trying my best to not punch Héctor right now. I'm tired of the games.

"D'atiao…" Héctor whispers, concern in his eyes.

"Leave, brother. Before ye make it worse," James orders.

Héctor grumbles and leaves towards the quarterdeck. While going up the steps, he briefly stumbles, holding his head. Taking a deep breath, he brushes it all off and proceeds to the helm. I look at James, and he smiles. James wouldn't hurt me, he isn't Pedro. He's the only one that's been genuine about liking me.

"Well. I'm the leader today, Red," James says, giddy. I smile, my mind drifting, the fathom touch of Pedro's hands on my body lingering on my skin.

I don't know what's worse.

The fact that my necklace has continued glowing all this time.

Being seen as an inconvenience.

Being seen as a money grab.

Or being seen as something I'm not.

Pedro

CHAPTER
TWELVE

Luz,

I pen this letter with regret gnawing at me. I was a fool, and my conscience now weighs upon me like an anchor. I ask for your forgiveness, for my words were laced with recklessness and folly. In the tempest of the moment, I let my pride overtake me, calling you a reward. I want to let you know you are not simply a means of gold to me; you are a woman with feelings, and unclear aspirations. I did not intend to hurt you any more than Córdova did.

I cannot rewrite the past, but I promise my words will not harm you any longer. I will see you at dusk.

~ H.

Also, James wishes for you to know Córdova has been reprimanded for his behavior, and it was quite the scandal.

I flip the parchment over, taking a quill and ink from Lydia's desk. I plan to send this letter right back to its author.

Héctor,

While all you deserve is a huge and heartfelt <u>fuck you</u>, ultimately, I accept your apology simply because I have other priorities, and your disrespect is NOT one of them. Just know that if you <u>ever</u> speak to me like that again, it'll be the last thing you do.

I'll see you tonight.

Luz

CHAPTER
THIRTEEN

It's been three days since Pedro's murder attempt, as evidenced by the tally marks beside my hammock. It has also been three days since I stumbled upon the letters meant for Sullivan, and the revelation of the crew's belief in me as a harbinger of destruction. Despite pondering, no legends or folklore surrounding a mythical siren of ruin or a Seer come to mind, making the past seven days confounding.

I just know time is running out.

Sullivan had mentioned getting to Haiti in around ten days. Three more days until I meet The Seer and the crew of *The Fury* may hurt me.

Since Pedro's unprovoked attack, I've kept to myself more than ever, secluding myself in Lydia and my shared quarters. I only come out at night, after making sure Pedro or those who helped him are nowhere to be seen. The murder attempt has made me restless.

Héctor has become more civil during our training sessions, after apologizing to me with that letter. I've almost disarmed him... but only when he claims to be lightheaded, needing a few minutes to recover, which doesn't really count. I'm not at his or even James' level, still, but I'm not as unskilled as I was when I first stepped foot on this ship.

He has also shared from his food supply with me, which he claims is much better for nutrition than the packs Pedro and Cyrus ration daily for the crew. Héctor's meals gravitate more toward dried fruits, pickled veggies, different crackers, and preserved meats and fish. The authentic pirate meals have thrown me off with each passing day, making me unsure of what truly is happening. Did I actually go back into the past? Each second that ticks by, the more convinced I am that maybe I did.

If I did, the food isn't as much of a problem as the lack of hygiene is. It's been almost a week since I showered, and I swear my skin has gotten darker with the grime. The abnormal amount of sweat I've lost has accumulated in my clothes and hair, making me go feral internally. The smell of the ship isn't helping either. This smell can't be replicated in an odd scheme of Oliver's.

Oliver.

With everything that's been going on, I haven't had time to mourn my relationship properly. In a fit of anger I ended it all, and I'm elated I did. I'm free of this courtship, of the expectations, the press, and hate. Now, Oliver can be with whoever he wants. With whoever his manager wants him to be with for more publicity. Someone who isn't *me*.

It still doesn't make this whole thing any less confusing.

The minor thing bringing me happiness is that I stole one of Héctor's vinegar-based mouthwashes made of mint leaves, fennel, parsley, and cinnamon. I took it when I was rummaging in his room trying to find my necklace yesterday. It was a failed attempt, so to not leave empty-handed, I grabbed his second bottle. Not the best flavor in the world, but it does the job. His mistake was mentioning it to me when I commented he smelled like mint.

The sun blinds me as I step out onto the deck after using the bathroom, which they call the head. The crew is doing their duties while Sullivan is giving orders from the quarterdeck. I walk around a bit disoriented, when I bump into Lydia, who's hauling two huge burlap sacks of sheathed swords and cutlasses across the deck.

Today, she's wearing a blue vest, brown breeches, and black boots, along with her black tricorn hat. Her muscled arms have tattoos and scars, like a true badass. She catches me staring and smiles, handing me a sack without hesitation.

Lydia Brennan. Aunt of Anne Bonny. Based on portraits I've seen of Anne, Lydia resembles her. How did they find someone who has an eerily resemblance to a drawing?

"The beauty has come out to get some sun, aye?" she asks, smirking. I follow her downstairs, dragging the sack behind me, unlike her who was carrying both sacks down her back.

"Aye," I reply and she looks satisfied, but as always, my curiosity gets the better of me. "What made you become a pirate, Miss Brennan?"

"Never call me Miss. That's not who I am." We head down to the lower decks and put the sacks inside a barrel. "And I did it to escape an arranged marriage. Does that satisfy Her Majesty?"

"I didn't mean it in a bad way." She eyes me weirdly, as if I was making a joke at her expense. "I just meant that we need more she-pirates. Girl power. You're truly an inspiration. To me, to other women."

"Am I now?"

"Yes. I meant every word."

Lydia tilts her head to the right, her gaze softening. She chuckles softly. "Ye know, most lasses wish death upon me on account of me bein' a she-pirate... but not ye. Even some men here have doubted my ability to lead. 'Tis refreshing to see someone who respects me upfront without wanting anythin' in return."

I bow my head and she puts her arm around me, leading me back to the main deck. She seems so genuine, so in character about being Lydia Brennan that it's making me doubt myself. It's making me doubt everything around me.

What if it's all real?

"Lass, stop pesterin' my first mate and make yerself useful." A deep voice commands. It's Captain Sullivan.

Lydia tips her hat to me and leaves to the quarterdeck. Sullivan hands me a broom and walks off with his cane.

My mind trails to the letters as I sweep. *My loving Sully. September 6th, 1689. November 4th is prevalent. July 31st, 1675.* It all bounces around in my mind, taunting the fuck out of me.

Could it be true?

I accidentally hit someone's boot with the broom. It's Sullivan again. He eyes me, suspiciously, and takes a huge inhale from his pipe, the smell of tobacco intoxicating my sinuses and brain.

"I ain't give ye it for ye to gaze upon me," he informs, his eyebrows raised in question.

"Sorry," I mumble and continue sweeping.

He doesn't move. Instead, he leans against a wall and watches me. A thousand possibilities roam through my mind as I sweep. Could The Seer truly be speaking of me in that letter? Could I really be in the past? Why *me*?

How much is the reward they're all getting for keeping me alive?

"Ye remind me of someone, lass," he states, exhaling the tobacco smoke in my direction. I cough a bit, flailing my arms. I look up at him, confused. "Only she wasn't as tall as ye. Same nose, scowl, and spirit..."

"Who?" I ask. Could they be confusing me with someone else? That makes much more sense than me time traveling. "What was her name?"

"She was as gorgeous as can be, deadly as the sea. Spared my life when her job was to take it." He sighs, looking down at his cane. "Her name was Casiguaya, perhaps ye knew her given that ye have her jewel."

Casiguaya. The one from the letters. "Oh, no. The necklace belonged to my grandmother. I don't know Casiguaya. You all have the wrong person, I assure you. I'm not the omen of chaos or a siren."

Captain Sullivan side-eyes me, raising his eyebrow. "James told ye, eh? Well, lass, did he also mention that Aycayias are a sight to behold? And forgive me for bein' forward, but ye is a sight. Ye've bewitched a couple of my men. They don't know whether to kill ye or be with ye. That in itself has brought them mental ruin."

I laugh. "All men are vexed by beautiful women. They see us and immediately lust over us like hounds."

"So ye concur?"

"I don't concur. If I wanted to cause chaos aboard this ship, I would've done so already." I sigh, wiping my forehead. "But Casiguaya. You mentioned she tried murdering you. Do you recall why?"

One side of his mouth turns upward, a wistful smile on his lips. "Ah, what else for, lass? I'm a man. Her people take the lives of men." He takes another long inhale of his pipe, releasing the second puff of smoke away from me, thank goodness. "That's what sirens do. They enchant us with their song, makin' a man forget his worries. They promise us the perfect life, full of riches and our deepest desires, and just when we're ready to give it all up for them, they attack without remorse."

"And you think I'd do that?"

He smirks. "Ye look like ye'd murder Villanueva in his sleep if it wasn't for me or the quartermaster."

A small smile comes to my lips. He's not wrong there. Héctor's the reason I'm trapped in this ship. Him and Sullivan.

"Ye were in my quarters three nights ago, weren't ye?" Sullivan asks, looking at me out of the corner of his eye. *Oh no.* "Córdova informed me ye came out of my room in a rush. Did ye find what ye were looking for, lass?"

"I was looking for you," I lie, my palms sweating as I clasp them together. I clear my throat, averting my eyes.

He moves in closer and I accidentally catch his menacing gaze on mine. Not once is eye contact broken. "Yer lying. Ye have something of mine, I fear, and I'd like it back."

Before I can defend myself, a bell above us rings, startling me. Everyone around us moves frantically, shouting orders, and readying themselves with weapons.

James slides down the mast, jumping on the deck.

"Father. I mean, Cap'n! Ship ahead! Flying TT colors!" James urges, taking out his cutlass. "Perfect timing for the hit we had planned."

"TT?" I ask, whirling my head around to him.

"Transatlantic trade ship." James hands me a dagger, taking the broom away from me. Did he say, transatlantic trade? As in a *slave trade* ship?

"Look alive, crew," Captain Sullivan orders, holding the pipe. "We're goin' huntin'!"

Sullivan barks commands as he leaves my side, but I follow him, not wanting to be left behind. "I'm sorry, *hunting*? What's going on?"

He sighs and turns back to me, taking out his sword. "Lass, there's a lot goin' on right now ye won't understand. But by joining this crew, ye've become part of the Marauders. We rid the seas of the filthy men who bring my brothers and sisters to this new world. We give them a choice. Join our crew to fight, or live a free life in Tortuga. Now, lass, either ye fight the same way ye fought my second mate." He places the pipe inside his coat. "Or stay out of the way."

He spits on the ground and runs off to the quarterdeck.

CHAPTER
FOURTEEN

This can't be happening.

The Marauders were a secret society of misfits, sailors, criminals, and escaped slaves that intercepted the East India Company and the Atlantic Slave Trade, robbing the ships of its gold, riches, and products of commerce. They helped slow the commerce for a while, recruiting over three-hundred people.

However, there was a subdivision, directed by Uriah Anderson and none other than Sullivan Edwards, intending to set their African siblings free of the colonizer's torment and torture. They killed the white generals and admirals in charge, stole all valuables and rescued the people. I've always thought of Uriah and Sullivan as heroes. Two men commandeering a whole movement to help combat the hate and prejudice in the Caribbean. What I didn't know is the fact that Sullivan could be Black.

The research took me forever to do, since there was barely any word of it, but I found documents and letters written by Uriah and Sullivan, both taunting the East India Company and Johann Nau in their clean and crisp handwriting.

This can't be a coincidence.

"All hands on deck, gents! We're havin' the blood of the enemy for supper!" Sullivan yells, cackling afterward.

I watch as everyone goes to their positions, getting their weapons ready. I grip the dagger James handed to me, a peculiar ache in my stomach tells me something is very wrong.

I climb up to the crow's nest, wanting to see what James saw from above. A ship approaches, the wind against their favor. This can't possibly be a trade ship. It simply can't. What if they are people coming for me? Searching for me?

Maybe that's why they're so hellbent on taking it down.

The speed of *The Fury* picks up, the sails pushing us towards the oncoming ship. Everyone down below itches to get a chance at destruction. I push the few loose strands of hair back, cold pricks racing up and down my spine. I take out my phone inside my satchel, attempting to get a bar of signal. I'm down to my last seven percent. If I'm going to get help, it has to be now before my phone completely dies.

"What is that?" a voice yells, startling me to the point where I nearly drop my phone. It's Héctor, hauling himself up next to me. *No.* Now they know I have a phone. No, no, no. I should've checked my surroundings.

"It's nothing," I state, trying to put it away, but it slips from my hands to the wooden platform onto his boots.

We both bend down to pick it up, but he grabs it first, twirling it around his hand. A look of bewilderment crosses his face as he mutters to himself in his language. He inspects my phone from various angles. He takes out his dagger, tapping the tip on the screen, which causes the screen to turn on. He gasps, his body rigid, as he examines the picture that I set as my background, which is me, Oliver, Nico, and Octavia in a sunflower field.

Héctor's breathing turns irregular, his movements tense.

"Is-Is this… Nau?" he asks, pointing at the screen with his dagger.

"No, that's Oliver Bennett," I say, hoping Oliver's name brings recognition. "Give it back, please."

"The woman in the background. Is that—"

A loud chirping notification goes off, informing me the phone battery has gone down to five percent. He stabs the screen with his dagger, muttering something about demons. I gasp as the screen cracks and falters.

"What did you do!" I shriek, trying to take the phone away from him.

"This is witchcraft! The work of demons! Darkness follows you! You are the evil they speak of!" Héctor accuses, removing the dagger from the screen and launching the phone overboard. With a small splash, my phone is never to be seen again.

I fall to my knees, my lips quivering. No. *He did not.* "You monster. I hate you so much." My eyes water. My last chance to connect with someone has been stabbed and flung into the ocean.

A faint cackle erupts below, drawing me back to this infernal reality.

"Stay out of the way, princesa." Héctor commands.

I stand, rage radiating throughout my entire body. "You can't tell me what to do!"

He sighs, the corners of his lips pointing downward. "I am. And I will."

With that, he climbs back down. Leaving me in my misery. I watch him from above. Before leaving, he rubs his temples, and then his eyes, as if his head hurt. He gives orders to the others, marching off.

This is witchcraft.

Darkness follows you.

Stay out of the way.

Should I listen to him? Or should I try taking this chance at escaping? I still don't have my necklace, but frankly, I'm considering if it's even worth it anymore. If they want it, they can have it. I simply don't want them to have me.

But I'm not listening to him. I'm not staying out of the way. That ship is my last chance at getting home.

I climb down, determined to make enough noise to draw attention to myself from the other ship. I think of James' fiddle, but I don't want to ruin it for him. A gun. Pistols. Wait. I've seen Pedro carry antique hand grenades. What if I throw one up in the air as high as possible?

Yes.

Now I just have to take one from him.

"¡Muévanse! Man those cannons and wait for my command!" a voice orders. Speak of the Devil himself.

Standing amidst the frantic yet enthusiastic activity on the deck, I realize that I'm the only one who is not taking this as seriously as they are. They are all geared up and ready to go murder whoever they encounter. Loading their pistols with gunpowder, arming themselves to the brim with daggers and cutlasses. Héctor places an arrow inside a wooden crafted crossbow, his hands working quickly under the ever-growing tension. My body suppresses a shiver. They're not really going to kill people are they? Will a fight really take place? Or is this ruse about to be done?

What if it's not a ruse at all...

Still. I must try to get out of this.

I discreetly go after Pedro, noticing how much closer the other ship is to ours. I'm expecting the attack to take place any minute now. As I try to catch him, a million thoughts run through my head. What if he tries to kill me again?

Let him.

He stops abruptly before going up the quarterdeck staircase and turns with a snarl in his face. He's wearing eyeliner and his clothing is damp, stuck to his skin.

"¿Qué queréis, querida? Didn't get enough the first time?" he asks, crossing his arms and flipping his waves away from his forehead.

"I just want a grenade," I state, crossing my arms too. I glance furtively over my shoulder, ensuring Héctor isn't watching me. "I want to help, but I'm better with grenades."

He raises his eyebrow, smirking. He gets close to my face, his breath a mix of liquor and fish. "I find that hard to believe. Apenas podéis manejar la espada." This is going to be as hard as I imagined. If not, more difficult. I want to run for safety, as far as I can, but my ego doesn't allow me to do so.

"Ay, por favor. Como si tu fueras tan perfecto con ella," I provoke.

His breath catches. I've hit a nerve by telling him he's not perfect at his swordsmanship. I've never seen him with it before, but something tells me this man is even better than Héctor.

"Playing with fire, eh?" Pedro asks.

He takes out a rusty smaller version of a cannonball, spinning it around in his hands. The grenade holds a little twine in the middle, surely where a person lights it up before it explodes. This means that to blow this grenade up, I need a bit of fire. But where can I find a fire near where I want to throw the grenade?

"Try not to kill yerself with this, mi amor." He places the grenade in my hand, but doesn't let go of it. "Kill any of my men, and I will personally make yer death slow, painful, and dreadful. Savvy?" He releases the grenade and leaves.

Yes.

I look around, desperate to find a way to light this up. I didn't think he'd actually hand it to me. The longer I take to think, the faster the other ship approaches. Time is running out. I need fire.

"Brennan! Take us port-side. Close enough to swing over!" Sullivan commands above the scatter of voices. He had gone up to the quarterdeck, but I don't see him there anymore.

"Aye!" Lydia says. She's up in the quarterdeck at the helm.

Pedro stands on the very edge of the ship behind her, held by nothing more than a rope in his hand. His other hand is at his waistcoat, gripping his pistol. Everyone is frantically preparing for the attack.

"We leave no survivors if it's just white men!" Sullivan exclaims. He puts an eyeglass into hit coat pocket and marches to me. I hide the grenade Pedro handed over, not wanting him to catch up to my plan.

Sullivan trudges to the quarterdeck. As my anxiety rises, so does the wind, pushing us forward toward the enemy ship. I rub my fingers against the rusty iron grenade, fear stirring in the pit of my stomach.

The ship is almost the same size as *The Fury*, only a tad smaller. Its color is an amber brown, flying a blue flag with a white-lettered logo. It's an East India Trading Company ship. James mentioned earlier it was a transatlantic trade ship, but looking at the historical facts, was there ever any difference between the two?

"Fire the cannons at the bow!" Sullivan orders. Pedro runs down the steps, pushing us out of the way, to repeat his command to the crew below deck manning the cannons.

The first cannon blows, the ship vibrating under me. I lose my footing but use James as my anchor to stay standing. The fired cannonball successfully hit the ship in front of us. Faint screams arise from the other ship, a small cloud of smoke eroding from the hit.

How were the sound and motion effects of the cannon so accurate?

This can't be real... It just *can't* be real.

Now that the ship has slowed down, and ours has sped up, some pirates tie themselves on the ropes and swing towards the other ship. They swing with such ease; it makes me wish I knew how to do that. Amongst the ones swinging? Héctor. He looks like he's done this countless times, with his wooden crossbow tightly held by straps on his back and his cutlass in the scabbard.

Clashing swords, screams, gunshots, and orders can be heard from the enemy ship. While I told Héctor I hated him, I hope nothing happens to him. He can't die before I kill him myself for throwing my phone into the ocean.

My body is weighed down, and I feel like I'm going to throw up. The smell of smoke and blood makes me nauseous. Perspiration beads on my brows, and I take long slow breaths, imprisoned by the negative thoughts screaming in my head.

This has to be special effects.

"Córdova! Hit 'em from above!" Sullivan orders and Pedro runs to the rope ladder, climbing it two steps at a time. A longer gun hangs from his back, like a rifle.

The ship nears our left by mere miles and I watch as Héctor and a few of the pirates fight white men in the same outfit Oliver's Nau wore. Grunts and shouts echo across the decks.

"No cargo, Captain!" Art screams from the other ship.

"Burn it to hell!" Sullivan orders loud enough for the others to hear. I don't know how Sullivan's actor hasn't gotten voice loss due to the constant commandeering.

More cannons fire from underneath, breaking that ship apart at the seams. Two men light torches and loose wood on fire, throwing it to the ship so it burns down. How convenient for me. What am I meant to do now? My grenade won't be noticed amidst this chaos. The most I can do is try to stop this.

I run up and grab a torch as well, my hand shaking under the weight of the burning wood. I can do this. I can end this scheme once and for all. I hasten my pace to the edge and stop dead in my tracks. I've never seen so much blood and dead bodies before. I want to gag, but one hand holds a torch, the other grips a grenade. Could this be the fake blood we use for filming? It must be. They can't be killing those men… can they? But what if they are?

My head spins, dread gnawing at my insides viciously.

I don't know what to make of this. I want to run and hide. I don't want to be here. Some tears fog up my eyesight, but I wipe them away with my dirty sleeve. I do what I decided to do. Lowering the torch, I ignite the twine wrapped around the grenade. Swiftly, I hurl the flaming wood toward the ship, landing on the rails. A white man onboard extinguishes the fire with water, pointing a pistol at me after. As the rope burns close to its end, I inhale deeply and propel the grenade into the enemy ship's port side.

If it's fake, nothing will happen.

The explosion causes a couple of us to get thrown backward, landing on our backs. Debris and wood chips land all around me, scratching my body. The ringing in my ears grows louder, as do the faint screams. Sitting up, my vision blurs, and I cover my mouth, a scream lodged in my throat. I stare mindlessly at the blurred figures as I'm paralyzed on the deck. I don't know if throwing that grenade made things better or worse for me. But it confirmed one thing.

It's all very real.

CHAPTER
FIFTEEN

I sit desensitized on the staircase, dried blood on my hands. I replay the explosion over and over. Everything was real. From the grenade blowing up, to the blood that dripped from the men into the ocean, to the enemy ship being burnt down.

No one from our crew died. A few were injured. But no one died.

It's all real.

I'm in the past.

Admiral Nau isn't being portrayed by Oliver. Johann Nau is himself. With Oliver's face, stature and physical attributes.

Johann must be Oliver's ancestor.

Oliver's mother is French.

He's a Nau from her side.

That's why the resemblance between the two is uncanny.

A roaring laugh and a rough pull upward brings me out of my stupor.

"Who knew ye'd be on our side after all this time, querida!" Pedro exclaims, spinning me around. He's utterly and completely bloody, his black waves underneath his hat are plastered to his sweaty forehead. Excitement fills his eyes, his grin mischievous, as if he enjoyed killing those men.

You're real...

"Not bad," Héctor acknowledges. He strolls to us, his black straight hair damp with the blood of his apparent enemies. As irksome as he is, his smile and eyes are an alluring song, drawing me in with its sense of wonder, relief, and adventure.

You're real too...

I stand there unblinking, trying to process what these two men have told me. Men who tried murdering me... now complimenting me on my ability to blow up the trade ship.

"Ye did well with the grenade, queen of ruin," Pedro admits, his eyes studying my body. "I shall remember how ye allowed us to succeed in this hit." He tips his hat, leaving.

Maybe now I don't have to worry about him choking me in my sleep.

But as content as I am, I still keep waiting for someone to yell the word *cut.*

"That wasn't really a slave trade ship, was it?" I ask Héctor, the muscles in my jaw tense.

"Aye, it was," he replies, removing the arrow from his crossbow and placing both on top of the staircase. "The men that were killed were men who harm others. Men who have done unspeakable things to those who look like James, you, and I."

My hands cover my chest as though trying to stop my racing heart from escaping. *No. He's lying.* "Well then... I, uh, I'm glad you're okay, second mate."

He pauses, his burning gaze held longer than it should. "That explosion must have concussed you for you to say that to me." He removes his stained shirt, not once taking his eyes off mine. It takes every inch of my body to not look down. "But likewise. And as much as I hate to agree with the quartermaster, you did well, princesa."

He smiles, grabbing his crossbow, and leaves.

I slump back down on the staircase. I slap a hand over my mouth to stifle the scream that wishes to escape from my throat. My stomach clenches, a sickening wave of terror washing me toward torment.

It's all real.

✿✿✿

"Are you going to be morose the entire evening, or do you want to continue working on your sword skills?" Héctor asks. I look up, expressionless, my hand on my chin.

He's changed to a beige, worn button-down. His hair is in a low ponytail, a few strands hanging over his face. His right cheekbone has a fresh bruise, but other than that, he's unscathed.

I look around, blinking rapidly as I try to process my surroundings. The sun is clocking out of its duties for the day, allowing the gorgeous moon to take over its shift. The crew has dispersed, faint laughter ringing throughout. Cyrus is passed out nearby, his tricorn hat over his face, a rum bottle barely held by his thick fingers. His snoring is drowned out by a whistling James lights up the lanterns for when the sky fully darkens later. Art and Pedro sit off to the side, playing a dice game, while keeping their eye on James. Have I really been sitting on that staircase in a catatonic stupor for the rest of the day?

I guess time goes fast when a person learns they time traveled.

"Let's do it," I remark, trying to push away the events from today. His brows furrow in confusion, but nods regardless.

More questions come to mind. Who is Héctor? Is he one of the Taínos that survived the hate and pain of the Europeans? He had also mentioned killing dozens of men and that he could do it again if he wanted to. Is he an actual murderer or was he saying that to terrify me into submission?

He motions for me to head to the deck, him coming behind me. He grabs two swords, his own and the one he lets me use. His sword has a black handle while the one I use is golden. It makes me wonder if he knows they took this gold from our islands. Stolen beyond repair, beaten out of us. Currently being displayed behind glass cases in museums, or used as decoration in cathedrals.

We stand and he counts down, officially beginning tonight's training as the sound of the ocean clashing against the rocking ship echoes in the night.

Art and Pedro's voices have become a background noise, intertwined with the sound of crashing waves, and clicking iron. Héctor teases me, trying to draw my attention back to him and his movements. I grimace, sliding back. He does a parkour move I taught him, and lands perfectly in front of me, smirking, and pinning me against the mast. He looks at my lips, at my eyes; just like that day I had the pistol against his neck. We stand there, our breathing synchronized. Our eyes refuse to disconnect.

"If you wanted me to pin you to the mast, you could have simply said so, princesa," Héctor taunts, smiling.

"In your dreams, second mate," I breathe, pressing my cutlass against his stomach. His gaze lands on my lips for two seconds before he finds my eyes once more.

"Perhaps you are the star of my wildest dreams." He takes a step closer, our bodies almost touching. My breath trembles as he releases me, a twinkle in his eyes. *What's happening to me?*

I grip the handle and swing my cutlass, but he blocks the hit with ease, smirking. We stand there, gasping for air.

"Is that so? And what do those dreams entail, my kind sir?"

His gaze locks onto mine as he lowers his blade. His lips rise on the corner. "You ask a lot of questions, Luz." I never knew my name could sound so... *melodic.*

I roll my eyes, stepping back. "And you answer too few, Héctor."

"Fine. With every hit you block, I shall answer a question of yours."

He lunges at me, and instead of running, I bring my cutlass up, weakly blocking his. "Why'd you kidnap me?"

"I did not kidnap you. I am protecting us. Protecting me."

I push him and his blade off me. "What?"

He sighs, swinging at me but I block it again. "I meant that with you under our supervision, you cannot keep running rampant and cause chaos and mischief everywhere you go."

My brows furrow together. "I'm not the one causing trouble. Besides, you and Pedro seemed pretty ecstatic when I blew up that enemy ship!" I throw a hit at him and he blocks it. And another. And a third. "So by the looks of it, I'm only chaotic when it's convenient for you!" My voice has raised, my blood boiling.

It's like I'm hitting a wall with him repeatedly, and I can't break through to find what he wants.

He slides out of the way, blocking my cutlass. "Not the one causing problems? Explain why every time you are exasperated the sky breaks." He throws a hit and my blade vibrates in my hand. "How every single one of us who interacts with you ends up in trouble." I grunt, becoming dominant in the fight once more. He struggles, holding his sword with two hands. "How Nau is hell-bent on finding you, but did not kill you when he easily could have."

I tighten my grip on the handle, swinging my cutlass with so much force, it's getting hard for him to block my hits. While I'm furious at him, I feel myself getting stronger and faster. More in tune with my movements and the cutlass with the passing of days. More acclimated to the constant movements and fight sequences. Even though I've always been considered a bigger woman—I actually love my curves, stretch marks, and plush extremities—my fitness levels have always been top-notch because knowing how to parkour can get tiring if you aren't used to it. Which is what others refuse to see.

"Luz!" He calls out. "Wa- wait!" But I don't stop. Me? *Chaotic?* Yeah, right.

I've cornered him. "How's that chaos for you? Huh? Answer me!"

"LUZ!"

He lunges at me and cuts my forearm with the tip of his cutlass. With a stinging arm, I drop my weapon, cursing in Spanish. A sharp, burning sensation shoots upward, my entire limb tingling. The shirt sleeve has ripped, slowly soaking with my warm blood. Angered at this whole situation, I stride to the opposite side of the ship. I'm especially mad at the fact that I threw a literal grenade, causing an explosion, and confirming to them I am indeed a harbinger of destruction.

And most importantly, I'm furious that everything is real and I can't blame it on Oliver.

"I am terribly sorry, d'nanichi, please forgive me," Héctor says behind me, his voice soft. *D'nanichi?* That's a new one. It feels more kind and accepting than princesa, yet I don't like it one bit. "Give me your arm."

Reluctantly, I do as told, more blood pooling. He rips off a piece of the sleeve from his shirt, rolling it around my forearm to contain the bleeding. His fingers caress my skin as he fixes the fabric. I don't know how, but this killer has soft hands. Very unlike what I assumed pirate hands to feel like. I expected callouses, bumps, cuts and scars even. But no. They're smooth, as if he had lathered them in some sort of seventeenth century lotion.

Instead of looking into his eyes, I lower my gaze to the wooden ring on his index finger. Héctor ties the cloth in a tender manner, and his fingers fall away. Part of me wishes he would continue. I push the thought away, remembering he's a killer, and I need to dislike him. I dislike him. He stole my necklace, kidnapped me, shot at me, and threw my phone into the ocean after stabbing it. He's simply getting tolerable as the days go by.

"Turns out training won't help me clear my head by the looks of it," I say, changing the topic. The last thing I need is for him to call me out too.

"I understand," he says, storing our swords away. As he does that, I study the tattoo at the nape of his neck, where his ponytail is. It's a Taíno symbol. A hollow circle, with semi circles around it, resembling a sunflower or even the sun. He catches me staring so I avert my eyes. "Would you like to learn to read a map?"

I stare at him, stunned. Suddenly, it hits me. Second mates take responsibility for navigational charts, sailing instruments, and keeping watch. I read about this when I was younger. Learning that fact actually made me obsessed with astronomy and the stars for a few months.

The coincidence is so eerie, chills run through my neck.

"Sure, why not?" I shrug, the art inked into his body running through my mind. If I am in the past, then the tattoo confirms he is indeed Taíno.

He smiles and guides me to a barrel with a satchel on top. He then unrolls a yellow scroll from the bag and sets it down on the surface between us. It's a map of the Atlantic Ocean and the Caribbean, but it's unlike any map I've ever seen. La Hispaniola, La Florida, Tortuga, Cuba, Fort Nassau, Port Royal, San Juan Bautista, and even the West Indies are labeled in fancy script. This isn't a replica or printing paper.

This is authentic.

"Where did you get this?" I inquire, gazing up at him.

A playful glint in his eye accompanies a soft chuckle. "How ironic. I recall when *I* asked you that and you dismissed me. Repeatedly."

I roll my eyes, a smile creeping on my lips. "I'm being serious."

"Well, if you must know..." He drifts off, smoothing his hair back. "I sketched it. From memory." *He* made this? "I sketch all our maps and charts, which helps the Captain. It is part of my role as second mate."

I run my fingers through Puerto Rico's drawing and its name, feeling the rough dry ink added to the parchment. There's a star over the capital city, calling it San Juan Bautista instead. The name was anointed during the era of colonization.

Tears come to my eyes. I miss my home. I miss my life.

I catch Héctor staring at me, a quizzical expression on his face. I wipe my tears away with the sleeve that's intact. The urge to cry gets stronger by the second, my chest tightening. I haven't cried or mourned my old life since the first night I was here. I haven't wanted to show them my vulnerable side, but it's getting tough to do so.

Everything continues piling up on me and I can't keep up. My thoughts are racing, not allowing me to focus on getting out of here alive. My heart is pounding, my palms are sweaty. It's as if I'm being pulled out to sea, drowning with the waves that engulfed me the first night.

I leave Héctor's side abruptly, covering my face with my hands, and scream into the dark abyss. It feels like the right thing to do. It's the only thing I can do if I'm being honest. I take my hands away, wipe my last tears, plaster a smile, and stroll back to his side. A major breakdown creeps in the back of my mind, but I will not lose it in front of him. Just like I never broke down in front of my family. Thankfully, he simply stares saying nothing.

Thunder crackles in the sky, the wind picking up. A few sprinkles of rain fall upon us, grazing out skin delicately.

"Am I amusing you?" I snap. I clear my throat, removing all signs of wanting to cry.

"No. I—Are you alright?" Héctor asks, his voice so affectionate it scares me. His hand reaches toward mine, but he stops himself. My heart sinks a little. Wait. *Why?*

"I'm fine. I want to go home."

"Where is your home?" I point at Puerto Rico, not once taking my eyes away from him. "You are from Borik- Puerto Rico?"

"Yes."

"Why were you in Port Royal then?"

I blow air through my lips. "I don't know. I was there not feeling good enough, I guess. Pleasing others to keep them happy." A wave of longing engulfs me. I slump on the deck, bringing my knees to my chest as a tear escapes my eye. "It doesn't matter, though. I just want to go home. Not my fake home, my *actual* home, Puerto Rico."

He watches me intently. "Well, if it helps, you are worth plenty. Believe me," Héctor says, kneeling in front of me. "Did you know the North Star is used as a navigational tool?"

He's changing the subject.

"Héctor, what—"

"Some call it Polaris. My bibi called it another karaya in the turey. *Another moon in the sky.*" He offers me his hand. I take it, allowing him to guide me up to the quarterdeck. "I simply call it the North Star. My... father taught me how to use it to measure the angle between the horizon and the sky to accurately determine not only my location but the latitude as well. It can help you find your way home."

Our hands break apart, the heat from his fingers falling away. "Wait, why are you telling me this?"

We stand to the side, gazing out at the never-ending sea and the swirling navy and violet sky. The sun is barely on the horizon, the littlest ray of light shining hazily upon us. The gentle sea breeze spritzes my skin. The humidity diminishes with the disappearing sun. It's absolutely breathtaking. Awe overtakes me, feeling a deep appreciation for the majestic scene before me.

All the anger and frustration I had evaporates, a sense of peace washing over me like gentle waves that greet the coast.

I glance at Héctor, and meet his eyes. Has he been looking at me all this time?

My skin goes hot as he averts his gaze to the sea. He clears his throat, fidgeting with his fingers.

"Because you will get home. From the two of us, you were not taken nor deprived of it. You can go home while I cannot. So I focus on the stars, on the horizon. Those are my home," Héctor confides. His eyes find mine once more. "It is in your name, Luz Karina. Star that lights the way is what I interpret from your name. The stars will lead you. I promise."

I blush. He must've overheard me and James speaking that first day because I never told him my middle name. I'm glad he did, because I like how it sounds when he says it. "Wait...why can't you go home? If I can find my impossible journey home, surely you can find a way too."

He smiles, but it's sad. Uncertain. Ashamed. "Who wants to go to a home that no longer exists?" He taps on the rail, twice. "Practice is over. Rest. One ship down is a lot of excitement for someone not used to it. I shall see you tomorrow."

"But—"

"Good night, d'nanichi." There's that word again. *D'nanichi.*

Before I can ask him what it means, he walks over to the helm. The conversation is over. Shocked by the sudden change in personality, I leave. What was that? The softness in his voice. The reassurance. The *care.*

I smile as I head downstairs, liking this strangely tender version of him.

CHAPTER
SIXTEEN

Nine tally marks. Nine days.

I open my eyes, facing the etched sticks I keep next to my provided hammock. Last night I had been consumed with overthinking and restlessness, the words found in the letters swimming around in my mind. Whoever The Seer is, she knew I was coming. I don't understand how I traveled to the past, but I believe she might be the answer to everything. One more day for it all to be revealed.

Whenever I fell asleep, strange dreams surrounding my grandmother, my necklace, the ocean, and Héctor plagued me. My grandma ordering him to protect me. That she chose him specifically for me. My necklace shines once more, but this time controlling the seas themselves. Héctor telling me he'd rather die than live a life without me as sirens dragged me deeper into the depths. Once again the ominous figure made an appearance, its golden sword aimed straight at my heart while blood trailed down my nose.

The most unbelievable part of that dream was Héctor. That man would rather die than live a life *with* me. And I would too.

I turn to the other side and my heart jumps to my throat.

"Jesus, Brennan," I mumble, throwing my arm over my eyes.

"Good morrow, beautiful." Lydia grins. "Rough night?" Her fingers hover over the makeshift bandage on my arm.

I sit up, covering the bloody cloth with my other hand. "I'm fine."

"Come. It's past dawn. Let's get our day started, eh, Narváez?"

I groan. "It's too early."

"The earlier, the better." She stands, shaking my hammock. "Get up, princess."

"I'm going…"

Time to distract myself with the duties Lydia has planned for me. I use the head and cleanse my face and forearm with a damp rag. I need soap. I need my skincare products. Sunscreen. I need a shower. Toothpaste. I miss feeling clean. I miss when I didn't have a second skin made of filth.

I return to Lydia's room where she's polishing a couple of knives. She gifts me five silver daggers, and throws her arm around me, leading me toward the deck. She was right; the sun has barely risen. I'm greeted by the bustling activity and the winding down of the night watch, finishing up their duties before going to sleep.

I sigh when I don't see Héctor. I don't know if I can face him after last night.

We head below deck to grab some food. As the quartermaster, Pedro is in charge of rationing meals with the help of Cyrus.

"There she is, the queen of ruin that won us the ship," Cyrus says, handing me a wrapped bundle.

"Not the queen of ruin," I reiterate, rolling my eyes.

"Well, whoever ye is... ye've got an admirer now," Cyrus elbows Pedro, "eh?"

Pedro averts his eyes, handing Lydia a bundle. "Shut it, Khan."

Cyrus cackles, taking a sip of rum. "See? Yer red!" Pedro smacks his head.

"And I'm nauseous," Lydia interjects, pulling me upstairs.

.Opening my bundle, my breakfast consists of saltfish, three dense wheat crackers, an apple, and water. I wish I had more nutrients. But if the pirates can sustain themselves with these meals, so can I.

At least this isn't as bad as the rigorous diets my mother placed me on while I was growing up. My mother's an almond mom, and having a plus-sized daughter is something she considered a gift from the devil himself. She'd make me skip breakfast, had me exercise two hours daily, made me take part in sports, sent me to horrendous weight loss camps where they ridiculed those who couldn't lose weight. To her horror, all that resulted in my body refusing to conform to what she wanted.

What she hated the most was that, unlike her, I genuinely liked how I looked. Every time I felt confident about my appearance, she'd take it upon herself to compare me with Abel or to reminisce on the good old days where she was so tiny, she could still fit in a child's clothing as a teen.

La belleza cuesta, she'd say repeatedly. Bullying me, sending me off to yet another weight loss camp. If it wasn't my hair, it was my body. If it wasn't my body, it was my unmedicated ADHD. She always found something unworthy of a Narváez in me, stating I was becoming more and more like

Mami Julia, my father's mother. Still, my mother never got what she wanted, causing the turbulent relationship between me and her.

Lydia goes off to do her morning duties and I sit off to the side, my body feeling sluggish as I eat. I mustn't crack. Tears and anger will only get me consequences. It will only bring disagreements and outbursts from the crew claiming I'll bring ruin. Possibly even death. I must stay agreeable and cooperative. I can't break again like I did last night.

By the time I finish eating, Lydia asks me to join her for the rest of the day. However, part of me believes it's her way of monitoring me. Still, it's nice to be around someone who doesn't trigger my impulsive thoughts. She teaches me how much value each item aboard *The Fury* has when using pieces of eight—silver and gold coins used during the 17th and 18th centuries—in trades, and how to climb the ropes attached to the mast with ease. With each task I successfully accomplish and comprehend killing no one unprompted, she warms up to me a bit more. Enough to even teach me how to aim knives and daggers at a piece of wood the crew uses as target practice.

After a while, she leaves to complete her duties, so I practice knife throwing by myself.

I clutch the cool steel of the dagger in my hands, my mind a tempest of conflicting emotions. I twirl the knife around, the sensation strangely calming. I take a deep breath, blocking out the murmurs of onlookers who have gathered to witness what I'm up to. My vision narrows as I focus solely on the wooden target ahead. I throw the first blade and the world around me fades into oblivion.

You aren't ready. *Woosh.* You half-blooded whore. *Woosh.* You helped destroy an East India Company ship. *Woosh.* You're in the past. *Woosh.*

With each throw, a surge of energy grows in my body, giving me a renewed sense of mental, and emotional clarity. My brain fog slowly lifts, helping me concentrate on the target in front of me.

My right arm gets heavy from the repeated movement, but I don't stop. The knives hit the board with more aggression as each negative thought circles my mind, getting closer and closer to the circle drawn in the middle. Maybe this can be my new therapy and Abel's picture can be in the middle.

By imagining his irritating face in the center of the wooden plank, I've successfully hit the target at least ten times in a row. Héctor should've trained me to throw knives instead of getting me to sword fight. I've finally found something I'm good at. I had to bring up all the negative words that have been said to me throughout my twenty-four years of life, but it got me to hit the target.

"Who knew ye had such a great aim," Lydia states proudly.

"I didn't know either," I say sheepishly. "I just imagined my brother's face in the target. That did the trick by the looks of it."

She chuckles, taking out her knives and joining me on the plank next to mine. "Ye and yer brother ain't get along?" Her knife hits the exact center on the first try.

"No." I throw another, this one bouncing off the board. "He's the ideal son. *Be more like him*, everyone says."

"Ah. Well, my brother, Dean, died young. I have a babe of a sister." The next knife lands next to the one she previously threw in the center. "When Dean passed, my mother was devastated. We no longer had an income. We were poor ye see, the three of us born out of wedlock. My mama was a seamstress, but that wasn't enough to feed three hungry mouths. So, I became him. I was suddenly Dean Brennan, sailor. He and I resembled each other, so no one noticed the difference. That was until my menses came and they caught me. They tortured me, raped me, threw me to sea. I swam to the shore, hopped aboard a new world ship and escaped from Ireland to the Caribbean, leaving my mama and sister behind."

Swallowing hard, I throw another one. This one lands on the outer circle. I can't imagine going through something as traumatic as that. "Was this before or after the arranged marriage?"

"Before. I took my brother's identity once more while in Santo Domingo, but realized my uncle lived there. He wanted to marry me off to some rich man named Cormac since I was of marrying age." She goes to take out the knives. "I ain't want that. I wanted freedom. The sea. So, on the day of my sentence, I encountered Sullivan, and he saved me. He gave me a home, a rank, respect. He knew of the sailor woman who dressed as a man. I'm indebted to him."

"He gave you a second chance at life." She nods. "What do you know of your sister?"

"Should be around twelve, I reckon. Ain't know much about her. Left her when she was merely four. Wonder what her life has become."

"I have a niece," I blurt out, gripping my knives. "She's ten. I love her more than anything in the world. I'd give everything to see her again, so I know how you feel."

She smiles, mutually understanding. Both of us miss someone dear to us. "All the love I have to give, I give it to James. He's the child I always wanted but can never have." A sharp pang in my chest. She's broken.

I laugh. "He reminds me of my niece. It's hard not to love him. Even if he helped lock me in that room nine days ago."

She chuckles, throwing a knife. "Men don't think rationally. I'm convinced the crew of *The Fury* share one brain." I snort. She's absolutely correct. "Héctor is known for being unable to do more than one task at a time. Which explains his lack of grace and etiquette upon meeting ye."

I side eye her, suppressing my laughter. "I'm convinced he doesn't have a sophisticated bone in his body. All he does is glare and roll his eyes."

"I've seen him be poised. It's... infrequent, but not impossible." She sighs, running her fingers through her hair. "Well, I shall like to meet this young lass ye speak of. One day, perhaps."

I nod and throw another knife. One day I'll see my Soledad. If I ever get back to the future. I've never missed someone so badly in my life.

Time passes and the next thing we know, dinnertime has arrived as the sun sets and the lively chatter on the deck slowly dies off. Lydia and I sit on some barrels as we feast on more saltfish, dried beans, dehydrated callaloo, and oranges. Lydia has had enough rum throughout the day to have slurred words and a cheerful outlook by now. She mentions her *spouse* awaits her in Tortuga; speaking in riddles for them. All I could figure out is that they have the most beautiful lilac eyes she has ever seen.

I continue the conversation, waiting for the perfect opportunity to hit her with all the questions I have. She's like the drunk tía who will spill anyone's secrets if allowed, which reminds me of my tía Estefanía.

"So, Narváez, are ye being courted by someone? A landlubber with yer appearance surely has many suitors at her feet," she remarks, taking another sip of her rum.

"No. Not anymore, at least," I say, sullenly.

"Aye? How about Héctor?" She puts her feet up on the barrel in front of us. "Ye have become rather close I've noticed."

I choke on my orange. Is she joking? "No, no. Never in my wildest dreams." I clear my throat, wiping my mouth with my dirty sleeve. "I don't like him, and he doesn't like me. The only reason we're constantly together is because he agreed to practice with me." *Also, because I'm sure he has my necklace, which I intend to get back.*

She raises her eyebrow, a smile slowly forming. "Well, I've known Héctor for quite a bit of time and I'll admit, he acts differently toward ye. Ye've definitely softened him."

"He's just being civil."

"That's not what Art said when he saw you two last night."

This time it's I who takes a sip of the rum. She laughs. *Softened* him? The only time I saw him empathetic was last night when he told me he didn't have a home to go to. Is this why he's doing this? Is this why they're all doing this? Fighting on the seas for the same cause?

"Lydia?" I ask.

"Yes, Luz?" Her tone is soft and loving. She has *never* called me Luz.

I take a deep breath. "Who's the Aycayia of Ruin?"

She eyes me, sighing. "James, I swear to The Seer herself I'll nail yer head to the mast."

"Lydia. Please. If you care about me, answer honestly." I hand her the rum back.

She sits up, her face sobering. Taking her feet off the barrel, she grabs the bottle. "The siren of destruction is a myth. A legend. An entity meant to conquer the seas and time itself, destroying everything in her path. The lore states that a soul with a pearl bathed in blood will rise from the tides. I told the tale to James when he was younger to scare him into doing his duties."

A soul with a pearl bathed in blood. An entity meant to destroy everything in her path. How strong is the alcohol these people have been taking?

"And you believe I'm her?"

"I can't say. After ye threw that grenade yesterday, it's unclear what yer intentions are. All I know is that The Seer will explain everything. I'm doin' this cause I'm sworn to Sullivan. Where he goes, I follow. And if his heart is set on taking ye to The Seer, then goddamn it I shall take ye to her even if it's the last thing I do."

Lydia takes another gulp of the rum. I watch her, my thoughts becoming scattered. I try to make sense of everything I've learned in the past two days, and what interacting with The Seer could actually mean. She must be a person of immense power to have the entire crew of *The Fury* doing her bidding. The hours have tripped over the minutes, racing to make the seconds go by quicker.

"What year is it?" I ask Lydia, sitting up.

"What?"

"Please, I just—"

"I'm havin' a bad day, and if I'm havin' a bad day, I'm makin' it everyone's dilemma," James announces, coming to us. "How in the infernal heavens is this said?"

James throws an open book on top of the barrel between us. Its pages are yellowed with age, its hardcover a dark brown. He shifts his weight from one foot to another, unable to stay still in one spot. He points at a word I've never heard before, but I decide to pronounce it with him. After a couple of tries, we mutually agree on how to pronounce it. Is it right? Who knows? But he seems satisfied. He takes the book in his hands and sits on the barrel, thanking me for the help.

"Before anyone moves any further," I declare, "what year is it?"

"It could be 1593. It could be 2258. Maybe even 1691," James teases, smirking with his eyebrow raised. "Who knows what year we're in, Red."

Lydia rolls her eyes, groaning. "Is ye ever serious?"

He chuckles. "I can be serious when I *die*, Miss Lydia."

Lydia asks him to read a passage from his book, changing the topic. His voice is hesitant, and he mispronounces various words, but he corrects himself, not once stopping or getting frustrated. I sit there in awe, watching as he gains more confidence as the paragraph goes by. The three of us spend the rest of the evening together, observing as the sun sets in the horizon. I've grown more and more accustomed to the ocean, and I won't lie that the day it all goes back to normal, it'll feel off not being surrounded by the vast sea.

Lydia stands, claiming that she has to do a last-minute chore before heading off to catch a bit of sleep before we arrive at our destination. Tortuga.

She stops short of the hallway, glancing at me. "And it's 1689, Narváez. Pay no mind to him," she says and leaves.

1689.

The Golden Age of Piracy.

Lydia

CHAPTER
SEVENTEEN

A fat Puerto Rican woman from the twenty-first century... trapped in the seventeenth century.

I see it. But I can't believe it.

Feeling like the weight of the world is crushing my shoulders, I take out the five daggers Lydia gifted me and throw them, James joining me. I focus on words I want to say out loud.

I wish I could go home. *Woosh.* Outer circle hit.

Why is this happening to me? *Woosh.* Outer circle hit.

Why the fuck am I in the seventeenth century? *Woosh.* Inner circle hit.

Johann Nau is very much real. *Woosh.* Center hit.

I remove my five daggers out of the wooden target, my heart racing inside my ears.

"Red, move before the next one lands on ye!" James teases.

I walk back, and he aims, his knife landing right in the center of the plank. "You're great at this."

He does a quick bow, tipping his hat. "Thank ye kindly." He tosses another, landing right in the center too. "Héctor wishes he were as good as me. He's got his swords and crossbow while I have my daggers."

I hurl one, but it ricochets on the plank. "I thought he taught you."

"He's far too impatient for this." He lobs a third and into the crevice it goes, knocking out the previous one. "Captain Sullivan taught me this."

"Is he your father?" The next one I launch punctures the outer circle.

"My real daddy died out there on those fields. I never met my mama. When I came aboard, Sully took me under his wing." Inner circle hit for him. "He and Lydia are the parents I ain't never had, Pedro as well. Everyone here treats me like their child, which I loathe, 'cause I'm perfectly capable of doin' things myself."

I stay quiet and toss my next dagger, hitting the center. His words bounce around in my mind. He's the child of colonization.

What horrors has he seen?

"I've also heard you call Héctor your brother?" I ask, changing the topic for his sake.

He nods. "Héctor was the one who found me, helped me escape The Ri—" he says but takes a deep trembling breath. Shaking his head, he hurls a knife. "He helped me escape, savvy?"

"Savvy." I turn to him, twisting a dagger around in my fingers. "Do you truly believe I could be the omen of destruction?"

He sucks in a breath. "Aye."

"Well, if I'm the siren of destruction, why is everyone warming up to me after blowing up that ship?"

James chuckles, shaking his head. "Wow, ye really ain't know?"

"Um, no."

"It proves that yer and yer destruction are on our side, not on Nau's or those who hunt us. Which is a relief considerin' everyone is out for us."

I pretend like I'm understanding, laughing nervously. "But it's not logical, James."

He snorts, tilting his head and smiling at me. "Red, ain't nothing here makes sense. My brother's Native to these lands Nau and his people stole, my mama's a one-eyed Irish she-pirate. I easily have around thirty drunk daddies. We're pirates who fight for the greater good. None of us are *logical* aboard this ship."

I chuckle and shrug. In a way, he's right. Nothing here makes sense, so why try to make it make sense?

"James, go rest. You do not want to be exhausted when we arrive at Tortuga," Héctor suggests. James rolls his eyes, ignoring him. "I know you like being around Luz, but I am sure she needs her own space. You can be quite a handful."

James mocks his brother, tossing the knife in a different direction, wedging itself in the wooden frame next to Héctor's face. He's leaning against the hall frame unfazed as he takes the dagger and peels the skin of a mango he holds in his right hand. His appearance takes both of us aback, silencing our laughter.

Héctor's hair is in a half-up, half-down hairstyle, and it's groomed enough to make me think about my hair, which has been in two frizzy French braids for days. He changed out of his filthy cream shirt and brown vest, wearing a loose black poet blouse that shows his chest, with the sleeves rolled up to his elbows. From head to toe, he's covered in black, except for the gold chains around his neck. I hate to admit it, but he looks... *nice.*

James whistles, laughing afterward. "Aye, lookin' like a true charmer tonight, ain't we?"

Héctor rolls his eyes. "What did I say, d'atiao?" he inquires, raising his eyebrow. I wonder what *d'atiao* means. It's not the first time I've heard it.

James sighs loudly, defeated, and tidies up his things. He struts down the hall, passing Héctor, who trips him playfully. James hisses at his brother, threatening to choke a chuckling Héctor in his sleep.

"I hope yer sleeping cushion is warm on both sides," James exclaims. "Good night, sweethearts!" He slams the door of his and Héctor's shared quarters. I throw a knife. I need to distract myself so I can stop staring at Héctor.

"He likes to play around. Forgive him," Héctor says, but I ignore him.

I force myself to focus on the daggers. While Oliver is attractive, Héctor surpasses him in his own way, his natural beauty drawing me toward him. If my grandma were alive, she'd say, "Ay, como si nunca hubieras visto hombres, Luz." *You're acting as if you've never seen a man before.*

I'm ashamed to be thinking about Héctor in such a manner instead of thinking of Oliver.

I push those feelings aside. I shouldn't be thinking about either of them.

I should be thinking about getting back home and finding my necklace. What if that was the source of travel? The strange light that emitted from it. That has to be what brought me here. I need to find it.

But it's not in Héctor's room, Lydia's or Sullivan's. It has to be in a different area of the ship.

The dagger slips from my fingers as I remember harsh words told to me a few days ago.

That infernal pearl continues glowin' like there's no tomorrow, clearly calling for its owner...

Pedro Córdova.

Of course.

"You stole from my personal supply earlier this week, did you not?" Héctor asks, smirking. He's cutting up his mango with the knife he took from James.

I shake my head, smiling, clasping my hands together in front of me. I rub my thumbs together. *Pedro has my necklace.* "I'm an honorable woman, Mr. Villanueva," I tease, and he smiles, sucking some mango from the skin. "That's a horrible and distasteful accusation."

He chuckles, his eyes looking at me playfully. "Much to learn indeed, fantastic liar you are, but your hands give it away rather easily."

I bend to grab the dagger I dropped, wondering how he figured out my giveaway for lying is fidgeting with my thumbs. It took Oliver a good year and a half to figure out. Héctor figured that out in mere *days.* Maybe even in a couple of minutes depending on my previous lies.

He must know I rummaged through his room for the necklace.

"Practice will have to be delayed tonight I fear," I say, shoving all my knives inside my satchel. I can't waste time. If we're almost to Tortuga, I need to find that necklace, and I need to find it now.

"Where are you going?" Héctor asks.

"I, uh, I need some time by myself," I say. He raises his eyebrow at me, but nods.

I leave.

Pedro fucking Córdova.

Heading toward the lower deck, my stomach churns. What will I encounter? I guide myself past the resting pirates, the stench of sweat making me gag. A few whistle at me, but my focus is on the opened door ahead. That has to be Pedro's room.

I put my most dazzling smile just to encounter a sobbing Cyrus thrown on a bed, with an exasperated Art comforting him.

"I simply want to give him the world," Cyrus cries.

Art rubs Cyrus' shoulder, sighing. He finds my gaze. "Is ye here to save me from," he gestures to Cyrus, "this?"

I shake my head. "I'm looking for Pedro's room."

"Opposite side, Narváez."

I turn. Pedro's room stares back at me, begging me to approach it. I jog past the hammocks and gently push open the door. Thankfully, it's unlocked.

"This better be a matter of life or death, querida, and, truthfully, I'd prefer the latter," Pedro hisses from the inside.

Fuck.

Pedro sits on his bed, sharpening his sword. His black waves cascade over his forehead, and he's shirtless, a single chain around his neck. His upper body is covered in grime and tattoos. His room reeks of sweat and tobacco. My heart gets stuck in my throat. I wasn't expecting him to be in his room so early.

"I came to see you, quartermaster," I say, trying to defuse the tension.

"Ah, by all means then, come inside," he snorts, looking up at me. Those fierce blue eyes stare straight into mine, daring me to step into his room. "Yo no muerdo, mi vida."

I laugh uncomfortably, but this must be done. Time to bring out my acting skills, even if my body refuses to cooperate. I force my legs to carry me inside, flashing my most photogenic smile. He stands, placing the sword on his bed and shutting the door behind us.

I twirl the end of my braid with my fingers, looking up at him through my lashes. My insides recoil.

If Héctor's room was messy, Pedro's room is much worse. With a heap of dirty clothes in the corner, a variety of polished pistols hanging on the wall and a bundle of grenades hanging from the ceiling, his room is the epitome of *fuck around and find out.* Where Héctor's room has bookshelves, Pedro has weapons upon weapons. The single oil lamp atop a flimsy, trashed desk lights his room weakly, giving his quarters an eerie feeling.

Attached on his windowsill is a small garden bed with a beautiful half dozen pink hibiscus flowers. That's... an *interesting* detail. My grandfather grew them, as does my father.

"I'll be the first to admit, I'm rather surprised ye seeked me out," he teases, lustfully. "Has Villanueva not pleased ye enough?"

"He's not quite what I'm looking for," I say, getting close to him. "I'm looking for someone... better. Stronger." The necklace isn't on his desk. Where could it be? In his pocket?

He raises an eyebrow, smirking. "Oh, is that so, querida?" His lip quivers as his body presses against mine.

I force myself to stay where I am. "Very much so, quartermaster." I gently place my hands on his soiled chest. Recoiling at this man's touch. The chain around his neck carries a singular silver ring, but it looks as if it was a woman's.

"Has anyone ever mentioned you have breathtaking blue eyes?" I lick my mouth. "Blue's my preferred color."

He grabs my neck, nearly choking me. But he doesn't. Instead, his lips hover mine. I freeze.

"I can't take ye like this," he whispers, pulling me closer. His other hand grazes my waist, caressing me. "Yer clearly drunk or else ye would've stayed away from me. I may be a pirate... but I ain't takin' advantage of ye."

Thank the Lord.

A knock on his door. "Córdova, have you—" Our heads turn and Héctor stands incredulous at the door. Pedro releases me, scowling. "Is this a bad time?" Héctor asks, clearing his throat.

"Aye, it is," Pedro snarls at Héctor. He shrugs me off, gently pushing me toward the door. "Get out, Villanueva. And take her with ye. She's drunk."

With that, he steps back and slams the door in my face, leaving me there without having time to investigate his room.

Well, that went great.

"What were you doing in there with Córdova?" Héctor asks, his whole upper body tense. "When you claimed you needed time alone, I did not know you planned to spend time alone with *him*."

"Oh, shut up," I snap, fixing my clothes. "I was fine."

"Clearly." He rolls his eyes, tugging on his sleeves. "He was ready to forgo his duties tonight with how he looked at you."

"I didn't peg you to be the jealous type, Villanueva. Why do you care about how the man looked at me?"

He scans my face, his eyes narrowing. "You were searching for your pendant, were you not?"

I walk across the crowd of sleeping pirates and he follows. I ignore the fact that he changed the topic. "He mentioned the jewel kept glowing the day he attempted to murder me, so I simply connected the dots."

He chuckles, shaking his head. "You need rest. You are obviously trying too hard to find something you will not attain."

The audacity of this man. "I won't rest until it's in my fingers."

"Then I guess you shall learn to live without sleep."

I stare him down, and he stares back. Pedro has to be the one who has it. I'm sure of it. But why give it to the man who tried killing me? I look away, clicking my tongue. We head to the deck, taking a breath of fresh air. I had Pedro *way* too close to me. I can still feel his sweat in my fingers.

"Héctor, I need to know exactly why you took it from me and why you refuse to give it back," I mention, my voice barely above a whisper.

Héctor sighs, rubbing his face. He saunters to the mast, but stumbles, falling on his side. I rush over to where he is, my mind racing with a bit of concern. He stands, clearing his throat, and fixing his hair, his gaze downcast. For the past few days, he's been stumbling or bumping into things. Is he naturally clumsy or might he have a vision problem?

"Are you alright?" I ask tenderly.

"I am quite fine, thank you," he says, genuinely grateful for my worry, "and I took the jewel from you because it is the conduit of your power. Without it, you could not hurt us, or me. You are less dangerous."

Now it's me who stumbles, my lips parting. I try to understand what he's saying. "I don't have powers. And if I wanted to hurt you, I would've done so already. I wouldn't have cared that you fell."

His lips quirk upward on one side, and he crosses his arms. His cheeks have a faint tint of maroon. "Oh, so you care about me, d'nanichi?"

I laugh, rolling my eyes. "You wish, second mate."

I gaze into his eyes, and it's as if I'm being pulled into the world of wonder, mystery, and horror behind them. A strange rush of warmth spreads throughout my body, causing my cheeks to grow hot.

"I also took it because of the inscription on the back," Héctor admits, shrugging his shoulders. "What did you say it meant?"

"My grandmother told me it meant *family first*, as a reminder that I should always put my family before anything," I mention, recalling the memory like it was yesterday.

The day she died, Mami Julia was meant to speak to me alone, but my mother refused to let her do so. The air was tense, doctors surrounded us. My grandmother seemed hesitant, irritated. As if she wanted to tell me a tremendous secret.

I never knew what it was she wanted to tell me.

But that same day she reminded me of the inscription. *Family first*, she had said. My mother had smiled, nodding along, claiming family, *blood* family, is more important than anything. No matter what.

"Are you certain?" Héctor asks, his brows furrowed together.

"Yes. I don't know the language it's in. But I know it means *family first*," I state, my hands coming up to where the jewel used to rest against my collarbone. The phantom weight reminds me of what I no longer own.

He smiles, but something sinister yet depressing hides behind those eyes. A secret lurks in his mind that he can't speak of yet.

"It has been a long day, and Córdova stated you are drunk, although you do not seem it. I suggest you sleep before we reach Tortuga," Héctor changes the topic.

"Before I go," I say, "what does the inscription mean? Why is it so important to you?"

"I cannot say. That was forbidden for me to speak of it with you." A chill runs through his body. "Anyhow, I must think of how to make you presentable for The Seer. She is a woman of grace and elegance, I cannot have you in filthy clothing before her. Go along now."

I sigh, ultimately, taking his advice and heading to my hammock to rest. I don't know when we will arrive at Tortuga, but it should be soon. It can't be too long. Maybe a couple of hours.

I enter the room quietly, just in case Lydia is asleep and, lo-and-behold, she is knocked out with her bottle of rum in hand. She snores softly, sleeping like someone who hasn't rested in days. Slowly, I approach my hammock and find a comfortable position. I've been so active all day my exhaustion is now hitting. I drink some water and face the wooden wall, wondering if this is truly my life. The nine tally marks look back at me.

Oliver comes to mind. His smile. His hair. His rich voice when he sings. Those strong hands that create the littlest pastries of delicacy. The comforting thoughts that replay in my mind slowly morph into depressing ones, as I remember the fact that I broke up with him right before I fell into the ocean. Five years of a steady relationship... Gone. Ended in a flash. He didn't deserve this. Yes, he messed up. Yes, he is a terrible listener. Yes, he's a very naïve person with my feelings and struggles. But he didn't deserve me breaking up with him out of nowhere.

Tears stream down my face. My chest hurts, and it feels like the room is closing in on me. I'm trapped with my own thoughts, drowning in this endless sea of pain and anguish. All the energy I felt evaporates, and I'm left with the withdrawal of missing my old life. My commodities. My niece. My friends. My family. All of it.

I close my eyes, hugging myself. Little by little, exhaustion overtakes my body. The next thing I know, I'm being shaken awake. I open my eyes and Lydia smiles above me. I notice that it's still dark outside. How much time has passed since I fell asleep? Thirty minutes? An hour? A few hours?

Nausea is the first sensation that overtakes me.

"Welcome to Tortuga, beautiful."

CHAPTER
EIGHTEEN

I don't know how to feel about reaching Tortuga. Part of me is ecstatic because it means I'm one step closer to getting answers. The other part of me has this eerie feeling in the pit of my stomach. As if this was only the beginning of it all.

I sit up, lightheaded, not knowing if I should make a tenth tally mark. Rubbing my eyes, I etch the line with one of my daggers. Ten days aboard *The Fury*, and of being stuck inside this nightmare.

Ten days of being considered the siren of ruin.

I grab my waterskin and take huge gulps of water, my throat feeling like the sand granules that rest on the coast. I do my vinegar rinse, sighing after. A soft knock startles me. Héctor comes in with fabrics in hand.

His hair is fully down this time, as if ready to seduce everyone he encounters. He's a pirate after all, who knows how many lovers he's got running rampant around the streets of Tortuga. His eyes land on mine but just as quickly, land on the fabrics he's holding. As if he were trying to avoid my gaze.

"This is for you," Héctor states, placing the items in my hand. The soft hug of cotton on my rough fingers is a welcoming feeling. "I refuse to let you step foot into The Seer's place looking like a stampede ran you over."

I roll my eyes. "Papito, you wish you looked this effortlessly good."

He chuckles, grabbing the handle. "Come on. Get up. We are leaving."

I throw the clothing inside the satchel and head toward the deck with him. My legs feel like jelly, my head is pounding. I want nothing else than to crawl back into my hammock and sleep.

Lydia is nowhere to be seen, which is not reassuring. Without her comforting, badass presence, how might the others behave with me nearby?

My thoughts grow more unsteady by the second. Oliver, Héctor, The Seer, the name the pirates have given me. It all fights in my head, wanting to be heard. I wipe my hands against my dirty clothing, the cut from my arm scarred. To distract myself, I make sure I have my personal items inside my satchel: my five sheathed daggers, the small bottle of vinegar I stole from Héctor, my half-empty water skin, the clothes I've been given, and a sweaty handkerchief. That's all I own at the moment.

And the letters I stole from Sullivan.

Unlike me, most of the crew is awake and ready to go. Their electrifying energy is contagious across the deck, their laughter and inside jokes bringing an air of familiarity. James stands off to the side, yawning and rubbing his eyes with the sleeve of his worn brown coat. Héctor fixes the fabric tied around James' neck, reminding him to not do anything *funny* on land. Since it's still nighttime, the humid heat is subdued, replaced by a cool ocean breeze instead. The smells of seldom-washed bodies, urine and rum wrinkle my nose. While it's not the best-smelling thing, I can't be complaining since I must be carrying the same odor they are.

The dock is as lit as Times Square on New Year's Eve. Various oil lamps and lanterns are hung on wooden posts and inns, lighting the alleyways and dock. People are asleep by the smaller ships or loading up provisions.

I'm not too far from the village. Maybe I could escape. Perhaps Sullivan trusts me more and relaxes his grip over me.

"Avast lads! We've arrived in Tortuga," Sullivan exclaims, rum bottle in hand. "Now, before I let ye go, I need my officers plus the harbinger of chaos to join me. The rest of ye are free to go!"

Harbinger of chaos.

The crew disembarks *The Fury* except for Lydia, Héctor, Pedro, Cyrus, and Art. James refuses to leave my side as I stand back. Art fixes his neck-length hair into a bun while Cyrus takes another chug of rum out of his bottle. How is he not dead from alcohol poisoning? Pedro looks indifferent to everything happening around him, looking at himself in a hand-held mirror as he fixes his black waves, tricorn hat held firmly between his thighs.

Lydia comes down from the quarterdeck, her shoulders held back proudly. Her new outfit makes her look more ravishing than ever. An olive-green blouse tucked inside a brown corset, black leather pants, a black coat, and her usual brown boots all scream of class and seduction. If she were a siren, I would know why. Her ginger pixie bob is combed underneath her black tricorn hat, and it looks like she's wearing the same eyeliner Pedro wears. Around her neck rests a necklace with a lavender seashell, which she fidgets with.

Héctor glances at me, his gaze calculating.

Sullivan approaches us, fixing his blue velvet coat. "Yer will have two hours to do as yer wish. After, the eight of us shall meet at Dolphin Cove and head to The Seer. Master Khan, have ye the payment?" he asks, and Cyrus nods, gesturing to a pocket in his gray coat. What more are they offering this woman? "Villanueva, Narváez, Córdova. I'd like to speak to the three of ye. Brennan, keep an eye on Khan, Zhào, and on mini Edwards. Yer free to go."

"Aye, Captain Edwards," Lydia says, nodding at the others.

Art and Cyrus leave, first singing a lively song. Cyrus takes out a second bottle of rum for Art, both of them ecstatic. James takes a bit of coaxing, but Lydia manages to drag him away. They leave, with Pedro, Héctor, and I staying back on the deck with Sullivan.

"I'm tasking the two of ye with keeping an eye on her," Sullivan orders. Pedro groans as Sullivan turns to a silent Héctor. "Don't think ye can go fuck whatever belladona ye encounter, and let this one loose. We came this far with her, I want her under yer gaze at all times, understood?"

"Aye," Héctor says, crossing his arms. "I will watch her."

"And to ensure ye do," Sullivan puts his hand on Pedro's shoulder, "Córdova has my permission to do with ye as he pleases should ye disobey. He ain't quartermaster for nothing."

"What?" Héctor shrieks. "I am an officer of this ship! I do not need this *whore* supervising me!"

Pedro's demeanor turns dark as he puts on his hat. He grabs Héctor by his shirt, pulling the second mate to his face. My heart stops. *No.* Héctor takes out a dagger, pointing it at Pedro's neck. My breaths become shallow as my eyes dart from one man to the other.

"Ye speak rather boldly for someone who is amongst the shortest here!" Pedro snarls.

"At least I make up for it in wit, which is something you lack!" Héctor seethes. "I have seen more intelligence in a barrel of rum than in that thick skull of yours!"

Pedro raises his clenched fist, but Sullivan breaks them apart with a single shove. Pedro curses in Spanish, taking deep breaths, while Héctor fixes his clothes, cursing in Arawak.

"I refuse to allow theatrics on *my* ship!" Sullivan commands. "Ye will all listen to me or I shall kill all of ye! Savvy?"

"Aye, Captain," the three of us mumble.

"Alright, get off. If ye wanna cockfight, it'll be done outside." I make to leave but Sullivan pulls me backward. "If ye run off, I'll personally lead the hunt for ye, savvy?" I nod, fear churning in my stomach.

Sullivan releases me, adjusting his coat. I rub my arm, a faint pain eroding from it. Pedro leaves to the cement dock, his stomps echoing as he descends the gangway. Héctor leads me down, Pedro mumbling death threats in Spanish.

"Come on, ye two!" James rushes us, and Lydia chuckles. The quartermaster strolls ahead, alone.

Our journey into the village of Tortuga begins.

The palm leaves dance in the breeze, insects chirping faintly. The fresh breath of air is pleasurable, compared to the stench from the ship. My legs take a minute to adjust to land, feeling the waves and ripples underneath my feet, but the others are wandering the path with ease.

Lydia suggests heading to a place called The Sunken Shard for a warm meal and company, and James wholeheartedly agrees.

"I do not see why not," Héctor shrugs.

"I can't wait to see Maggie," James swoons.

"Ye will be seeing no one," Lydia scolds.

"Ay, por Dios, let the boy live," Pedro barks from ahead, not once looking at us.

We arrive at what I can only describe as downtown Tortuga. A small collection of wooden taverns, inns, and brothels with thatched roofs are nestled among the palm trees and lush foliage. The deeper we saunter into the village, the narrower the streets become. Paved surfaces are non-existent, instead it's a dirt road lined with palm trees and fruit trees. We even pass loose barking dogs scavenging for their supper. The clucking of chickens fills the air, reminding me of the finca I grew up in Puerto Rico with Mami Julia and Papi Gustavo.

Just like in Port Royal, the structures and buildings of Tortuga are made of a mix of wood and brick, sturdier than the pieces on the set I worked on. All reminders of the life and people I left behind in my time.

The environment is loud and cheery, with plenty of commotion to go around. Many women in brightly colored dresses like the one I wore ten days ago flirt and cling to some of the crew members as we pass them by, speaking of broken promises and a pleasurable night. The sounds of accordions and untuned fiddles accompany us.

Nobody walks past us sober. Their slurred words and laughter remind me of Abel. Of Johann Nau. Of Cyrus even. Everyone around us is intoxicated by the drink.

An inebriated white man grabs my arm, his clothes covered in filth and vomit. I shove him off, and he stumbles face first into a horse trough a few feet away.

"They will not approach if they see you in my arms, d'nanichi" Héctor whispers. I glare at him, eventually letting him do as he suggests. He places his arm around my waist as we walk, and that single touch makes my whole body melt. The rest of the time, his eyes go dark. Menacing. Threatening.

Men eye me with pleasure, but grumble once they see I'm accompanied by the second mate. James holds Lydia's hand as they talk so perhaps that's why they haven't approached her... however, she looks like she could choke anyone who dares breathe in her direction.

Finally, the four of us arrive at The Sunken Shard, its name written in curly script in a swaying sign above. Music bursts from the windows, as do lively conversations and flirtatious giggles. I separate myself from Héctor and look inside the window, the smell of food wafting in my direction, making me salivate. Meat, chicken, potatoes, freshly baked bread. All being served. So close to my grasp.

Lydia twirls James around as if they were ballroom dancing. He giggles, taking out a small pouch. Money. He's got the money. What if my necklace is inside that little bag too? They interlace their arms together and walk inside, receiving cheers from a few of *The Fury* crew. Two young girls dressed in burgundy and mustard yellow dresses with fancy updos yank James inside. I follow because, truthfully, I'm so hungry for a warm meal I could eat an entire horse, but Héctor grabs my arm.

"No running off, savvy?" Héctor warns, letting me go.

"I won't. I promise," I reassure. "I need a room, though."

Héctor pulls his head back, making a face. He chuckles nervously, fidgeting with the pistol tucked inside his pants.

"Luz, the rooms in the tavern are for prostitution," he states, a little too quickly. He tries to get more words out, but they come out a stuttering mess, one word intertwined with the next.

"You didn't let me change on the ship, so I kind of have no other choice."

He takes a deep breath, his face flushed. His fingers are tapping anxiously against his thigh and he can't look me in the eye. Rambling, he takes out a small, brown leather bag and leads me inside.

"One room, thanks," Héctor demands to a white man with brown eyes in his forties probably, throwing some gold coins on the desk reluctantly. The man eyes me, raising his eyebrow. Wood string music, laughter and jovial conversation fill my ears as we stare at each other.

"Ye sure ye ain't want one of the ones upstairs, Villanueva?" the man asks, taking the golden payment. Oh, so Héctor *has* been here before?

Héctor shakes his head. "No. Just hand me the keys, Frederick."

Frederick gives us a rusty, copper key, smiling mischievously. "It's nice to see ye give in to a beautiful woman for once. Indulge yerself. Stop bein' such a prude, boy."

I take the keys, my face turning hot and walk off. Héctor follows. "I hope you don't plan on coming upstairs with me," I say.

"I can live without seeing," Héctor gestures to my body and face, "all that."

He walks off and I head upstairs.

The staircase is nothing more than wooden creaky steps with women of various races in seductive clothing waiting to ensnare their next prey. One of them—a pretty brunette with gorgeous brown eyes—makes a move at me, biting her plump pink lip as I pass her. I simply smile, insisting I'm not the one she's looking for, but that there's a bitter yet attractive second mate who could use some company downstairs. Eager, she nods and leaves, on a mission to find Héctor.

Walking down the hall on the second story of the tavern, sounds of pleasure and laughter fill the hall, muffled by shut doors. I try my best to disregard every noise around me—especially one that sounds like the quartermaster's ecstatic voice—asking one innkeeper if the rooms have bathrooms. He shakes his head. Of course there are no bathrooms. This is 1689. So I ask him for a pail of water, clean rags, and soap, which is used primarily for domestic cleaning, not *bathing* during this time period. The innkeeper eyes me, but does as I say when I offer a tip involving three gold doubloons, which I believe are equal to fifteen dollars each.

I reach my room. If it weren't so run down, it could've had the potential to be fancy. Stained beige silk curtains engulf a four-poster bed, and the smell of roasting meat downstairs permeates the room. A broken mirror sits on the wall with a dusty wooden table underneath it. Candles illuminate the room on a rusty chandelier.

Cold breeze enters from the open window, subduing the humidity with the night air. It's not as suffocating as it feels during the day. The temperature reminds me of el campo where I grew up, where Mami Julia would scream at me to come inside to avoid el sereno, the nighttime air.

But this is not el campo. This is Tortuga.

I shut the curtain and throw myself on the bed, the faint odor of rose perfume and sweat hitting my nose. Unholy things have definitely happened in this room.

A knock on my door. The innkeeper has brought what I've asked for.

After he leaves, I undress and lower myself into the metal pail, ready for a sponge bath. The pail is the same width as a barrel, but half the height. It's not exactly what I had in mind, but I've missed the water, being clean, and having time to myself. The water's room temperature, but I don't care. I've never been so ecstatic to be clean before.

I clean a week of grime off my body, hair, and undergarments with the soap that smells faintly of lavender. My face is tender as I rub it, most definitely sunburnt. I wish I had my soaps and body washes. My lotions and oils. My conditioner for my straw-like hair. I'm just glad my period didn't start. It's set to begin in a few days based on the tallies I made.

By the time I'm done with everything, the previously crystal clear water has turned brown. I dry myself with the blankets, silently apologizing to my hair for the mistreatment I've given it. I scrunch up my undergarments, which dry rather quickly, thanks to the lack of humidity in the room.

I take out the new clothing I was given. A beige poet blouse, a scarlet vest the shade of my necklace, and some black pantaloons. The fabric feels clean and crisp against my clean body. While I don't feel completely clean, this is better than before. My skin, however, is brittle, screaming for moisture.

I don't know how people can go more than one day without bathing.

I braid my unruly curls again for convenience. With my hair tied down, I have one less thing to worry about. Looking at myself in the mirror, I take a deep breath. I truly look like a pirate, down to the tired eyes, sunburnt, freckled skin, and healing scrapes. It's only been ten days, but I look like I've aged months.

My resolve slowly deteriorates by the second. I press the pillow against my face and scream. Tears form in my eyes. I throw things around, as if I was in a rage room instead of a hostel. Pillows, blankets, my old clothes. Everything gets flung. I scream until my throat burns. Tired, I slide down the wall, a sob lodged in my throat. I bring my knees up to my chest, dropping my head between them.

I want to wake up from this nightmare. I want Octavia, Soledad, even Oliver. I want my grandmother even though she's dead.

Minutes pass by, an imaginary clock ticking in the back of my head. No one checks in on me.

I sigh and stand, my legs numb. I have to go back downstairs before they think I ran off and they send Pedro to kill me. However, if the voice I heard earlier belongs to him, I doubt he's going to stop his fun to hunt me down. I put on my black leather boots and Héctor's satchel, sighing. My eyes catch sight of various oil vials that sit on the desk, so I pick one up, the glorious scent of lavender and florals wafting up to my nose. I dab a good amount on my wrists, neck, and collarbone. A closet next to the desk holds outfits, and I find a black tricorn hat with a tag. I take it and put it on, surprised to find it fits comfortably on my head.

I dry my tears and smile. Hide the emotions. Don't feel them. Show them you have none. I don't even bother fixing the room. What I do here doesn't matter.

Nothing matters anymore, so why try?

CHAPTER NINETEEN

Standing on my tiptoes on the ground floor, I try to locate the group but cannot catch them over the ruckus. I glance at the door, considering my escape. Pedro is most likely busy, he won't kill me.

But if I run, he'll kill Héctor, and as much as he irritates me... I want him to *live*.

"Red!" James calls over the commotion. I lock eyes with him, smile and head toward the table he's in. I push the thoughts of escape into the deep crevices of my mind.

James sits with a brown-skinned teenage girl on his lap, giggling and flirting with each other, everyone else nonexistent to them. This infatuation reminds me of when Oliver and I began dating. As the years passed, the feeling decreased, replaced by a sense of emptiness, as if something was missing from my life.

Next to him, Lydia is playing the dice game Pedro and Art played two nights ago with a woman dressed in a pirate outfit as well, her long hair as golden as the sun. A silent and calculated Héctor is watching the game with a drink in hand, awaiting Lydia's next move. More men have congregated behind the three, placing bets. Lydia twirls the seashell necklace around her neck, bringing it to her lips. Finally, Lydia throws the dice and cheers erupt. She's won. The blonde pirate woman places her fist against the table, but raises her eyebrow at Lydia, as if to say *good game.*

The tune changes to a faster one, Lydia, the pirate woman, and a few of the men go dancing, while others down some drinks. My eyes fall on the food.

China crockery rests on the table, holding roasted turkey legs and chicken, potatoes, vegetables, fried saltfish, and fresh loaves of bread with slabs of butter. Ignoring everyone around me, I sit next to Héctor and load up a plate with a bit of everything. Especially bread. Tons and tons of bread. As soon as I taste everything, I gag. It's bland. Flavorless. As if I was eating a piece of wet paper instead of an aesthetically pleasing warm meal from a pirate tavern.

"What is wrong with it?" Héctor asks, suppressing his laughter. "I thought you were begging me for a meal."

"I need spices. The Europeans raided the world for spices, killing thousands, millions even, and this is what they created with them? I thought it was bad before, but this? This is definitely worse," I say. I force myself to eat the dry, gummy chicken, and flavorless vegetables since I need sustenance.

Some omen of destruction I am, spitting out food.

Only then do I realize what I said out loud. Héctor stares at me, stunned. I bite down on something else, looking at my plate instead. I should've lied or kept my mouth shut, now he's studying me. Like there's something about me he can't place but is certain about.

"I agree, d'nanichi. When my bakutu was alive, she utilized the herbs given by the earth. She would grind them with a siba, giving our Zemí an ahiahude, a blessing. Now, they plunder and kill and mock people like my bakutu." He breathes deeply, tightening his grip on the cup of wine. "People like me."

The way he speaks. Zemí. An Arawak word. *Now they plunder and kill and mock people. People like me.* The genocide of the natives. He's a Native alright... Taíno. The indigenous people the Puerto Rican government keeps trying to say are extinct. But they're not. They are everywhere in the Caribbean. They are in me. In him. They still exist and he speaks their language. Our language.

"When you speak of my people's history, there is passion, fury, and hatred. You speak as if it too was your experience," he says, fascinated. "I have never met someone so forthright." Héctor leans in a bit, and my heart stops. "How did you live with such a powerful voice surrounded by the invaders of our land?"

I open my mouth to answer, but Cyrus stumbles over to us with a brown-haired man in hand. They're both so drunk, they spill wine over us. It lands everywhere on the table, and while I hate the food, I raise my plate, protecting it from the rapidly moving liquid.

"Watch it, Cyrus!" Héctor hisses, wiping wine from his black pants.

"Sorry," Cyrus mumbles, the man next to him giggling.

"I'll go get rags," I say, lowering the plate to a different section of the table.

Héctor shakes his head. "No, I got it. I will be right back."

He leaves toward the bar, flipping his hair back. As I continue eating, I study him, my eyes never leaving him. Cyrus and the guy sit next to me, with Cyrus feeding the man grapes. Art cackles at the spectacle from the dance floor. The person behind the bar nods and Héctor sits, fidgeting with his ring.

The tune changes to a slower paced song, low enough for conversations to be heard, but loud enough to fill the air with a sensual vibe. I rip a piece of the bread, watching as a beautiful blonde woman with flowy curls and a seductive green dress approaches Héctor, her eyes filled with mischief and desire. He stands, placing an obvious distance between him and her. She's talking, twirling his hair on her finger. He grabs her delicate hand, pushing it away. His shoulders are tense and he avoids direct eye contact with her, as if seeking an escape route.

My stomach tightens with a peculiar feeling as she flirts shamelessly with him. While I should feel satisfaction at his unease, all it does is remind me of parties I used to attend with Oliver, where executives and the press would get handsy with all the actors, to the point of us feeling uncomfortable. Oliver persisted through it, but I would end it quickly by blowing a whistle in their face. Yes, call me irritating, but hey, it worked.

The woman persists, pulling him by his shirt, her laughter like a siren's call. A spark ignites within me and all I wish is for her to leave him alone. I may not tolerate him, but I tolerate disrespect and the breaking of boundaries even more. And who knows? Maybe if I go to his rescue, he'll tell me where my necklace is afterward. Placing my utensils on the table, I stand, his gaze darting to me, his brows slightly furrowed.

I smile and reach his side, placing my arm on his shoulder. "Hey, what's taking so long?" I ask, leaning into him. "You said you'd be right back."

Héctor locks eyes with me, the tension in the air palpable. "I apologize, my love. I got held up."

She studies me, pursing her lips together. "And you are?"

"His wife, from *The Fury* crew." I eye her and she averts her gaze. I turn to Héctor. "Are you coming back soon?"

"Yes, I am, sweetheart." He looks around for the bartender and they're nowhere to be seen. "If he ever bothers to appear." He locks eyes with the girl. "Listen, Katherine, like I have told you before, I am not interested in your services."

She scoffs and marches off, pushing a man out of the way. Héctor sighs, running a hand through his hair.

"You okay?" I ask.

"Yes, thank you. You did not have to intervene," he says, a hint of gratitude in his tone.

I shrug, taking the seat next to him. He sits too, a bit of smeared lipstick on his cheek. "It looked like you needed saving." I reach out to his face. "She left a bit of cosmetics on you, hold on."

I pull my sleeve down, using it to wipe away the red stain. His breath catches and his eyes widen as I trail my hand tenderly down the side of his cheek. My heart races as I finish, but I don't remove my touch. Héctor takes my hand in his, bringing it to his lips, his dark, twinkling eyes on mine. That single kiss makes my entire body shiver and part of me wants him to do it again.

My hand grazes Héctor lips, and he inhales the scent of lavender I rubbed on my wrist. His eyes shimmer with a glint of desire, capturing my attention with their intense gaze. As his jaw clenches, his bewitching stare radiates a combination of yearning and longing that speaks volumes without uttering a single word.

While I try to keep a serious expression, my demeanor betrays me, softening as he lovingly looks into my brown eyes. A delicate dance between my emotions and this new sensation stirs within me, a soft blush grazing my cheeks.

"What are you doing?" I whisper, not breaking eye contact.

He rubs my hand with his thumb. "Showing my appreciation," he says. We both lean in, my heart beating so hard it threatens to rip out of my chest.

"Here ye are," Frederick says. "Sorry about that."

I drop my hand and look away, my face growing hot.

He kidnapped you, Luz. Snap out of it. You aren't a Stockholm victim.

"Thank you," Héctor says, taking the rags. "Let us go back."

He leads me to the table, where Art is scolding Cyrus for scamming him. Héctor cleans the wine as I sit to finish my meal. Lydia is dancing, while James feeds his girl. Héctor speaks to Art about the next hit they plan to do aboard *The Fury*, glancing at me every once in a while. I keep my mouth shut for the rest of the time, just as I do whenever I join my family for Thanksgiving and Navidades.

Unfortunately, my nerves slowly unhinge by the second. I'm going to meet The Seer. This powerful woman who sees and knows all. Who knows what type of person she truly is?

I finish my meal in silence, belly full of bland food. But hey, can't complain. I try some wine, spitting it back out when I realize it's very strong. I'll stick to drinking water for now. If I'm to face The Seer, I want to do it sober.

Despite disliking the meal, I find myself recharged with a bit of energy. Héctor clears my plate as I gravitate toward a window, seeking solitude away from him and the others. I maintain my position within a few feet of the table, ensuring that if Pedro comes downstairs, I'll be close to the second mate.

I watch the panorama outside. The hairs in the back of my neck stand and my arms get sudden goosebumps. I observe every person who passes by. Pirates, saloon girls, drunk men. I see nothing out of the ordinary. I don't see Johann either. Or the three men that were with him from the first night. I breathe deeply. Must be the wine I tried.

"Cálmate mija, se te va a fundir el cerebro," I tell myself, rubbing my temples.

I pivot to face the commotion inside when an unexpected collision with Héctor startles me. I clutch my chest, instinctively. He arches an eyebrow, folding his arms in front of him.

"One of these days, you are going to give me a heart attack," I admit, my heart beating fast. "How are you so good at sneaking around?"

"When you are a master criminal, such as myself, you must know how to blend in," he teases, shaking his head. "Help me gather the others. It is time to walk to Dolphin Cove."

Lydia joins us quickly, wanting nothing more than to leave. James, while sober, doesn't want to let go of the gorgeous girl on his lap. They give each other a quick peck on the lips and speak of promises I know they won't intend to keep. Héctor laughs at the spectacle, telling James that as soon as he leaves, he'll probably find another girl to seduce. James shrugs, stating that he'll be back, and leaves back into the crowd.

Cyrus is heavily intoxicated, and it takes Lydia grabbing his coat and physically dragging him away to get to leave. Art joins us by himself, laughing at a very disheveled and euphoric Pedro coming down the stairs. Fixing his weatherbeaten coat and hair, he joins us with a grin.

"Ready to eat, crew?" Pedro asks, rubbing his hands together.

"Well, *someone* had fun," I tease, looking up at him through my eyelashes. "We're literally leaving, like, *now.*"

His face feigns surprise. "No, the fuck we aren't."

He runs toward the table we sat in, grabbing leftover food and throwing it inside his satchel. Once Pedro and James both come back, we leave The Sunken Shard and head to Dolphin Cove.

The air outside is a nice, pleasant contrast from the inside of the tavern, where the body heat made it feel like it was daytime. The night sky is clear, the stars shining brightly overhead. The moon casts a silvery light over the village, along with the torches and lanterns, casting flickering shadows on the walls, brightening the path we're walking on.

The farther we walk, the fainter the smell of wood smoke, salty sea air, and fish. We pass a couple shacks, their windows open to let in the cool night air. Pirates pass us by, some drunk, some sober yet drinking, others smoking pipes and cigars. The sound of crickets and insects grow louder from the foliage and palm trees.

Cyrus sings a lively shanty, slurring his words, and Art joins him, interlacing his arm with the bo'sun's. Pedro eats the food he took from the tavern, the grease dripping down his fingers. Lydia puts her strong arm around me, complimenting my new outfit. Héctor twists the wooden ring around his finger as we walk, anxious. I'm about to ask if he's okay when James takes out a fiddle from his satchel. I watch, my mouth wide open. How did he sneak out a whole instrument? That must be what he went back into the tavern for.

He plays it to accompany the shanty Cyrus and Art are singing. But even with the energized ambiance, I feel like throwing up my dinner.

"James, lad, play my favorite tune!" Lydia calls out, letting me go. James changes up the tune to a faster one. Cyrus, Art, and Lydia cheer and sing in unison, not caring about being heard or seen. I wish I had zero care in the world. They're not the ones about to come face to face with a mysterious, powerful being.

Desten, sirèn nan ruine... Desten...

I glance around, my heart wanting to pop out of my chest. The voice was rich and accented, with an eerie quality that I quite can't place.

"Did you hear that?" I ask Héctor above the noise.

"Hear what?" he asks.

Ou pral peye... You will pay...

It sounds like Haitian Creole, which is familiar to me because I've heard Octavia speak it before. It's official. I need a psychiatrist.

Art and Lydia dance, and now that he's finished, Pedro joins in, spinning Cyrus around as they both laugh. Memories of when Mami Julia was alive resurface as I take everything in. When she and I hosted random dance parties on the weekends, busting out neon eighties clothing. She especially enjoyed dancing in the rain, letting the music guide us under tender drizzles. Sometimes Papi Gustavo joined as well and they could dance for hours, staring into each other's eyes as they connected their bodies.

I miss those beautiful days. When both of my paternal grandparents still lived. Papi Gustavo's death saddened me, but Mami Julia's destroyed me.

James ends the song, and we clap for him, whooping and cheering. He truly is talented with that fiddle. James bows dramatically and puts the instrument in his bag, smiling big. Pedro rubs James' shoulder and James responds to this affection by taking Pedro's hat and running off, cackling. Pedro and Lydia chase after the mischievous fifteen-year-old, warning him to not stray far. Cyrus and Art follow, their arms interlaced as they slur another shanty.

Even though the street is deserted besides the seven of us, I still can't shake the feeling that we're being followed. My heart races as the feeling intensifies, but I try telling myself that it must be my imagination. Just like the voices I heard earlier.

"Luz," Héctor says. While the rest of the group moves ahead, unconcerned with our delay, he positions himself in front of me, wearing a worried expression. "Are you alright?"

"No, yes, I'm fine," I lie. "I've never seen you so *relaxed* before, oh, lord of bitterness."

He chuckles, rolling his eyes. "You continue mocking an officer of *The Fury*. I should punish you. For real this time." I snort, knowing damn well he's going to do nothing of the sort. He puts his hand inside his brown leather satchel, but just as quickly takes it out. "D'nanichi. Who did your jewel belong to? Who gave it to you?"

I sigh. "My grandmother. Technically, my mom gave it to me, but it belonged to my grandmother before she passed. It's the only possession I have of her I'm able to carry daily." I kick a rock away from us, taking a shuddering breath.

Héctor nods. "Do you see this ring?" He shows me the wooden ring that he wears on his left index finger. "It too belonged to my bakutu. Her father had carved it for her brother, but they murdered him years before my mother was born. When I turned a mere ten, she passed it onto me. I have had it for fifteen years since. It is as if my bakutu was traveling with me aboard *The Fury*." Bakutu. Grandmother. He speaks of his grandmother the same way I speak of Mami Julia.

"Did she pass away as well?" We walk, with him offering his arm to me. I take it, just in case the quartermaster decides to shoot us down.

"No. She is alive. I have not seen her for the past five years." He takes a deep breath, reminiscing of his old memories. "I could not risk putting her in danger, I would kill myself if something happened to her."

"It must be so hard not seeing her." He nods, looking at the ground as we walk. "Mine passed away eight years ago. I was sixteen. Which is why you must understand why the jewel means so much to me."

"I understand."

We stop walking and he puts his hand inside the satchel once more.

Héctor pulls out my necklace. I gasp, taking a step forward. He holds it in his firm hands, caressing the jewel.

"Héctor. What are you doing? I thought Sullivan and The Seer warned against giving it back to me," I recall. "I don't want us getting in trouble. I already have enough on my plate."

"I will only give it back against my better judgment because it might bring you ease with what is coming," he admits. I reach out and he pulls it back. "However. If you run, I will personally hunt you for the rest of your days."

I laugh. "I won't run, I promise, but I'd love to see you try."

"You promise?"

"I promise. When have I lied to you, Villanueva?"

This time it's he who cackles. "Every day, Narváez."

I laugh and he orders me to turn around. His soft hands graze my back, my neck. The weight of the jewel is noticeable on my collarbone, but so are his warm fingers on my skin. I can't believe he's simply giving it back to me.

Lydia was right. He's softened up. I smile at the thought.

Once he's finished, I pivot to meet his gaze, finding him looking back at me. In the moonlit night, his eyes appear gentle and they gleam with a soft twinkle.

"Thank you, Héctor," I express. "I assure you, I won't run. I refuse to die by Sullivan's or Pedro's hand. I'd rather die by The Seer. I *love* ominous women."

He smiles kindly. "You are most welcome," he reassures. "And look at you. Finally, making an intelligent decision for once."

"Don't push it, pirate boy."

He holds his arm out, gesturing to me to take it. "Let us walk. We do not want to fall behind, do we?" he asks.

In only minutes, I'll finally have some answers.

CHAPTER TWENTY

"Took ye all long enough," Captain Sullivan scolds. "Come. The Seer is not a patient woman and we're already behind."

We say nothing as we approach the sullen dock. Sullivan is smoking a cigar underneath a lanterned post, holding the cane in his right hand. Even now, it feels like all eyes are on me, studying my every move. Next to the Captain sits a wooden canoe tied to the dock, swaying to the beat of the ocean. Surely we aren't getting in *that*.

"Zhào, Khan, Córdova, Villanueva. Prepare the longboat," Sullivan orders, but Cyrus runs off to a barrel, vomiting inside. The others groan and roll their eyes. Sullivan grimaces, throwing the cigar against the ground and stomping on it. "James, Brennan, bring some sense into Khan. I ain't want him soiling my boat." He turns to me. "Come, lass."

The guys fix the canoe up, taking out the wooden oars as they converse about the night's events and what's coming. Lydia glares at Cyrus, arms crossed, while James offers some water. Captain Sullivan comes to me, pulling my arm toward a few tied barrels, away from the officers of *The Fury*. The hairs in the back of my neck stand, chills running through my entire body. The street is deserted except for the eight of us, the only sound coming from the crew. Yet I can't shake the feeling that I'm being followed. Especially if those voices I heard earlier were real.

Sullivan notices my necklace and sighs. "Does Villanueva ever listen? It's like speakin' to a child," he says, releasing me. His breath smells of rum. "Whatever. I ain't gonna quarrel ye for it, but ye better not run off or I'll shoot ye down."

"I won't." I chuckle awkwardly, but stop when Sullivan raises his eyebrows. "Kinda hard to run away now, isn't it?"

Just as I shift away, he swiftly pulls me back in place. My lips quiver, and a familiar dread washes over me. I have no one to blame but myself.

"Ye best not mock me, girl." He releases me, tapping his cane against the ground. "Now, The Seer. She's not a force to be meddled with. I suggest ye stay quiet unless told to speak. Don't touch anything, don't run. Embarrass me, lass, and I will have no remorse in letting the quartermaster kill ye in any way he wishes. Savvy?"

"Yes."

"We're ready," Pedro says, joining our side.

Sullivan tips his hat and departs, cane echoing on the ground. Pedro and I exchange glares, but he motions for me to walk ahead. We reach the docked canoe. Cyrus, pale and shivering, drinks water as Art scolds him. Lydia hands oars to Héctor and Pedro.

Sullivan grabs James' arm and pulls him to the side, scolding him softly as he fixes the collar of James' shirt. James nods and Sullivan grabs his face, enunciating his words to the child. The entire exchange mesmerizes me, and I know James is loved in the same way I love Sole. If not more.

Sullivan taps his shoulders, and James jumps in the longboat, tilting it from side to side. Lydia hands me a damp, wooden oar and nods. We're ready to go by the looks of it.

The seven of us go into the canoe one at a time, trying not to tip it over with our weight. Murky water surrounds us, sloshing as the keelless boat gains more people. My heart races and my hands get sweaty, threatening to let my oar slip from my fingers.

I cautiously dip my oar into the waters of the swamp, helping the officers push our small canoe forward into the woods. Sullivan directs us toward a narrow path in between bald cypresses, the dense water making sloshing noises against the structure. A single oil lantern illuminates our path hung on the very front by Sullivan, where he sits with a recovering Cyrus.

The deeper we go, the heavier the air stenches of decaying vegetation and stagnant water. The silence is loud, broken only by the sound of our oars breaking the water's thick surface, toads croaking. Something slithers into the bubbling water all around us. A log passes us by as we row, but my paranoia convinces me it was *not* a log.

The further we go, the more darkness engulfs us.

A loud splash nearby startles me, causing me to cling to Art, who's sitting next to me. I glance around, searching for the source of the sound, but there's nothing. It's as if the swamp swallowed the noise whole. My hands tremble, and my breathing becomes erratic as I fight to stay calm.

"How much farther?" I shudder. *Fuck.* I release Art's arm and go back to rowing.

"Ye ain't scared of quagmires are ye, lass?" Art mocks, snorting.

"No, Art. I'd just like to *live.*"

"Ain't nothing to be afraid of, Red. Art's scent scares 'em away," James says from the back. Some of us force a chuckle. I don't think any of us wants to be here any more than I want to be here.

"Ye wish yer smelled as manly as me, lad," Art exclaims without missing a beat. "And I doubt they'll grab ye, Narváez. Unless I push ye overboard."

"Leave her be," Héctor chimes in. "No one will push anybody overboard. No matter how badly we want to do so, aye, Córdova?" Pedro hits the back of his head. Héctor pushes him. The canoe tilts with their movements, causing my fingers on the oar to accidentally brush on the murky water. I wipe it off, hysterical.

"I'm this close of pushin' ye," Pedro hisses. "Please continue talkin' so I can speed up the process."

I don't know whose brilliant idea it was to seat them together, but if we can get to where we're going without tipping this boat around, it'll be a miracle. Pedro and Héctor seated together... It's like trying to mix oil and water in one container.

"Once we get to The Seer's place, I am going to kill you," Héctor threatens, gripping the oar.

"Me encantaría ver eso," Pedro shoots back.

"Córdova, Villanueva," Sullivan warns from the front.

"Kill yourself, Córdova."

"Not before I kill ye, Villanueva."

"I'm going to die surrounded by fucking children," I mumble.

"No. The actual *child* is being a God-sent angel. Those two are bloody idiots," James says, and Lydia shushes him. "What? Ye know I'm right, Miss Lydia!"

"Oi, Narváez... is that a snake?" Art taunts, pointing to my left.

"ENOUGH I SAY!" Sullivan commands. "Put some respect on these here waters."

You could hear a pin drop.

The silence is oppressive, my anxiety mounting with each passing second. I study the twisted hollow trees, their branches gnarled and reaching out like skeletal fingers. The vines and mosses hang thick above us, giving the entire swamp an almost supernatural appearance.

My heart beats in my ears. Every rustle of a leaf, every trickle of water, every movement of my oar sends my nerves into overdrive.

Faint laughter. The crew must hear it too because some of them tense up. My breath shudders, my eyes dart all around. The canoe bumps something, and Sullivan curses, trying to guide the canoe away from what we hit.

A scream is lodged in my throat.

It's a severed head. It's lifeless eyes staring back at us.

This sight makes my stomach churn, a feeling of dread settling over me like a cloak.

"We move on," Sullivan says.

We pass more severed heads impaled on torches, which make a narrow path, all in various stages of decomposition and decay. I cover my mouth and nose, holding in the bile building in my throat. The overwhelming, pungent odor of the decapitated heads overwhelms me, clinging to our clothing, to our skin. It'll be impossible to escape. Shivers run down my spine. Art taps his foot next to me, his fingers gripped around the oar.

What type of person is The Seer? Who could do such a thing?

The further we paddle, the denser the mist becomes, suffocating us. The sounds of the swamp creatures fill my ears, their cries and chirps adding to the eerie atmosphere.

Soti pandan w kapab, Luz, a regal, deep voice whispers around me. The same one from earlier.

I bite down on my tongue to prevent myself from screaming. My stomach clenches, my mouth goes dry. Fear floods my body like a tidal wave. I don't know what I just heard, but I do know this: I have to get out of here.

I grip my oar tightly, my knuckles turning white from the hold I have on them. The mist slowly clears, a glimmer of light in the distance. It draws me in, calling out to me.

The more we float down the swamp, the more light we receive, and the less severed heads we pass. A child's laughter comes from my right and I whirl my head to the same direction. A pair of yellow eyes in the darkness stare right back at me, chills running throughout my entire body. I blink, and they're gone.

The flicker of light comes from a small wooden shack, adorned with wind chimes and seashells. A window faces the swamp, the curtain drawn. Here, the sounds are more intense. Mosquitoes and flies congregate on the oil lamps in front of the shack. Smoke arises from the chimney.

Pote fi a ban mwen... Bring the girl to me...

Two intertwined voices say this. I can't pinpoint the second, but it's dainty, feminine.

Sullivan grumbles, taking a deep breath. He heard that too. He must've.

We pull the boat up to the muddy shore, whispers carried on the wind. One by one, we get out carefully, in order to avoid touching the murky water. When it's my turn, Héctor offers me his hand, but I get out without his help. This whole eerie environment might creep me out, but that doesn't make me helpless. Placing my boots against the soggy ground, I sigh, grateful to not be on the water.

Sullivan throws the oars back in the canoe as Pedro ties the boat against a tree.

"Let's go, crew. She awaits," Sullivan orders.

I survived the swampy waters, and the head on spears, but as we walk toward the cabin, I can't shake the feeling that the worst is yet to come.

As we stand outside, Sullivan takes something from a lightheaded Cyrus. A medallion, made of pure gold with an emerald in the middle. That must be The Seer's payment. Worth more than me, probably. Sullivan nears the door and without knocking, the door opens by itself; the hinges creaking loudly into the night. The candlelight by the entrance flickers, low whispers surround us. They talk of death, sacrifice, catastrophe.

They're the voices of the dead.

Oh, no. I've seen horror movies.

No, thank you.

Héctor and I are the last ones in, a chilling gust of wind causing the door to slam shut behind us. I lose my footing and Héctor grabs my arm, taking out his dagger. I look at him, my eyebrow raised. Is he scared? He catches me studying him and coughs, averting his gaze.

"Cannot have you running off, savvy?" Héctor taunts.

While the shack looks small from the outside, it's ginormous on the inside. More wind chimes hang from the ceiling, along with dried herbs. There are furs thrown on a bench, seashells on a table. That same table holds yellowed scrolls, inks, and tea leaves. I even see coffee beans in a mortar, waiting to be ground up into the typical coffee grounds. The sweet smell of incense and dried flowers has overtaken the natural swamp scent.

A wind chime made entirely of antique forks and spoons hangs above. Next to it, shelves hold various jars. From what looks like oils with herbs, to cinnamon sticks, to dry rice. I'm surprised there's not a jar with eyes. Or intestines. Or a human sku—no wait. There it is. A human skull sits on the wall, followed by the bones of an animal. Jars of pigs' feet, tongues, and even severed fingers rest on a shelf underneath the bones.

Louder whispers carry inside the room.

I lean into Héctor, my head resting on his shoulder. His grip on my arm is still strong.

"So, you know how I promised I wouldn't run?" I mutter.

His eyes meet mine. "Mhm," is all he says.

I cover my necklace with my right hand, my fingers tightening around it. "I may have to break that promise."

"Only if you take me with you."

"Deal."

Glass suddenly breaks near us. Both of us jump, startled. It's James, who dropped a jar filled with what looks like caviar to the hollow wooden floor. Sullivan groans, cursing under his breath.

Héctor releases me, pulling James away from the mess. "Goddamn it, James! This is not a place for mischief!" he scolds, his voice hushed yet tense. James balances himself from foot to foot, his eyes roaming the other jars.

"Leave him be, Villanueva, it's not like The Collector of Souls will pop up and drag him to the shadows," Pedro says, rolling his eyes.

"He may if James continues touchin' things that don't belong to him," Sullivan scolds. He must read James' expression because he glares at his energetic son. "Put a single finger on anything else, boy, and I'll cut it off."

That stops our dear fifteen-year-old from causing trouble.

The light from the oil lamps dim, loud footsteps coming our way. They moved a red velvet curtain to the side. A figure of around Héctor's height approaches. My heart lodges in my throat. Her copper locs reach well below her knees and are adorned with gold embellishments, and small seashells. A dress made of mismatched earth-toned fabrics hugs her upper body and then widens at her waist. The beige sleeves drag on the floor, like a wedding veil. She's thin but well-fed, clearly unaffected by the severed heads on her doorstep. Her face is hidden underneath a wooden mask with white symbols, like tribal paint. Her threatening, yet inviting violet eyes gaze into mine. I don't know why, but those eyes feel familiar. Her dainty dark-skinned hands are interlaced together in front of her. A hedgehog lies on her smooth ebony shoulder.

"Hello, Luz," The Seer says, removing her mask. "Long time no see, sè."

I stumble backwards, stepping on Héctor's boots. He grabs my arm and prevents me from hitting the floor, but my widened eyes stay on the infamous Seer.

On the person whom everyone fears and respects.

The one from the letters. The one Sullivan told me to obey.

The woman who has my fate in her hands.

No.

She has two golden piercings, a septum and an eyebrow ring. I take a minute to process it, but I'm looking into the bright violet eyes and unmistakably well-defined face of Octavia Guillebeaux.

Octavia

CHAPTER
TWNETY-ONE

Octavia and I met in our first year of college, six years ago. They assigned us to the same dorm room as incoming college freshmen. She was attempting to major in nursing ,while I had gone in through the pre-pharmacy track to keep my family happy. We clicked right away and found out that we both had a common problem: we both went into medicine to please our families. Eventually, the both of us dropped our programs and got into what we truly wanted. Me, with a double degree in history and theater performance, while interning in museums and libraries. Octavia went after her astronomy degree, obsessed with the stars and the universe, always believing they tell stories.

Octavia has always had a following on social media thanks to her unusual astronomy and astrology videos, using math, astronomy, and physics to relate the stars, skies, and planets to past events that have happened, and future situations that end up coming true. That's the reason she's popular online. Because of her unnatural ability to predict what is to come, her religious family disowned her, leaving her to fend for herself.

Emotionally, financially, mentally... Octavia has always been alone. As far as I know, I haven't met anyone from the Guillebeaux family, and she's an only child, unlike Oliver and I.

It can't be her.

Octavia, who wouldn't be caught dead wearing mismatched outfits and refuses to leave her home if she even has a bad hair day. Octavia, who hates anything that crawls on four legs or slithers. Octavia, who always tells me, *I'd rather die*, when I tell her to imagine being alive in whatever time period I'm ranting about. The woman who is incapable of killing anything, much less *display* it on her front porch like *decoration*.

Sullivan approaches me, pointing at Octavia. "Ye know Nadège, lass?" he asks.

"No. I don't know *Nadège*." I cross my arms, not taking my eyes off her. "I know *Octavia*."

Héctor touches my shoulder, his expression quizzical. "She is the woman you had on your witchcraft box that imprisoned souls, is she not?"

My phone. The background picture of me, Nico, Oliver and Octavia.

"Y-yes."

She smiles, placing the wooden mask atop a table. "It's truly me, sè," she reassures, her voice calm and mature. *Sè.* Sister. "I am the woman in the witchcraft box, as Héctor says." No. She can't be. We're at least three centuries in the past.

"What the hell is going on?" I snap. "Is this some type of sick joke?" I laugh. "You people really managed to convince me I time traveled? And where is the grandmaster of it all, huh?" I glance around, searching for Oliver.

Whispers amongst the pirates erupt. A soft breeze outside causes the wind chimes to create an eerie tune, like a lullaby sung to monsters instead of children.

Art, Cyrus, and Pedro talk quietly amongst themselves, their words intangible. James and Héctor give each other a look, not needing words to understand unspoken thoughts. Lydia simply leans against the shelf with the jars, silently watching everything unfold. Her eyes don't leave Octavia. Sullivan, however, stands as still as a statue in front of the door, his eyebrow raised. The hand that doesn't hold the cane hovers over his pistol.

"Great job everyone, that's a wrap! Your services are no longer needed," is all I say.

Faint laughter. A man's this time. I glance around but none of the officers are laughing. My gaze falls upon the door once more. Sullivan smirks, crossing his arms. *Try it*, he mouths.

Octavia approaches me, and the pirates make a clear path for her. Out of the corner of my eye, Héctor holds his temple with his left hand, wincing in pain, just like he did whenever he stumbled aboard *The Fury*. She clears her throat, bringing my short attention span to her. She smells of sweet spices, like cinnamon and anise.

She stops a mere foot away from me, her violet eyes staring into mine. "Luz. This isn't a game," she says. *Oh, bless her little heart.* "This is all real. We're in the past."

"Babe, how much is Oliver paying you? Like be for real. How much did he spend on this?" I ask. The wind outside bristles causing the window shutters to tremble back and forth. I turn to everyone. "Just how much did the king of Broadway pay for—"

Octavia touches my temples and a tremendous flash of light blinds me.

Images run through my mind, moving faster than I can comprehend. In the first, I am facing Octavia as she shuffles some cards. *But why can't I tell her,* Octavia asks, *this is too much for her, she will lose everything.* I raise my finger as if to scold her, but it's not my finger. A strange voice speaks in an unfamiliar language, and she nods, sighing. *Fine,* she says, *but I've seen how it ends... and he gets involved. The last thing we want is for my brother to arise from the shadows.*

A second image. This time I am Octavia, on my knees, looking up at a raging Oliver. But it's not Oliver. He looks like Nau. *You will never be the man you want to be,* Octavia seethes, *and when she comes from the future, she will kick your ass.* He smirks, *and when she does, you'll be the first I'll kill.* A third. This time I watch as Héctor clutches his chest as he stands, taking deep breaths. *It is decided, you'll bring her to me before Nau steals her,* Octavia demands, a doll in her hands, *understood?* Héctor glares at her, placing his hands on the table. *Aye,* he says, gasping, *but let it be known this is against my will, savvy?* Octavia scoffs, grabbing his chin. *You'll thank me when the time comes, and when you do... all I'll say is I told you so.*

Octavia's face comes into focus.

A soft "no" escapes my lips as I walk backward, away from her. I end up accidentally hitting the shelf with my body. The jars shake, the contents inside clanking together. Blood rushes to my cheeks, my breathing unstable.

"What the hell was that?" I ask between gasps.

"My power. Like I said, this is all real. They're real. You're real. We're all in the year 1689," she states. *Power?*

No.

I time traveled. Someway, somehow, what brought *me* here, possibly brought *her* here as well. Unless... she's telling the truth.

"If you're really Octavia, why did Sullivan call you Nadège?" I ask, my voice a hoarse whisper. "What fucking year is it?" A shutter opens with force. "What do you mean *power*?"

She sighs. "It's my Creole name. My real name is Nadège Guillebeaux, but in our time, I go by Octavia Nadège Guillebeaux." She tilts her head, studying me. "It's November 1689, Luz. Your necklace glowed, you got pulled into the ocean and thus, arrived here. In the seventeenth century."

"So... I truly traveled to the past?"

She nods.

My thoughts are a jumbled mess, swirling around my head. I keep repeating what she just told me, as if it would somehow make this less real. The wind outside picks up, the wind chimes around the cabin twinkling together viciously.

It is Octavia. *My* Octavia. With a different name and peculiar eyes, living in a shack surrounded by severed heads in pitchforks and spears. But it's her.

"Let us sit, shall we? I think that is best," Octavia says, gesturing for them to sit.

The crew accommodate themselves on the benches and seats around the wooden table, not a word being said between them. Even James is silent. The table holds a mortar and pestle, a jar with coffee grounds, various seashells, tea leaves, and even animal bones. She gently places the hedgehog on her shoulder atop the table and inserts her hand into a pouch on her dress.

She turns, a sad smile on her lips. She reaches her hand out to me, nodding softly.

"Luz? Come sit, please," she encourages. "It'll help."

I take her hand and she leads me to a wooden chair with a plush fur covering. I sit down, dumbfounded.

My heart races, my mind a blur of anxious thoughts. I take deep breaths, trying to calm myself down, but I can't. My chest feels tight, constricting even. The gusts outside grow stronger by the second, hitting the shack, causing it to tremble. The branches surrounding the swamp rustle together; the air feels charged with a dark energy.

My mind can't seem to process the fact that my best friend, the person whom I've called my other half for six years, could stand right in front of me, revered by pirates everywhere. I tap my foot against the wooden floor, placing my hands on the nape of my neck.

"Octavia Guillebeaux, I demand an answer. An explanation. Anything," I snap, gesturing with my hands. "Did you time travel, too?"

She sighs, leaning against the table. "No. I didn't time travel. This is my home, where I live," she declares. "Where I have lived for the past century."

"Girl, what do you mean *where I've lived for the past century?* What are you even saying?"

My voice borders on the edge of hysteria, my accent creeping to show up. I take deep shuddering breaths, my hands shaking. I glare at her, awaiting her answer, but I can't. I stand, causing the chair to fall to the ground loudly.

Octavia reaches out and grabs both of my trembling hands, interlacing her slender fingers with mine. They're soft, and reassuring. Staring into her violet eyes, something hits me. Is this why she always wears contacts? I always assumed her eye color to be lighter, like blue or gray, since she claimed she constantly received hate for their natural pigmentation.

"I'm The Seer, an immortal entity who sees things past, present, and future. I give advice, guide those who seek to be guided. I can also share my visions or things I have experienced, as you saw. I work with The Greats as an intermediary between humanity and them. Some mortals call us Lwa, believing us to be a part of ancient Voodoo, but we're not quite that. I'd say we're more spiritual based. By we, I mean me and my brother. He works with The Greats, too. They created us," she explains, releasing my hands.

"I'm sorry, The Greats?" I ask. The shack creaks with the intensity of the wind, howling as if it were the screams of the dead. James says something under his breath, but Sullivan shushes him with a look. "Who are they?"

"They're Gods."

I chuckle, rubbing my face. "And *brother*? Last I recall you were an *only child*."

"Yes, I know I lied by saying I was an only child, but I have a twin brother. Younger by three minutes. He's The Collector of Souls. I reckon you heard the quartermaster speak of him."

I simply glare at her. She's speaking to me, and I'm listening, but I'm not understanding. "You have a brother. A twin, no less. And he's immortal too. Both full of magic."

"Yes. But where I work with the light and guide those in need, he works with the dark, collecting the souls of all who pass. He sets the ways of our death."

I shake my head. "Okay, so he's the grim reaper, but the Caribbean version. And he's important to all this... why?"

"Because we should not invoke his name," Lydia intervenes. "It doesn't matter how powerful a person may be, he's got more power and can eliminate ye in a second. We know the tale of the dark master."

"He and I were eternally damned, sè," Octavia declares, shrugging. "Me doomed to foresee, him doomed to be a part of the dark. We've lived a thousand lifetimes and will live a thousand more. We come from the same creator, but are two sides of one coin."

I sit there, spiraling into a pit of despair, unable to escape her words, her confession.

The wind builds up to a howling gale, whistling through the gaps in the windows and doors of the shack. Thunder cracks from the distance and the shutters slam from the force of the wind. Rain falls outside, gradually picking up.

"You're lying to me," is all I say. I tug on my braids, not knowing what else to do with my hands. No one makes a move to close the shutters. "This is all a lie, and you know I hate it when I'm lied to."

"Luz, how else could you explain my being here?" she asks, her voice melodic. "You time-traveled, I'm an immortal entity. That is the truth. What other thing do you want me to say? Th-that Oliver paid for this? Oliver Bennett? The man of *convenience*? The man who pays for everything instead of doing it himself... coming up with a scheme like *this*? I want you to do the math, quickly."

I want to run away, to hide from the truth, but there's nowhere to go.

"Then... you... you lied to me. For six years, you lied to me," I breathe out, my chest tightening. "Six years of friendship. All a lie! How could you keep this from me?"

Thunder rumbles outside, the rain coming inside the shack.

She sighs and looks back at the crew. I turn to face them and they're quietly invested in the conversation, hanging onto every word we say. I glance at Héctor for any confirmation that

Octavia could be lying, but astonishment overtakes his expression. As if he can't believe what's going on. Truthfully, neither can *I.*

A lightning bolt hits the swamp. James does the sign of the cross, just like the one I did when I took part in church. The growing hurricane takes on a relentless quality, threatening to break this cabin apart hinge by hinge. Pedro grabs his pistol, glaring at me. Lydia places her hand on his, her eyebrow raised in warning.

"I had to lie, Luz. My whole life is one complicated lie," Octavia states, walking to a shelf and grabbing a glass bottle. "I don't just shout it out to the heavens. Like, *hi, I'm immortal. I can see your future, how are you? No, wait, don't answer... I know.*" She takes a gulp of the liquid inside. "I know everything. I'm cursed with the gift of knowledge, of foresight. The Gre–Gods love twins, so they chose us, made us who we are."

I laugh. Not shy laughter, but loud and full of hysteria. It was all a lie. A façade. My heart is pounding inside my chest, and I tug on the ends of my braids.

Sullivan stands and shuts the shutters to prevent possible flooding inside.

"'Acho mija, no jodas," I spit out. I let go of my braids, marching toward her. "You're telling me you see everything, right? And you're immortal. So, that means you saw me getting kidnapped by this... this crew and just let it happen? Coño, te pasaste."

She chuckles nervously, biting her lip. "To be fair, I kind of scared them into bringing you here. I think I showed you."

This takes me aback, my eyebrows raised. The hurricane stirs outside. "What did you just say to me?"

"Um… they weren't supposed to kidnap you, per se. More like, bring you under your own free will. Right, Héctor?"

I whirl my head at Héctor, fuming. "YOU!" I yell.

He raises his hands up protectively. "SHE PUT A CURSE ON ME!" he yells, trying to put the blame on her. "She said that if I did not take you to the captain, she would curse me to drown for all eternity!"

My eyes slice to Octavia again. She grips the bottle with her fingers. "You did WHAT? Just to get *me* here? Why didn't you just get me *yourself?*"

"I'm a wanted woman, okay? A fugitive. Johann is after me, and he swore to kill me if he ever saw me. And I'm not much help dead, am I…" Octavia trails off, taking deep breaths. "I couldn't go get you. As much as I wanted to. So I told them where you'd be." She takes a sip of rum. "Sullivan?"

Sullivan sighs, walking over to Octavia and taking the bottle from her. "Nadè—Octavia admitted that ye were coming thanks to a vision. She couldn't intervene, as Nau is after her too," Sullivan explains, crossing his arms. "Villanueva was told and ordered to find ye in Port Royal, and bring ye to me before Nau encountered ye. However, ye had already gotten into trouble with Nau. We were to bring ye here in exchange for a reward. Fifty pieces of gold per man for bringing the girl with the pearl to The Seer."

I throw my satchel on the table. The crew stares at me, silent. Watching my every move. Anxiously awaiting to see what will happen next. If it wasn't for the thunderstorm roaring outside, one could hear a pin drop. I ignore their gaze, closing my eyes. I lean on the table, my weight supported by my hands.

"Héctor… my necklace. Were you ordered to take it too?" I ask, opening my eyes and facing him.

Héctor shifts in his seat, putting his hair behind his ear.

"No. He did that all by himself, just like I knew he would," Octavia says, grabbing the hedgehog from the table. "He's a pirate after all. One sign of treasure and he takes it. Once a thief, always a thief, unfortunately."

"You should not speak about me in such a way, Seer," Héctor threatens, standing. "I am not the one who lied."

"No, no, no. Let's bring it all back to the fucking table," I snap. "You lied to me and stole my necklace without remorse." I point at Sullivan. "You encouraged a kidnapping, and carried out said kidnapping. I can't believe I ever considered you my idol." I point at Octavia, outraged. "And you. You... La cagaste, mi amor. Not only did you lie to me, you had to kidnap my ass." I laugh, sighing after. "Everyone here lied to me. I bet I'm not even the siren of ruin! There's not a fucking prophecy. Just more lies!"

What a shit show. This has to be a nightmare. A very vivid nightmare.

"There is a prophecy," she admits. "But that's not mine to tell."

Anger builds up inside me, like a thunderstorm gathering on the horizon. My fists are clenched tightly against my temples, my nails digging into the palms of my hands.

"Not yours to tell?" I growl. "What *is* yours to tell? Your lies?"

She takes a shuddering breath, tears in her eyes. "I'm truly sorry about everything. I wanted to tell you. I did. But I couldn't. It's forbidden for me to say unless absolutely necessary."

"That's not helping your case." I study her, her stance, her expression. "Was any of what we went through real?"

"It was all real, sè. We became friends naturally. You were the first I met after a century of solitude. You reminded me of what it means to have a best friend, a sister. I've no true family other than you and Oliver. And my brother."

This is too much to hear, too much to bear, and I feel like I'm about to scream.

"D'nanichi, are you alright?" Héctor asks softly, hesitantly approaching me. His fingers caress my arm, but I pull away from him.

"Am I alright? Are you joking? I'm perfectly fine," I say, humorlessly. I turn my head to Octavia, grabbing her shoulders. "Octavia Guillebeaux, why am I here?" The wind picks up once more. It's like we're inside a tornado, the noise and chaos overwhelming my senses. "Why. Am. I. Here? *Tell me.* What do me and this prophecy have in common?"

The room slowly gets unnaturally warmer, closing in on me. My eyes get teary, but I don't feel the urge to cry. I feel the urge to scream. The fingers on my temples feel damp and sweaty. My feet and knees get overtaken by a peculiar tingly sensation, my heart beating inside my throat. A sudden high pitch bell rings amidst the cyclone outside, startling me.

What in the hell is that?

"I knew this was going to be a hard thing to do, so I brought some reinforcements," Octavia warns.

Reinforcements?

Octavia looks at the crew, and somehow they understand. The room quiets down once more, Sullivan stepping out of the way, back toward his seat. The storm outside calms itself, down to the point of a gentle sprinkle.

Nearby candles blow out without any wind. This time the whispers remind me of the ones that caused me to fall in the ocean. Soft, insidious mumbles carried throughout in a menacing tone. They're warning me, telling me something. A cold sweat breaks in my forehead. This is my imagination.

"Luz, I need you to understand, we're not against you. We're with you, okay? Until the end, sè," Octavia reassures, grabbing the door handle.

The door slowly opens. The thunderstorm outside completely stops. All the nighttime sounds around me cut out, my ears ringing instead. My eyes must be messing with me. I take a weak step forward, towards her, but feel nauseous instead. I have to lean against the table to steady myself.

"No puede ser," I mumble.

I try to steady my vision to look at her more clearly, but it's hard to do so. The ringing around me gets so loud, I have to cover my ears, but it's not enough. The lights from the oil lamps increase in strength, blinding me. Laughter surrounds me, taunts that remind me that this is really and truly happening to me.

Her long salt-and-pepper hair is loose and damp from the rain, reaching her waist. Her soft bronze-colored skin shines as bright as the ocean when the sun rises, as if she doused an entire gallon of lotion on her body before arriving here. On her collarbone lies a familiar necklace with a beautiful sapphire jewel, reminding me of one I haven't seen in eight years.

A thin golden headpiece with a V shape sits atop her head, an uncut gem as blue as the deep sea resting between her arched brows. Her outfit, a clean and crisp beige tunic like dress, tied at the waist, resembling a ghost.

She must be.

Because she's dead.

They buried her. Taken from me, never to return.

My grandmother. Mami Julia.

Who died eight years ago?

"Hola, mija," her soft voice says as she hesitantly walks inside.

I slowly slide to the ground, my head clashing against the wooden, hollow floor. I blink rapidly, everything around me goes in slow motion. My name is called repeatedly, various voices fighting for dominance. An eerie melody begging me to stay with them. The smell of blood fills my sinuses, the colors gold and black clash in the shadows behind blurry figures. The image of my very alive grandmother shows up in my mind as I succumb to the darkness, a high-pitched ringing drowning everything.

She's alive.

CHAPTER
TWENTY-TWO

I awake with the pungent scent of burning incense and dried herbs surrounding me.

Hushed voices rise and fall, but they overlap, making it hard to identify who's talking. I move my head around, but it's pounding so I stop. This must be the beginning of one of my infernal migraines.

I shut my eyes once more, bringing my sweaty hands up to my face. I'm thankful for the plush fabric underneath my head and the soft mattress I'm laying on. It's as if I'm floating on a cloud, my body lightweight. I bury my head in the satiny materials, a small part of me hoping that I've woken up at home, in my bed. Maybe everything I experienced was a vivid nightmare with no way out. Maybe it was an out-of-body experience.

I open my eyes, the flickering lights of the candles to the side casting eerie shadows on the walls of the dimly lit room. This is not my bedroom. This is real.

My grandmother is alive.

Same luscious salt-and-pepper hair, semi-wrinkled face, and moisturized bronze skin. It's all the same, as if she were ageless. But no. It can't be her. *I buried her.* I saw her dead upon the hospital bed. Lifeless, cold, shriveled up.

But it can't be.

I remember the day she died vividly.

The weather had been out of sorts for the week, a category four hurricane hitting Puerto Rico. We almost missed our flights to provide treatments for her in Lehigh Valley, Pennsylvania, where my family and I moved after I turned thirteen.

That last day of her life, our family had been there. Her two sons, their wives and my cousins. We were all there for her. She was the matriarch of the Narváez family. Our elder. The one we treated with utmost respect and love, especially after Papi Gustavo passed. She was our rock. The person who kept peace between the Narváezes and the Garcías—my mother's family.

Mami Julia had wanted to speak to me alone, but my mother forbade it, claiming I was far too young to hear omens of death and things that would've scarred me for life. Her and my father got into a huge argument as the thunderstorm outside the hospital room brewed.

We all stepped away, taking my parents' hateful words from her. In the end, she passed alone in the room. No nurses, no doctors, no family. Just the sound of machines, pouring rain, and roaring thunder.

Alone, afraid, cold.

Neglected.

I never knew what it was she wanted to tell me.

I stir in the bed, my chest as hollow as the day she died.

I place my feet on the hollow wooden ground, grabbing my temples. I concentrate on taking deep breaths, my anger rising like it never has before. My mind races with all the lies, secrets, and betrayals that I've been kept in the dark to all my life. It's as if someone has plunged a sharp knife into my back, creating pressure throughout my entire body.

Everyone lied to me.

Groaning, I stand, coming face to face with a twine and cloth doll hung from the ceiling with a piece of rope around its neck. Chills run throughout my entire body. The sound of low, breathy chants fill the air, and a strange energy pulses through the air, making the hairs on the back of my neck stand.

Velvet curtains drape over a small window above a table covered in candles and a burning incense stick. A dreamcatcher hangs over me, but not a store-bought one that reeks of colonization. This one is made of black webbing, with dark feathers and seashells. The shelves around the room accommodate peculiar objects, from raw crystals and geodes, to jars filled with bones and feathers, antique books, and a small golden chest adorned with jewels. Strange white symbols are etched into the walls. Along with various sets of numbers that catch my attention.

11041689. 11141689. 11271689. 12041689. 02281690. 06071691.

They're all the same length. Coordinates? Probably not. Coordinates are around fifteen digits. I take a second but realization hits me. *Dates.* They're dates.

I try my best to use my skills of rapid memorization I learned as an actress to remember them. *November 4th, 1689,* already happened. *November 14th, 1689.* It has to be today since it's been ten days. The next date is *November 27th, 1689.*

A date that is yet to come.

"D'nanichi." I turn my head to the front of the room and Héctor walks toward me, his face awash with concern. "Would you like anything?"

I shake my head; the numbers replaying in my head like a mantra. November 27th, 1689 keeps being highlighted. I want nothing from him. I need nothing other than explanations.

"Where's everyone? Where's Octavia? Where is the woman who walked in?" I ask, my voice devoid of all emotions. "How long was I out?"

"You fainted for a few minutes. Everyone else is in the main room, including the older woman. She sent me to check on you." He leans against the doorframe. "How is your head?"

"My head is the least of my worries." I walk over to him, determined to find the truth once and for all, but he stops me. "Don't. I have enough issues right now. I don't need a man's pity."

"I was not going to pity you." He offers me some water, and I take it reluctantly. "I am simply here to check if you are well."

I finish drinking, the dryness in my throat subsiding. "I'm fine." I hand him the waterskin, holding his gaze. "Octavia mentioned you were coerced into taking me?"

He stands there, shifting his weight from foot to foot. He fidgets with the wooden ring on his index finger, as if trying to vanish. "The Seer and Sullivan had conversed a few months back, deciding I would be the best person to find you and bring you to them before Nau took you instead. I did not want to, but she claimed it had to be me, that only *I* was capable. I am a pirate, but I have never kidnapped someone." He runs a hand through his hair. "However, The Seer can be very convincing."

Héctor stops twisting the ring around, his jaw clenched. His body tenses up, taking short, shuddering breaths. A knot of worry forms in my stomach, twisting and turning like the tide under a hurricane. What did Octavia do to him? My mind races with every possibility, from the most irrelevant thing to the worst-case scenario.

"She has a cursed doll of me somewhere around this cabin, and I do not know where it could be," Héctor says, his shoulders tensed. "She grabbed the doll, and threw it into a pail of water that day, emotionless. I was choking by the second. I could not move, could not escape." He takes a deep shuddering breath, bringing a hand up to his neck. "All I could feel was the saltwater drowning me, filling my lungs. It was simply me and her in the room. No one saw as I became disoriented, physically exhausted trying to fight off invisible water demons that were not there." His hands tremble as he closes them into fists. "She raised it from the bucket, asking if I had changed my mind. Still, I refused, so she threw it inside once more. I could not take it anymore and I forced myself to gain enough composure and consciousness to agree. Then, and only then, did she remove the doll from the pail completely."

My thoughts scramble, searching for something to say, but I can't. Every time I open my mouth, the words seem spent, as if I had been rid of all my vocabulary. Octavia created a doll like the one she has hung near the bed I woke up in, and used it to coerce him into taking me. She *drowned* this man.

"Afterward she explained to me that *a girl with a pearl of prophecy is the one you seek. Bring her to us*," Héctor mentions. "I did not know it was going to be you, but once I saw Nau after you, it confirmed all suspicions."

"So, the two of us were just scared into compliance, huh?"

He shrugs, an eyebrow raised. "It seems we are simply pawns in a matter much bigger than the both of us."

It's not until he says it, it clicks. *Pawns.* Surrounded by lies, deceit, fear. My emotions are a mess, running into each other. My stomach churns, making me nauseous. This anger and betrayal I feel are both intertwined, and the realization that I'm a piece in someone's games doesn't sit right with me.

"If you think we're pawns, why'd you take my necklace? You were ordered to take *me*, not *it*. That was on your own free will apparently," I state. "Still, you were warned against giving it back to me, weren't you?"

"I was looking out for myself at first, truthfully," he explains. "I immediately recognized it as the jewel pirates and sailors alike spoke of in their legends. It drew me in, called to me. I snapped out of it and figured if I took it, if I had something you cared about, you would follow me with little to no fight, making the whole situation much more bearable."

"For who? For you or for me?"

After holding my stare, I head into the living room, wanting nothing more than to understand what's happening and what exactly they dragged me into. Everyone is huddled around the table. My gaze lands on *her*. My grandmother. All speaking to each other, the words *catastrophe, ruin, sacrifice,* and *prophecy* jumping out.

The storm outside picks up once more, the wind pounding on the shutters, demanding to be let inside. I clench my hands into fists, a fire burning within me. A seething rage that I've never felt before.

If she's alive... She lied to me.

I just can't believe it. I refuse to believe she's real. No. They have to be playing tricks on me.

"Are you an apparition?" I snap. Everyone quiets down, their faces turned to me. The woman with Mami Julia's appearance shakes her head, approaching me. I step back. "No. No me toques. Mami Julia is dead. Who are you?"

Héctor joins my side, not saying anything.

"Mi Luz," her voice is soft and accented, just like it was before she died. "It's me. I am her. Although, I've always somewhat disliked my modern name. I'm sorry you had to find out this way, but we're desperate."

"Find out *what*? What do you mean by a *modern name*?" I ask.

"In your time, I was Juliana Arroyo Martínez, widow of Gustavo Narváez Córdova. But my real name, my true birth given name is Casiguaya." She brings her hands to her chest, twirling the jewel on her necklace.

The others have various expressions in their faces, ranging from shock to astonishment to bewilderment. James is intently listening, fascinated by the words being spoken. Next to him, Pedro sits up, bringing a hand to his mouth. I've never seen that man any less than certain, and the knot in my stomach grows.

All I can do is stand there, staring into her eyes. One brown, the color I'm used to. The other, however, is cerulean like the ocean that surrounded me for the past ten days.

Casiguaya. The woman from the letters. She's Casiguaya. She's the love of Sully's life. The one he claimed I reminded him off.

It was *her*.

That's why the handwriting seemed similar to Mami Julia's.

Because it was *hers*.

The powerful gale makes the branches outside creak and moan like they're in pain. The cabin shakes with every gust, the sound of the wind so loud it drowns my rapid heartbeat. It's like a freight train is passing by, relentless.

"I just... I-I can't," I stammer, "I d-don't—"

"Luisa," Octavia says, gesturing to the two chairs in front of us. "I suggest you sit down for this. Please."

"Vente, mi amor, sit," Casiguaya says. I can't even bring myself to call her Mami Julia.

I lower myself to the chair closest to me, and Héctor sits on the left, putting his hand on my shoulder reassuringly. The crew sits quietly, awaiting to see what will happen next.

The more I try to control my fury and confusion, the more it seems to grow. It's like a living thing, taking over my body and mind. Not allowing me to think clearly of what I've been told about.

"Okay. You all have five minutes to give me a logical explanation as to what the hell is going on or I'm bolting out that door and swimming the hell out of here," I snap. "What exactly am I meant to do? How are you even *here*? I saw you *die*. I *mourned* for you."

"I didn't die, mi amor. Like Octavia, I am an immortal entity. But unlike her, they chose me to take life. To watch over our ancestors. To protect them from harm," Casiguaya explains calmly, as if this made any sense. "I have to explain myself to you, and I need you to listen."

I sit there, blinking quietly ahead, my already overstimulated mind struggling to process what I've learned. My body feels heavy, as if weighed down by an anchor, yet a sense of hollowness refuses to leave my chest. It's as if I were watching everything from a distance, detached and disconnected.

"How did you come to be an immortal entity?" I ask, every muscle in my body tense, like a coiled spring ready to snap back at any second.

"Long ago, I was born a mortal woman," she explains. "Casiguaya was my name in Borikén, and I lived in the Guainia region of our island. They considered me the most beautiful in the village, which brought a curse upon me. The curse of greed. When the Spanish came in 1493, they raided our island, stole our resources. A couple of months later, they arrived in my region. They saw me and decided they wanted to own me. They took my innocence, my family, my people." Her voice cracks, and she shuts her eyes, breathing slowly. Lydia comforts her, grabbing her shoulders, while Art offers her a clean rag. The others stay quiet, averting their eyes to Casiguaya's vulnerability.

This is the history our education system has hidden from us. The history that no one wants to learn about. Women raped, communities murdered. Because the Europeans believed themselves to be greater than them. Tears flood my own eyes.

Casiguaya's story.

Our story.

She sighs, patting her eyes dry with the cloth Art provided her. "They dragged me and a few of my sisters onto their vessels for their amusement, their pleasure," she continues. "So, I threw myself overboard. Into what I feared the most. The sea. Treacherous, mysterious, without an owner. But as I fell, I didn't see death. I saw life. The ocean called me. Drew me in. Atabeira and Guabancex took pity on me and my sisters, and gave us a chance to come back stronger than before."

I recognize those names from Mami Julia's legends. "Atabeira. Guabancex. The ancestral spirits of the Taínos," I recall, and she nods.

My heart pounds inside my chest like a jackhammer. Short gasps come out of my mouth, my hands shaking uncontrollably underneath the wooden table. Tears threaten to escape, but I blink rapidly, pushing them away.

Héctor grabs my hand, a corner of his lips upward in a reassuring manner. Part of me wants to remove my fingers from his touch, but the other part of me, the hidden side, wishes to do nothing more than grab his hand and run.

With my free hand, I wipe my tears away and see the pirates glancing at me. Sullivan watches me with tenderness, just as he did the day he mentioned Casiguaya. Pedro continues with confusion, while James, Art, and Cyrus are intrigued and eager. Lydia and Octavia lock eyes, then turn to me and Héctor.

"In my new life, I was reborn as an Aycayia," she tells me. "One of the most beautiful creatures in the sea, cursed to enchant men to their deaths with my voice. I thirsted for hearts with a soul so dark, it could be ink. The darker the soul, the more appetizing. And who, as a native, do I know to have a dark soul? The Spanish. The English. The Portuguese. The French. All those men that came to conquer us. To extinguish us. To replace us. I gave my fallen sisters and daughters an opportunity to join me and rid the seas from them. And they did."

I rub my temples. She's an Aycayia. The Aycayia from the Neo-Taíno myths. Her people, the stuff of nightmares. *She* is the one I've been fearing all along.

I can't comprehend it.

"So, if you take life, how did you not kill Papi Gustavo?" I ask, rubbing my face. But I don't want this information. I mean I do, but I want to know why I'm here.

"I had renounced my title as queen to explore the new world, so when I met him, I was not ridden with thoughts and a need for death. I was simply... existing like I did before it all. Basically, once an Aycayia renounces her title, she becomes mortal until her mortal form expires, and without our magic, we pass from strong illnesses, like cancer, Alzeheimer's, among others. I had tried desperately to speak to you, but your mother forbade it..." She never takes her multicolored eyes off mine, and I squirm on my seat. "My mortal self passed away from cancer, but thanks to Octavia, I was reborn in my siren self again, retaking my title of queen."

This is my grandmother. Otherwise, how would she know of the argument? Of the secret left untold?

To experience her passing eight years ago, and now she's back like nothing changed. Like *I* didn't change. The news is too much for me to handle. It's a tidal wave, washing me away further from the shore.

The draft outside comes through the gaps of the wooden walls, making the flames of the candles flicker and dance. James does the sign of the cross again, closing his eyes and leaning his head on Art's shoulder. Art whispers something in James' ear, attempting to calm the boy. The wind and rain seems to come in from all directions, trying to tear this cabin apart piece by piece.

Cyrus mumbles incoherently, taking out a rum bottle and toasting it to the thunderstorm outside. In mere seconds, his rum is gone. I want nothing more than to do as he's doing. I too want to get drunk beyond comprehension or sanity. But I can't.

Pedro is glaring at Héctor, and vice versa. Héctor takes out a dagger, placing it on the table in front of us. Lydia places her hand around her necklace, taking deep breaths, her eyes wide open as she studies the room.

Octavia and Mami Julia are the only two unfazed by the storm outside. Sullivan studies Mami Julia, speechless yet enamored. His brows are furrowed together, and he's taken off his feathered tricorn hat, revealing his salt and pepper locs. His eyes are unfocused, all over her face. As if he can't believe she's here with us.

He looks at her like she's the only one in the room, and she does the same, giving him the same look she gave Papi Gustavo. A look I thought was only reserved for my grandfather. They're lost in each other's eyes. We don't exist to him. We are nothing compared to his loving Casiguaya.

"Grandmother, aye?" Sullivan asks. "I knew ye reminded me of someone."

"Ay, Sully," Mami Julia sighs, waving him off as her face turns a deep shade of maroon. "It was long ago. This is not the time for us to speak of our previous affairs."

"Yes, this is not the time for... *affairs*," I snap, my hands sweating. "I'm trying to understand what exactly I'm meant to do, and bringing up old *flings* is not helping." I wipe them on my pants. "*Octavia* is here. *You're* here. Just... help me understand everything."

"I'm sorry, mi amor—"

"Just *stop*. Por favor."

My breathing turns to sharp gasps, my heart pounding so hard it feels like it is trying its hardest to burst open inside of my chest. In that moment, everything slowly spirals out of control, and I'm at the dangerous mercy of my own emotions.

"Why was this another one of your lies?" I snap, my eyes daggers on Octavia.

"The Seer has no part in my deceit," Mami Julia states, coming to Octavia's defense. "In your lifetime, I was searching for prey, but I became enamored with the technology, with the people. I became enamored with your grandfather that same day as well. I tried to kill him, but I could not. He already had my heart and the men who take an Aycayia's heart are bonded with the Aycayia for life. Once given to them, we cannot kill them." She sighs. "That is the truth. Please do not blame Octavia."

With her words, it feels like I'm drowning in a never-ending sea of uncertainty. Tears well in my eyes, hot and painful, fighting to break through the shell of numbness and rage that envelops me. I stand, silent, my heart heavy with the truths I've learned without rest. I want to scream, to sob, to fight. To do something other than stand here like an emotionally unstable person, but nothing is happening.

"What am I meant to do?" I ask. Octavia and Mami Julia stare at each other and then at me.

I walk away from the table, bringing my hands up to my eyes. Being alone with my thoughts, my pain, my sense of betrayal is becoming too much. Tears flow soundlessly down my face, each a painful reminder that I lived a life of deception and hidden truths.

Rain pours outside. Steady, like a waterfall.

"WHAT AM I MEANT TO DO?" I cry out, sniffling. "Don't just sit there! Answer me!"

Mami Julia sighs. "Luz..."

Footsteps approach me. I wipe my tears and see Mami Julia reaching out to me, Héctor standing next to his chair in a protective stance.

I need answers.

This can't continue.

I take a deep breath, calming myself enough to lock eyes with my grandmother once more. "Why am I here, Mami Julia? What is the secret you could never tell?"

"You're here because you need to fulfill your destiny," Mami Julia admits. "You're here because of that, my dear Aycayia of Destruction." She points at my necklace. I look down, taking it in my hands. It's glowing, the shimmering red light pulsating, the cause of me arriving in the past, just as I suspected. "¿Te acuerdas de la bahía bioluminiscente? In Vieques?" I nod. I vaguely remember going there around ten years ago. But what does the Mosquito Bay have to do with me being here? "Before you arrived, did the necklace glow? Did the water follow? Just like la bahía bioluminiscente?"

It did. My necklace shimmered a bright red, calling out to me, drawing me in, like a siren enchanting men. When I got pulled into the water, the same glow surrounded me, but it wasn't like Mosquito Bay. It wasn't blue and green, it was fiery red. My long silence must give away my answer because Mami Julia smiles reassuringly.

"That's how you traveled. The necklace is magic. It lulled you to the sea, to your destiny," Mami Julia says. "You are my granddaughter, which means you have my blood coursing through your veins. You're a siren. The siren of *ruin*, no less." She caresses my cheek, running her delicate fingers down one of my braids. "That was the secret I could never tell."

I sniffle, releasing my necklace. "I'm not an Aycayia, Mami."

She chuckles, shaking her head. "Yes, you are. You have power, and your necklace helps intensify it. Whatever you feel, it triples it. That hurricane outside is simply a mere taste of what you can do." She smiles, satisfaction and pride in her eyes. "You are what the prophecy speaks of. You are the destroyer of the seas. And you, mi Luz, are here because *we need you.*"

I raise my eyebrow, keeping my distance from her. "Need me to do what exactly?"

"To come into your power and kill Johann Nau once and for all."

CHAPTER TWENTY-THREE

When I was little, maybe seven or so, my grandmother would fill my head with urban legends, claiming that they held truths and lessons. I remember being invested in each and every one of those stories, convinced she held secret knowledge to our Puerto Rican heritage. El vampiro de Moca, la Llorona from Coamo, las Aycayias del Caribe, a few others I'm pretty sure she made up on the spot. These were the stories of my youth that lulled me to sleep, stories I was convinced were real. I used to fantasize about La Llorona taking my brother to the depths with her, and of catching el vampiro at night, placing intricate traps for it.

That was until I grew up and realized most of these were fake. Used by parents to scare their children into being obedient.

Now, I stand here, in disbelief. The downpour outside has ceased all at once.

The crew has told me repeatedly that I'm the Aycayia of Destruction, one of the mythical creatures used to terrify children. The siren of a so-called prophecy.

The one to *murder* Johann Nau.

"I'm s-sorry, ¿q-qué tú d-dijiste?" I stammer, my head pounding. My focus is solely on her, blurring out the rest of the crew. It's just us, right now. "No digas disparates. Powers? I don't have any powers."

"No son disparates, mija," she calmly states. "You have powers. What do you think causes that typhoon outside?"

My mind races, trying to make sense of the impossible. It's as if she grabbed a rug from underneath me and pulled it out with force.

No. It can't be. Then that means—

"That's what I told her. What all of us told her," James interjects, standing and leaning on the table. "We told her that ain't no coincidence in the weather matching her mood. That ain't no coincidence in Nau letting her *live.*"

The world seems to blur, as if the shock is slowly altering my vision. "No. It can't be," I mumble, holding my chest.

I stumble, hitting my hip with a smaller table. Glass breaks. The pain is nothing compared to the pull in my chest. *Air.* I need air. The room rapidly grows warmer, the flickering candlelight heating the small living room. Rapid footsteps approach me, holding me up. It's Héctor. I grip my chest, my breaths turning into short gasps.

It feels as if I'm choking, gagging on the lies and secrets that are being revealed to me.

"James," Héctor calls out. "Come help me. Quickly!"

James rushes over to us, as does Octavia and Mami Julia. The sound of muffled voices surrounds me, incoherent whispers that graze my ears. I'm lost in a never-ending sea of disbelief as they fan me, and try to bring me back to reality.

You have power, Mami Julia said.

Those three words replay in my mind repeatedly as I try to control my breathing, but they remain nonsensical, like a puzzle with missing pieces. I can't do anything else but come to terms with the impossible reality that has been thrust upon me.

You have power.

You're an Aycayia.

Kill Johann Nau once and for all.

"For someone considered the evil in the seas, she sure is rather weak," Pedro comments from afar. "Look at her, weeping. Crying. It's as if she would prefer Nau to *live*."

I stand up straight, holding my shoulders back. All the anger I had felt coming back into my body.

Héctor releases me, taking out his pistol and aiming it at Pedro. The others gasp. "I suggest you refrain from speaking, Córdova, or else the hell that will be unleashed is mine." Héctor commands.

Pedro smirks. "Pull the trigger, Villanueva. Let's see how much of a man ye are."

"Do *not* spill blood in my house!" Octavia screeches. "I recently deep cleaned my floors, and James already spilled my ethically sourced caviar on them."

"If I were the evil in these fucking seas, Pedro, I'd have killed you already," I snap, regaining my composure. I turn to my grandmother, my gaze a sharp dagger. Héctor lowers his pistol, his shoulders tense. "What is this fucking prophecy? How does it speak of me? Why am I a siren of *ruin* specifically?"

"Each Aycayia has a role when they're made. I'm Queen Aycayia. My second in command is the Aycayia of War. You, however, the heir to my throne, are the Aycayia of Destruction," Mami Julia explains. "You have the power to control the seas, time, and the weather. You have our song. You are the one sailors and pirates alike fear, just like us."

"What?"

"She speaks the truth," Héctor admits. "Every pirate knows of the chaos bringer who wears a pendant the color of blood. The jewel of the siren of ruin. It is what drew me in when we first met."

I face him, my eyebrows raised in question. His eyes show a plethora of emotions, ranging from certainty to concern. I give him a pleading look to tell me otherwise. To tell me that this is a joke, that James was messing with me. But he shakes his head, refusing to let me feed into my delusion.

"James told me that everywhere I went, ruin followed," I recall, my insides recoiling. "And that I was just as bad as Nau, if not more. I'm not him. I'm not a raging colonizer with a personal vendetta against inclusion!"

"I'm not saying you are," Mami Julia reassures. "But you do have the power to control the seas and the weather. To sing men to their deaths. To travel through time, and live a long life. And with that comes ruin." She grabs my arms, then my cheeks, caressing them. "You are the most dangerous of us, Luz. Our line is powerful, but you have more power in one finger than all of us combined, mi amor."

Nope.

James, Cyrus, and Art stare at me flabbergasted, while Pedro scoffs and reveals a bottle of rum, taking a swig from it. Mami Julia steps back from me, smiling and twirling the raw sapphire on her necklace. My hands hover over my own, my heart throbbing inside my ears.

I'm a powerful entity? A *dangerous* one at that?

I'm not even acknowledged at home. What makes my grandmother and everyone else think that I have power in an era where I don't even have rights as a woman and a person of color?

Here and in my time, I am nothing.

"Luz," Octavia calls, drawing my attention to her. "I can feel your mind racing. *Yes*, this is happening. *Yes*, this is real."

I scoff, crossing my arms. The wind outside picks up again, the wind chimes singing an eerie, twisted melody. James squeezes himself between Art and Cyrus, petting the hedgehog. Octavia heads to the table, informing Lydia to grab the jar with animal bones in it. Lydia nods and does as she's told, mesmerized by Octavia's beauty and ethereal aura. They all talk amongst themselves, Pedro sighing exasperated in the middle of a conversation, but never taking his eyes off of me.

The rain turns to a gentle sprinkle, the wind to a tender breeze.

Could this really be my doing? Have I really caused the weather that has been unstable and rancorous?

When Mami Julia died, any time I felt upset, the day Oliver proposed.

Any time thunder cracked above us on the ship whenever rage filled my body.

All *me*.

"I'm still fuming at the fact that you wrote a letter to Sullivan, to warn him of my arrival, yet couldn't write me, your *best friend*, a letter explaining what the hell would happen to *me*," I scold, taking out the proof I stole from Sullivan's drawers.

She sighs. "I tried writing you countless letters in our time, or flat out telling you, but every time I tried, I got a vision of how you are being informed would actually worsen your path, guiding you away from your course and your destiny. It was better for you to know nothing," she admits nonchalantly, gesturing to the empty seats around the table. I shake my head, staying back. I will *not* be sitting down. "That's fine. Let me explain."

I stay where I am, as does Héctor, who's tapping his foot against the unsteady wooden floorboards. Besides Octavia, he and I are the only ones standing, leaning against the wall. He mumbles quietly to himself, his face a swirl of emotions. I can't tell what he's thinking. He's probably trying to make sure I don't swing the door open and take off with their canoe. Mami Julia heads to a chair, her eyes never leaving my face.

The candlelight dims, and all voices hush as if we were in a movie theater. The wind outside subsides entirely, eerie whispers encircle us in their mysterious nature. Octavia throws seashells on the table, opening a yellowed scroll after. The hairs on the back of my neck stand, goosebumps taking over my entire body. I don't know what's scarier: the lights dimming in an ominous manner or James being extremely quiet for the first time since I met him.

"For years, runaway sailors and pirates have used the seas to escape torment," Octavia begins. I clench my hands into fists while they're crossed, the wind chimes on the door softly dancing in the swamp. "The seas have been used to escape bondage, injustice. Amongst us they hide in Tortuga, Port Royal, Saint Mary's Island, New Providence, Nassau. Where war has been brewing. Hiding from the horrors of the world. Colonization, genocide, sickness. Those unable to hide have chosen the sea. For death is better than chains. Death is paradise."

Slavery.

"You speak of slavery and the genocide of the indigenous tribes in the Caribbean. I understand how it occurred, why and what came afterward. I've studied it for years," I admit. "We still experience its effects in our time. Colorism. Racism. Misplacement. Entitlement. Things that plague our daily lives as people of color."

"Yes. As someone who has lived throughout centuries, humans have not changed. Maybe gotten better at hiding their disdain for us, but their hateful nature? Still within them." She takes out a couple of tea leaves, smelling them and breaking them up into little pieces, blowing them in my direction. I flail my hand, pushing the bitter taste away from my lips. "However, how does one fight evil?"

"I'm not following," I say.

"Just listen, okay?"

She chants in Creole and takes deep breaths. More ominous, spine-chilling whispers. She opens her eyes and begins reading from the scroll.

"Time will collide.
The sea shall divide.
The conqueror to rise and change the tides.
When thy oceans bleed, darkened skies cracked,
The soul with a pearl bathed in blood shall rise.
With bitter seas, shouting winds, death as black as night.
Through pain and gloom,
Blood and gold intertwined.
Conquer the seas, the souls, even time.
One evil shall fall, another will rise.
A never-ending reign of ruin until one dies.

"Our prophecy speaks of the Aycayia of Ruin, a powerful entity of chaos and destruction that will rise from the sea with a powerful pearl," Octavia finishes. "She is to conquer the seas, souls, time itself. She will rise through endless pain and gloom, yearning for freedom and power. She'll change the tides, enrobing us with her darkness and reign of ruin. She is to fight evil with evil." She closes the scroll.

I stand there, aghast. Me? Fight evil with evil? A reign of ruin?

Thunder rumbles as my heart races.

"And where the fuck does this prophecy say that I have to kill *Johann Nau*? I'm sorry, but the man dies on June 7th 1692. That's almost three years from now. It can't be changed," I state. "Besides, he already tried killing me. I'm not trying to experience that again."

"You are the only one he will let near. If he wanted to kill you, he would have done so already," Mami Julia informs.

I roll my eyes. "Oh, so I assume those gunshots fired at me were a warm welcome to the past."

"You're not listening. You're the siren of *ruin*. Everything you touch, you *change*. The flow of time, history itself, the tides. Not to mention you've also ruined certain matters involving The Collector I shall not discuss," Octavia says. "Johann Nau knows this. He thinks you will join him in his quest to rid the seas of pirates and those who are like us. He wishes to conquer the seas, and how better to do that than be joined by the siren of catastrophe? Which is why he let you live. He's searched for you his entire life. He won't kill you the moment he finds you."

Everyone mumbles around me, commenting their thoughts to each other. I stay quiet, repeating what Octavia recited over and over in my head. Speaking of reigns of ruin, evils rising, oceans burning, it doesn't make sense that I'm the one who's supposed to do all this. It can't be me. This so-called prophecy can't be speaking of me.

"Octavia… this is a man who cannot be killed. It's been written. His destiny is to fall to the earthquake that'll happen in 1692," I say. "Not before."

She smirks. "Yes. It's been written. But when has history ever been certain and proven?" she asks, grabbing her hedgehog from the table. "You as a historian know that *certain* men change historical facts and twist them as they please. Placing themselves as unsung heroes, especially when it comes to our history." She scoffs, a ginger loc falling over her forehead. "Our *saviors.* Once and forevermore."

I take a few steps toward her, resisting the urge to reach out and shake her. "You're saying Johann won't die in the earthquake?" More thunder reverberates in the night sky. A second storm just waiting to happen.

"I can't confirm nor deny." She glances around, her eyes shimmering. "But who's to say he didn't die before?"

I can't just murder someone. No matter how horrible he may be.

I've killed no one.

"Luz, every one of us has had unsavory encounters with the Admiral as we tried assassinating him," Héctor says. His face comes into focus, his deep brown eyes staring intently into mine. "And each of us has failed miserably. No one has gotten close to him in years. He is a hard man to catch, but he seeks *you.* He wishes to create chaos and catastrophe in the West Indies, much more than what he currently brings, and who better to do it with than the siren of ruin?"

"Which means ye can betray him and end him, querida," Pedro chimes in.

Octavia hastens toward me, nodding. "This is your destiny, Luz. Whether you like it or not, Johann Nau is to die by your hand. You are the siren of ruin. You'll split the seas, change the tides... and come into your power. The fate of history rests in your hands. It always has."

"And ultimately, one of us will die. *A never-ending reign of chaos until one dies*. That's what you said right?" I ask, hysteria rising in me. "One of us will die, and it'll most likely be me!"

They say nothing. But their silence is enough for me.

I glare at Mami Julia and Octavia. The two who kept secrets from me. "Neither of you once thought, *hey maybe we should tell her she's going to time travel and die in the fucking 1680's trying to kill the murderous ancestor of her ex!*" I yell, hail accompanying the wind and rain. "Why does it have to be me? Why can't either of you do it? You– you can sing him to death!" I point at Octavia, my hands shaking. "And you! You can see where he's going to be!"

Mami Julia hugs herself, her eyes down-turned. "It can only be you," she says. "No matter how much any of us tries... It has to be you, mi amor."

"Fate prevents us from doing so. Believe me, I've tried. Everyone in this room has tried. And he always seems to slip away at just the right time," Octavia chimes in. "It is written in the stars. You and Johann are cosmically bound. It is your destiny."

"And if I don't want to do so?"

"Luz... if you don't kill Johann, thousands upon thousands of your fellow brothers and sisters will die by his hand. Including us. One by one, he will hunt us down, leaving you for last."

Second by second, the walls come closer, threatening to crush me. I'm nothing. I can't help. I just want to live my life like I did a week ago. Pulling on the end of my braids, jitters run throughout my entire body. Both hot flashes and chills course through me, confusing me. A terrible combination. The wind chimes made of utensils faintly rock with the breeze I create, the candles are slowly being lit back by Octavia. Everyone whispers, but I pay no mind to their words as the prophecy dances around in my mind.

The prophecy where I, like Johann, am the evil in these seas.

Tears well in my eyes.

I want to go back to my old life.

Where the press and Abel were my evil. Where Octavia was just Octavia and not the immortal Seer who has a brother called The Collector. Where my grandmother is dead and buried six feet underground because of her cancer. Where a non-lethal, non-deadly version of Oliver exists.

"No, no, no," I mutter, grabbing my chest.

Only I am the one able to kill one of the contributors to the mass genocide of my ancestors in the Caribbean.

Not my grandmother. Not Octavia. Not even the crew of *The Fury.*

Me.

I head to the front door, grip the handle with my shaking hand, and slam it shut, leaving that infernal shrinking shack and everyone who ever took me as a fool behind me. Especially my newfound responsibilities as a killer.

CHAPTER
TWENTY-FOUR

Insect sounds remind me immediately of where I am. I can't leave unless I take the canoe back to mainland Tortuga, and frankly, I'm not trying to be devoured by whatever lurks beneath the water.

The rain has turned to a sprinkle, the wind and hail have ceased. Far ahead, I'm greeted by the severed heads my best friend has put up as decoration around her cursed marsh. The air is thick with the fragrance of the surrounding foliage, the damp earth beneath my feet releasing a rich, earthy aroma that fills my senses. I can hear the occasional croak of a frog in the distance, as if singing along to the sounds of nature. The scent of decomposition from earlier has dissipated, no longer making me gag.

I have nowhere to go. I'm bound to this godforsaken swamp until I either decide to go back inside and ask for a ride or someone comes out and takes me where I ask to go. In all honesty, I should try to leave by myself to ensure I'm not followed.

The mud squelches beneath my boots as I walk around, attempting to find a way out of this swap, but it's futile. Octavia literally lives on a secluded island. It's just her and her heads. Murky water encircles her shack, the mangroves stick out, their threatening shadows making me unsteady. A small, winding path is in between the eerie mangroves. The water levels have risen with the relentless downpour in this path, creating small streams that wind through the underbrush. The flickering light of dancing fireflies reflects on the water. My gut decides against it.

Frustrated, I circle back around to an area with a fluttering oil lamp, plopping myself down on the damp moss. Bringing my knees to my chest, my whole body feels as tense as a boulder, as static as rusty parts. My heart races so quickly, it could be a grenade waiting to explode. The last time I felt it this way was when I first began learning parkour.

I don't cry, for all my tears have been spent.

Instead, all that can be found is anger.

Betrayal.

Denial.

Fear.

Prophecies, pirates, sirens, voodoo, the dead being alive again. Magic. Impossible things. Fairy tales, urban legends, folklores, and nightmares. *Especially* nightmares.

What Mami Julia is the product of.

And I am too.

The Aycayia of Destruction. The firstborn girl in the Narváez family.

The heir to a powerful line.

Dangerous, more like.

The sounds of the night are loud enough to cloud my thoughts, but not loud enough to control my edge. I wish they would drown me, engulf me until I could hear no more. Maybe then I might make some sense of this. While the air refreshes me, the dampness seeps into my clothes, weighing me down deeper into the ground.

I take off my necklace and keep it in my hands, studying it. A raw-cut, polished ruby glistens against the light from the lamp, its color as dull as always. The back with an inscription that only Héctor could read and understand.

I throw the necklace into the satchel, disgusted. I can't believe this little thing is the mastermind behind my current struggles. This useless rock that brought me to the seventeenth century so that I may make a catastrophic yet very tempting difference in this world full of colonization and hate.

What a fucking joke.

I chuckle humorlessly, shaking my head. I should've let Héctor have it that first night. I should've let Nau kill me. Johann fucking Nau, the son of Jean-David Nau, the most ruthless pirate of the Caribbean. The man who tortured his prisoners for *fun*. The man who sliced off portions of his victims with a sword. Who burned people alive, their screams unheard in the night. And he's Oliver's ancestor. Oliver Bennett, one of the most naïve, *harmless* men I know, is related to a vicious killer who committed mass genocide without remorse.

I don't know what's worse, accepting I time traveled, that I have to murder Johann, or that I have powers.

I sigh, taking out a dagger as the gentle rain falls over me.

"There are poisonous animals out here, Luz," Héctor warns from behind me. I whirl my head toward him, seeing how he's keeping his distance. As if I would snap at any second and kill him with my bare hands.

"Come to see a woman in her misery?" I snap.

"Your grandmother wants to make sure you are alright. I have not come to relish in your confusion, as surprising as that may sound to you."

I roll my eyes. So high and mighty. "Surely she can't have her prize pig roaming around, having that last taste of freedom before it's slaughtered." I turn to face the swamp again, the rain slowly picking up once more.

There's rustling behind me and he ends up sitting next to me. I groan and scoot away from him. Everything seems to be on a mission to infuriate me. From the insects that hid during the torrential downfall and have come out to resume their activities, to the way my cotton beige shirt feels on my skin, to a few strands of misplaced curls that have broken free from the braid I put them in.

"I have a question for you, second mate, and I better be told the truth or I swear I'll gut you like a fish," I threaten, ripping out a handful of wet grass and moss. The rain falls on the murky water, creating a deep, echoing melody.

"I promise I will not lie to you," Héctor says. "Although, you gutting me would involve having your undivided attention and I would not be opposed to that."

His playful smile warms me up, allowing me to forget all my worries and negative emotions. His deep brown eyes seem to twinkle under the lantern, and my mind struggles in forming a coherent sentence in response to his teasing. The pitter-patter of raindrops provide a soothing rhythm to this moment, falling on our hats then down our clothes and body.

What's happening to me?

"Villanueva. Is that your attempt at trying to make me feel better?"

Héctor chuckles, twisting the wooden ring on his index finger. "Is it working?"

Kind of... "No."

He laughs, looking ahead. "What was your question then, princess of ruin?"

I bring my fingers up to my necklace, never taking my eyes off him. "My necklace. How could you understand the inscription on the back?"

He blows air out of his mouth, wiping the corner of his lips. "It is written in my language. It says inaru bo bara. *Woman of Great Death.*" My expression must come across as bewildered because he sighs and plays with the moriviví next to him. All of them are already closed from the rain. "Woman of Great Death. Aycayia of Ruin. The two are intertwined. The prophecy speaks of death as black as night, and with you being a siren of destruction, death is bound to follow you. Just like The Collector follows those who have evaded their end."

I glance at the swamp in front of me, mulling the severity of his words. A knot forms in my stomach, uneasiness rising in my chest. A lightning bolt flashes the sky. Woman of Great Death. Regardless of whether I want to or not, death will follow me. Someone will die. It's a matter of *when* and *who.*

My breathing becomes shallow once more, and each inhale feels unsatisfactory to my lungs. It's like I'm drowning in a sea of revelations, a sea of death and souls whose blood will inevitably be on my hands. The rain diminishes from a steady pour to a gentle sprinkle that falls over us in a beautiful melody.

"D'nanichi," Héctor says softly. "I know we all lied to you, kidnapped you, and expect you to do the right thing instead of joining Nau in his quest to exterminate my people." He takes off his ring, scooting a bit closer to me. "But I know what it feels to be overwhelmed. I know your pendant may not bring you much comfort at the moment, and I assume you want nothing more than to run and forget us."

"I do. I want to hide, to escape," I admit. "I do not want to kill a man. I don't want anyone to die because of me." Tears well up in my eyes, my hands trembling. "I need to stay away from others. I refuse to cause anyone's death. No matter how horrible they may be."

He smiles sadly, taking my hand. "I know you do not want to murder him, but if you do not kill him, many more will die. Dozens upon dozens. Thousands upon thousands. You claimed he dies in three years. Imagine how many lives will be lost to him if he does not fall before."

Héctor places the wooden ring on my palm and closes my fingers around it. I look at him, aghast. He releases my hand, quickly crossing his arms.

"Why are you giving me this?"

"Like I said, I know your jewel may not provide much comfort, but that ring has always helped keep me steady in moments of uncertainty. I will let you have it for a few minutes while you regain composure. Twist it around your finger. It will be cathartic." He messes with the moriviví again. "Now, do not run off with it."

I smirk, a tear falling down my cheek. "Maybe I should, given that you took my necklace and kidnapped me."

He smiles. "I shall give you a five-minute head start this time."

"Why are you being so nice to me?"

He shrugs, taking a deep breath. "Perhaps I am making up for my actions and all the distress I caused."

I put the ring on my index finger, and while it's loose, I twist it around like he suggested. The wooden sensation brings relief to my skin. "Thank you. However, it'll take a lot to make up for when you shot at me as well... remember? Maybe you could take me inland and we'll call it even."

He sucks in a breath, chuckling awkwardly. "I shall try my best then." He scoots back and stands. "I will get the canoe ready and take you where you wish to go, then. But just... think about what you are meant to do, okay?" I nod. He brushes off the moss and plants from his hands. "Do not lose my ring or I will not hesitate to push you into the water. You seemed rather afraid of the reptiles."

I snort, laughing after. "Try that and I'll put your soul in another of the witchcraft boxes that you threw into the sea." He rolls his eyes, his mouth upturned on the side. "But I won't. You, while a thief, kept my necklace safe, so I'll keep your possession protected."

Héctor nods and walks away. A small part of me wants to call out for him. It wants me to cry on his shoulder, to ask for his expertise as someone who has killed people. How does he cope with it? How does he *live*?

I look back at the ominous trees, cicadas becoming louder by the second. Twisting the ring, ideas of how I may live in the seventeenth century arise. Maybe I can trade my necklace on the mainland for a house away from everyone. Since I'm not getting home, I might as well try to establish myself here. I can try to live in 1689. Where racism, oppression, misogyny, and sexism are the norm. Where I will probably be burned at a stake for being too outspoken. Where I will continue being called a half-blood.

I can't do this.

Twigs snap nearby.

The hairs on my neck stand, my heart races. I stand quickly, taking out one of my daggers. More twigs snap.

Someone is watching me. The paranoia I felt earlier is back and stronger than ever. I was right. Someone was following me.

"Come out! Now!" I yell.

I can't believe I'm daring an invisible danger to face me head-on. Me, who has a small dagger as a weapon. Me, a person who's never stabbed anyone before.

Come out they do. And by *they*, I mean a brown hare.

I sigh, laughing and relaxing. I can't believe I let this little thing get the best of me. I put the dagger back in my satchel, wondering why Héctor is taking forever to come back. The quicker I get to the mainland and leave this nightmare, the better.

The quicker I can escape this cursed swamp, the more I can stay in denial.

"Never let your guard down, siren," a brusque French-accented voice taunts behind me.

Before I can turn around and punch them, there's fingers around my throat, pulling me backward and restricting my airflow. I thrash around and reach for the dagger I put away, but I can't. They're pressing my neck harder and harder, making me gag and leaving me unable to scream.

My body weakens by the second, my adrenaline slowly disappearing. They release their grip and I let out a small scream, which causes their fingers to dig so deeply into my skin, I swear I can feel the fingernails in my throat.

Ultimately, they win.

My body goes limp and my eyes go dark, all my worries melting away.

CHAPTER TWENTY-FIVE

My nose brings me to consciousness before anything else. The pungent, metallic notes of blood lingers around me, but the putrid smell of decaying, rotting flesh makes me want to vomit, the food from earlier threatening to make a vicious reappearance.

I cough, gripping my chest, my throat. The odor reminds me of the time my cousin Nico and I played deep en el campo, and encountered a decomposing pig. Both of us stood there, watching as the maggots ate away at its skin, how the flies made a feast of its foul body. The scent of the dead pig was three times worse than this one, and when Mami Julia found us, she refused to let us into the house, dousing us in a weird bath of water, vinegar, and lemons.

Nothing like reminiscing the trauma of nine-year-old Nico and I.

This room is dark, except for the flickering light of a candle. The sound of water dripping above me reminds me of an unforgiving sea, which makes me assume I'm somewhere below deck. Perhaps lower.

I'm inside a ship once more.

A decomposing body lies only feet away from me, its arms tied with chains. Maggots are eating away its putrid flesh, and I taste metallic bile in my throat. I scurry away from it, tripping over a small stool.

I fall on dampened hay, my chest tightening.

My throat feels raw as I cough, my body weakened and sore. How am I not dead? Whoever sneaked up behind me was choking the life out of me.

I would rather be dead than be near a festering body.

I'm inside a cell, rusted iron bars caked with grime encasing me. It's barely large enough for a single person to lie down, with a ceiling only a few inches above my head. A hollow wooden floor with the sound of crashing waves comes from underneath. An eerily cold breeze surrounds me in a room where there are no windows or ventilation to let in any fresh air. The walls are made of rough, splintered wood, some of it eaten away by termites or clawed out by nails. My hands sweat, and I cover my mouth to keep from crying.

The floor of the cell is covered in filth, debris, and hay, a few rats scavenging for scraps in the cell next to mine. The ship rocks and sways with the motion of the sea, a faint creaking of the ship's hull making my nerves stir. Voices and laughter are distant, oblivious to the prisoner inside the cage.

I reach for my satchel, wanting to arm myself, but end up grabbing air instead. All my belongings have been taken. My weapons, my necklace, my waterskin. Except for Héctor's ring, safe on my index finger.

Thank God.

"Do not look so terrified, my dear," says the brusque voice from earlier. "'Tis simply a body."

Standing to the side, leaning against the beam stands a proud Johann Nau, with my necklace in one hand and my satchel in the other.

Instead of wearing the powdered wig, which is the norm for Royal Navy men, his natural blond hair is tied in a low ponytail. He wears a navy blue coat with a train that hits his knees, adorned with gold embellishments and buttons. Underneath, a simple white linen button shirt tucked into white pantaloons. His black leather boots match his half beaver hat, also adorned with gold.

He *is* Oliver. Same face, same build, same hair color. The only thing that's changed are his eyes. As blue as the ocean.

Angered at his presence and audacity, I stand, feeling the rough wood under my feet. I've been left barefoot, making me squirm at the thought of touching decay and excrement. I drag myself towards the cell door, grabbing on to the rusty bars.

"You!" I yell. "What did you do to me? Where am I?"

"That's the greeting I get after all this time? Tsk, tsk, tsk." Johann grins, walking over to stand in front of me. The iron bars separate us. "I thought you would be delighted to see me, my dear Luz. Or should I say, *siren of ruin.*"

My breathing staggers. How did he learn my name? I *never* told him. Did he follow us and that's how he heard it? He must've hidden in the swirling path with the mangroves. That's how he kidnapped me from The Seer's place. He was probably the one I felt watching me at Tortuga. It was *him* all along.

"What do you want, Nau?" I ask, staring right into his ice-cold eyes.

"Straight to the point, I love that," he declares, smiling. The necklace dangles in his hand, taunting me. "I want you."

"Excuse me?"

"I said that I want you and I got you. I own you now."

"You will not own me."

"Unfortunately, you are *not* looking very free right now, are we?"

You must kill Johann Nau.

I reach out to choke him, but he steps back, smirking. These bars are in the way. He inspects my face, my body, his tongue wetting his lips. I grip the iron keeping us apart, wanting nothing more than to rip out his eyes. Johann throws the necklace in his pocket, the satchel around his body.

Another uniformed man enters the room, his shoulders held back and a smirk on his mouth. His filthy hands hold iron shackles. Unlike Johann, this man wears a powdered wig underneath his hat. Johann unlocks my cell door, talking to the other man. While they're both distracted, I take off Héctor's ring, hiding it inside the pocket sewn into my vest. Johann will not take this ring from me.

Even if I die, I'll try my best to give it back to its owner.

Johann swings the cell door open, marching toward me. I stand strong, hiding my shivering breaths. I refuse to fight him with no weapons. He grabs me firmly from behind while the other man places the shackles around my wrists, the rough metal chafing against my skin.

When the man is finished shackling my arms in front of me, Johann caresses my cheek with his sweaty hand, eyeing my neck as he grins. Johann's presence looms over me, making me feel small and vulnerable. It's uncanny how Oliver looks exactly like this monster.

But Oliver is *not* this monster.

I stand frozen in place, even though my body is screaming at me to run, to move, to do *anything.*

He takes a deep breath, licking his lips. "Lavender," he whispers, leaning in. "It's such a shame you resemble the impure. You have the body of a goddess, and the smell of one."

"And you, Admiral, resemble those whose tears I drink for breakfast," I state, clenching my hands into fists. My knees tremble ever so lightly. "Tell me, how does it feel knowing you're going to end up crying at my feet like a weakling?"

For the second time since meeting him, Johann's face reddens, his nostrils flaring like a bull's. His expression goes dark, reminding me of demons. He slaps me suddenly. I stumble, but catch myself, fixing my posture. A sharp, burning sensation pulsating on my cheek.

"You forget your place, whore," Johann snarls, gripping my arm. He yanks me out of the cell.

Anger rises in me like a flame, and I stay in place, refusing to move."No. You forget *yours*."

"And what would my place be, pray tell?"

"Six feet under, rotting in hell." I spit at his feet.

The ship sways with force, the waves hitting the port and starboard sides, begging to be let in my vicinity. The man that brought my shackles discreetly walks away from me, taking deep breaths. That must be the power Mami Julia and Octavia mentioned. The power everyone mentions. No. It must've been a coincidence. Johann stares me down, and I glare right back. I will not be completely at his mercy.

I approach him, forcing myself to be within at least five inches of his tense body. "So high and mighty. Claiming to rid the seas from evil," I grit through my teeth, "but you'll never get rid of us."

The corner of his mouth twitches, and he grabs my chin. "I've already begun getting rid of you all, my dear," Johann purrs, his breath smelling of liquor. "I could get rid of you right now, but I quite enjoy seeing you chained and to my mercy."

"I'll never be at your mercy."

Johann's brows furrow as he lets out a heavy sigh. Abruptly, he takes out his pistol and presses it against my temple. I take a deep breath, my gaze never leaving his. A surge of adrenaline enters my body, making me tremble under his scrutinous glare.

"Move. Or I will move you by force," he orders. I inhale and walk.

I wish I had it in me to hurt those who have hurt me. To give them exactly as they deserve. Without remorse. Unfortunately, I'm not that way. No matter how many times I've been hurt, abused, racially profiled, or sexually assaulted, I don't have it in my heart to become like those who claim they are children of God. Preaching His word, but then turn right around with their vile behavior and poisonous mentalities that target anyone different from them. Making it their life's mission to prey upon those who have been silenced and ignored by the various systems put in place. Systems that benefit them. Always and forever.

Johann tugs on my arm, bringing my focus back to him and my surroundings. The smell of unwashed bodies and liquor fill my nose. Beige linen hammocks hang from the beams with twine and rope, a few holding snoring men. Those awake and completing their duties have stopped to observe the new prisoner aboard their vessel. They whistle and catcall as Johann parades me toward the wooden steps. My nostrils flare as I glare at them.

I pull away from Johann's grip and all he does is hold on tighter, pressing the barrel of his pistol deeper into my sunburnt skin.

As we ascend, the sun blinds me, and the chatter of male voices fill my ears.

How long has it been?

I flinch at the sun that's shining through the light gray clouds, my eyes unsteady. The sun is far past its highest point, which means it has to be after noon. The refreshing spray from the waves hits my face as we arrive on deck, refreshing my disoriented senses. While the temperature is hot, the humidity is subdued, making it much more comfortable to breathe in these conditions.

The Glory is grand, and they have spared no expense in assembling it. Fresh navy paint with golden accents intertwined between. Brand new canvas sails flap with the wind, commandeering us to who knows where. Men shout orders in English, calmly navigating the seas, as if nothing could faze them. As if they owned the very seas themselves.

Which, historically, they do.

Johann and I reach the area where the officers' quarters are. He opens a door and leads me inside, slamming it shut with the tip of his foot. Removing the pistol away from my temple, he pushes me onto a wooden chair with a plush blue cushion. The shackles feel heavy on my wrists, the air reeks of sweat and rum. With a gold chandelier, blue velvet curtains, a collection of shiny new swords and cutlasses, a map of the Atlantic Ocean as tall and wide as a bulletin board, I have no problem assuming that these are the Admiral's quarters.

Adorned with gold directly sourced from the islands, I presume.

He drags a chair in front of me, sitting as he watches me without saying a word. Avoiding his scrutinizing gaze, more gold adornments catch my eye. A grand antique mahogany table sits next to us, with scrolls, ship figurines, and an opened map on top. A pristine set of golden knives and quills rest upon the table, all ingrained and stamped with a symbol I've seen before. His four-poster bed in the corner of the room holds lush pillows, folded cotton blankets, and a shut book, a mosquito net surrounding it. The screech of seagulls, crashing waves, and voices carry through the windows.

Next to the bed stands a tall wooden wardrobe with golden handles and a big, golden cursive N lettered on each door. A wooden bookcase showcases bottles filled with liquid, more books, shot glasses, pistols, and even peculiar artifacts and relics.

Now I see where Oliver got his expensive taste from.

"Find my quarters to your liking?" he asks, drawing my attention back to him.

His mysterious blue eyes study me, his and Oliver's features battling in my head. Blending with each other. Oliver. Not Oliver. Part of me wants to warm up to him, give him what he wants, simply because my mind believes he's Oliver. The other part of me wants to fight and push him overboard, saving myself and hundreds more from the pain he's inflicted all these years.

Maybe the prophecy of having to kill Johann Nau isn't so bad. He hasn't killed me yet. He's been trying to negotiate. If he wanted me dead, he would've done so that first night, or even last night.

Maybe I *can* use my evil to rid the seas of his evil.

"I'm assuming you brought me here to negotiate? And by the looks of it, you're trying to win me over with your grandeur," I conclude. "Unfortunately, it's not working. I'm not easily impressed with the gold sourced from my people."

"Observant, I see," he says. "I'm surprised that you would defend those who fear you."

My eyes glimpse the knife set lying next to me.

Don't do it, my inner voice tells me.

"Better to be feared than loved, right, Admiral? Is that not your philosophy? Hundreds, no, *thousands* cower at your feet. There's no need for love. Fear is all that matters."

I glance at the knives again. *Don't. Do. It.*

Johann smirks, tipping his hat. "Let us come to an agreement then, shall we? Marry me. Join me in my quest to control the tides once and for all, and I shall let the crew of *The Fury* live. Or everyone you've ever loved will die."

"Why do you want more power? You already have it all, do you not? Only pirates and children believe in legends. Surely an intelligent man with common sense understands this." Maybe I can convince him to let me go, but it's not looking like that will happen.

"My dear, before I became all this, I, too, roamed the seas as a beast. Filthing the oceans with my beliefs. Hunting for treasure. My father, Francois l'Olonnais, was the most ruthless pirate the West Indies ever saw. A true leader and inspiration."

Luz, you better leave those knives alone. "The Flail of the Spanish."

"So you've heard of him." He nods, gripping the satchel around his body with his fingers. "But I, too, have heard of you. Of the siren of ruin who can control the skies and tides with simply a thought. Whose voice can bring down armies. Whose single touch can break the flow of time. My father gave his life to try and find you. I gave my youth, but ultimately the law caught up to me. Even as an Admiral, I've spent countless nights trying to continue what my father could not achieve. But, I've finally achieved it. Making me better than my father ever was."

My eyes widen, and my mouth drops slightly. "You're jeopardizing your job, your future, for a pirate's tale? It's not real, Johann. Contrary to what the prophecy states, or what legend foretold."

He slaps his hand on the table; the utensils shake from the hit. "Don't tell me what's real or not real. This job, this uniform is a façade." He spits on the ground, making a face. "I'm first and foremost a pirate at heart. I'll always be a pirate, hunting for the worthiest treasure. Which is you."

"You're wrong. This is all a farce."

"You lie, my dear. And I don't like liars. Now, what will it be? Do we have a bargain?"

"No. My answer is no. Fuck you and your shitty bargain."

He chuckles as if he expected this from me. My palms grow sweaty, his mocking snicker making my stomach churn. Frankly, I would've preferred for him to be enraged than nonchalant. It's as if he's got more planned beneath that vicious sneer.

He stands, heading to his bookshelf. This is it. My chance to fulfill the prophecy and go home. I'm taking my chance.

Luz. Don't you fucking dare.

Ignoring my inner voice, I grab the nearest blade, careful as to not make too much noise with my shackles. It's smooth in my trembling hand, and immediately I fear dropping it, alerting him of my intentions. The wind picks up outside with my anxiety, my heart racing a mile per minute. I attack Johann from behind, aiming for his torso, but I panic and accidentally stab his left arm through his thin clothes instead.

Oh, my God. I stabbed *Johann Nau.*

The Shadow of the Flail.

However, he's right-handed.

All I've done is anger him.

I remove the blade from his body, dropping it on the ground. This helps me come back to reality. With him holding his arm, I run out of his quarters, back toward the deck. I don't know what I'm going to do.

I should've thought this through.

Why am I a do-first, think-later person? This is definitely my unmedicated ADHD taking the lead, because there's no way I stabbed Johann Nau without thinking this through.

Johann's booming voice commands me to stop, but I keep running away from him. Away from everyone. My heart pounds within my chest, fueling my rapid, panicked breaths as I push my body to its limits. His men attempt to catch me, but I use the thick area of the shackles to hit the bridge of their nose, giving me a few seconds of escape. My muscles strain as I propel my body toward the rail. As my eyes dart around, I realize... I have to jump.

The cacophony of pounding footsteps as I climb over the rail amplifies my dread. The world around me blurs into a thundering haze, my focus solely on the gray skies ahead, and on the instinctual drive to jump into the sea.

Even if I'm shackled, death is better than whatever consequence I'll have to face.

Hands pull me backward as I look down at the roaring waves. Those five seconds of hesitation gave them the chance to catch me. Two men grip my arms, keeping me in place.

"That... was a mistake, my dear," Johann taunts, holding his side.

His hand is bloody and red. But not even being stabbed slows him down. He seems quicker. His other hand holds a sword, and instantly I fear for my life. Everyone has gone quiet. Not even a whisper can be heard. I'm going to die.

"Johann..." I manage to get out.

"Admiral Nau to you, you half-blooded sea wench!" he yells.

What happens next is so quick, I almost miss it. Almost. Johann brings his sword down in an arc, and searing pain explodes across my cheek.

CHAPTER
TWENTY-SIX

My shackled hands go up to my cheek and come away bloody.

He could've killed me.

But he didn't.

This is simply a warning of the things to come aboard his ship.

A scene unfolds with him bearing gritted teeth, a clenched jaw, and a throbbing blue vein on his forehead as he bellows in French. His wide-eyed fury causes spittle to reach my face, making me freeze like a deer in headlights. Regrettably, my attempts only resulted in a slight skin nick, leading him to dismiss the medic's help with disdain.

Johann's breathing turns shallow, his posture rigid. He throws his sword on the deck, the delicate iron clanking against the wood. He stomps toward me, his nostrils flaring, and punches me in my stomach, knocking all the wind out of me. My shoulders curl inwardly, pain flaring up from my abdomen. I fall a bit, but the men hold me up, laughing at me. An acidic taste comes to my throat.

Johann grabs my face, pressing his rough fingertips into my cheeks. "You dare injure me, whore?" he snarls. He forces me to face him, the ache in my abdomen thumping. "Those scurvy dogs corrupted you."

"I was corrupted by no one," I seethe. "I did that all on my own because you are a despicable son of a bitch!" I spit on him.

He stands there, watching me, his left eye twitching. Now I've done it.

"Gents, this *woman* has decided to disobey me." Johann chuckles humorlessly. Everyone quiets down, listening to their cult leader. "Do we, as men, accept disrespect from a whore?"

"No, sir!" they reply, glaring at me.

Thunder cracks above me, the sky slowly turning gray.

"What do we do to those that disobey us?"

"We punish them!" a man whoops, and the rest agree. The two men release me, pushing me toward Johann.

Punishment?

No.

Gentle drops of rain fall from the sky. They're small and delicate, yet sharp as daggers on our skin.

Johann and his father were known for their cruel punishments on their victims and enemies. Both had no remorse, enjoying the pain. Relishing it.

No, no, no.

He yanks me forward and unshackles me, two different men appearing on either side of me. My eyes dart from Johann to the men holding me as my breathing becomes ragged. I fall, hitting the deck sideways, but they hold me down. My heart pounds so hard in my chest that I fear it may rip open. The cold grip of fear takes a hold of me with each second that passes, paralyzing me with its icy touch.

"Johann, don't do this," I plead, tears falling down my cheeks as Johann reveals a sharpened knife. "I'm sorry! Please, it won't happen again!"

I squirm, attempting to get free, but two more men approach, firmly holding my legs down against the wooden deck. Panic arises in me. I sob, my heart beating so fast that it echoes in my ears. I'm stuck in place, sobbing, waiting for the inevitable to happen. Laughter mixes with the wind, eager cheers from behind. The adrenaline pushes down, crushing my lungs and leaving me unable to breathe correctly.

Johann squats down, smiling, pressing the knife against my neck. The once-soft raindrops now fall onto us in thick sheets, pounding against the deck, causing the entire world around me to transform into something ominous.

"It's too late, my dear," Johann declares, smiling. "Not to worry, I've heard sirens don't feel pain."

"Johann, please!" I'm sobbing uncontrollably now, my whole body shivering. "I won't try anything again! Please!"

The sky darkens to a shade of black, to where it could easily be dusk. The wind picks up, causing the sails to sway violently from their knots, struggling the onslaught of the zephyr. Mutters erupt throughout the ship, most in awe.

He positions himself directly on top of my left arm, pulling the sleeve of my blouse up. The tip of his knife splits the skin of my forearm open with a soaring pain. I scream as he cuts me, tears falling. Never had I felt a pain so blinding, so excruciating.

The rain pours so heavily it has become difficult to see more than a few feet. I could not only feel the weight of the rain on my skin but also Johann's, the knife piercing like a million tiny needles. The searing agony radiates from my arm to every fiber of my being. My muscles tense at his touch, trying to protect my body from the onslaught of pain he's creating. More screams. More begging. It feels like I'm being torn apart from the inside out.

The conqueror to rise and change the tides.

I don't feel like much of a conqueror.

Smiling, he removes the tip of the blade, inserting it right next to the incision he's making. The pain in my body, doubling, no, tripling. My breaths come in quick gasps, my skin hot and clammy even under the rain. Every nerve ending in my body seems to be on fire as I writhe in agony, unable to find relief as he cuts me open. The downpour does nothing to bring me solace from the ache. Johann's eyes twinkle under my torment, his mouth moving, but no words come out.

One evil shall fall, another will rise.

He's the evil in these seas.

The pain is so intense, I start to lose my grip on reality. It's consuming me whole, like a whirlpool sucking me in and devouring me from the inside out. This is it. This is how I die.

The rain loses its intensity, going from a rancorous storm to a steady fall. My focus diminishes by the second, my mind showing flashes of Soledad, Octavia, Mami Julia, James, Lydia, and even Héctor.

I understand my ancestors now.

Death would be better than this.

I'm drowning in my pain, unable to come up for air. Laughter surrounds me, encircling me in this never-ending nightmare. Little by little, my screams diminish. My vision blurs from my tears, my body goes limp. The rain nearly ceases.

A never-ending reign of ruin until one dies.

Please... God... Let me die...

By the time he's done, no more screams escape my body. I stare at the beautiful gray as the tears slowly drain from my eyes. No more rain or wind. Just ominous stillness. My entire arm aches as does my collarbone, the warm blood dripping down onto the wet deck. He could kill me right now and I wouldn't even feel it.

"Stand her up," Johann's voice says faintly. As if he was miles away instead of right in front of me. Maybe the one that's miles away is *me.*

My body goes flaccid as I'm harshly pulled upwards by four powerful hands. I'm a rag doll to them, unable to stand up straight, unable to set a firm grip on the deck. My eyes lazily open and close, the crew's bodies blurring and blending with each other's. Fuzzy balls of white are all I see.

A hazy Johann stands in front of me, holding my face firmly in his hands. His breath smells of liquor, his lips are stained red as if he licked my blood. His blond hair is plastered to his skin, as are his clothes.

Death as black as night.

You must kill Johann Nau.

No. Kill me instead...

"That's what you get for attacking me. Next time, it'll be worse, darling," he snarls at me. His face barely comes into focus, devoid of all energy.

"I don't think we should provoke her any more, Admiral," a second voice chimes in. Younger, muddled.

"Don't be afraid, Clarke. Take her to the cell and bring her back to the moment. The wench seems pretty out of it. I shall be along."

I should've listened.

I should've obeyed.

I'm dragged away, back toward the hold where my decomposing friend and oncoming days of agonizing pain surely await me. My eyes can't focus, but I try my hardest to keep them open. The clanking of iron sounds near me and I'm thrown forward, landing on damp hay. As the iron creaks, warm water falls on me.

My arm and eyes sting so bad, I cry out in pain. Salt water. An open wound.

This brings me to the moment.

As well as the flapping fish and guts tossed onto me.

I push the fish off of me hysterically, as the live fish flap on the wood next to me, searching for the water they were just yanked out of. As they die all around me, I scurry backward, away from them. My clothes, my skin, my hair. All covered in remains.

The men laugh, clearly satisfied with my reaction. All but one. He seems uncomfortable, secluding himself. Looking at the ground instead of me. They leave as Johann enters the hold, their menacing laughter haunting me.

Weak, covered in fish guts, and with the smell of decay becoming stronger by the second, I throw up until nothing stays in my stomach. This is a nightmare.

I crawl to the other side of the cell, shivering and weak. Johann stands on the other side of the bars, smirking as he watches me.

Awake and in infernal pain, tears come to my eyes as the word *halfbreed* stares at me, bright red blood oozing out of each of the slurred letters carved into my forearm. On my collarbone, I can make out the upside down *Y* I had seen on Héctor's arm. He carved me there too.

While I never cared much for Royal Navy history, I do recall them being painted as pacifists. Another fact that was whitewashed. It doesn't surprise me. All of our history is whitewashed.

This doesn't look very pacific and holy to me.

"Now, my dear sirène," Johann begins. "Let us get down to more important matters. We could rule the seas together. Controlling the tides, the oceans. The feared admiral with the beautiful sirène at his side. You shall marry me two nights from today."

The way he's speaking reminds me a lot of Oliver. Soft voice, full of tranquility. Oliver is different from this man. Better. Kinder. Genuine.

Oliver wouldn't do this to me.

"I don't want to marry you."

"I'm not really asking you. Matrimony will bind you to me, therefore granting me your power. It is decided."

He exits the hold, leaving me there.

I look down at my bleeding arm.

Halfbreed.

Mestiza. Crossbreed. Bastard.

The names colonizers called my ancestors. Labels assigned to my people and I by those in power. Words that have been uttered in disgrace and hate, flung toward us unprovoked. Now he's branded it onto me, so it can mock me for the rest of my days.

I take out Héctor's wooden ring, putting it on my index finger with twitching hands. I twist it around and around, attempting to feel that cathartic feeling he promised.

Does he even know I'm gone? He must know. But I doubt he cares. If he does, it's simply to get his most prized possession back.

I cry, wiping away the blood on my arm and my collarbone, wanting nothing more than to escape this insult that's been branded onto me.

But I can't. Because that's what I am.

And that's what I'll always be.

No matter where I go.
Go back to where you came from. You people. Your kind.
A half-breed.
An abomination.

CHAPTER
TWENTY-SEVEN

A long shadow is cast on the ground of my cell. My heart pounds with every step taken toward me. An eerie presence lingers in my body; a strange, unsettling energy sending chills down my spine. Johann appears with a sharp dagger in his hand, claiming that he needs to carve the word whore on my forehead.

I desperately try to scurry away from him, but my legs turn to jelly. The surrounding air thickens. My pulse races, he approaches. He laughs, holding me down with his left hand. I try to fight him off, but I can't. I plead with him to let me go. He ignores me, his menacing figure looming over me. The tip of his dagger splits my skin in an agonizing nick.

I jolt awake, panic arising in me.

I'm alone, I'm safe.

He can't hurt me.

I crawl over to a corner, cocooning myself for protection, my tongue as dry as the sand on the shore. My body is riddled with cramps, my head tender, my breasts sore. All indications that my period might've begun or will begin soon. Just what I needed.

My arm, forearm, and cheek are numb, all with a dull ache that refuses to leave my body. I take deep breaths, counting to ten. *He's not here.* My forearm has stopped bleeding, and now angry, red clots have formed in each letter. *Halfbreed.* My helpless screams from the torture inflicted to me replay in my memory, the agonizing pain lurking in every crevice of my curves. The taunting laughter from the crew causes me to cover my ears as the world crushes my chest.

Oliver did this to me.

No.

Johann did this.

I can't let my fragile mind blur the two men together. Oliver is not the nightmare. Johann is. But how can one differentiate between the beast beneath the cupboard when they have taken the same appearance?

The laughter turns to a whisper, and I uncover my ears, unable to find a comfortable position to sit in. Hugging my knees, I twist Héctor's ring. Each turn reminding me of him, of the crew from *The Fury*, of the prophecy.

Time will collide.

Are they okay? Did Johann and his crew ambush them in Octavia's shack? Are Octavia and my grandmother okay? Is James alright? They have to be.

I need them alive.

If they're alive... might they be looking for me? Part of me lights up at the hope that they're out there looking for me. Some of them were irritating, but they never tortured me.

Through pain and gloom.

The smooth wooden ring feels warm on my finger, providing me with a bit of comfort after the horror Johann put me through. Did he put the crew through horrors as well? Héctor vaguely mentioned that they've all had unsavory encounters with Johann and the East India Company. I bet what happened to me was merely a taste of what he's capable of.

One evil shall fall, another will rise.

Footsteps approach.

"Good morrow, beautiful!" a voice hollers.

"Go. Away," I order, my gaze daggers at this strange man. I take off Héctor's ring discreetly.

The man arrives at the cell door with a smile that reaches his brown eyes. "The Admiral sends for you."

"Fuck you, fuck him, fuck everyone!"

He unlocks the cell and walks in, rubbing his hands together.

"Fiery, ain't we?" He throws a kiss at me, biting his chapped lips after. "Move. Before we carve more on the other arm."

I scramble to stand. The last thing I want is to experience the pain from yesterday. I can't go through that again. I walk toward him, smoothing down my vest, throwing the ring inside the pocket. Holding my shoulders back, he shackles my blistered wrists, my gaze never leaving his. The iron feels cool against my raw skin; however, the shackles feel tighter and heavier than the first pair they put me in. Surely to avoid a stunt like the one I tried.

He grasps my arm and pulls me to meet my tormenter.

I'm paraded through the hold and below decks, where sleeping men lay and the pungent, musty odor of unwashed bodies is intensified by humidity and sweat. The smell aboard *The Fury* was bad, but some of them tried keeping themselves clean, such as Héctor, Cyrus, James, and Lydia. Here, none of them care. Just like their predecessors when they arrived at what they called the "New World."

History states how my ancestors received the Europeans with incense and oils. Many will say it's because they were paving the way and honoring their saviors with gifts. If you research the truth—the hidden truth buried by those who consider themselves the ultimate race—is that Europeans carried an overpowering and unpleasant scent that lingered in the air, causing the indigenous people to burn scented sticks just to breathe clean air.

"You truly are a defenseless woman," the brown-eyed man says. "Maybe I'll pay you a visit after dusk."

"Maybe I'll kill you before you do," I snarl through gritted teeth.

"Move along, whore."

Watery light hits my eyes as we ascend the stairs to the deck, fog consuming us whole. Is it morning? Night? How many days has it been?

The scent of the sea is strong and crisp in my sinuses, mingling with the tang of salt. It possesses a refreshing quality, offering a welcome respite from the bitter, rotten odors that surrounded me in the hold. The pure breeze carries a faint hint of seaweed, evoking images of very distant shores that offer me freedom.

Men in navy blue coats and powdered wigs under beaver hats maintain the deck, rigging lines, sweeping, and taking inventory of their weapons and cannons. The wood creaks with the gentle sway of the vessel, a reminder that I'm at the sea's mercy and it at mine.

The man leads me toward the officers' quarters. To Johann's room.

One knock. Pause. Another knock. Then he opens the door.

"The wench, Admiral," he announces, and pushes me inside. The door slams shut behind me, leaving me with the evil in the seas.

Johann sits on his bed, taking a gulp from the bottle he's holding. His upper body is shirtless, revealing the gauze wrapped around his left bicep. His fluffed, blond hair cascades to the side, down to his neck. His jaw clenches as he watches me with his piercing, hooded blue eyes. But just as he's observing me, I'm studying him.

The eye shape. The square chin. The high cheekbones. The blond hair.

Oliver Bennett.

"Tonight, we shall marry," Johann declares, sitting upright, his elbows on his knees. "Through marriage, we'll join forces. The choice to do it all willingly, however, falls onto you."

"Johann Nau," I articulate. "I'd rather die than marry you."

He chuckles. "Unfortunately, I'm not that merciful, my dear." He sighs, pushing a few strands of hair back. "I thought the punishment would bring you to your senses. I'm not someone you want to cross, siren of ruin."

"Nor am I, *Little Shadow.*" He sucks in his breath. My whole body is ridden with tremors. Seeing him reminds me of what he did. Of what he could do if I step out of line again, but I force myself to continue speaking. "Yes. I know that name. The name you're called when others mock you. Tell me, Johann, how many times did you hear it as a pirate before the Company made you pledge your allegiance to them?" I force myself to approach him. "Little Shadow. Never the first. Always the last. Had no choice but to save his own—"

"Enough!" He grabs my arms, pulling me to him. He takes quick breaths, angered at my remarks. "You will do as I say!"

If there's one thing I'm good at besides history, parkour, and being so unbearable no one can stand being in my vicinity, it's acting.

"Fine," I utter, and he releases me. "I'll marry you and join you in your quest. If, and only if, you do a favor for me."

"What shall you like, my dear?" he asks, resigned.

"You must ensure the crew of *The Fury* are not harmed. In fact, they will receive letters of marque, ensuring their pardon. For each member of the crew. Every. Single. One."

Johann's jaw clenches. "No."

I force myself to chuckle, stepping away from him. "Then you can kiss this alliance goodbye." I run my fingers through the mahogany tabletop, looking at him through my lashes. Time to embrace my role as the *siren of ruin*. "Good luck staying alive on June 7th, 1692 without me, Admiral."

Johann stands still, his brows furrowing together as a puzzled expression creases his face. His gaze shifts from my eyes to my hands back up to my eyes, as if trying to make sense of my words. A subtle snark plays upon my lips, my chin slightly lifted, my shoulders held back. Even if my breathing turns shallow and the flashbacks of what he did return... I hold the reins. My screams echo in my head, his smirk, the laughter. I clasp my sweaty hands together, my nails digging into my palms. My arm feels like a thousand tons, my body weakened and beat from the traumatic events. I can't cry. I can't freak. I have him right where I want him.

While my body wishes to shrink back, and distance myself from him, my gaze is steady and unyielding, locking with Johann's with an unwavering intensity. His sadistic blue eyes seem lost and without focus, and eyebrows lift ever so slightly, challenging my words to him. There's nothing a pirate fears more than dying.

"What'd you just say?" he asks, hoarsely.

"You heard me. You're to die if you don't do as I suggest," I say nonchalantly, clasping my hands together. "I will make the ground shake, and the Earth will split in half. My wrath will surround you. You won't be able to escape it or me. Wherever you go, death shall follow. And you'll die on that date. Alone, forgotten, mocked. Forever."

He coughs, forcing himself to never waver. "That's too soon. That's... in less than three years."

I nod. "Exactly. The odds are not looking in your favor if you continue working by yourself. I must be close to you. I'll marry you, but the only way to do that is to grant the crew from *The Fury* immunity. Along with the woman known as The Seer."

Johann steps away from me, facing one of his windows. The watery sunlight steadily leaves the vicinity, letting me know that it's about to be nighttime. He brings his hand to his mouth, biting his nails. His head tilts to the right side, which is something Oliver does whenever he doesn't understand certain things. Johann's shoulders are slightly slumped, his weight shifting from his left leg to his right.

I stand there, not wanting to have my skin carved again for attempting to injure this man. My thoughts go to the crew of *The Fury*. At least if I'm stuck with Johann until one of us kills the other, I'll try to ensure they're safe and protected. With Letters of Marque, not even the king himself can lay a finger on them. I wonder if they're looking out for me the same way I'm looking out for them.

At the very least, thinking about them helps me forget the repercussions I've brought upon telling Johann his death date.

"Deal," is all he says, not looking at me.

"I beg your pardon?" I ask.

Johann spins halfway, his eyebrows raised. "I agree to your terms. I shall grant them my immunity, while being saved from your wrath. They don't deserve it, but it's a small price to prevent eternal damnation."

I smile. "That's fantastic. Now be a good boy and take these off."

Johann scoffs, but for the first time since I met him he does as he's told. Once the shackles are removed from my wrists, I rub my raw skin. He stands in front of me, his eyes on my lips. His breathing is shallow, and I recoil under his stare, wanting to be anywhere but so close to this murderous colonizer.

Johann stops looking at me long enough to offer me a waterskin. Bigger than the average size, filled to the brim. Water. My parched lips quiver in anticipation as I clutch the drink with my calloused hands. I rip the cap open, the scent of hydration wafting through the air. As the room temperature liquid touches my tongue, my eyes close momentarily as I gulp the entire thing in five swallows. A content sigh escapes my lips after I finish the container, the weight of my thirst being lifted for the first time. My senses feel more stable, more focused.

"Now that your thirst is quenched, we shall marry," Johann commands. "At dusk."

"Sure."

I could laugh at this entire situation. In my time, I refused to marry Oliver to the point where I broke off our relationship. Now, I have to marry his murderous, sadistic ancestor in order to ensure my livelihood. When I was aboard *The Fury*, James kept messing with Héctor and I, stating that our arguments were that of a married couple. Repeatedly, we both answered we preferred death to being betrothed to each other. The funny part is I actually wouldn't mind marrying Héctor after experiencing literal torture at the hands of Johann. But I can't admit that.

I smile to myself. Not here.

❧❧❧

Time to become property.

Johann seems tranquil as he holds out his arm to me. Reluctantly, I take it as he leads me out. My stomach churns, and faint lightning cracks from the sky, clearly connected to my emotions. I don't think there's any more denying it.

I have powers. The question is, how do I control them?

Up in the quarterdeck, an older white man with gray hair, wrinkly pale skin, and a black clergy robe greets. My eyes go to his hands, which are holding a Bible and a wooden rosary. A priest. He will marry us tonight.

"Admiral Nau de Vernay, may God bless you in this union," the priest says, doing the cross motion to Johann. The priest turns to me and does the same motion, but doesn't speak to me. As if I was invisible to him.

I've seen that look of disgust before. In people from my time.

Half-breed.

Go back to your country.

Puerto Rico is owned by the United States, therefore we own you animals.

Johann and I hold hands as the priest speaks. He looks at me with curiosity, with interest, with lust. Not an ounce of fear can be found in his eyes. A cold sweat breaks in my body, my knees weaken, the skies crack open. A gentle spring rain falls over us, the raindrops piercing our skin like blades.

277

Conquer the seas, the souls, even time.

I say goodbye to my freedom. My life.

One evil shall fall...

Will he try to consummate the marriage after?

Oh God, I hope not.

Another will rise...

"Do you take Admiral Johann-Laurent Nau de Vernay as your husband? To love, cherish, and obey till death do you part?" the priest asks me.

No, I don't. Fuck him. "I do," I say, a smile on my face.

"May this union be blessed by God. Admiral Nau, you may kiss your bride. God shall forgive her of her past sins, of her mixed status. Now, she becomes yours."

A never-ending reign of ruin until one dies.

Johann licks his lips and kisses me. I freeze under his touch, a small strained noise escaping my lips. The rain stops, but thunder rumbles in the sky.

"Let's celebrate, lads!" Johann exclaims, raising our hands together in accomplishment. He then leaves me and heads down the deck, joining a group of men who've begun drinking.

I'm officially married to the son of the most ruthless pirate that ever stepped foot in the Caribbean.

With Johann and the crew downing their liquor in excitement, I sit on the staircase, the cool night breeze refreshing my sinuses. I take deep breaths, attempting to relax, but I can't. My period cramps are strong, making me yearn for tea or ibuprofen. Due to the lack of menstrual products, I have a free flow, staining my pants and creating one of the most uncomfortable sensations I've ever experienced.

Also, because I don't know what awaits me.

Only God knows.

And Octavia.

Did she know I was going to get kidnapped by Johann? Is that why she and my grandmother sent Héctor out to be with me that night?

She must've known and never told me.

My stomach groans, reminding me I have not fed it since the night at the tavern with the officers of *The Fury*. Hunger has taken a toll on me. Dizziness, headaches, stomach cramps. I've gotten weaker by the minute.

The night sky twinkles against the ocean, giving a sense of tranquility. After days of being locked down there, I'd give anything to stay up here, surrounded by the beautiful yet mysterious sea. The home of my grandmother, the home of her power source passed down to me.

I wish I could take out Héctor's ring to find some comfort in this never-ending hate, fear, and torture. But I can't risk anyone seeing it.

"Come, my dear," Johann approaches me, calling me out of my thoughts.

"No, I'm fine here," I say, shaking my head. Johann ignores me and grabs my arms, pulling me towards him. He plants a wet kiss on my lips, and I recoil under his touch. I break the kiss apart, my trembling hands against his chest. "Get off me, Johann."

His eyes darken, turning to slits. "As my wife, you must do as I say."

"No. Just 'cause we're *married* doesn't mean I have to obey you. This is a *partnership*, not an *ownership*, Little Shadow."

Johann's face is set ablaze with wrath. His nostrils flare with each heavy breath, and he's just a volcano of rage threatening to erupt. My body tenses as his muscles ripple along his temples. Quick, shallow gasps betray my composure. The breeze picks up, chills rising on the back of my neck.

"You push your luck," he says.

"No," I snap. "I can't be owned. By you, or anyone aboard this fucking ship!"

Johann reaches out and grabs my braids with one hand, pulling them with such force that sudden jolts of pain radiate from my scalp to my neck. I curse him out in Spanish and try to push him off, instead he drags me to where he pleases. Every rough tug sends a sharp, throbbing sensation all over my head.

"What the fuck is wrong with you?" I scream, grabbing his hands as he pulls me down the stairs.

"You may be the omen of catastrophe, but you're still a *woman*!" he yells, leading my hunched body down the wooden steps. "I'm above you, now and forevermore!"

Johann hauls me to the hold, our rushed footsteps echoing amidst my curses in Spanish. I order this man to let me go, promising a hell to be unleashed. Johann says nothing as the ship sways with force.

More struggling. More pulling.

Swinging the cell door open, he pushes me inside, grimacing. I land on my chest, atop clustered, dampened hay, all the air blown out of me. Tension runs throughout my scalp, a lingering tenderness all over my neck and head.

I turn to him, spitting out hay.

"Maybe you are above me, but this woman is the one that can prevent you from dying in three years!" I remind him, standing up. "You can't run from what's foretold, Nau!"

Johann shuts the cell door, locking it afterward.

"I make my own fate! I'm the holder of my own fucking destiny!" he yells, hitting the iron bars with his fists.

Johann's face is red. His muscles tighten and bulge with an intense surge of negative energy. A storm brews within him. His body is a vessel for the unrestrained power of his fury. An eerie feeling lingers in my body; a strange, unsettling energy sending chills down my spine.

"It's time you learn who's in charge," he seethes. Gripping the iron bars so tightly, his knuckles are white. "You might hold the power of the seas, but I hold the power of God. Here... I am God."

Johann leaves me there, and I scream in frustration.

CHAPTER TWENTY-EIGHT

I don't know how long it's been since the wedding. I've no window in my cell, no way to tell whether it's night or day. My seconds, minutes, days have blurred together. My stomach has been roaring non-stop, weakening me each minute. My cellmate keeps decomposing as the seconds go by. He no longer haunts my nightmares. But truth be told, he's the least of my worries. The smell of sweat, blood, urine, and rotting fish has become a friend to me, dimming my other senses.

They brought me a thick chunk of bread, an apple, and water six times. I don't want to get ahead of myself, but I assume it's been three days. I can't be too sure.

The scar on my arm keeps taunting me. Reminding me of what they did to me. The pain has become bearable by now, and delicate scabs have formed on each letter. My energy has dwindled, and even the simplest task of hanging on has become daunting and overwhelming. Fatigue consumes me, both physically and mentally, leaving me devoid of motivation.

I lay in my corner, facing the ceiling as the ship sways. The rhythm of the waves has become calm. Along with Héctor's ring. I've even spoken to it twice, as if I was speaking to Héctor, James, Octavia, Mami Julia, or Soledad. I'm way past feeling embarrassed for doing so. I've asked the ring if its beautiful, sassy owner is coming for me. If the owner's crew is trying to find me.

I want them to find me. To give the Admiral and his crew hell. Unfortunately, some were content to get rid of me.

Have they doomed me with Johann?

Speaking of Johann, he hasn't come to see me at all. He keeps sending different officers to me and it's never the same man. They all differ in age, height, eye color, but they're all the same in behavior. Various men join those in charge of bringing me supplies, and they take their precious time with me. They call me names, throw buckets of water on me, aim knives at my head as if I were a target. Thanks to them, I now have knicks on my ears, neck, and shoulders.

A couple of them even came in as I slept, trying to take advantage of me but a loud, harsh voice outside told them to leave me be. I don't know who the kind soul who scolded them was, but I'm forever grateful to them. Scorned, those men forcefully took my hair out of my braids and ripped my scarlet vest to shreds, leaving me in the bloodstained beige blouse and brown pants I was given.

As I slowly twist the wooden ring around my finger, sanity leaves my body by the second. The cell door unlocks once more, startling me. In comes a man, probably around my age or so with a blade in hand. Great, another one trying to perfect his aim. His uniform is clean and crisp, his wig freshly powdered. I stay far from him, not trusting his intentions. I hide the ring in my fingers, waiting for the perfect opportunity to throw it inside the pocket in my pants.

"Come, Admiral Nau summons you," he announces.

"That worthless son of—" I hiss and curse in Spanish, reluctantly walking over to the man.

I spot the twine I used to tie the ends of my braids and rush to grab them, placing my hair in two low ponytails with frizzy strands loose around my face.

The man leads me out of the cell, putting his arm around my waist. We walk, and the higher we go, the more I see that it's daytime.

Tears form in my eyes. A clear, azure sky with a radiant sun beams its warm embrace upon us, painting the world in a tapestry of beautiful light and color. The welcoming breeze brings a bracing freshness, whispering stories of those who have chosen the sea. I inhale its intoxicating essence, the air's crispness cleansing my spirit and soul.

How many days has it truly been?

I'm led to the quarterdeck this time where Johann stands at the helm, his hair down and blowing with the ocean wind. He glances at me, his eyes landing on my filthy clothing and ruined hair.

"It seems three days has been enough," Johann says, smirking. It felt like an eternity to me. The man who brought me upstairs departs. "I hope you've learned your lesson by now, my dear."

"Maybe I have. Maybe I haven't."

"Oh, really? What a shame. I was just about to bargain with you. It involved your precious *Fury* crew."

I raise my eyebrow, stepping back. "Unless you've got their Letters of Marque I asked for inside that coat of yours, I'm not interested in any shitty bargain you may offer."

He signals another man to take hold of the helm. Johann comes up to me. "Well, siren, perhaps you'd be interested in knowing I've decided that we will grant the wretched *Fury* their cursed Letters of Marque. As shall leniency for the witch. They shall be pardoned and allowed to roam the seas."

I take a breath of relief. I've ruined a lot of things since I arrived in the seventeenth century. I'm just glad I could do something well, even if it means my soul will be given to the devil himself.

The knot in my stomach loosens. "Thank you," is all I say.

"However," he says. *There's a but.* There's always a *but* with men like him. "Your filthy scalawag Héctor will be pardoned for his crimes of piracy, *not* for his crimes against the East India Company committed in his youth."

This takes me aback. I stand frozen in place. "Crimes against the Company?"

He smirks. "Didn't he tell you?" Johann leads me to the rail, overlooking the sea. From far away, a figure appears in front of us. "Our dear Monsieur Villanueva worked for the Company. He was employed in it for quite some time, actually. I'm not surprised he didn't tell you. He's rather good at lying."

My mouth falls agape, my eyes widening in disbelief as the weight of what has been told settles upon me. No. *He's lying.* Héctor would never work for such a place. No. A surge of emotions ripple, sending tremors that threaten to shatter the façade of my composure. The gentle breeze turns to a rough wind, causing *The Glory* to pick up its speed.

"No. You're lying," I stammer. "He would never work there. Why should I believe you?"

"Why should you?" Johann asks, tsking after. "Let's learn a story about our dear Héctor, shall we? That filth worked under my command. I knew and worked with his father, a respectable Spaniard man. Before being murdered by his own son, he wanted to ensure Héctor had a respectable job and rank, but because of the system we have in place, it wasn't attainable for our dear, loving pirate."

Héctor killed his own father?

I have killed dozens of men with my bare hands.

I could kill you in the blink of an eye if I wished to do so.

I can truly be the monster you speak of.

No. Héctor's murders couldn't have come from working with The East India Company.

My chest tightens as Johann's words mull in my mind. The caste system. Racism. Hate. Héctor is of mixed heritage, but he's not white in skin, making his rank in society lower than it should be. Is this why he worked with the Company? For a *rank*?

Johann sighs, frustrated. "I gave his father his wish and took Héctor under my wing at seventeen. My apprentice, my second in command. He commandeered the smaller ships for the East India Company. It all went remarkably well. Or so we believed. Until he was caught conspiring in piracy, against the company. Against *me*. He harmed our commerce more than I care to admit by helping to plan those hits that ruined our ships, setting us behind by more than a year. All of our cargo and trading materials sunk deep into the sea. As his overseer, I was punished for his foolishness while he roams free, evading the law."

My hand instinctively comes up to my chest to anchor myself. I have to find some sense of stability amidst the swirling storm of emotions that engulf me. The world seems to tilt on its axis, leaving me momentarily disoriented. My heart pounds in my chest, the rapid rhythm echoing my inner turmoil.

There must be more to the story that Johann isn't telling me. But his story is too detailed to be blasphemy. Héctor *did* work for the East India Company. He commandeered ships. Worked with Johann. That's why there's so much resentment between the two. That's why Johann tried murdering him. Héctor *backstabbed* him.

But if Héctor had a high-ranking job where he would be less discriminated against, why mess it up? Johann stated that what Héctor did was so bad, commerce was set back by more than a year.

"How'd you find this out?" I ask, my voice barely a whisper.

"Well, my wife, Villanueva's motto has always been *dead men tell no tales*, but he made the mistake of leaving someone alive. One of his old crewmates. Héctor allowed him to live. His biggest and worst mistake," Johann states, pushing an out-of-place curl behind my ear. "For a minute, the pirate forgot who he worked for. He forgot I see and know everything. So, we caught him. I found him myself conspiring with the enemy."

The wind turns to a gale, tears well up in my eyes. The sky darkens. Héctor lied to me too. *They all did.* Claiming that I stand for everything Johann stands for, when in reality it was *him*. He killed, he stole, he worked for the enemy. Disbelief merges with anger, hurt, betrayal. The ground beneath me seems unsteady, and the very foundation of my reality shattered. I want nothing more than to get rid of his ring.

The sky closes in on me, threatening to crush me. This revelation stirs doubts, the little trust I had placed in Héctor diminishing by the second. I take quick breaths, wiping the tears from my eyes. I refuse to let Johann see me cry.

Johann smiles, his hair cascading over his forehead.

"Hurts, doesn't it?" Johann says. "Appearances are never what they seem, my dear."

"I..." I drift off, placing my head in my hands. My body shivers, thunder cracks above us. "Y-you're lying to me."

"What reasons do I have to lie to you? Since the day we met, I've been nothing but straightforward." Johann caresses my shoulder, his lips hover near my ear. "And you know what's the worst of it all? I can tell you *care* about the filth."

I brush him off, wiping my eyes. "No. I don't care for him."

"If you didn't, you wouldn't be *this* appalled at his actions." He chuckles humorlessly. "Him, you, me. We're the same. We're all *monsters.*"

I move away, my hands trembling. "No. You're wrong. I'm not a monster. *You're* the monster."

Johann grabs my hand, kissing it. I recoil under his touch. "Here's the thing about monsters, my dear siren of destruction. They aren't born, they're made." I avert my eyes, but he grabs my chin, forcing me to look into his eyes. "You can lie to yourself as much as you'd like, but I see it in your eyes. The fury, the resentment, the hatred. It was all there before I carved anything. You're just like me."

A bell rings above us before I can say anything else. Johann releases me, and I let a couple of tears fall. My breath shudders. The air crackles with energy as an amalgamation of shouts, commands, and footsteps intertwine, creating a symphony of chaos.

Out of the corner of my eye, a surge of bodies move through the wooden, polished deck, each man absorbed in their own urgency. The clatter of hastened footsteps reverberates against the wooden floorboards, and voices blend, forming a harsh cacophony of accents and yells.

"Admiral, a pirate ship approaches!" an officer exclaims behind us. Could it be *The Fury*?

"Scarlet colors?" Johann asks, taking out his eyeglass. A small ship half the size of *The Glory* is on its way to us, the wind against their favor.

"Nay, emerald."

"*The Serpent.*" Johann grips my arm. "This is your chance to earn those letters."

"This wasn't part of the agreement."

"It is now. Help us defeat *The Serpent*, and those letters are yours." He releases me, putting his eyeglass away, and takes out my necklace from his inner coat pocket. I want to cry. It's glowing, calling out to me. "Every pirate knows this jewel is the one that grants you the power to create catastrophe. With it, you'll win us *The Serpent.*"

Johann puts my necklace around me, his rough fingers brushing against my skin. My mind goes back to the time Héctor did the same before we encountered Octavia. My breath catches, one last tear trailing down my cheek. Johann's hands leave the nape of my neck, going down to my arms. The weight of the necklace feels foreign to my collarbone.

"Control the tides if you want your crew to be pardoned," Johann threatens. "You only get this one opportunity to prove you are truly devoted to me."

"I– I can't. I don't..." I stammer, my chest tightening.

He walks down the stairs, taking out his sword. "Get me to victory. Let your inner power be unleashed, or suffer the consequences that will come if you cannot do so."

Johann disappears into the commotion.

I have to use my powers.

So far, they've been activated without me even trying. They're connected to my emotions. Anxiety coils around me like a constricting serpent, squeezing my chest with its icy grip. What's going to happen if I can't control it? What's going to happen if I *fail?* What would happen if I do gain control of my powers but use them against Johann in front of his crew? Doubt clouds my thoughts, as well as the sky above us.

"To your stations, men!" Johann orders. He glares at me from downstairs, threatening me to step out of line.

Closing my eyes, I attempt to focus my thoughts while the men anticipate their nearing attack, reaching deep within to tap into these catastrophic abilities I have. A surge of anticipation bubbles in me, mingling with a tingling sensation that spreads through my limbs. Whispers surround me in the language I've heard before from Mami Julia and Héctor. Arawak. They're beautiful, sending shivers down my spine. Fear grips my heart as the wind turns to a ravenous tempest, pushing the ship forward roughly.

I open my eyes, gasps coming in short and shallow. Pacing back and forth, I rub my temples. If I don't do this, Johann will punish me. If I do this, innocent people die.

One evil shall fall, another will rise.

I can't do this. I can't let innocent people die.

Johann is the one who should die. Not them.

They've done crimes, but they haven't tortured.

I refuse to be like Johann.

"I'm not a monster," I whisper, clutching my necklace.

The first cannon of *The Glory* goes off, taking me off my balance.

Johann

CHAPTER
TWENTY-NINE

*T*he *Serpent* receives a hit on the port side of its vessel, the waves churning underneath. The sky has turned a light gray; the wind pushes us forward. Smoke arises from their ship, and frantic men shout orders to strike back. Even if I try to help them, part of me knows that their small ship is no match for *The Glory*, whose members are driven by greed. Their emerald pirate flag waves viciously with the wind, ripping from the mast.

The Glory closes in on its target, shouts of anticipation carried by the salty breeze. The flapping of tattered sails and creaking timber fill my ears as the crew prepares themselves for the impending attack, a mix of exhilaration and trepidation in the air.

Get me to victory, my dear siren.

I already am without meaning to. The wind refuses to be in the pirates' favor.

Another cannon fires, knocking me off my feet. I grab onto the barrel next to me to avoid hitting the ground. Shouts of urgency arise from The Serpent, as well as smoke and flames.

If I could control the wind or water, maybe I could lead them away.

With the speed augmentation, the ships stand side by side on the swaying waves. The pirate captain bellows orders with a hoarse cry, and the ships' gunmen fire at us. They've no cannons to defend themselves with. Thunderous booms echo across the water as *The Glory*'s cannonballs tear through the air, finding their target with devastating precision.

They lost before it all began.

I bring my hands in front of me, taking deep breaths. I don't know if this will work, but I have to try to save them. This isn't a fair fight.

The ocean churns underneath us, and I'm struggling to gain control of the water. I can't rein the tempest I've been told I can unleash. I can barely create a mere sprinkle now that I need it.

I take deep breaths as the men of *The Glory* shout and swing over to the other ship. The clash iron echoes, as do yells and groans of pain. Johann ties himself with a rope, and I focus on him.

My screams replay in my mind. The agonizing pain.

As he swings, I do a motion with my hand and the ships sway, with The Serpent moving farther away from us. I jump in elation. It worked. But my excitement is cut short with Johann's death glare when he lands on *The Serpent.*

Three cannons go off in a row, causing me to fall on my knees. Wooden planks from The Serpent splinter, the metal groans, and their defenses slowly crumble to the relentless assault *The Glory* brings. Pirates jump overboard, others killed by their murderous opponents.

Ocean, please. Do something. Help them survive.

Nothing happens.

I can't regain the minimal control I had.

Blades glint in the dim light as they clash with defenders. Shouts, curses and the metallic ring of swords carry with the wind. The air is thick with the acrid scent of gunpowder, smoke, ash, and blood.

This is a lost war.

"Lluvia," I whisper. I need rain. Nothing comes. I take off my glowing necklace, glaring at it. "Coño, you're supposed to help me!"

The infernal rains have come whenever I'm nervous, confused, or in pain. Now that I need them, they refuse to come.

I sprint down the stairs, mixing with the bodies of the crew members. Frustration simmers within me, radiating an aura of tension that takes over my entire body. My fingers tighten around my necklace, and I remind myself to not throw it into the ocean.

Men aim their rifles and pistols at the pirates across us, killing them off.

My chest compresses as they shoot a man in the eye, blood escaping his nostrils and eye socket. A sharp rain falls over us. *Finally.*

"Find the ones below, take them aboard *The Glory!*" Johann commands. His cult followers run downstairs, and the others swing back to *The Glory* before it's too late.

Slowly but surely, the officers return. I simply tune them out, watching the devastation unfold.

Lurid tongues of fire leap from *The Serpent*'s breaking splitting remains, devouring the wood and canvasses that had once comprised its proud and menacing structure. The scent of burning wood and scorched metal fills the air, both a pungent reminder of destruction that took place. Sparks dance and scatter in the sky, carried away by the searing winds that fan the flames higher.

The once colorful sails of *The Serpent* are reduced to ashen tatters, floating in the fiery maelstrom. The mast, once a steady centerpiece, now stands twisted, unable to withstand *The Glory*'s assault. Red embers shower down upon the ship's deck, igniting small fires that mirror the main one, consuming the vessel whole. Most of the pirates are dead, marooned in the burning waters below, or taken prisoner. Screams from the ones who leaped into the sea erupt and they cling to fragments of their home's wreckage, their only lifeline in the sea of ruin.

My heart breaks for them, and I know for a fact their histories have been altered. If it weren't for me, *The Glory* wouldn't have taken this route and would have never encountered *The Serpent*. I've ruined their histories, cutting their bloodlines short.

Maybe I truly am the Aycayia of Ruin.

All I do is mess things up.

Johann swings over, throwing his sword onto the ship and marching straight to me. His face turns crimson with a rage that consumes his entire being. His previously composed and greedy demeanor shatters like fragile glass. Veins pulsate on his forehead, his fists transformed into tightly wound balls of fury. My body trembles as waves of fear wash over me, pulling out to a tempest. I keep my necklace hidden in my left hand. Perhaps he's forgotten about it by now.

"What the hell was that?" he asks, shaking me roughly. "You are my wife! I am God! You do not disobey God!"

"It was an accident!" I shudder. "I swear it was!"

"Admiral! What do we do with the prisoners?" one officer asks.

Johann glances from me to the quartet of men brought aboard. "Prove it was an accident," Johann growls.

"What?"

"You'll prove it was an error. Right now."

Johann pushes me away, commanding the quartet to be bound and brought to their knees. They have various injuries, the worst being a second-degree burn from the fire. My eye catches on the youngest of the four. A young boy, no older than James, with eyes the color of mahogany and soiled beige skin. He's tearing up, the blood from a long cut in his cheek dripping onto his brown coat.

They tied the prisoners' hands behind their backs, their hats taken away, revealing scruffy hair of various colors. Each pirate has an officer of *The Glory* standing behind them, knives drawn. *The Serpent* sinks into the sea with groans, the rain of wood chips and ash settling over us.

Johann takes out a pistol, loading it. His wet blond hair cascades over his creased forehead, his shoulders tense as he does. He guides me forward to the young pirate who caught my eye. Johann stands behind me, stopping us a mere inches from the boy. He kisses my cheek as he hands me the pistol, tightening his fingers around mine. He presses the barrel against the boy's forehead, pushing his light brown hair to the side. My eyes meet the young pirate's, and he begs me not to pull the trigger.

"If you're truly on my side now, pull it, my dear," Johann purrs in my ear.

I take deep breaths, my brown eyes never leaving the child's. I can't kill him. The wind picks up around us; the sails flap against each other.

"Please don't make me do this," I beg, tears forming in my eyes.

Johann cocks the pistol in my hand, and the boy trembles. Johann's crew watches intently. The officers hold the bound pirates down, preventing them from intervening.

"If you're truly the siren of ruin, if you're truly on my side, you'll do as I say," Johann says. "Killing this insignificant sea rat should be no problem."

The boy cries, his lip quivering. I grip the gun, tears streaming down my cheeks. I can't kill him. It'd be like killing James, and I can't kill James.

"The one I'd have no problem killing, Admiral, is you," I grit through my teeth, elbowing Johann in the face. He nearly drops the pistol and I step away, but two crew members grab me. I thrash in their grips, but it's futile.

"That was a mistake," Johann seethes, fixing the pistol in his hand. "Let it be known that every member of *The Serpent* was exterminated by the H.M.S. *Glory*."

His crew cheers as Johann aims the gun at the oldest pirate. I close my eyes just as he shoots the old man in cold blood. One by one, they're shot. The pit of my stomach churns, twisting and turning like a tempestuous sea. My legs feel weak underneath me as they bring the pirates to their horrible ends.

"Force her head in this direction, I want her to see this," Johann commands. My eyes remain closed as they forced my head forward. "Open your eyes, wench." I don't. "I said, open them!"

I reluctantly do as I'm told, seeing Johann put away his pistol and take out his sword instead. Thunder rumbles above us.

"No. No!" I scream, being held in place.

"Now, his death will be much more agonizing, thanks to you."

Johann stabs the young pirate through the stomach, removing the blade. The boy falls to his side, groaning and whimpering. I'm released and rush to the boy's side, kneeling in front of him. He's sobbing, curled into a ball. His breaths have turned to gasps. In this position, he looks no older than my Soledad.

"You're okay. Breathe. Think of the ocean. Of the vast seas you'll get to explore now," I reassure him. Tears fall down my eyes, as rain gently hits us from above. "Just breathe, okay? Can you do that for me?"

He sobs, hugging himself. Seeing him in this pain, I do what my grandmother did to comfort me when younger. I hum the song she used to sing to me when I was little. No words, just a beautiful, mesmerizing melody that could leave even the toughest person entranced. I caress his brown waves as his shaking diminishes, his breaths becoming slower by the second. I continue with the song, not caring about the crew. They're invisible to me. The boy visibly relaxes with my voice, shutting his eyes. His chest is barely moving now, his blood covering the deck. I lean over him, my lips over his ear.

"It'll be safe where you're going, baby," I whisper. "You'll no longer hurt. No longer be hunted. Just a life full of endless adventures and happiness." He lets out one shivering breath, his body slumping completely.

I give his forehead a kiss, controlling the urge to scream, sob, and kill everyone aboard this ship. I'm yanked to my feet, giving me no time to mourn the young boy who passed away in my bloodied hands.

CHAPTER THIRTY

My teary eyes refuse to leave the pirate boy's lifeless body. "Clarke, Green, hold her tight," Johann commands as I'm dragged backward.

Johann paces back and forth, shouting commands in French. Two pairs of hands hold me as I mourn the boy I never knew, his pain and hurt still in my body as if it was my own. Behind me, two men talk about what an inconvenience this was. No mentions of the lives lost or the pirate ship that got blown up. No mentions of the boy that bled out on their ship.

"That was a nice thing ye did for him," the man holding me whispers in my right ear. His voice sounds vaguely familiar to me. A muddled English accent. I turn to face him, immediately taken aback by his appearance.

He resembles a much younger Pedro, even with his powdered wig atop his head. But my blurry vision could be playing tricks on me. His eyebrows are black, giving away that he's naturally dark-haired. His soiled skin is beige and freckled yet sunkissed by the long hours under the harsh sun, just like Pedro's. His hollow eyes are the color of the ocean. His face is thin from the lack of proper nutrition, with a cleft chin, clenched jaw, and strong stature.

Based on his looks, he must be no older than eighteen.

I swallow hard. I'm seeing things. "I couldn't just let him die alone," I say as others hasten to do whatever Johann has commanded them to do.

"Maybe ye ain't as evil as they say," he says. "But then again, ye caused the heavens to break apart that one night."

"I don't know about that, mister…"

"Clarke. Luke Clarke, actually." *Clarke.* He's the one that spoke up after I was tortured. The one that told Johann to leave me alone. "Still, one evil will reign us all. Will it be him… or will it be ye?"

I open my mouth to answer, but calloused fingers grab my cheeks. I grip my necklace that hides in my left hand.

Johann.

"I've about had it with you!" Johann yells, spit getting on my face. "How hard can it be to obey me? I don't care if you're the siren of ruin, I've more rank than you. All you've done is refuse to aid me, and I'm exhausted."

Johann punches my stomach, all the wind being released from me. I groan, but go back to keeping a serious expression. While the dull ache consumes me, Johann rips the necklace from my fingers, pocketing it. The men release me, and I fall to my knees, taking deep breaths.

"Stand up," Johann commands. When I don't, he yanks me upward, dragging me across the slippery deck. "Move."

We descend the staircase that leads to the lower decks. We pass empty hammocks and weapons thrown around the ground. Johann pulls me past the hold, and part of me feels relieved. The other part grows anxious.

We reach a secluded area hidden deep within *The Glory*. The smell of defecation and blood overtake my senses. This is a hundred times worse than the smell in the cell I was in. It feels much more concentrated, with no way out.

Johann takes out some keys, kneels, and unlocks a trapdoor.

My guesses where he was leading me could not have been more wrong.

My heart races. *No.*

He wouldn't dare.

"Surprise," Johann announces with a flourish. "This is the punishment for whores who refuse to listen."

It's a crawl space. Dark and eerie. It looks like it's three feet in width by four feet in length. Maybe five feet deep? I have a feeling that it's less. No. No.

I can't go back into an enclosed space. Please.

My face must show horror because he laughs at me, standing up. He grabs my arms, pulling me toward the door. I hold my weight in place, my feet roughly dragging across the wooden floor as I fail.

My heartbeat drums in my ears and my neck.

I've never felt more nauseous in my entire life than I do right now.

Between the pain, the smell, and my rising anxiety, I feel like I could throw up.

Death is better than this.

"Please, don't make me go in there," I shriek.

"You don't want to aid me in my quest? You don't want to join me? Fine. Until then, you stay in here," he says nonchalantly. "Consider this a late wedding gift."

"No! Don't do this, Johann, please. Don't make me stay there. Please!"

"Rest easy, my dear."

Johann pushes me inside the crawl space, and I fall on my knees, scraping them underneath my brown-stained pants. I grab the sides of the space to haul myself up, but I'm greeted by his pistol. Aimed right at me.

No remorse can be detected in his demeanor.

"Make a move to get out and I shall empty this entire pistol on you," he threatens.

"Do it. I'd actually prefer it." Tears form in my eyes. My body convulses with each sob I stifle, my shoulders and chest heaving as they release all the anguish, pain, and trauma inside my body. Once the tears begin, I can't stop them. They're a torrential out-pour of emotions that unfortunately let Johann know he won.

He laughs. "I won't give you the satisfaction of death." He gestures for me to lower myself back down into the space. He catches sight of the slur carved on my arm and smirks. "And don't worry about your scars, my dear. I told Héctor your time aboard my ship would be memorable for the night I took you."

His grin is the last thing I see as he shuts the trap door above me, locking it and enclosing me in a suffocating darkness.

I hyperventilate, the walls closing in on me, the nightmares of my youth haunting my mind, my soul. It's as if I was six years old again, locked inside a wooden chest for hours by Abel when we were left unsupervised. My heart races as if trying to escape both my chest and the enclosure. A surge of panic courses through my veins. The air inside feels thick, suffocating me.

The walls are inching closer in this darkened space, and my deep breaths become shallow, refusing to provide the relief I so desperately seek. Sweat beads from my forehead, and my palms grow damp as I push the wooden walls around me. My trembling hands bang on the smooth surface, hoping to find a secret door. But I can't. I'm trapped in here.

Blood pounds inside my ears, my heart violently thudding in my chest, threatening to escape my body. I bring my shaky hands to my temples, closing my eyes as my feet tingle.

I need to get out.

Negative thoughts flood my mind, reminding me there is no way out. I strain my eyes, trying to make out any glimmer of light, any hint of freedom. But all I see is the impenetrable darkness that has made me prisoner. My whole body is overcome by chills, my stomach contracts, and I taste bile in the back of my throat.

I slump back down on the rough unsanded wood, defeated. Completely blinded and surrounded by my very old childhood friend.

Darkness.

This infernal shadow. An empty void.

Not once in my adulthood did I think I'd be back in the place of torment.

How much more physical torture will this man put me through just to get me to obey?

With shaking hands, I take out Héctor's ring, twisting it around my index finger as I hug myself. I shiver, even though it's hot and humid. I cry, memories rushing through my mind like a broken record. Héctor, Soledad, James, Mami Julia, Octavia. The crew of *The Fury.*

I want to tell them to stay away. I no longer want to be saved. I don't want them to risk experiencing this. Their legacies and histories must continue. I need them to leave me be. I just want to die. I want death.

Unlike when I was in the cell with a decomposing corpse, I don't have the strength to bang on the trapdoor above me. Much less scream to capture someone's attention so I can be let out.

For the first time, I accept my fate.

CHAPTER
THIRTY-ONE

T *hrough pain and gloom,*
   Blood and gold intertwined.
Conquer the seas, the souls, even time.

During the oppressive darkness, a glimmer of hope appears as the trap door creaks open, allowing a slender beam of light to pierce through the imprisoning gloom. The soft glow spills into the area, illuminating the shadows and dispelling the heaviness that had settled. The smell of liquor wafts up to my nose. With dried tears, a numb heart, and stinging eyes, I look up.

I have no idea how long it's been. Nor do I care. Blood and cold sweat covers my body. My nose is runny from crying non-stop.

Three silhouettes stand above, lit by some oil lamps behind them. One of the men's faces, a younger man my age, scrunches up in disgust, his features contorting. His body instinctively recoils at my sight, his blue eyes darting away from me. The other, a shorter man the age of my father probably, chuckles down at me, as if me being tortured brought him sheer happiness. His eyes crinkle at the corner as a wide grin spreads across his lips. A third person stands off to the side.

Johann.

He laughs, his hands behind his back.

"Good morrow," Johann chirps, his blonde hair loose, a few strands cascading over his forehead. "Tell me, my love, did you enjoy your time?"

"Fuck you, Johann," I spit out. I don't know how I have it in me to cuss him out, but I do. "Get me out of here. Now."

"What a shame. It seems that spending some time in the breaker did nothing to you." Johann brings his hands forward, and in them is a gray fur blob. I blink rapidly, my eyes adjusting a bit and it's actually a mouse. No. "Let us speed this process up, shall we?"

It's not a mouse.

It's a *rat*.

Its once sleek, gray fur is now matted and disheveled, a testament to its journeys through *The Glory*.

Johann stretches his arms above me, the rat gripped tightly in his fingers.

"This should get me answers," he says. "And correct your behavior."

My pulse quickens, my bottom lip quivers. My senses heighten and I become hyper aware of every detail. From the ship that sways with force, to the screeching rat, to my nails digging into the rotting walls. Sounds become sharper, echoes form in my ears. My eyes dart from Johann to the rat to the men, trying to stay one step ahead of the impending peril.

"You said that when I die, buildings will fall over me, and you'd cause the Earth to split apart. Will that be my manner of death, regardless?" Johann asks, the rat squirming in his soiled hands. "Answer me!"

"I don't know!" I weep. "I don't know! It's written in history that you died in the earthquake. I don't know what would happen if you die another day!"

"Why haven't you been able to control your power?"

"I don't know!" He raises his eyebrow, neither lowering the rat nor removing it from above me. "I don't know! Please!"

"The prophecy The Seer told you about. It states one evil shall fall and another will rise. I know because I heard it." I cry, my chest aching. "If you're the evil that shall rise, why haven't you joined me?" He lowers the rat, not releasing it.

"Because I refuse to be forced into it!"

He smirks, shaking his head. "Wrong answer, my dear."

His fingers release the rat.

Time slows as the rat falls into the enclosure. My body breaks out in cold sweat, my skin clammy with horror. The ship rocks from side to side, causing the three men to lose their balance. Nausea churns in the pit of my stomach, a deep-seated dread refusing to leave me as the rat scurries around. My body breaks out in goosebumps at the thought of having to share a space with such an animal. I gag involuntarily, my throat tightening to keep down the bile that rises.

Don't let it bite you, Luz. They carry diseases...

With adrenaline coursing through my veins, I fix my eyes on the edge. I have to get out. I'm pushed back down, crying hysterically. Laughter rings out above me as they throw a few apples into the crawlspace. Then the darkness consumes me once more, the lock above me clasping together.

No.

No.

I scream.

My heart pounds inside my chest, a relentless drumbeat signaling the urgency of this moment. The rat squeaks as it tries to find a way out, running all over our shared enclosure, touching my feet with its furry mouth and damp fur. Time seems to both slow down and accelerate, creating a disorienting sense of urgency.

I bang on the door with my fists, choking on my sobs. My healing arms hurt from the hits, but I keep going.

"Johann, please get me out!" I sob. "Please. I promise I'll obey, please! Let me out!"

I can hear muffled laughter enjoying my misery amidst my pounding on the door.

Because this space isn't deep enough for me to stand, I crawl towards a corner to try to avoid the rat, but it comes after me as if it could smell my fear. It must be smelling my body odor, sweat, and blood.

"I swear I'll do what you ask. Please. Just let me out!"

A loud stomp on the door startles me, dust settling over me like a sheet. The rat's rough fur caresses my feet and hands, its rough texture making me shriek as I try everything in my power to get it away. Its paws scratch my exposed calf. I kick it away, and it makes a strange noise. I probably angered it.

The taste of metal reaches my mouth and I throw up, acid cutting my throat. My whole body shivers, my chest tightens and I retreat to a corner, sobbing loudly. I bring my knees up to my chest. My disposition deteriorates by the second as the rat scurries through our space. It even climbs on my legs, and I push it away repeatedly with my bare hands, the feeling of its damp fur encrusting itself into my brain.

The walls are closing in on me faster, squeezing the life out of me. Every fiber of my being screams for release. For the open space that lies beyond these oppressive walls that mock me.

The laughter eventually dies above me, and the rat goes to work on my waste, which makes me want to open my mouth and release more. My stomach churns and all the hunger disappears.

"Let me out..."

The first thirteen years of my life lived in Puerto Rico, where I grew up on Papi Gustavo's finca. Mice and pests were recurrent houseguests there. For that reason, I've always disliked them.

I've never wanted to die more than I do right now. But, I remember how sometimes Abel would stomp on them, killing them instantly.

Now that it's distracted, I drag myself near the rat and kick it repeatedly, pressing it against the wall. It's screeching and squealing, but eventually its insides splatter over my feet.

My body tenses, and I struggle to breathe. I recoil back as I kick the remains away from me, creating a fair distance from the corpse. My feet feel wet, blood seeping into my skin. Emotions swirl together, creating a turbulent storm within me, leaving me helpless and trapped in my turmoil.

I just killed something.

My body grows increasingly fatigued, muscles aching and my limbs heavy with the weight of trauma. My eyelids droop heavily. *No.* I have to stay alert. But my body yearns for rest, longing for the solace of sleep to ease my panic. I can't surrender to the sweet embrace of slumber.

I twist the ring around my finger, wondering what might arise from the shadows. What worse things will happen if I succumb? Fear outweighs any physical need for rest. The silence is oppressive, punctuated by the sound of my heart racing.

My thoughts become fragmented, the lines between what's real and not blurring together. The prophecy jumps around in my mind, as if Octavia herself was telling it for the first time. Still, I resist her beautiful lullaby, afraid of confronting what comes next.

The conqueror will rise...

The internal battle between weariness and fear rages on, and each passing second only deepens my exhaustion, yet I persist, clinging to wakefulness with a desperate determination.

In the deep stillness within the dark, a haunting melody permeates the air, a call that sends shivers down my spine. The ethereal notes drift through the darkness. It's a tune that feels out of place, that transcends time and space itself, tugging at the deepest recesses of my soul. Calling for me, enticing me.

The harmony rises and falls, undulating like the beautiful tide. Its mournful wails and enchanting trills make me forget all the horrors. It carries a subtle enchantment that reminds me of the whispers that brought me to the seventeenth century.

The song wraps itself around my senses, sinking into my consciousness like beautiful tendrils of mist. It talks of promises that invite my eyelids to drop deeper, exhaustion taking over me like never before.

Sleep...

I let my eyes close and take a shuddering breath. The call hangs in the air like a phantom's lament.

My resolve continues to be tested as I grapple with the conflicting desires to find comfort in sleep, evading the terrors that surround me. And with the mesmerizing whispers that call for me, it's a war that I eventually lose.

I lose all consciousness as one final thought crosses my mind.

If I'm going to die, I'm going to die on my own terms.

CHAPTER
THIRTY-TWO

"One for sorrow, two for mirth, three for a wedding, four for a birth," I sing weakly as I twist the ring over and over again on my finger. *"Five for silver, six for gold, seven for a secret never to be told."* I laugh, bringing my knees closer to my chest. *"Secrets. Gold. Blood. Souls. Death as black as night. 11271689."* My fingers tremble. *"Change the tides. Tides. Time. Change them!"*

My body feels dry, inside and out. My throat has become a barren wasteland, tightening and screaming for water. I don't remember what it is to not feel dizzy. My pulse has been racing all the time, causing me to shift in positions but nothing is comfortable.

I need water. Food. Sleep.

Therapy. Six for gold.

12041689.

My face feels thinner, my fingers gaunt. I've urinated less and less, the smell becoming stronger each time because of the lack of hydration.

How long has it been? I laugh.

Seconds. Minutes. Days. Seven secrets never to be told.

Conquer the seas, the souls, even time.

I continue twisting the ring, humming my grandmother's lullaby to myself.

The one I sang to the boy Johann murdered in front of me. The young one who reminded me of James and Soledad.

When thy oceans bleed, darkened skies cracked...

Johann has replaced my memories of OliverJohann has replaced my memories of Oliver. Green eyes have now turned blue. Dark humor has now turned deadly. Loving, tender care turned into physical threats and assaults. I no longer know how to differentiate between the two.

Oliver. Johann.

They're equal.

One evil shall fall, another will rise.

Footsteps come and go above, causing dust to settle over like a thick curtain. One minute it's loud, the next, conversations are being carried away like the waves that sway the ship. The crew of the H.M.S. *Glory* has continued with their lives, as if they didn't have a person locked in an area that's no bigger than a coffee table.

A never-ending reign of ruin until one dies.

The history books have not adequately described the cruelty this crew imposed on the Caribbean. Rats, forced marriages, physical assault, sexual assault, psychological torture, murder, enslavement. And that's just the *surface* of their crimes.

11271689. 11271689. 12041689. 12041689.

I sing the prophecy and dates, which I've memorized quickly from years and years of practice. A random thought enters my mind as I do: what could be Héctor's crimes? They surely have to be minimal compared to these men. But because he's indigenous, he's the Caribbean's most wanted fugitive.

Oh, Héctor. How I miss your death glares and playful threats.

My laugh turns to a stifled sob. Three for a wedding.

Crows peck my eyes.

Sirens drown me.

My mind, once a sanctuary of clarity and coherence, becomes a labyrinth of fragmented thoughts. Tears stream uncontrollably down my face, my cries coming in raw, guttural bursts. My body convulses with each sob. My brain wanders into uncharted territories, bringing up unpleasant memories of my youth. Papi Gustavo's death. Abel's mistreatment. Weight loss camp. My thoughts trail into recent events. The flash of a smile. A pair of golden eyes. The sound of a fiddle.

The soul with a pearl bathed in blood shall rise.

I hum through my sobs, twisting the ring with such force, I fear I may break it in half, like Johann broke me.

Suddenly, the air feels lighter, and it's easier to breathe. Even with the faint smell of tobacco. I blink, covering my face with my hands, my eyes straining to adjust to the gleam.

The trap door opens, the light flooding my crawl space with a brilliance that erases any lingering trace of darkness. It reveals details previously hidden by the shadows, such as the bloodied wood and the smashed rat I killed in my fit of panic. It lays in a pool of blood, reminding me I am its killer.

"Are you listening to me?" a voice asks, exasperated. Johann stands above me with a cigar in his mouth. "Answer me, wench."

"Death as black as night," I mutter, wiping my eyes. "Six for gold. 11271689."

"Ugh. I need a siren, not a songbird." He reaches in, grabbing my arm. I flinch. "Get up."

"One for sorrow, two for mirth..."

I uncurl my body from my crouched position, standing as I hum the prophecy. My muscles, now accustomed to the compression, release their iron grip on my cracking joints, a rush of relief coursing through my body. I straight my legs, my back, stretching. The weight of my upper body shifts, relieving the strain on my knees and lower back. I stumble, my footing unstable on the swaying ship.

Johann hauls me up with ease. I flex my toes on the wooden floorboards.

"Water..."

"Here," Johann states, handing me a waterskin. My trembling fingers open it with difficulty. "I don't want you dead. Not yet."

I take a slow gulp of the water, since I've heard that you can't take rabid swallows after a long time of no hydration. Johann watches me, taking a puff of his cigar. I drink some more water, my strength slowly resurfacing. A dull ache refuses to leave my injuries, and the need to itch my scars nags at me.

"Let's go," Johann orders, taking back the waterskin, placing its strap around his torso with ease. "We haven't got all day."

I force my weakened legs to move. Placing one foot in front of the other. The barrel of a pistol is suddenly placed against my back, urging me to hasten my pace. I expected no less from the man who has brought me torment. Johann guides me upstairs, the pistol digging into my skin.

The first light of dawn breaks over the horizon as I climb the stairs, bathing the Caribbean sea in a watery yet golden glow. The warm sea breeze carries the faint scent of brine, mingled with the rich aroma of fresh wax, damp sails, and morning dew. A few *Glory* members stir from their swaying slumber. Upstairs, the rhythmic lapping of waves against the ship's hull fill my ears as seagulls soar overhead, their cries harmonizing with the low chatter of the crew.

"Move, woman," Johann barks.

I roll my eyes, swaying to the rhythm of the waves. "An evil shall fall..."

Johann pulls me toward the officers' quarters and I shiver, hugging myself tightly. I am now a product of the oppression and mistreatment my ancestors went through, and if they could survive these horrors and persevere through them, I can survive this sadistic white man.

The iron hinges of a door being opened bring me back to the moment.

Johann has brought me to his bedroom once more. It's neat, as if he deep-cleaned before coming to get me. The aroma of roasted fish and veggies waft up to my nose, making me salivate. A half-eaten spread of food sits on his desk, with a lit wax candle. Fish, veggies, white bread, water, and even wine. My mouth waters, but nausea also forms because next to the main platter is my necklace. Untouched, pristine, glowing. Ready for me to take it. The urge to steal everything on Johann's desk fills my body with a newfound adrenaline.

Johann shuts the door, and without permission, I speed to the table, grabbing bread and fish. As I gobble down the flavorless food, the urge to eat food from my time comes. Maybe some asopa'o con tostones. Some bacalaítos. Arroz con gandules. Shit, a Caesar salad with fries on the side.

Behind me, the Admiral chuckles. My eyes never leave my necklace, and I calculate the best way to steal it back from him.

Johann paces around the desk, watching me eat. I take a swig of water, gasping after.

"Finished?" Johann asks, an apple in his slender fingers. I freeze at the sight. Apples. It's what he and his officers have given me. Bile in my throat, I stare out of the window. It's about to be a new day. "Will you obey me now? A day in the Soul Crusher can make any man bend. You spent *three* days in it."

I nod, wiping my sweaty hands on my ripped vest, and remember Héctor's ring on my finger. I don't think he's coming for me. I'm on my own. They all had unsavory encounters with Johann, nearly bringing them death. They won't risk coming. They're smarter than that.

Part of me relaxes. They're most likely safe and away from him. But *I'm* still with him. And I have gotten nono closer to murdering this man than I am at getting home.

"I'll obey," I mutter, facing him. He's studying me, holding a stack of beige letters in his hand. I put my hands behind my back, taking off the ring, my eyes never leaving the parchment.

The Letters of Marque.

"Good." He grins. "I want to witness your powers. Sing to me, enchant me. Explain the cursed prophecy to me." Placing down the letters, he sits on his desk, taking one of the folded parchments out from the stack.

It doesn't take a rocket scientist to know who it belongs to.

Héctor.

"If you bring out any tricks, this shall end in the fire. I promised I will grant the filthy crew of *The Fury* and the witch leniency. And I will," he says, fanning himself with the letter. "If, and only if, you keep your part of the bargain."

"I shall try my best, husband." I put my hands into my pockets, throwing the ring there.

"No. You won't try. You will *do*." Johann places Héctor's letter over the burning candle on the table. No, no, *no*. The parchment burns and flies off. There goes Héctor's half pardon.

"Why would you do that!"

"I promised the Letters of Marque to the crew. But they will be valid if you do *something*. Prove to me you are once and for all on my side. If you should fail, these shall be void and I will try the crewI will try the crew for their crimes. I will burn each and every one of these. Which means they shall be hung. Starting with that sea filth."

I break eye contact with Johann.

While I'm rather rancorous at Héctor's involvement with the East India Company, it doesn't mean he should get hung. None of them deserve to die for their past crimes. If they've escaped death this long, they can escape it until the day of their deaths.

Blowing air through my pursed lips, I place my hands on the nape of my neck. How am I going to create rain? Last time I tried, it didn't come on command. I'm very new to this since my grandmother and Octavia failed to tell me how to control my power, my emotions. TThe stronger the emotion, the stronger the weather effect.

I'm going to have to wing it.

Time to bring out my skills as an actress.

"As you know, Admiral, I can control the tide, call on the rains, stop time even. I can make hurricanes by lifting a single finger. I can make you travel to worlds unimaginable with a single thoughht," I lie, knowing damn well I'm incapable of doing any of those things.

"Show me," Johann orders, intrigued.

Héctor's Letter of Marque keeps burning. The crisp paper flakes floating around us, as my thoughts go to his face, his smile. I can't be his cause of death. No matter how horrible the second mate's crimes may be. Johann can't keep getting away with this. With his hate, with his vendetta against pirates and people of color. Someone has to stop him.

Maybe that someone can truly be me...

Thoughts swirl and churn, a whirlwind of frustration casting a subtle ripple inside my mind. My breaths become heavier as the letter burns. I close my eyes, digging my nails into my neck. Water. Rain. Something. My jaw clenches, my brows furrow together as the tidal wave drowns me.

"Ay bendito sea Dios," I mumble, my knees buckling.

"I'm not a patient man."

If anyone out there is listening, please. *Help me.*

Sprinkles of rain fall outside. I open my eyes, whirling my head back to the window. I laugh.

Thank God.

Johann marches over to me, blowing out the flame on the corner of the parchment. I did it. But inside, I'm a nervous wreck. Just how far will this get me?

"Now that wasn't so hard, was it?" he teases, elated.

"It's not as strong as it could be," I admit.

"And it shall remain that way. We don't want you overpowering me, do we?"

Fucking coward. "Of course not, Admiral." I flash my most convincing smile, letting him know I'm going to cooperate. If only for a minute.

He heads to the table, grabbing my necklace. "What does the prophecy speak of? I've seen the original and I couldn't understand the Godforsaken language it was written in."

"Simply because you are of an ignorant mind, it doesn't mean languages different from yours are inferior." I take a deep breath. "But it speaks of an evil that will fall in these seas so that another may rise."

"Who will die? The pirates?"

"Perhaps. No one can really say. I just know the time of prophecy is upon us. A never-ending reign of ruin will begin when we least expect it. One can only assume that once the first evil is eliminated, the other will take its rightful place, reigning over everything. The tide, the seas, time. Even people."

"Do you believe it speaks of me? Do you believe I'm the evil that should fall in order for you to rise?" I shrug, my eyes on my necklace. "I'm not the evil that roams the seas without order. I'm its savior," Johann gestures at himself for emphasis, his mannerisms reminding me of Oliver.

I suck in a breath. *Stay quiet.* But I don't. "You'll never be its savior. You plunder and loot other countries for its riches. You're the executioner. The one who brings pain, misfortune, and poverty. Those people you capture and imprison are a thousand times the person you wish you were, *Little Shadow.*"

Johann's expression darkens. Furious, he grabs one of his golden daggers and aims it at me. While my knees threaten to buckle, my burning gaze never leaves his.

"If you hurt me once more, I will unleash the oceans on you without remorse," I snap. He glares at me, gripping the knife with his fingers. "You call yourself God? You're not God, and you never will be." His trembling hand points the blade at me, his nostrils flaring.

"You cannot speak to me like—" I grab a knife from his table, pressing it against his neck. He stops speaking. Johann fears death. All pirates do.

"I am and I will." The tip of the knife pierces his sandy beige skin. "What are you going to do? Burn me? Hang me?

Do it. See how long you last without me." I throw the blade back on the table, the metal clanking against the plates.

Never again shall he hurt me. Never again shall he or anyone put their hands on me.

Johann clears his throat, hurling his dagger back on the table. "Fine. I see where your loyalties lie."

My whole life, I've taken Abel's mental and physical abuse without retaliating. I've accepted Johann's torture and abuse aboard this godforsaken ship. I've accepted taunts, insults, slurs, and hate.

Well, no more.

No more will I be the people pleaser who's afraid of what others might think. No more will I be stepped on.

This pain Johann brought me has lit a spark that is ready to burn down villages.

I will conquer the seas.

I will make him fall so that I may rise.

My reign of ruin will begin.

No matter what or who stands in my way... I will burn the world down.

CHAPTER
THIRTY-THREE

A church bell chimes in the distance.

Johann chuckles, rubbing his hands together. "Welcome to Port Royal, my dear," he says. "We'll see just how much your loyalty to the pirates will save you."

Port Royal. Where it all began.

Johann shackles my wrists together in front of me, tugging at the chains. The iron is cool against my skin, weighing not only my arms but my whole body downward. Johann searches for something in his closet, and I study the bruises on my arms which range from purple to green.

The word *halfbreed* stares back at me, dark brown scabs formed in each letter, making the word more pronounced.

I shudder, not letting my emotions and memories take the best of me. I can't break down. Not as the laughter echoes in my mind. Not as the feeling of the rat fur runs throughout my body.

I don't need this.

Not here, not now.

Taking advantage of the fact Johann's rummaging through the closet, I swiftly grab my necklace, hiding it inside my fists. Its smooth material feels soft in my fingers, and immediately, it soothes me. I stand back where he left me and look out of the window, inconspicuously.

"Fight me and see what happens, savvy?" Johann warns, buttoning his coat.

He holds a powdered wig between his thighs. After he straightens his outfit, he places the wig on his head with a scowl, then leads me towards the door once more.

Whatever awaits me, at least I'll have a part of Mami Julia with me.

Slowly, I head toward the deck, conserving the last bit of energy in my body. The sunlight hits me at full blast, causing me to wince. Enthusiastic crew members fill the polished wooden deck, all giddy to get their feet on land. Crows soar above us, their eerie song reminding me of the uncertainty to come. My unfocused gaze lands on the landscape ahead, the salted sea breeze stinging my watery eyes.

The shimmering azure ocean is completely lined with merchant vessels, armada ships, and a few discreet pirate galleons. The masts of each ship are adorned with intricate riggings, their flags fluttering in the Jamaican breeze. Sailors, fishermen, and Royal Navy guards go about their business.

"No, no, no! You call that a knot?" Johann yells, releasing me. "Fucking Navy men."

Johann trots over to the men he's scolding at while the gangplank from *The Glory* lowers to the cement dock. The men tidy up their uniforms, eager to leave. The cacophony of boots and cheerful chatter drown out the crow's song.

One for sorrow, two for mirth. A never-ending reign of chaos.

I lower my gaze to my bare legs as I slump against the wooden mast, unable to twist Héctor's ring around my finger. How's he faring without it? He mentioned he twisted it whenever he felt anxious or uncertain. A small spark inside me lights up at the possibility of seeing him and *The Fury* crew again, but they're much smarter than that.

The waistband of my pants hangs on my stomach, no longer being able to be held on my waist. The weight of the shackles around my wrists pulls me down, and I grip the mast with my hands, my nails digging into the wood. I'm nearly to the ground when muscular hands hold me up, steadying me amidst my lightheadedness.

"Thank you," I say. I look up. It's Luke Clarke, the young officer who asked if I was going to reign over the seas. "It seems our paths keep being intertwined, Mister Clarke."

A sheepish smile shows on his cracked lips, his blue eyes twinkling with a hint of mischief. "It seems they are, Miss...?" he asks, offering me a waterskin with his free hand.

I snatch the leather container from his thin hands, taking a huge gulp of the room temperature water. "Luz Narváez García."

The water quenches my never-ending thirst, strengthening my body as it descends. I down the whole thing, twisting it so the few last drops of water aren't wasted.

"Luz. Light," he says. "Luke. Also, light." He lowers his head, rubbing his forehead. "How horrible we must seem to ye." His touch is gentle, unlike everyone else's. "I promise ye, we ain't all savages. Some of us have good intentions."

"If you're so good, why are you here then? What's your story?"

"'Tis long and winded. Destiny intertwined. That's why our paths have aligned, siren of ruin."

Johann appears in front of us and eyes Luke strangelly. Luke lowers his gaze, releases, and disappears into the mass of uniformed men disembarking *The Glory.*

Once everyone has left, Johann drags me by my arm. The sanded wood of the gangplank is rough under my exposed skin. The moment the sole of my foot touches the concrete, heat sears it, making me jump and cling to Johann. He pushes me off, cursing. We're moving on.

As we reach inland, locals and citizens intertwine with those of higher-ranks. Alabaster-skinned women wear white linen bonnets that cover their hair entirely, their frocks ankle-length and muddled in color. The men's outfits range from rugged sailors' attire to the rich garments of wealthy merchants, with a variety of vests, collars, flowing capes, and even golden adornments. I hear enough of their conversations to catch their old English accents.

People gawk and whisper when they see me, my frizzy curls, my bloodstained pirate clothing. But my skin color and non-European features repulse them most.

I focus ahead, biting my chapped lips.

Iron clashes against iron as the blacksmith creates new weapons, and horses gallop past us, dragging carriages behind them. Warehouses with stout walls and large doors surround us as we enter the town square. A market with fresh produce fills up with buyers for the day. The church with a golden bell stands tall, its highest peak a bronze cross. The courthouse holds golden scales in the front, signifying justice. Both have glass-stained windows and well-manicured gardens with loose roosters and chickens. Small chatter fills the air, as does the smell of freshly caught seafood, spices, and baking breads.

In the middle of the square stand the gallows.

But they're not empty.

A light-skinned man hangs from the noose, his limp, lifeless body displayed for the masses. His pirate clothing is dirty and bloody, like mine. His neck is twisted to the side, his brown matted waves cascade over his forehead. My breathing turns shallow as I meet the glossy eyes of the corpse.

"That's to be your fate," Johann mocks.

"What?" I shriek.

Johann smirks, raising his eyebrow. "What? Did you think I was going to let you disrespect me?" He yanks me forward, cackling at his own deceit. "I won't lie when I say I'm going to regret this in the future, but you showed me where your loyalties lie. I'm willing to risk my death if it'll ensure *yours.* If I can't have your power, then no one can."

He leads me toward the pristine courthouse, my legs turning to jelly. Still, I move at a brisk pace. If Johann yells at me in front of all these people, he will surely be cheered on or even joined.

Swinging the door open, the men inside stand at attention when they see him.

The courthouse, like *The Glory,* spent no expense on bragging about their grandeur. Adornments of gold, bronze, and silver stand all around. A British flag and an East India Company flag hang from the wall. A huge burlap canvas with the Company logo rests above the main hall. An upside down Y, with the letters E, I and Co in the spaces available. The odd scar on Héctor's arm and on my collarbone.

What could it possibly mean?

"Move," Johann dictates, dragging me forward with one rough pull.

Three white men stroll toward us, all wearing powdered wigs and fancier Navy outfits. Clean, crisp, ironed. Johann tenses when he sees them, but then relaxes, as if a reflex from all his years of being a pirate. The men glance at me, then at Johann, waiting for an explanation of the chained woman of color the Admiral has marched into the courthouse.

"Admiral Nau, what a pleasant surprise. I believed you to be en route to Anguilla, to aid our ships against the Frenchmen stationed there," the shortest man says. He's older with a clean-shaven face. Johann tenses again. The Nine Years' War. Johann participated in it, but his hunt for me has diverged his path. "To what do I owe the pleasure of this visit?"

"Judge Brown, I've brought the Queen's thief. Found while we took port on Port-de-Paix," Johann lies. *The Queen's thief? Port-de-Paix?* He's avoiding telling them he stepped foot on Tortuga, which would annul his deal with the British Navy. "Unfortunately, the wench threw the stolen jewels into the ocean before we could capture her."

"This is the proclaimed Queen's thief? This... woman? How did she get past the guards and leave Fort Nassau without being caught?" Judge Brown looks unconvinced.

Not once does Johann stutter, though. "Witchcraft. She's done it before my eyes." My mouth hangs open while Johann looks smug. *Witchcraft!*

"What other crimes will they try her for?"

"Thievery, witchcraft, kidnapping, attempt of murder, piracy, and impersonation of a Spanish royal. I believe the sentence for this is a hanging. To be done before noon, I presume?"

"I've done nothing of the sort!" I shout, pulling my arm away from him.

"Silence, witch!" Judge Brown orders, glaring daggers at me. "Admiral Nau, I cannot thank you enough for bringing this to our attention. We will carry out her sentence in four days at the strike of noon. 'Tis unfortunately our earliest. We shan't tolerate witchcraft in the West Indies. That is not of our Lord and Savior."

The two white men next to the Judge approach, and Johann hands me to them. They tower over me, both easily at least six foot two. I turn my head back to Johann and spit on him, cursing him in Spanish after. One maman grips my arms from behind while the other pulls his arm back, punching me in the face without remorse. My eyes water, my nose turns numb, and a loud, high-pitched noise rings in the background. Sharp pain erupts from my nose, making it hard to breathe. The punch has made it hard to focus. My surroundings slowly spin.

Gasping for air, I pull at them, trying to get free. "He kidnapped me from Tortuga! His treaty should be nullified. I implore you—"

"I'll execute you myself if you don't shut that filthy, bastardized mouth of yours!" The Judge hisses. "Gentlemen, take her to the holding cells!"

❧❧❧

I'm pushed roughly inside a cell, my shoulder blade and left ankle receiving most of my impact. An excruciating wave of pain engulfs me, rendering me momentarily paralyzed. The throbbing ache intensifies with every second that passes, and tears come to my eyes. The wall is built with thick stones, a small window above me allowing a sliver of sunlight in. *Click.* The heavy, iron-barred door is locked, trapping me in with only damp hay, a rusty chamber pot, and a disappearing will to live. Minimal ventilation can be felt in the air, with a lingering odor of dampness.

"Looks like we got a beauty in our presence," one prisoner hisses. He's got beige skin and discoloration spots on his face. "Showin' us her ankles and everythin'."

"If these bars weren't in between," another says, licking his lips.

Ignoring the catcalls, I open my hands and drop my necklace down onto my lap. The imprint of the scripture behind the jewel is marked on my right palm. Inaru bo bara. *Woman of Great Death.* I wipe my swollen and tender nose, my fingers coming away bloody. Blood trickles down to my lips, leaving a warm, metallic taste in my mouth.

With little energy, I drag myself toward the wall, leaning my head forward. Some of the blood unfortunately detours to my throat, burning my esophagus like battery acid. The rest stains everything. My exposed calves, the hay beneath me, my pants, my shackles even.

Eventually, the blood subdues and so do the catcalls. My vision has stabilized enough to see my ankle has swollen up to the size of the grenade I threw almost three weeks ago.

With much struggle, I place my necklace around my neck, regaining some self-identity. If I'm to die, I'll die with the thing that connects me to my grandmother. Once I clasp the ends together, a sudden surge of energy overpowers my body, triggering a downpour outside. My breathing turns to rapid gasps, my lips quivering. The pain I feel leaves, replaced by anger, by fury... by the overwhelming urge to destroy everything in my path.

I didn't feel this when Johann attacked *The Serpent.* This... this feels *nice.*

Ripples of energy course through my veins, and the surrounding atmosphere stirs as if the very air molecules around me were responding to my presence. My palms tingle with a cool sensation, and rainwater enters the windows, directing themselves toward the prisoner across from me. It twirls in a mesmerizing dance, obedient to my unreliable will, choking him without remorse. I'm entranced by the water. The others gasp, imploring me to stop. But I don't.

My breaths turn to maniacal laughter, and I crave this power. It's addicting, and I want it all. However, as the rush of unimaginable strength courses through my entire being, my body feels strained. The water beam dissipates, and my breathing becomes labored. Dizziness creeps into my senses. My body wavers, the tension becomes too much.

"No..." I mutter, my hands trembling.

I drag myself to a corner, my consciousness threatening to escape me. I lean my head back against the wall, giving into my sudden desire to slumber. I'm much safer here than I ever was in *The Glory*.

I slump to the side. The surrounding noises dim.

Darkness overcomes my senses.

My power came... and just as quickly... it left.

Now I want nothing more than to feel it once again.

CHAPTER
THIRTY-FOUR

"*W*ake up. It's not your time, siren queen," the gloomy figure sings, his voice deep and playful. Shadows consume him. "Finish my rhyme. Finish it before it's too late. Seven for a secret never to be told. Eight for a kiss. Nine for a wish..." He urges me to continue.

His golden staff shines against the twinkling twilight, threatening to take my very life as he presses its tip against my chest. Right where my heart lies.

"Ten for a bird you must not miss..." I finish, my voice far and detached.

He claps, a bit of my strength returning. I cannot see his faceI cannot see his face underneath a black cloak. A chill creeps up my spine, sending shivers down my back. The atmosphere is heavy with an unsettling stillness as if time itself came to a halt, his shadows reach me. The cells are bathed in a darkness that's impenetrable, choking the others to their deaths.

"Time ticks, queen of ruin," he warns, removing the staff from my chest. "But not yours. It's been two days. Hurry and *fulfill your destiny before I do it for you... and let me tell you... you won't like that."*

As consciousness slowly returns, my mind feels disconnected from reality. How long has it been? Am I still in the cell? Who is that cloaked apparition? What does it want? My thoughts are fragmented, unable to recall what happened in the dream. I blink my eyes repeatedly, trying to focus, but everything appears hazy.

A mild headache appears as I try to adjust to being awake. My body feels sluggish, uncoordinated, tense. As if I had been asleep for days instead of hours. Seconds have blended with each other, unable to let me form a coherent thought.

I sit up, lightheaded. My senses sharpen little by little, and I'm still inside my cell. Outside, rain falls. My ankle has turned a bright red. The blood in my hands and legs has dried. My sinuses are clogged up.

The feeling I'm looking for is nowhere to be found. The sweet ecstasy I felt when I put on my necklace, triggering my power by accident.

It felt invigorating, giving me the strength I need. It amplified the awareness in my surroundings and my need for revenge on Johann Nau for the pain he inflicted on me. Now, it's left me empty inside. I've only had a taste of what I could do, and I'm addicted already. If only I could control them.

Don't...

All at once, the rain outside stops.

"Yer alive!" A young voice exclaims. Luke stands on the other side of the bars with a wooden tray in his hands and clears his throat.

"Why wouldn't I be? Can't let Johann miss the chance to kill me," I say groggily.

Luke sets the items down on a stool, unlocks my cell and heads inside with the tray, locking himself with me. I flinch as he approaches, but he simply sets the tray on the ground and offers me the waterskin that hangs across his body. I rip it from his hands, drinking slow gulps of the room temperature water. While it's difficult to twist the leather container with my shackled hands, I manage to do it so as to not miss a single drop.

"Thank you," I say. Voices stir from a few prisoners, but Luke silences them with a glare. I don't feel parched or weakened. I feel energized. In pain because of my injuries, but *alive.*

"Yer welcome," he says, kneeling down in front of me. "I– I brought supper, if yer interested."

I nod.

On the tray sits a delicate china bowl, its contents a rich and hearty broth, accompanied by a chunk of white bread, a peeled orange, and a bronze cup. My eyes linger on the spread, but my wrists are bound by the unyielding shackles, rendering me unable to indulge in the food before me like a civilized human being.

"Hopefully this gives ye the nourishment ye require," he says, silence encompassing us.

"Well, I'd love to eat it, but I can't feed myself like this," I say, tilting my head and pointing at the shackles with my lips.

He exhales loudly. "I ain't got a problem feeding ye."

"No, I don't need hel–"

He chuckles. "Lass. I want ye to process what ye just told me."

I sigh. "Fine." I'm past feeling embarrassed, if I'm being honest. "How long was I... asleep?"

Luke brings a spoonful of broth up to my mouth, his blue eyes never leaving my face. "A little over two days." *Two days?* I swallow the bland chicken soup. "I kept checking that ye were alive, and alas, ye are."

"Wow... dos días..."

Luke rips a chunk of bread and feeds it to me, not saying anything. He wipes my mouth with his sleeve, his eyes brightening. "Ye know, I heard that before ye fainted, ye drowned a man with yer power." Luke leans forward, his pupils slightly dilated. "Is it true?"

I shrug and stay quiet, the urge to feel the power back in my mind, in my soul. I've never felt a more satisfying thing. Imagine the satisfaction if I could unleash it on Johann. He continues feeding me in silence, the prisoners muttering amongst themselves.

Luke mentioned I was unconscious for two days. Could that have been my power's doing? I finally controlled it and ended up with absolutely zero energy after.

"Is it true ye can control time? How about the seas? Oh, perhaps sing men to death?" he asks, raising the filled spoon to my lips. It seems he *cannot* be in a quiet environment for long.

I shake my head. "No."

"But ye can call storms, right? Yer the siren of ruin, call one."

"I can't, Luke." I point at the bread and he feeds me a chunk. "I don't know how. Which is why I'm getting killed, remember?"

He breaks off a second chunk. "How is ye the siren of the prophecy if ye can't control the *ruin*? What type of siren are you?"

"A bad one, by the looks of it?"

He scoffs, raising his eyebrow. "Can I trade ye for the siren of war, then?"

My eyes widen as he grabs the spoon. "There's a siren of *war*?"

He pulls the utensil away from my mouth. "Unbelievable."

I roll my eyes, adjusting my position on the damp floor. "How are you so annoying? Just feed me and go. I don't know why you're trying to hold a conversation."

"For yer information, I'm not *irritating*, I was simply stating *facts*."

"Oh, you want facts?" I tilt my head, glaring right into his blue eyes. "Okay, then kid—"

"I'm not a kid. I'm a man. I'm seven–I'm one and twenty." He averts his eyes, feeding me another piece of bread.

I chuckle. "Well. Are you *seven* or *twenty-one*? Because you look rather *young* for the latter."

He fidgets with the hem of his coat. "I was blessed with incredible good looks."

"And he's conceited, too."

"I ain't conceited, just aware of my good looks."

I snort, and he chuckles. The numbers keep replaying in my head. *Seven. Seven.*

It hits me.

"You're seventeen, aren't you?" I ask, declining the food. I feel like I could burst.

Luke's breath trembles as he wipes my mouth. "No. I-I'm n-not."

My eyes narrow. "The crew doesn't know you're just a kid... Do they?"

He places the fragile bowl down, finding my eyes. "Ye cannot say anything. I'm doin' this for my family." Luke averts his gaze, picking up the cutlery.

"You're hunting down pirates and people of color for your *family*? You must all be horrible peo—"

"No! Ye wouldn't understand." He points the knife at me. "Don't tell anyone my true age or—"

"I won't."

He lowers the knife, bringing the cup to my lips. It's water. "Rest up, siren of ruin. I'll be back in the morrow."

I drink to the very last drop, and he removes the goblet from my mouth. "Oh joy. I get to see you again."

He stands, grabbing the tray with the leftover food. "Don't push yer luck, or I'll kill ye."

I laugh. "Please get in line, babe. You're like the *fifth* person to say that to me."

He snickers. "My family says that to me all the time as well, especially my younger brother when I misplace the items he worked hard to... attain."

"You miss them?" He nods. "Well. At least one of us will get to see our family soon."

He smiles, but his eyes are glossy, his jaw clenched. A lock of dark hair comes from underneath his powdered wig. He pushes it back up. "If ye need anything, just hold on 'til the morrow, alright? Hang in there." I glare at him. "Too soon?"

"Way too soon."

With that, Luke departs and locks my cell, smiling before he leaves.

I don't know why... but he feels eerily familiar.

As if I *knew* him.

CHAPTER THIRTY-FIVE

"Hear ye, hear ye!" a voice yells faintly. "The Queen's Thief will die at noon! Join us in bringing justice to the Crown of England!"

It's the day of my sentence.

Heavy footsteps approach.

Judge Brown and a second man show themselves, malicious smiles forming on their lips.

"Rise, criminal," Judge Brown remarks. "It's time to bring ye to justice once and for all."

***

I limp between Judge Brown and the officer, my ankle screaming for help every time I press my foot against the ground. Luke Clarke trails the three of us, his tread quiet. Thankfully, they don't rush me, but they seem annoyed at my slow stride.

The courthouse is devoid of its officers. Johann is nowhere to be seen, which strikes me as strange. He'd take any opportunity to taunt me, to mock me for not obeying him as my superior. As my savior.

Unleash your power, Luz...

I take deep breaths, silencing the voice in my head. My odds against three people aren't that great, especially since I can't control it. But it's my last chance to escape.

I focus my gaze ahead, wanting to release the power that runs through my veins. But once more, nothing happens. I can't call it on command. It's futile.

Their pace quickens, and I struggle to keep up. Pain shoots upward from my ankle.

"Where's the Admiral? " I ask.

"Silence, wench. You have no voice here." Judge Brown snarls.

"Perhaps I could aid ye both in parading the bitch around," Luke Clarke says from behind. His accent is muffled, forced. "She can barely walk and we want to be done today, aye?"

The judge nods. "Absolutely. Lead her to the gallows, sir."

Luke grabs my arm, pulling me gently to his body.

The door swings open and I squint, blinded by the light.

The rain clouds have dispersed, rays of sunlight piercing through the dissipating mist, casting a golden glow across the town square. Puddles have formed in the uneven cobblestone pathways, the moist greenery glistening under the watery sun. The smell of damp earth and wet dog mingles with the salty twang of the nearby sea, creating an interesting aroma that permeates the air.

The villagers have emerged from their homes, their quick footsteps creating rhythmic patterns as they attempt to see the girl that's being hung. Market stalls have closed, traders close their crates. The sounds of haggling, laughter, and insults fill the air, my heart beating under their relentless words.

Children run along with dolls hanging from makeshift nooses on sticks. Their boots splash in the puddles, and their laughter echoes in my mind.

From young to old, everyone has gathered to see the death of the Queen's Thief at noon.

"Where's Nau?" I ask.

"Preparing for the reading of the crimes," Luke conveys.

"Don't answer her questions, lad. She's a witch. She's using witchcraft to beguile you," Judge Brown commands with a grimace. Luke nods and quiets down.

Crossbreed.

Witch.

Criminal.

Harlot.

My heart races as the villagers' slurs impale me like arrows. They throw pebbles and spit in my direction, further degrading me. Despite their cruelty, I keep my head held high, refusing to show any weakness. Each step becomes a struggle, and the taunts grow unbearable with every passing moment.

Tears pool in my eyes. The sky darkens overhead, yet I attempt to maintain a stoic facade. I'm not revealing to Johann that he has triumphed, even as I approach the brink of mortality. Inhaling deeply, the sky gradually brightens once more.

My teary gaze fixates on the noose. The corpse from four days ago was removed, and the platform beneath reset. Perched upon it, Johann Nau wears a fresh uniform and wig, a sly smirk adorning his face as he clutches a scroll in his hand. At the sight of him, a sudden surge of emotions courses through my veins. I lift my eyes to meet his gaze, my jaw clenching.

He did this to me.

The wind picks up. My brown eyes do not leave his blue ones.

A second person stands on the platform with Johann. In an all-black ensemble and machete by his waist, I know this man is the executioner.

The death bringer.

"Walk faster, witch," Judge Brown orders, pulling me roughly.

I land on the injured foot and wince. It's definitely sprained. Any last-minute attempt to escape is thwarted because of my ankle. Can't run. Can barely walk. Luke holds me up by my waist, allowing me to have a sprinkle of dignity as I walk one last time. Judge Brown eyes the both of us with disgust. I let a couple of tears fall and wipe them away quickly, not letting them see me at my weakest.

"Clearly, the whore has a spell on you, lad. Hopefully, once dead, the spell breaks," the judge retorts, rolling his eyes. "We walk forward, no exceptions."

"I don't want to die. Please don't take me up there," I plead quietly, taking as much weight as I can off my leg.

"I cannot intervene," Luke admits, regret in his voice.

We arrive at the gallows. The judge goes up the stairs with ease while Luke drags me up them. One step closer to death, to seeing Papi Gustavo.

To escape this hell.

At the top, I'm met by Johann. He pulls me close to him, kissing my cheek.

If you're to die, he should die with you, the voice in my head says.

Power courses through my body once more, as if it didn't have an owner. I reach out, my grip tightening around Johann's throat. My soiled fingers dig into his tender flesh. He fights desperately, but emotions surge in me, a rabid mix of anger and control. We both struggle atop the flimsy, wooden platform.

Kill him...

A rush of adrenaline floods my body, blurring any rational thoughts. The judge and executioner try to separate us, but a strong wind pushes them away. The screams of horror from the crowd only fill my urge to hurt him. Johann's face turns red, then purple, contorted with rage and a predatory focus on how to get loose from my deadly grip.

Johann gasps for air, and a twisted satisfaction rises in me. Just as I dig my fingers deeper, I see Oliver. Flickers of doubt and remorse flash in my mind, a brief recognition of the person I once loved arising. In a panic, I release Johann, my chest falling and rising rapidly. Johann coughs, touching his neck. The wind around us stops.

I'm yanked backward and slapped in the face by the judge, a few unruly dark brown curls loosening from the twine holding them back. The grip on me tightens, pulling me to the platform. Johann wipes his mouth, taking deep breaths.

The executioner positions the noose around my neck, taking my matted, frizzy hair out of the way. Then, and only then, does Johann notice the necklace that I stole back from him. His eyes open wide, his head faintly shaking. The noose is tightly secured, the rough, stale rope scratching my neck.

I keep my gaze on the horizon. I press my lips tightly together, trying to contain all the emotions within. My face muscles tense up and my forehead wrinkles as I tune out the crowd below. I take deep breaths, holding it momentarily to suppress any outward signs of vulnerability. I clench my fists in front of me, the shackles tight on my wrists.

If I'm to die, I will be strong.

Johann clears his throat, opening the scroll. The judge steps behind me. The executioner moves closer to the wooden lever.

"We are gathered here today to witness the sentencing of the proclaimed Queen's Thief," Johann reads. His voice starts out hoarse and ends in a strong, commanding tone.

The crowd quiets down, not wanting to miss anything.

"The Queen's Thief is to be tried for the following crimes. Theft of Her Majesty's jewels, impersonation of a Spanish royal, piracy, fornication, kidnapping, blasphemy, and witchcraft. Her sentence is death by hanging."

"Any last words, witch?" Judge Brown asks. The executioner grips the lever.

I take a deep breath, my eyes slicing to Johann's.

"You all may have won this war, this twisted lie you preach, but mark my words," I yell loud enough for everyone to hear. "Evil never truly dies, it only slumbers awaiting its chance to rise again." I glare at Johann one last time. "I will rise again, and just watch. I'll become your worst nightmare."

The sky is azure without a cloud in sight.

I raise my chin, looking dead ahead.

They can kill me. But evil will prevail. He will forever be haunted. By my memory.

The platform trembles under my feet.

And a single firework whistles, bursting wide open in the middle of the bright blue sky.

CHAPTER
THIRTY-SIX

A firework.
In 1689.

Everyone is taken aback, including me.

What's going on?

Deep whistles scatter and whispers from the crowd. Another firework explodes in the sky. Screams erupt from the eager people of Port Royal.

Next to me, Johann breathes hard, his whole body shaking. "Find who's delaying this and stop them, now!" he orders above the commotion.

Woosh. The executioner drops to his knees, an arrow impaled in his neck.

The crowd panics, making way for a mysterious figure heading to the gallows. With a sword dragging on the ground, their face concealed by a hat, and adorned in lavish pirate attire, they strike fear. Trapped in the square, the townspeople brace for the unknown.

A third firework.

Woosh. Next goes the judge, falling from the platform. An arrow in his heart.

"*The Fury!*" Johann hisses, his face reddened. *The Fury?* "Men of the Navy! Stop them!"

The mysterious person reaches the gallows, not looking up once. Johann's men hurry to load their pistols and weapons, aiming randomly at the crowd. Civilians drop dead.

Woosh. A third arrow barely misses a stomping Johann. I turn my head from the direction of the arrows, but only catch a person in a black cloak atop the rooftop of the courthouse. They slide down a pole, disappearing.

"Down with the Royal Navy!" Sullivan's voice bellows.

"Down with them all!" the crew members echo back.

The Fury is here.

They came.

The town square becomes a battleground, filled with screams and chaos. Merchants quickly lock up their shops, finding shelter behind secure doors. The trapped citizens, blocked by *The Fury*, are forced to endure the turmoil. Sullivan spearheads the charge, mercilessly taking down Royal Navy adversaries.

I laugh, elated. Words can't describe the relief I feel. *The Fury* members' eyes are filled with fierce determination, their weapons ranging from cutlasses, to flintlock pistols and even muskets. The atmosphere is charged with the scent of gunpowder, mingling with the salty sea breeze.

The Royal Navy men in crisped and polished uniforms attempt to form a disciplined line, their bayonets glinting in the fading light. A second commander, a much older man, barks orders with authority while Johann composes himself, ready to restore order and justice. The clash of steel echoes through the square along with screams. Muskets roar to life, sending clouds of smoke into the air as lead balls whiz toward their targets.

Townsfolk run off, running for their lives.

I steal a glance at Johann. His face turns crimson, the scroll crumpled in rage, nostrils flaring. Hatred fills his eyes as he clutches the lever, controlling the noose around my neck.

No.

Thunder cracks overhead. My neck is moments from breaking when Luke intervenes, shoving Johann off the lever, and he tumbles down the steps, losing his wig mid-fall. I gasp in disbelief, my eyes locked on Luke.

What the hell just happened?

Luke comes up to me, sword in hand. He grabs me by the noose. His ocean blue eyes gaze into mine.

"Yo se que vos no podéis correr, but I need ye to run. Run, Aycayia of Destruction," Luke orders, cutting off the rope above, and letting me free of the noose. My shackles then follow, the skin around my wrists raw and red.

"You son of a bi—" Johann yells coming up the steps.

"Run, lass. Run!" Luke commands and pulls the lever.

I fall through the platform, screaming. I expect to hit the ground, but I don't. S. Someone grabs me from underneath, their hands at my waist before I fall on the cobblestone path.

"Vos se va and a death sentence is brought upon ye," a voice taunts. Pedro. He gently sets me on the ground, and I embrace him. He tenses up, but returns the gesture, his cold blue eyes highlighted by fresh black eyeliner. "Yer a menace, aye?"

"Nice to see you, too," I say. Pedro tips his hat, taking out a pistol. "Pedro, my ankle. I can't run. It's injured."

"You!" Johann screams. Both of us look up, watching as he grabs Luke by the collar of his coat. "You let her *go*? Dishonor on your family, Officer Clarke!"

Pedro snorts, sure of himself.

"No, señor Nau. Dishonor on your family!" Luke yells, throwing away his wig. It reveals a mane of dark curls that reach the nape of his neck. "¡Y mi nombre es Lucas Córdova!"

I gasp. *Lucas Córdova. Pedro Córdova.*

I should've known. They could be twins.

Lucas stabs the man coming up the stairs, fighting off Johann.

"¿Tu hijo?" I ask Pedro. He nods. Pedro has a kid? He's a *father*?

I was right when I said Pedro could've been related to Lucas Córdova, but I never imagined Pedro to be Lucas' *father*. I also never imagined Lucas—one of the deadliest Spanish pirate captains known to history—to be a skinny seventeen-year-old *kid*.

"Váyase por esa dirección." Pedro points straight ahead to an alley at the farthest side of the town square, in between the clatter of frantic bodies. "I know yer injured, but it'll be healed. We need ye to run. We have it from here. Go!"

He heads off, shooting a Royal Navy officer in the eye. The officer's body drops to the ground with a thud. Another comes up to him and Pedro shoots this one in the neck, running off.

"Stop her! She cannot escape!" Johann screams, and I move.

Every step is agony, as if I was being stabbed repeatedly on my ankle.

I bolt ahead. Wind rises, rain drizzles fall. My heart races, and my breaths are uneven. After weeks of being confined, running drains me. Ankle in agony, body weakened by hunger. I sprint to the alley Pedro pointed out, skillfully dodging townsfolk and preoccupied Royal Navy officers.

Screams come from all around, as well as commands. I glimpse a few of the crew members fighting like there's no tomorrow.

A lecherous man halts my path, but swift Black hands end his life in a headlock. His lifeless body drops to the ground, and Sullivan stands behind him. I cry out, rushing to Sullivan's arms, embraced and lifted.

"Thank you for that," I whimper. His coat is burgundy, covered with the blood of his enemies.

"Truly a survivor ye are," he observes, his locs loose behind him. "Ye need to run to where Córdova told you. I'll be soon. We shall drink ale in victory afterward!"

"Be careful... please."

He smirks. "Careful ain't in my vocabulary, lass. Go!"

A Royal Navy officer's cry pierces the air as Lydia's blade finds its mark. I find the scene a few feet away, where she thrusts him to the ground, delivering a knockout blow to another officer with a single punch. Locking eyes with me, she nods, a smile gracing her lips before she swiftly advances toward a third man. His sword clatters from his grip, sliding across the ground to my feet.

I reach for the sword, but get knocked down. I clutch the blade, raising it. He looms above, pistol aimed at my head—the same man who assaulted me on *The Glory*. I fix the sword on his groin, unwavering. A surge courses through me.

"The Admiral should've killed you when he had the chance." He smirks, his chest falling and rising.

"You should've never put your hands on me."

I kick his groin with my uninjured leg,, and he falls forward, on top of me. The blade I hold enters his abdomen. Blood drips down from his lips to my face. I push him off of me, removing my new sword from his body. He groans miserably, holding his bleeding injury.

I stand over him as he squirms in his last moments, the bloody sword still in my hand.

I made my first move to kill without my powers.

And it *succeeded*.

On *The Glory*, I panicked and couldn't kill Johann. With this man, my fight-or-flight instinct took over, and I acted without thought, but still I was aware of my actions. Trembling, I step back, unable to look away as he bleeds into the ground.

He is my first kill.

"Red, stop looking at him!" James yells. He appears in front of me, sweaty and bloody, grabbing my shoulders. I just *killed* someone. "Red, it's okay, breathe, the first kill is always a memorable one. I need ye to breathe." I can't get the feeling of death out of my fingers. I'm a murderer. Now I truly am no better than Johann. "We have to go. Follow the plan. Nau is after ye, he won't let ye run off a second time alive."

He releases me and grabs my free hand.

We jog. The zephyr wakes me up.

"Wait, James," I beg, out of breath. "How is Pedro's son involved in this if he was a member of *The Glory*? How does he even have a *son*?"

"Well, Red. When a man and a woman—" I give James a look, and he laughs. I don't need a lesson on reproduction. Not right now. "Lucas is one of us. He's been undercover for two years aboard *The Glory*, helping us intercept the commerce. He's doin' what Héctor did—Lucas is under the orders of the Cap'n and The Seer."

I nod. Nothing is as it seems.

We dodge people running, dying. Their screams and the clash of swords are embedded into my mind. James tells me to hang on, that we're almost at the rendezvous point. I go along with what he says. I trust him.

He wouldn't hurt me.

He's not Johann.

For the first time in a while, I'm safe.

Even as I hold the bloody sword that brought the end to that *Glory* crew member.

The more James and I jog, evading people, the more secluded the area becomes. We arrive at an alleyway, where I see Octavia. I begin crying, but out of joy. I run up to her, embracing her. Her arms tighten around me, tears in her eyes. She smells of gardenias and citrus, smells that remind me of home.

I relax, even amidst the chaos.

I break apart and look at her. She's wearing a brown dress with black tights underneath, held at the waist with a black corset. Her ginger locs are down and tied back with a bandana. No sword, but a small sheathed dagger at her hip.

"Here she is. Alive. Just as we planned," James announces, taking deep breaths.

"Now, we just need—" Octavia begins, but is cut off by a loud voice giving commands.

The three of us turn and encounter a raging Héctor, slashing the throat of a man, while kicking another in the shin. The one he kicked falls to the ground, and Héctor shoots him with the pistol in his right hand.

Héctor strides toward us, hair in a low ponytail, face covered in sweat. His beige shirt and brown vest bear the stains of a bloody massacre, as if he's taken thousands of lives in five minutes. A wooden crossbow and empty quiver rest on his back. Blood drips from his cutlass, leaving a crimson trail on the dirt and cobblestone.

"D'nanichi," he calls out, running to me and tossing his weapon to the ground.

I swallow my pride and ego and throw myself on him, embracing him hard. I've missed him. *Badly.*

"Let me look at you," he says, putting his warm hands on my face. Dark circles pronounce his unsteady, hollow eyes as he bores his gaze into mine. There's slight hysteria in his voice. "Are you alright? What did they do to you?"

My heart races, a small knot forming in my stomach as he caresses my face. My palms grow sweaty, this display of affection creating a tumultuous internal struggle. Does he feel pity for me? Is this mere politeness? Does he feel bad? Technically, he's the last person who saw me before Johann took me. My soul grapples with a swirl of conflicting desires. His affection and reassurance comforts me, but it also makes me afraid.

"I'm fine," I lie, pulling away from him. "I swear. I'm fine."

He releases my face and looks at me. *All of me.* My bloody clothing, bruises, cuts, swollen ankle, my matted hair. His expression changes when he catches sight of my left arm. He pulls it forward, the word *halfbreed* staring right at the both of us. His breath quickens, his body tenses. His eyes are dark when they find mine.

"Who—who did this to you?" he asks, his fingers caressing the letters carved on my skin.

"Héctor, it's noth—"

"Who did this to you? I need names." He drops my arm, his eyes full of wrath. "Names, Luz, and do not lie to me."

"Héctor, we have to stick to the plan," Octavia warns him.

"Fuck the plan." He caresses my cheek with tenderness, even as his demeanor turns bloodthirsty and murderous. "Did Nau do this to you?" His tone is soft when he speaks to me, a stark difference at the hostility toward Octavia and James. "Please, I am begging you. Was it him?"

My breath trembles, tears coming to my eyes. "Yes, he did this," I say. "And everyone in the crew watched and laughed as he—"

My voice breaks and a tear falls down my cheek. He wipes it away, affectionately.

He turns away from us, cursing in Arawak furiously. He rubs his temples, kicking away his cutlass. I've never heard him like this before. James tries calling him, but Héctor glares at him. A look that could kill us all if allowed. Then, he punches a rotten wall of wood next to us. Once, twice. Until he breaks the wall through.

I grab his face in my hands, his eyes red and wrathful. My heart tugs, and a sudden itch for Johann's head on a platter enters my body.

"I am fine," he lies, grabbing my hands. "I promise."

"Héctor, we have to go. The plan," Octavia informs. "James—"

"James, you go with them. I will deal with Nau," Héctor intervenes, releasing me. James and Octavia look at each other, confused.

"Wait. That ain't part of the plan. We agreed to—" James starts, but Héctor yanks him by the collar of his shirt. I've never seen Héctor with such hostility and fury.

With such a need for *vengeance*.

"You will listen to me. I do not care what any of you have to say. You leave Nau to me. You take her to safety. Now. And do not wait for me." He releases James, picking his bloody sword up from the ground.

"But Héctor—"

"I said NOW! The Admiral is mine to deal with! This is between me and him."

"Héctor, what are you doing?" I ask, lightheaded. "I don't know what the plan is, but you heard them. The prophecy. It's me. If you do it, you'll die."

He smiles weakly. "The moment he took you, I knew I had no intentions of following any plan that did not involve his fucking blood on my hands. I will kill him for putting his filthy hands on you. He will suffer the same way he made you suffer. And I will enjoy it." Héctor comes up to me, his trembling hand on my cheek. While his voice softens, his gaze is as murderous as can be. "Even if I die, I will make them all pay for what they did to you, d'nanichi."

Angered, James marches to us, clutching Héctor's shoulders, compelling him to face the furious, yet disheartened child. "Ye would sacrifice yerself to ensure his blood lands on yer hands instead of hers?" James asks, releasing Héctor. Both stay quiet, glaring at each other.

Héctor's gaze lands on me, and I know he's struggling to not touch me. "Always."

I don't want him to die for me. I try to say something to him, but my voice catches in my throat. I long for his embrace, for his arms around me. But the outside part of me struggles with showing him my vulnerability.

"This ain't have to happen this way, brother!" James exclaims.

As the uproar of navy men and pirates continues, Héctor sighs and moves strides to me. His hand cups my cheek, his unwavering gaze fixed on mine. I lean into his touch and he smiles weakly.

"I could live a thousand lifetimes, and in each of those, I will always sacrifice myself for her," Héctor admits, placing an out-of-place curl behind my ear.

With that, Héctor runs back into the commotion, stabbing every Royal Navy officer he encounters in his way. Their cries of agony echoing as they drop to the ground like flies.

CHAPTER THIRTY-SEVEN

"Well, shit," Octavia exclaims.

Screams of agony arise from the crowd. The three of us stand there, not knowing what to do.

A bloodied Sullivan materializes from the crowd, glancing back at Héctor. Even from where I stand, his demeanor exudes a powerful and intimidating presence. Deep lines of tension show in his face, along with a rigid jaw, narrowed brown eyes and a hostile gaze. One of his fists clenches, his back straight as he marches over to us. He shoots a man down without even looking at him, his locs swaying behind him.

"Guillebeaux, why the fuck is my second mate back in there?" Sullivan yells, putting away his pistol. He's breathing heavy, age catching up to his body from the strenuous movements.

"Because he refuses to listen, that's why!" Octavia yells back. "I can't control what he does!"

"He'll get himself killed." He throws his hat on the ground, sweat embedded on his forehead and brows. "James ain't goin' to—" He screams, frustration overtaking him.

"Fath–Captain!" James says, running up to him, sheathing his bloody sword.

Sullivan takes deep breaths, putting his hands on James' shoulders, but his squinted eyes turn to Octavia. "What'll happen now, Seer?" Sullivan asks. "Ye know what the next part of the plan encompasses."

James gets loose from Sullivan's grip and paces back and forth, his hands shaking. "I ain't able to do Héctor's part!" James grabs Octavia, his eyes impossibly widened in alarm. "Don't make me do this without him!"

From the alleyway, I watch as Héctor stabs everyone he encounters. Men, women. Anyone in his path will meet death until he reaches his primary target.

Sullivan tries to calm down a hysterical James, stopping him dead in his tracks. Whispering in his ear. The sounds of dying and pain surround us. I can't take this anymore. I refuse to be a pawn for any longer. I step forward and grab Octavia, fighting the urge to shake her body.

"What plan are they talking about, Tay?" I ask.

She pushes a loose loc behind her ear, her frantic purple eyes finding mine. "We were to intervene in your sentence and take you to *The Fury*. Alive. However, between us and *The Fury* stand The Ringmasters. Vicious men with sick tendencies. The original plan was to have you, me, Héctor, and James head to *The Fury*, with Héctor being the one who faced them. He was supposed to stay as far away as possible from Nau, but—"

"But Villanueva's reckless behavior changed everything," Sullivan interjects. "I ain't lettin' my son face those bastards alone. We're goin' and we're goin' now."

"Captain Edwards, are you certain you want to take Héctor's place?" Octavia asks, grabbing my hand.

"Nau! Come out here and stop hiding like the fucking coward you are, you bastard!" Héctor yells faintly. It takes everything in me to not turn back and stop him.

Sullivan chuckles humorlessly. "I ain't got much of a choice, do I?" He points at James. "What of him? Will he be alright?"

James takes a deep quivering breath, and Octavia nods. "He's protected, Captain. I assure you." James somewhat relaxes, but anxiety lingers in his demeanor, making him appear younger than he is. Sullivan whispers in his ear, and James nods, unsheathing his sword. Octavia turns to me next, squeezing my hand. "Luz, I need you to walk a bit more. I know you're weak, but I need you to hold on, okay?" I nod.

The four of us begin our journey with haste.

We walk through alleys and secluded areas, trying our best to be silent as we sneak around.

James goes in front, bloody sword in hand. He's humming a song to himself and fidgeting with the handle, trying to stay composed. I'm behind him, with the sword I used to make my first kill.

I need to concentrate.

I need to get Héctor's rage out of my mind. The way he held me, the way his trembling fingers caressed me.

"A mole rat could hear yer footsteps, James, and they're fucking deaf," Sullivan remarks from the rear. "Walk quieter." James does as he's told.

Octavia chuckles behind me, her hands devoid of weapons. She must be good at hand to hand combat. Then again, she *sees* everything coming.

Looking back at Sullivan, he's tense as can be, pistol in his hand at the ready. His footsteps are heavy, as he walks with a limp. His eyes scan all their surroundings, waiting for what may arise from the shadows.

"Stop right there! In the name of the King!"

We whirl our heads around, and a white man with a cutlass charges at us. His eyes are thirsty for blood, and the closest to him is Sullivan. However, before Sullivan can shoot him down, Octavia twirls toward the man, taking out her dagger. With one move, she slits his neck. His body falls limp to the ground with a loud thud, a pool of thick blood growing under his head. Sullivan looks up at her, lowering his pistol.

"He would do horrible things. The world will not miss him," Octavia justifies, wiping the bloody dagger with the hem of her brown dress. "More will come."

"Ye've changed, Seer," Sullivan remarks.

"Appearances can be deceiving, Captain."

Sullivan nods, and we continue walking.

Octavia Guillebeaux, who wouldn't hurt a fly in our time, has killed a person in five seconds.

Without *remorse.*

Two people have died at our hands and both have me unsettled. How do people murder without guilt? Surely they must feel some type of way afterward?

Octavia cries out in pain, doubling over. I limp to her, helping her stand straight. She's holding her chest and neck with such urgency one would think she's being murdered.

"What's happening?" I ask as she heaves. Her eyelids move quickly, Creole escaping her lips quietly. "Octavia!"

"I've seen this before," James says, holding her other side. He's snapping with his free hand, trying to recall information. "She's... she's Seeing things. Yes!" Sullivan scans the area, making sure we're alone. "When what's coming is near, it manifests physical pain, I think. Especially death."

Octavia's eyes flutter open, gasps come between breaths. She looks straight at me, tears in her eyes. Her eyebrows are creased as her knees buckle underneath her. She pushes James off, paranoid.

"Death. Death shall come. Hands ripped apart, bodies drowned, destiny fulfilled. Death will come." She reiterates, her voice thick with horror. Her hand grips her neck. "We must go."

"And go we shall, let us move," Sullivan insists.

Sullivan holds a teary-eyed Octavia, helping her along while James and I stand in front. I didn't know Seeing things such as death brought her physical pain. Imagine being immortal, but feel death upon your body each time you See it. Not a cost all would take.

"Take a left here," she groans.

I've seen this place before. Only it was recently dawn and fog covered the marina. It's where I first boarded *The Fury*.

Reaching this dock feels easy. *Too* easy. Out of the frying pan and into the fire, as they say.

A loud bell goes off near us, startling me. Octavia seems unfazed by it, but her stance grows defensive, pushing Sullivan away from her body. James' hands tremble as he raises his sword, his eyes scanning all surroundings. All of his confidence, his sense of security has evaporated.

"James. They can't hurt you anymore," Octavia reassures him.

Sullivan rushes to James, grabbing his shoulders. He leans down, meeting James at eye height.

"Remember what I've taught ye. Ye is important. Ye is of value. Ye is my *son*," Sullivan says, doing the sign of the cross over James. "They won't take that away from ye, I assure ye." Sullivan releases him, nodding.

"Has my prized lost boy returned to me?" a voice taunts. A white man appears from the shadows, his face tethered and old. He holds a wooden club, a sheathed sword at his waist. He wears an all-brown ensemble, his hair gray. His rolled sleeves reveal countless scars. "Long time no see, Wilson."

"I no longer answer to that name!" James shouts, feigning confidence. "Run along before I tear ye apart!" The man laughs.

"'Tis my prize indeed," the man says. James' sword falls to the ground, his shaky fingers forbidding him from picking it back up. "Tell me, boy. How does it feel knowing you've amounted to nothing without us?"

"Say one more word, Peterson!" Sullivan orders, aiming his pistol at this man's head. "I'm bein' merciful."

The man—Peterson—laughs. "If it isn't Sullivan Edwards. The most wanted pirate of the West Indies," Peterson jeers while approaching, but Sullivan shoots at a barrel behind him. A warning. Peterson stays back. "You took my favorite performer, and I'd like him back."

"You better back the fuck up!" I yell, my sword in hand. It takes all the power in me to step in front of James. Power courses through my veins, just like it did when I was in the cell. "Leave him be!"

Thunder roars above us, the breeze turns to a violent gust.

Peterson raises his club. "He's coming back home."

"We are his home," Octavia interferes, dagger in hand. She stands next to me, shielding James from Peterson.

Peterson laughs, and more men emerge from the shadows, surrounding us from all sides. They all wear brown as well. Eight large men with swords against an injured woman, a Seer with a dagger, an older pirate Captain, and a fifteen-year-old who's on the verge of a nervous breakdown.

I'd say our odds aren't great.

Trembling, James grabs his cutlass, tears in his eyes. He points it at everyone, hysterically spinning around. His chest falls and rises quickly, a scream visibly lodged in his throat. James is always so cheerful. So full of life and wonder. Seeing him like this causes something in me to turn sour.

"Leave us be, we want no trouble," Octavia states, not lowering her dagger. She throws a glance at me, warning me.

"Trouble began when our little lost boy ran away from home," Peterson states. "Give us what we require, and we'll be on our way."

"He's my son. Ye ain't takin' him anywhere," Sullivan declares.

Peterson laughs. "He's no son of yours. He's a bastard."

"I suggest you shut that white mouth of yours before I finish you," I remark, my fingers tightening around my cutlass. He scoffs.

Peterson swings the club at me, but misses. Sullivan, in retaliation, kills a man of his.

The fighting begins.

Octavia hurts the men with ease, their groans as they fall to the ground in agony. The sounds of blades piercing skin should unsettle me, but I think we're well beyond me freaking out.

Sullivan shoots down the endless supply of men arising from the shadows. He shoots one and two more take their place. Like a Hydra. When his bullets run out, he throws his pistol away and takes out his cutlass, stabbing every man that dares approach him.

My focus is on Peterson.

He unsheathes his sword as ripples of energy course through my body. More whispers. An eerie Arawakan harmony fills my ears. My breathing quickens. Full of rage, I try every move that Héctor taught me, but miss constantly. Peterson mocks me, cutting me with every attempt. He will not take James. No matter what becomes of me.

"Puppet, you are disappointing me. This ain't a fair fight," he taunts, smirking. I swipe at him again and he dodges, laughing. "You're the lost boy's protector? Or is he your protector? Hard to tell."

I charge at him, and he punches my side. I stumble backward, pins and needles erupting from my body. The adrenaline subsided. *No.* I drop my stolen sword, wishing I could kill him at once. Peterson pushes me to the ground, and my body refuses to cooperate in letting me get up. I cough up the dust circling me. He kicks away my sword, which glides across the rough dirt.

Peterson bends down and grabs my neck, his thick fingers cutting my air supply. Desperate, I attempt to pry his hands open with weak fingers, but it's futile. My air flow decreases by the second, my vision going dark.

"Ye will no longer torment me!" James screams behind us and the next thing I know, Peterson releases me, grabbing his side.

Coughing, I look up at the spectacle. James stabbed him. Unfortunately, Peterson still lives, charging at James. James, while strong, is nervous, causing his usually smooth moves to be slippery and unfocused. Sullivan is screaming and pushing people off of him, calling out for James. Octavia drops her dagger after a man punches her. A second man grabs her from the front. She knees him in the groin and takes his pistol, shooting them both down with such grace, you'd wonder if she was ever a ballerina.

Peterson bats James' sword out of his hands. He grabs James by the neck, raising him easily a couple feet off the ground. James kicks him, and he's released, falling onto his knees. Finally, my body cooperates and allows me to get up, running towards Peterson. Both of us struggle—two seething dancers attempting to gouge each other's eyes out. He elbows my face, a dull ache presenting itself as I fall backward. My head hits the ground. Everything around me spins.

"James! Narváez!" Sullivan cries out, punching a man unconscious.

A high-pitched screech roars inside my ears. My vision decreases, but I see James coming to his feet without a weapon. Peterson's focus isn't on me, though. It's on James.

Peterson knees James' stomach, and James falls, curling up into a ball. He's crying out in pain. Sullivan calls out for him once more. Peterson raises his sword high above his head, gaining momentum.

"No," I mumble, moving to my side. The wind is relentless. I'm devoid of any power. "No."

"Say yer last words, Wilson," Peterson taunts as James groans. "The little bird has sung its last note."

"James!" Sullivan yells between breaths.

James holds his stomach, but not once does he stop looking at Peterson, the bringer of his nightmares. Peterson smirks, readying his sword. I drag myself over to James, distracting Peterson for the briefest of seconds.

Peterson swipes his sword.

I'm too late.

At the last second, Sullivan dives in front of us. Peterson never stops his swinging weapon.

"NO!" James screams.

Sullivan's head disconnects from his limp body, both falling to the gravel with a deafening thud.

Sullivan

CHAPTER
THIRTY-EIGHT

I scream frantically, watching as blood pools around Sullivan's decapitated body.

"NO!" James screams. I heave acidic waste near me as James hugs the headless corpse. His cry sounds like a thousand lost souls calling out to their families.

I can't process what I've witnessed.

Sullivan. Beheaded. Murdered.

My chest tightens and my whole body trembles. Thunder cracks in the darkening sky.

"One of these fuckers down, three more to go," Peterson taunts over James' screams. He smirks as he approaches me with the sword.

I make no sigsign to move. I can't. My whole body is frozen in place, my muscles have constricted, and my heart skips beats. I can't comprehend what I saw. All sounds mute themselves.

"Father, please. Come back!" James weeps in the distance, not caring about Peterson. "Please. Please!"

Adrenaline courses through my body once more, my hair whipping behind me. Rain pours over us. My emotional pain dissipates as James sobs. I grip the gravel and dirt around me, my knuckles turning white. The docked ships sway with the storm, their wooden planks creaking.

Ethereal singing echoes in an unfamiliar language. Rain turns to a monsoon, pushing and pulling us in every direction. I spot Mami Julia marching to us, a need for death in her eyes. Her mouth is moving,, and the rain avoids her, parting ways. As she gets closer, she swivels her arms in front of her, causing a thirty-foot wave to build on the ocean. The rainwater pricks out skin.

"Steady, men!" Peterson shouts over the raging winds. "Bring her down!"

Mami Julia stops her ethereal singing, along with the rain. "YOU KILLED THE MAN I LOVED. NOW I KILL YOU!" Mami Julia screams, the winds knocking over every one of Peterson's goonies.

One by one, they are thrown into the water. Dragging them into the thirty-foot wave that threatens the horizon. Peterson tries to run, but the wave grabs him, pulling him toward her.

She's closer now, her face contorted with rage. Her eyes red, her glare looks like it could easily kill an armada of men.

"You fucked up, blanco," is all she says. In my years of knowing her, she was never this furious, vulnerable, raw. This is the power of Queen Aycayia at work. Beautiful. Dangerous. Relentless.

My squinted eyes land on Sullivan's corpse. Octavia runs to us, tears in her eyes.

"James—" Octavia begins.

James looks up, his eyes bloodshot. "FIX HIM, SEER. HEAL HIM. PLEASE!"

"I can't! I CAN'T! I'M SORRY!"

More thunder cracks above us. My chest hurts, my throat burns. Seeing James broken like this, I embrace the darkness within me. Power surges through my veins and I feel the pricks of rain against my skin. My lips quiver, my breaths turn shallow. The feeling from the cell has returned.

With a sudden burst of energy, I stand, the rain parting away from James, Octavia, and I. The waves get higher, ships blow up one by one.

Without having to control it, a tidal wave grows on the dock. Mami Julia turns to face me, worry on her face. Peterson's remaining men scramble to run. I simply stand in the middle of it all, my eyes dead on Peterson. I raise my arm to point the wave in its indicated direction, but I'm yanked backward. I blink rapidly, breaking out of my murderous fog, and the water retreats to its home.

"No. He's not yours to kill," Octavia states, pulling on my arm.

Mami Julia controls a wave, sending Peterson to the depths. No more men are on the dock. Hopefully that's the last we see of them.

The waves retreat, yet the rain continues. Mami Julia falls to her knees, screaming, choking on her sobs. When Papi Gustavo died, she sobbed just like this. Twice she has lost the men she loved. Twice has she screamed like this.

My heart breaks once more.

James weeps while Sullivan's corpse lays in his hands. Weakness overtakes me, and I fall, a sob escaping me. Octavia is crying with her hands pressed to her temples.

Why must the good people be taken from us while the bad ones survive?

"One of ye heal him," James begs. "One of ye *will* heal my father."

I glance at Octavia through my tears and she looks back at me, her lip quivering. "Nothing can be done, James," Octavia whimpers.

James' eyes darken as he stands. "Bullshit!" He looks from me, to Octavia, to Mami Julia. He clenches his jaw as he presses his hands into fists. "The three of ye have magic. More magic that I've ever seen! And yer tellin' me NONE OF YE WILL DO SHIT?" More tears fall down his cheeks. "HEAL HIM, SEER."

"James. No magic can bring him back... and even if it could, it wouldn't be him. It would be... something dark." Octavia takes a deep breath, hugging herself. "My powers come from the light, from the spiritual. Not from the darkness."

"They're coming. We have to go," Mami Julia warns. She holds her chest, her hand trembling. Her gray hair clings to her face and neck. "Child. We must go." She reaches over to James, touching his cheek, but he steps back.

"Stab me," James orders. The rain stops all at once.

"What?" I breathe out. "James. Please don't say that. We need to go." His eyes slice to mine.

"No. I ain't able to continue this fight without my father. He took me in, fed me, was there for me. Don't ye get it? I killed him. He's dead 'cause of *me*." He covers his ears, panting. "I DID THIS! This is *my* fucking fault! So *kill* me!"

More voices boom in the distance.

They're coming.

My heart aches for him. I reach out, but stop myself. "James, it's not your—"

"She's right, James. It's not your fault," Mami Julia interjects, glaring at me. "It's Héctor's. Héctor did this. If he had stuck to the fucking plan, Sully wouldn't have taken his place."

A gasp escapes my lips. Certainly she doesn't mean this. I study her stance, her quiet, trembling rage. Oh, she means it. She meant *every* word. "Mami, no estás ayudando."

"We don't have time to play the blame game!" Octavia yells.

Octavia picks up an abandoned sword, her dagger, and Peterson's splinted club. An armada of men have risen from the shadows, their footsteps are the sound of impending death. A gunshot goes off, and Mami Julia creates a water barrier in front of us, blocking the men from getting to us.

"James. You can mourn on the ship, when you are safe," Octavia assures him, but I don't think our words will get through to him. He's listening, just not comprehending. The water barrier dissipates.

He lowers his hands and stands up straight, picking Sullivan's sword up. "No. Go on without me. I deserve to pay for my consequences. If I die, I die." He looks at me, grief and guilt intertwined on his face.

"There they are! Stop them! Don't let them get away!" the leader of the group yells.

No.

"*The Fury* is right there," Octavia urges, taking away his sword.

Down at the very edge of the dock rests *The Fury* amongst the few ships that survived the torrential downpour. Is that how we're leaving? Wouldn't they be able to catch us?

"These assholes can never get enough, huh?" Mami Julia growls. She tilts her head to the side, panting.

The wind picks up, and she chuckles. Watching her, she exudes vengeful energy. Queen Aycayia is craving blood, and she won't stop until she gets it. She closes her eyes, feeling the rain against her skin as they fire more shots. Without looking, she sends water in front of us, blocking each bullet. Grunts and complaints come from the men's mouths.

James watches, mesmerized, his eyes barely open. Octavia hugs herself, watching the spectacle.

"The three of you go," Mami Julia orders.

"No," I say. "We aren't leaving you either!"

"Yes, you are."

She opens her eyes, and I come face to face with two murderous turquoise irises. Gills have appeared on her neck, her pearly-white teeth turned sharp. She looks like a true Aycayia. Beautiful yet terrifying.

When I move toward her, she creates a sudden seawall in front of me, separating her from the three of us. The water flows freely, like a waterfall without beginning or end. It disappears when it hits the concrete. Sullivan's body is on the other side of the barrier, causing James to hit the wall with his fists, crying.

I scream her name. I can't lose her too.

My grandmother sings a single syllable from the other side, her voice rising and falling. A deadly lullaby. Footsteps soften, water splashes.

"Cover yer ears! She's a siren!" a man yells. Groans. Gargling.

From far away, more voices join. I whirl my head around, but Octavia calls my name, forbidding me from investigating the source of the harmony. The melody rises and falls, enticing anyone in their vicinity. James covers his ears, the enthralling song increasing in volume.

"We have to go now!" Octavia shrieks, pulling me backward.

"I can't just leave her!"

"It must happen this way. Trust me, Luz."

Despair is in her face. Against my better judgment, I let Mami Julia and Sullivan go. I say goodbye to them in my heart.

Tears swell in my eyes, mourning my grandmother for a second time. Mourning Captain Sullivan Edwards.

"James. We have to go," I cry, my chest aching.

"No! Ye can't make me!" he screams. "I ain't leavin' him!"

If we're to leave, we have to drag him. I pick up his upper body, Octavia grabs onto his legs, shushing him. He thrashes around, crying, begging us to let him die. We hasten to the swaying ships, every step I take in agony. The eerie tune carries in the wind, Octavia and I unaffected by it.

❧❧❧

We finally reach *The Fury*. There's no wooden platform, just three ropes hanging from the side of the ship. Octavia and I release a numb James. Octavia grabs onto a rope, urging me to climb as well. She hands the other to James, and he takes it, disassociated.

She and I study his robotic, lethargic movements. He hauls himself up a few inches, glancing down at the roaring ocean below us. *He's gonna do it.* We head to him, and Octavia cuts the rope above him with a single swipe of her sword. James lands on the ground, crouching, his ears covered, his whole body shaking.

In a swift move, Octavia steals a bundle of ropes from a broken canoe, unraveling them with steady hands. She loops them around James' waist, securing him tightly to the main hanging rope. I watch as she takes a set of thinner cords and ties his legs together, creating a secure cocoon. Her movements are deliberate yet quick.

James is so zoned out, he doesn't fight or struggle. He lets Octavia do as she wishes. Silent tears fall down his cheeks.

She stands him up, placing his hands on the main rope. "Do not let go, you hear me?"

He nods.

A single groan joins the eerie melody as the voices weaken.

Mami Julia.

"It's for your own good," Octavia reassures him, signaling for me to come. "We have to go."

The water barrier dematerialises, returning to its home.

Mami Julia's surrounded by dead men, but this time she isn't alone. From the water, sirens drag themselves onto the dock, drenched in sea water. Their bodies are mesmerizing, a terrifying combination of a deadly lionfish tail with the bronze upper body of a woman. Their hands are talons that dig into the concrete, dorsal fins at their backs. Onyx, straight hair is plastered to their skin, which is adorned with red and white tribal paint.

Their voices are breathtaking, and the new men stop dead in their tracks, listening to their enchanting harmony. One by one, the sirens yank a mesmerized man into the ocean, never to be seen again.

"Hurry," Octavia urges, hauling herself up on the rope.

My gaze lands on James. He's gripping the main rope tightly, keeping his eyes closed. I want to embrace and comfort him. Not yet. Not until we're safe. While Octavia climbs with ease, my arms strain as the ship rocks back and forth.

A bullet is fired from a distance. Mami Julia groans, the sirens crying out for her.

No. Not her, too.

The seductive song ends. Men come out of their trance, screaming commands. Bullets fire, whooshing past me. A few sirens yell, followed by the clashing of the sea.

"Luz. Don't you look back!" Octavia warns from above, throwing herself over the rail.

The ship sways with force, threatening to lose my grip on the rope. *The Fury* is docked, bound to its place on this sector of the marina by the rope bindings. A bullet enters the ship less than a foot away from me. My chest tightening, I take a deep breath and lower myself back down.

The wind picks up. Screams, gunshots, and groans is all I can hear behind me. Not once do I look back.

Limping, I reach for the sword Octavia left on the concrete dock. A bullet clashes with it, breaking apart the tip. All I need is the smallest bit of sharpness. Two ropes hold *The Fury*. A thin one, which I cut with a single swipe of this sword, and a thicker one. Sawing the line turns out to be much strenuous than I thought. My body slowly shuts down, my lungs working overtime from the constant activity, trauma, and terror.

A searing ache erupts from my right arm. I cry out in pain, dropping the remnants of my sword. Blood pools on the sleeve of my shirt. A bullet has nicked my skin.

Screams. A female groan. I look back.

Mami Julia is on her knees, hugging herself, a gun on her forehead.

"No!" I scream, the thicker rope splitting in half. *The Fury* is released, pushed away by the waves, Octavia yelling my name.

Mami Julia's eyes widen in surprise, and with a flick of her wrist, a ravenous wave flings me backward into the ocean, separating me from my grandmother.

I descend into the tumultuous waves, broken and alone.

CHAPTER
THIRTY-NINE

I'm trapped, caught within a swirling maelstrom of crashing waves. The ocean's wrath seems insurmountable as towering walls of water engulf me completely. I swim up, the currents tugging at my weary body. Each attempt to escape proves futile as the sheer force pushes me away, rendering my cries for help inaudible.

Something grabs onto my hands, heaving me upward, their grip firm on my skin. I'm hoisted out of the swirling abyss, immense relief filling my body. I cough, pushing my hair back from my face. My chest burns from the water I swallowed. I'm surrounded by the vast, calming ocean, meters away from everything.

"You are too late, d'itu," a soft--spoken voice says. Her accent, like Héctor's, is muddled, combined as if she spoke over three languages. "She has been taken."

Behind me is one of the most beautiful women I've ever laid eyes on. She looks like she could be my age, her skin darker than Mami Julia's. Her jet-black hair is adorned with small braids and shells. Her ears are pointed, pierced with golden earrings. Her lips are plump and two-toned, her nose hooked and crooked. An obsidian gemstone necklace similar to mine lies on her collarbone. Her features all scream of regal beauty.

"You need to learn to control your power. Instead, you let *it* command you," she says, gripping my left arm. Slowly, we swim toward *The Fury* which has stopped a few miles away from the dock. From afar, Octavia hauls James up. "You are the inaru they call Luz, no?"

I nod, not knowing what inaru means. "I'm Luz, Jul– Casiguaya's granddaughter."

Her mouth upturns slightly. "Curiama, Aycayia of War." She shrugs, studying me. "Most call me Ria."

"I didn't know you were *real.*"

She chuckles. "I am very real."

An ethereal, soprano harmony vocalizes a few feet away. One by one, Aycayias bring their heads to the surface, surrounding me and Ria. Five bewitching bronze faces stare right back at us. Their long hair is as dark as midnight, their physical attributes hypnotic. Their eyes are all one brown, one turquoise. One matching the earth, the other matching the sky and seas. Ria, like me, is the only one with brown eyes.

Ria catches me staring, raising her eyebrow. "You are a curious one, are you not?" I avert my eyes. "Casiguaya warned us you ask a lot of questions, so, before you ask, inaru, I was blending in with the mortals. That is why my eyes differ. They shall return to their natural shade soon."

"I didn't mean to stare."

The current turns unnaturally still. Ria speaks to the sirens in Arawak, her tone urgent and demanding respect. Their expressions range from reverence to bloodthirst. They nod, retreating into the sea.

"Come. We mustn't waste time," Ria says, pulling me toward The Fury.

"Who took her? Help me swim to the dock, I can get to her if—"

"We all lost today, and we nearly lost you. You're the only Aycayia of Destruction we've got. We can't risk losing you."

We near the ship. "What's the difference between being a siren of war and being a siren of ruin?"

"We are the generals, the warriors of the sea. I lead our army. You, however, are capable of mass devastation. We can only destroy in our proximity, whereas you have a broader spectrum. You can even lead mortal armies."

"I'll throw down the ladder, hold on!" Octavia cries from the top, hysterical. James is no longer hanging from the side of the ship.

I glance at Ria. "Wait. How am I the evil one?"

She raises her eyebrow at me, her fingers on my necklace. "Evil resides in all of us, inaru. The question is, will you let it out? You can either contain them and hinder your potential; or become who you were meant to be."

Octavia flings the ladder down, where it hits the wood with a loud thud. "What does it mean if I like how I feel when I use my powers, even if I can't control them?"

Ria chuckles, tapping the ladder. "Then do not, but just know, too much power and you'll be corrupted beyond saving. You will turn on even those you love. That's why you're dangerous." She places my hands on the wooden steps. "Rest now, Aycayia of Destruction. This is just the beginning. You must end the man who claims the seas. End those who dare hurt our ituno. You are the daughter of daughters. Do not let your grandmother's sacrifice be in vain."

"Thank you, Ria."

"Seneko kakona, d'ituno. We shall meet again."

Ria helps me climb onto the ladder without slipping. My whole body trembles as her words replay in my mind. *You'll be corrupted beyond saving... you're dangerous...*

Am I being corrupted? If I am... Why do I like how it feels?

The water weighs heavy on me as I ascend the steps, straining to maintain a tight grip. Sea water spritzes my face, stinging my wounds and eyes. I dare not get teary, for I fear I might lose my calm after losing my grandmother.

"Just a few more steps," Octavia calls out above me, her hair disheveled. She's holding on tightly to the wooden rail. She probably lost her footing when Mami Julia made the ship move.

I climb the last few steps and arrive at the top, my legs unsteady from the movement. I scan the ocean, Ria and the sirens are nowhere to be seen. My hands are raw and red, a blister or two appearing. I slump to the floor, resting my ankle. Octavia takes a deep breath, rubbing her temples, and paces back and forth. James sits off in a corner, hugging his knees and staring off into the distance.

"Was any of what happened supposed to happen?" I ask, rubbing my neck, the sensation of the noose still lingering. I lean my head against the wooden rail, the sea breeze refreshing us.

"I knew Héctor would change his portion of the plan regardless of what I said, that Sullivan would die, and your grandmother would choose to risk herself," she explains, sitting down next to me. She looks at the dainty silver and copper rings on her fingers. "I knew you'd take the necklace back from Johann without him noticing. That he'd hurt you and push you to the brink of death, but would not kill you. All this was written."

My chest compresses and my gaze ends on James. His eyes darken by the second, his breaths turn shallow. "Did you tell them?"

"I See what is to happen, but am forbidden to tell it until *after* it occurs." She exhales. "I'm meant to be a guide, Luz. I steer the way so that it all goes according to The Greats' plan. I keep the balance so that darkness doesn't take over. But it's getting really difficult to do so."

I nod. "Do you know how this all ends, then?"

She looks straight ahead, clenching her jaw. "Yes."

If she knows everything, did she know I was going to be taken?

Octavia stands, striding across the wooden deck. A satchel hangs from a nail under the staircase that leads to the quarterdeck. She removes two small vials from inside. One she hands to a silent James. When he doesn't grab it, she places it in his hand, his fingers tightening around the glass. She comes up to me, praying in Creole over the bottle.

"Were the sirens a part of the plan?" I ask.

"Very much so. I told you everything happens for a reason. Our choices and mistakes always lead to something bigger." She kneels in front of me, taking a deep breath.

"What happens now, then?"

She uncaps the vial, a strong herbal scent hitting my nostrils. "Mistakes will be corrected, life will be reborn, destinies intertwined." She chuckles awkwardly. "This is about to hurt. It won't be pleasant at all. But it'll help."

"What is it?"

She hands me the bottle. "Just drink it. Every last drop."

So I do. The mixture feels smooth and cool on my tongue. I can't explain the flavor. Earthy, herbal, somewhat watery. It numbs my senses as it descends my throat. I drink every drop, just like Octavia said.

That wasn't so bad.

Crack. The sound of my bones clicking together excruciatingly erupts from my ankle. I wince, holding on to the wooden rails behind me. I drop the bottle, and it breaks once it makes contact with the deck.

"What's happening to me?" I ask between gasps. "What in the hell did I just take?" Amidst the pain, a strong heat travels throughout my body and concentrates on my ankle.

"You're being healed. I warned you it was going to hurt," Octavia says, grabbing my face. "Focus on something else." The pain increases and I groan, my nails digging into the sanded wood. "It only works this way because you're half mortal. It's supposed to be more excruciating on mortals. Or so I've heard."

"What?" My heart races and chills form on my arms. "When are the others coming?" Heat radiates throughout my entire body, the feeling of waves making me more lightheaded than I was. "Will James be okay?"

"They're on their way, they'll be here soon on the longboats." She glances at a still James. "And James has a long way to go. He just saw his father die before his very eyes."

"Are they okay?" My vision blurs and my senses weaken. My hands lose their grip on the wood, my body lowering itself to the floor. "What's happening?" My voice echoes and slurs viciously.

"Focus on you. Let go." Her face becomes a blob, her voice a melody. "Sleep now. It shall be okay."

A bright white light surrounds me, and a soft voice sings. Lulling me to sleep.

CHAPTER FORTY

I awake to the sound of muffled voices.

My body, while weakened beyond comparison, no longer hurts.

Shifting my position, I find I'm on a soft surface. The plush cloth feels like silk against my skin. A material of comfort compared to the wooden floor I slept on *The Glory*.

I must be dreaming.

My throat feels as dry as sand, the earthy flavor of what I drank still in my mouth. What was that? A tonic? A magic potion?

Whatever it was, it drained all the pain away.

Opening my eyes, I come face to face with a smirking Johann.

"No!" I scream, sitting up. "You get the hell away from me!"

"D'nanichi, it is me!" a voice that doesn't belong to Johann pleads. I wipe my eyes and see Héctor instead, sitting on his knees. He's covered in blood, sweat, and fresh cuts. His whole appearance is disheveled, but it's Héctor. "It is me. You are safe."

I take deep breaths.

Héctor would never hurt me.

Looking around, I'm in his room aboard *The Fury*. On his bed. I catch sight of my ankle as I fix my position. It's no longer red and swollen. Whatever was in that drink worked.

"What happened? Where's Johann?" I ask, studying Héctor.

His nose is bruised, as if it was broken and pushed back into place. One of his eyes looks like it was punched, and there's a red gash going through his right eyebrow. A small nick on his lip catches my eyes, as does a huge red spot on his left cheek.

Héctor took a lot of hits. And that's just on his face.

"What happened to y—"

"I am fine," Héctor interrupts, his eyebrows creased together. "Nau still lives." That bastard is still alive. Maybe Octavia and Mami Julia were right. *It has to be me.* "How are you feeling?"

"Words can't describe what I'm feeling, Héctor." He grabs my hands, caressing them with his thumbs. "James. Octavia. Are they okay?"

"Focus on resting, alright?" His gaze lands on my arm, and I pull away, embarrassed.

"Did you hear—"

"About the Captain?" He looks away, his mouth downturned. "Yes, I have."

"How's James handling everything?"

"We do not know. He has not woken yet." His hands tremble, his eyes downcast. "I did this. I strayed from the path. I chose my need for revenge and in return I led our captain to his doom. I am the one responsible for this." He closes his eyes and takes a deep breath. "And it was all for nothing. Nau escaped. I did nothing but bring pain and misery to our crew."

My stomach churns, my muscles tense, my chest tightens. *Héctor did this*, Mami Julia's voice repeats in my head. No, he didn't. Johann did. His shoulders slump, but he catches himself, setting them back. I attempt to stand, but my legs refuse to cooperate, making me stumble. Héctor catches me, helping me sit back on his bed. I need to see James.

Héctor grabs my face tenderly. He pushes my hair out of the way, not once dropping his eyes from mine. Words don't have to be said to know what we're both feeling. He caresses my cheeks, his touch gentle on me.

"I cannot bear to see you this way," he whispers. "Let me clean you up."

"I can do it myself," I say. His hands fall away, standing.

Héctor brings over a prepared bucket with water, and clean, dry rags, all ready to go. As he sits next to me, he submerges the rag into the water and brings it up.

"You don't have to do this," I say.

"Please," he begs.

Reluctantly, I nod. Héctor grabs my right arm, gently wiping the blood on it. I study him, his face, his body. He's concentrated on what he's doing, not once breaking eye contact with his actions. He mutters to himself as he cleans me up. It sounds venomous. But not once does his touch get aggressive, instead, it gets more tender with each passing minute. My heart flutters, yet I feel safe.

When he wipes the dirt over a fresh bruise, I wince loudly and he stops, looking up at me with concern.

"Have I hurt you?" he asks.

"No, I'm okay," I breathe. He moves the rag onto my neck, but I defensively push him off. "I'm sorry, I didn't mean to do that."

"Do not worry. Is it because of what Nau did to you?"

I nod. "I can still feel the noose around my neck, if I'm being honest."

Héctor skips my neck and wipes my face. My attention is on him again. On his concentrated expression, his deep yet exhausted eyes. His jaw clenches, his brows furrowing together.

A splatter of blood runs along from his cheeks, to his forehead. There's a fresh cut on the bridge of his nose and beneath his left eye, both full of dried blood as well. Even though he looks like he just emerged from a battle, his beauty is marvelous.

His fingers graze my cheeks, gently brushing against my forehead and tracing my jawline. They linger on my lips, pausing at the crease, and my breath catches in my throat. As I gaze at him, he notices and withdraws his touch, edging away from me. A wave of disappointment washes over me.

"Why'd you stop?" I whisper.

"I feared I would hurt you," he admits, the corner of his eyes on the slur. "Luz, Nau had you for two weeks. What exactly did he do during that time frame?"

I clear my throat and look at my raw wrists, at my arm. I close my eyes, and the memory of Johann cutting me open replays in my mind in a matter of seconds.

The carving of the slur.

The decaying body in my cell.

The knives aimed at me for target practice.

The crawlspace with the rat.

The noose rubbing on my skin.

The infernal darkness that consumed me.

"It doesn't matter what he did. What's done is done," I say.

Héctor stands, his back facing me. His shoulders tense, and he rubs his temples, sighing. I go up to him, putting my hand on his shoulder, but he walks away from me, toward a burlap sack. He removes a few things from it, approaching me.

"This is from The Seer. She prepared it for you," he mentions, and hands me a package wrapped in parchment. He then grabs a leather bag. "There is some food in there. I assume Johann has not fed you. Please, eat, drink, and rest."

"Thank you," I say. A soft knock on his door and in comes Lydia with a fresh bruise and cut on her freckled, tanned face.

"Had to see for myself," she says, her body sweat glistening with the sunlight. "Ye look feverish, princess."

"Lydia!" I exclaim and jump on her, hugging her so hard I'm afraid of taking the air out of her. "I'm so sorry. About everything. Have you seen James?"

She releases me, putting her hands on my shoulders. "He's still asleep, Luz. He's safe, I assure ye." She clicks her tongue, nodding at Héctor. "I know I told ye to come to the gathering, but some of the crew is out for yer head so I suggest ye stay away. I'll update ye after."

He nods. "Yes, Captain."

Captain? "Wait. With Sullivan's death, the role wentent to Pedro. Is he okay?" I ask.

"He refused the position, so it passed on to me," she states, shrugging. "Villanueva. Please let Luz change so she can join the gathering."

"I will not leave her."

"Héctor. I'll be fine. I promise."

He walks over to me, his hands on my face. "I cannot bear to leave you by yourself once more."

"No one will hurt me here."

Héctor sighs, releasing me. "Fine, I shall go. Only because I respect you both." He takes one last look at me, hesitating, before walking out of the room.

"I'll stand at the door, aye? Five minutes."

I'm left by myself.

I slump on Héctor's bed, an overbearing feeling of loneliness overcoming my body. I open the package wrapped in parchment. A tear comes to my eyes. Clean and crisp fabrics. I caress the clothes Octavia has gifted me, thankful for the opportunity to forget these haunting memories.

Placing the outfit next to me, I undress and finish the job Héctor began with the rags. Cleaning my body of all the blood stuck to my skin. I'm thankful that my period has ended. I no longer have to be as uncomfortable.

While the concoction given to me by Octavia healed my injuries, my body is sore and my muscles have become rigid. My movements are slow, cleaning as much as I can without help. My waist has diminished, and the plushness I loved so much from my body has decreased. I still would be plus-sized in the future, but malnutrition has made me more socially acceptable.

I dress myself in the outfit I've been given. A gray poet blouse, black pants, undergarments, and a brown vest. I place Héctor's ring on my index finger, grateful it survived everything I experienced, just like I did. I detangle my damp hair with my fingers, some matting and knots unable to be loosened. It'll need to be cut. I grab the twine and tie my hair back in a low ponytail at the nape of my neck.

I glimpse the hammock where James sleeps. Memories of him fill my head, bringing tears to my eyes. His screams as he mourned Sullivan. His weeping, him begging us to kill him.

The tears come and I can't stop them. There are too many emotions rushing out of my body at once, racing to escape. Frustration, fear, loneliness, guilt.

Especially guilt.

Sullivan Edwards. My hero.

Beheaded thanks to me.

A brief knock brings me to my senses, and I wipe away my tears. Erasing all proof of emotions from my face. I don't want them to see Johann hurt and destroyed me beyond recognition.

Lydia comes in again, holding a pair of black leather boots in her pale hands.

"I figured we can't have ye barefoot on deck, so I bought ye these," she says. "When ye were on board, before ye know, *Nau*, James figured out ye and Héctor were around the same foot length. So, I stole one of Héctor's boots to measure with and bought ye a new pair."

I take them and put them on. The leather is cool and soft on my skin. The size is nearly exact to mine, just a tad bigger. They almost reach my knees, so I fold the pant legs and shove them inside. Standing up straight, the boots easily give me an inch of height.

"Thank you," I say.

"Come."

I nod, throwing the second satchel across my body and follow her. She leads me to below decks, where the pirates sleep. The entire lower area has transformed. The hammocks are put away, the round wooden table typically used for gambling and dice games dragged to the center of the space. Since the crew is no bigger than thirty people, we all can fit comfortably.

"Captain on deck, lads," Art proclaims, wearing a makeshift gauze sling on his left arm. Lydia's emerald eye goes dark, her shoulders tense.

Everyone gazes at me. A few of the men are injured, while most got away unscathed. Some men stand from their seats, their heads held high. Next to Art sits Octavia. Her hair is down, the bandana tied around her wrist.

"Come, Luz, sit," Octavia says, patting the chair next to hers. I force my legs to guide me to her.

I catch Pedro's deadly stare. He's leaning against a wall, his pistol in his hand and grenades hanging from his belt. His beige shirt, black vest, and black pants are stained with blood. His black curls are plastered to his forehead underneath his hat. He's received a few scratches and hits, but he looks like he could murder everyone in this room if given the chance.

"Let us begin, shall we?" Octavia informs. "Captain?"

Lydia clears her throat and stands straighter. "So we know of our casualties. Captain Sullivan was murdered by The Ringleader. Tim Lewis, Nicholas Raak, and Juan Dominguez perished in the town square. Our captured consist of Casiguaya, Lucas Córdova, Cyrus Khan, and Bob Jackson."

I wince. Four dead, four captured.

"Anything that can be done, Seer?" Art interjects, and all attention turns to Octavia.

"For now? No. But what is done will be undone. Not much can be shared, my dear Art. Patience," Octavia simply responds.

"And what of Villanueva, Captain?" Pedro interrupts, his demeanor of someone who wants blood. And I don't blame him. Lucas, a traitor to Nau, was captured as well. "Because of him, Edwards died. The leader of our cause, *gone.* His son? Who knows how he's managing. My son? *Captured.*"

The crew nods and murmurs in agreement. This is why Lydia warned him not to come. Pedro's out for his blood.

"Héctor Villanueva is not to blame," Octavia raises her voice. "We cannot control all the variables. This was Seen."

"Seen or not, crew members died and Nau still lives! Yes, we saved the lass, but at what cost?" Pedro raises his voice too, challenging her. He throws his hat to the side, his hair disheveled.

"Everything has a price."

"The price was predetermined, yet increased by his recklessness. He shall be punished!"

Octavia stands, slamming her fists on the table. "For he who is without sin, cast the first stone! Then and only then can he be punished, Pedro Córdova!"

Pedro slams his own fists at the table, pointing his pistol at Octavia afterward. Arguments erupt between the ones in favor of punishment and the ones against. Only Lydia, Art, and I stay quiet, watching everything. Octavia stands tall, simply glaring at Pedro as he yells at her in Spanish. She yells back, refusing to be disrespected.

Lydia stands, mumbling under her breath. Her shoulders are tense, and her six--foot figure seethes with the authority Sullivan once had on him. She moves quickly, taking out a knife from her belt and stabbing the middle of the table with it. This quiets everyone down, except Pedro. He turns to her, his nostrils flaring, the tip of his ears red.

"Héctor is the least of our worries. We must plan our second strike before Nau can plan his," Lydia states. "He was appointed second mate, and now he shall be my first mate. If ye wanted to punish him, ye should've taken this godforsaken role as captain instead! No punishment shall be carried out while I'm in charge!"

"Ye are too soft on him, as was Sullivan. Sullivan, at least, saw his bluff and reprimanded him. Ye, however, see him as a brother. Feelings and emotions are getting in the way of yer duty!" Pedro screams at her.

"Do *not* tell me how to do my job!"

"Then fuckin' do it correctly!"

For the first time since I've met her, she looks at him shocked, *pained*. This is her crew mate. Someone she *trusted*. Betrayal hangs in the air. Anger rises in my body.

Before Lydia can say anything to Pedro, I march to him and punch his nose. He stumbles backward. A few of the crew members gasp and Lydia stands there, stunned.

He holds his bloody nose, his eyes full of rage. "What the fuck!" he screams at me, spit getting in my face. "Ungrateful little shit!"

"We have a common enemy here, and that's Nau. We should spend our energy trying to bring him down, not on bringing each other down!" I yell.

"My dear Córdova," Octavia interjects, chuckling. He glares at her. "I suggest you listen to us. Never one to listen, always one to act. Beware the depths, the beast down below. That will be your end."

With that, Octavia smirks and walks away from this chaotic congregation, pretty satisfied with the confusion Pedro has on his face. I give him one last death glare before returning to my seat. Art's mouth turns slightly upward in one corner and he winks at me.

Pedro retreats to his place, wiping the blood away from his nose. Lydia glares at the crew, daring them to put one finger out of place.

"We'll take this day to rest and recover," Lydia orders. "Quartermaster, I relieve ye of yer post." Pedro protests, but she shuts him down immediately. "For today. Even though yer words drew blood, I've no intention of leaving ye without a job with Nau out for vengeance. Rest. We are all tired and have a burial rite before the sun sets. We shan't need a quartermaster today. Aye?"

"Aye," his voice is soft and resigned.

"I suggest we work together, quartermaster. Like Luz said, we have one common enemy, and that is Nau, savvy?"

"Aye, Captain."

"I release ye all from this gathering. I should like no confrontations today, crew." They all give their *aye's* and they all make to leave. "Narváez, I shall like to speak with ye. *Alone.*"

Everyone leaves, leaving me and the new captain of *The Fury* alone. She shifts in her seat, turning to me. Her shoulders relax as she releases a breath. She throws her hat on the table, rubbing her forehead.

"I can't guarantee Héctor's safety aboard this ship anymore. Half of the crew is furious at him, including the quartermaster. Stay away from both of them," she suggests. "Please plan to join us for our rituals later. Then we shall plan our strike." She places her hand on mine. "And I just want to say... thank ye for being there when *it* happened. The Ringmasters are sick people. I ain't know how James will react once he wakes."

Before I can open my mouth to speak, Art runs down the stairs.

"Captain!" Art yells out of breath. "It's James. He's attempting to shoot himself."

CHAPTER
FORTY-ONE

Lydia and I jump to our feet, following Art up the wooden stairs.

We're greeted by pandemonium on the deck.

Near the mast stands James, one pistol pressed against his lower jaw, another aimed at us in his other hand. He trembles as he scans his surroundings, yelling at everyone to stay back. He's choking on his sobs and no one dares enter his space in fear of him setting the trigger off. Front and center, closest to James, is Héctor, in a protective yet gentle stance. A lump rises in my throat, my stomach contracting. An intense energy surge grows within me, my heart rate increasing. The canvas flaps with the gusts of wind.

"D'atiao... give me the pistol," Héctor pleads.

"Stay back! Or I swear to God, I'll—" James shudders. "Just stay back!"

I approach him, my arms raised. James aims the pistol at me. "James..."

"Just take it from him!" an older pirate barks, rushing to him. James shoots the deck as a warning. I push the man back.

"Don't scream at him! You have no idea what he went through!" I turn to a shaking James, taking a deep breath. "James. You are loved. You are safe. I know it hurts, and that's okay. It's okay to feel that way." His bloodshot brown eyes land on mine. My heart breaks into a million little pieces. "Give me the pistol, please."

Héctor joins my side. "Losing a loved one hurts. You most likely feel like life itself has no purpose." He glances at me, but immediately his eyes go back to James. "I unders—"

"No!" James screams. "Ye ain't get to preach to me! This is *yer* fault! My father died 'cause of *ye*! Ye are *not* my brother! Stay away from me!"

Héctor's lips part slightly, his watery eyes widening in shock. A pained expression comes to his face and his breath staggers. He averts his gaze, lowering his defenses. A gentle rain falls over us. The crew watches the spectacle. Tears stream down James' face, the pistol still on his jaw.

I take a step closer. James watches me silently, but doesn't aim to hurt me. "James. Don't listen to them. Listen to me, okay? Can you do that?" I ask. He stays still. A minute of silence goes by. He nods. Relief washes over me. Nobody dares move a muscle. "I understand it feels overwhelming right now. I know you must be hurting and that your heart aches like you've been stabbed. But you're not alone. I'm right here with you, we all are."

He sobs, the pistol shaking in his hand. "I can't bear this pain anymore." Despair takes over him. "It hurts, Red. It really does."

Take a deep breath. Move two steps forward. "I'm here to listen to you. Your pain doesn't define you. You're stronger than you think, James. Yes, I know it feels like you're lost and have no purpose. Believe me, I know. I've gone through this."

Three more steps. "But there's always hope, even in the darkest moments." I stand in front of him. A mere six inches away from being able to take the weapon. "It's okay to mourn and cry. It's *okay.*"

James falls to his knees, weeping. I take both pistols away from him, handing them to Héctor. In a panic, Héctor shucks them overboard, never to be seen again. James reaches out to me, embracing me. I close my eyes, humming my grandmother's lullaby to him as I rock him on the deck. My body softens as I caress James' head. Tears stroll down my cheeks, rain falling over us in a gentle curtain.

"Let's get you out of those dirty clothes, okay?" I whisper, and he nods.

I help him stand, his knees shaking. Héctor takes a few steps forward, stretching his arms to James. Anguish is all I can see in his eyes.

"D'atiao…" Héctor trembles, his breathing shallow. They stare at each other.

James sobs hard again, and he runs, his arms outstretched. But he doesn't run to his brother for comfort. He sprints to *Pedro*, clinging to his clothes and body. Pedro tenses up, not knowing how to react to this sudden act of affection. James' knees give out, so the quartermaster holds him up, embracing the child back. Murmurs erupt around the deck. Pedro whispers things to James, rubbing his shoulders. He speaks tenderly and his gaze softens for the first time since I've met him.

No one expected James to run to Pedro Córdova.

"Back to yer stations!" Lydia commands and the crew disperses. Pedro stands James up, leading him down to the lower deck area, possibly to his quarters.

Héctor tries his hardest not to break down right there. He pushes his black hair back, clenching his hands into fists. His eyes are unfocused, roaming the crowd. His lips quiver and the rain makes it difficult to see if he's crying. Suddenly, he runs off. Climbing the ladder toward the crow's nest. I follow, but Octavia stands in my way with a hedgehog in her hand.

"No. Give him space," she cautions.

"What if he jumps, Octavia?" I ask, looking up at Héctor. He slumps on the floor, his face in his hands.

"He won't. He simply needs to be alone right now. James blamed him publicly for the Captain's death and told him they weren't brothers. He needs time to process everything. He'll be ready later."

I purse my lips together and release a breath. "When is 'later?'"

"After the parting ritual. For now, focus on you, okay?" She grabs my hand. "Gather your strength. Recover. Mourn. What is to come will not be easy."

A bell rings, signifying the time for the rituals has come. I've eaten, napped and hydrated myself, my mind and soul numb. Octavia has distracted herself by shuffling a deck of cards until the parting ceremony came, not saying a word to anyone. Lydia and Pedro felt it would be reasonable for the pirates to say goodbye to the four who perished in this battle, to help James. Octavia leads me out of Sullivan's room, refusing to let me touch anything.

The sun has begun its descent on the horizon, the soft hues of pink, orange, and gold spreading across the sky. An ethereal glow is cast on the water surface, turning the sea into a shimmering expanse of liquid gold. The waves gently lap against the side of the ship, creating a soothing soundtrack.

The crew slowly congregates on the deck, facing the setting sun. Four bundles lay on the wooden floor, all carefully wrapped and tied. Typically, the deceased pirate's body would be prepared and placed on a small wooden plank, both of which would be tilted and slid off into the depths of the sea, ensuring the individual would find eternal rest in the ocean they once called home. However, with the four bodies unable to be recovered, the bundles were created as a symbolic body that can be buried at sea.

Most of the pirates have a vacant look in their eyes. James hangs off to the side with an immobilized Pedro next to him. James grips one of Sullivan's pirate hats in his trembling fingers, his breathing shallow. Lydia stands behind the bundles, her hands clasped in front of her. Her skin looks paler under the setting sun. My shoulders slump as I near Octavia, my body lethargic.

I glance up at the crow's nest, a blank-faced Héctor descending the stairs. He scans the crowd and trudges to my side, his eyes red and puffy. His skin is flushed, his appearance disheveled. He says nothing to me, instead focusing on the horizon.

"Crew of *The Fury*," Lydia begins, her tone strong. "We gather here today to mourn the lives of four pirates who fought for a cause greater than them. Captain Sullivan Edwards, co-founder of the Marauders. Tim Lewis, a fantastic sleight of hand. Nicholas Raak, the one whose stories never ceased to amaze us. And Juan Dominguez, a lad ready to take on the world, leaving behind a daughter." Lydia removes her hat, taking a deep breath. She nods, Octavia approaches. "These men are part of our crew. Our family. They fought with honor. 'Til their last breath. Murdered by the hands of those we hate."

Four people died. Because they risked their lives to intercept my hanging. Lydia continues talking, my eyes and ears unfocus as Sullivan's death replays in my mind. James, injured and defenseless. Me, hurt and unable to protect him.

Sullivan, sacrificing himself to ensure his son lived. Tears form in my eyes. *I* did this.

Just like I caused the death of the man in the town square.

I remember how his soul drained from his cold eyes. How his skin went from a beige to a slight gray. The warmth of his splattered blood all over resurfaces, the smell of iron taking over my sinuses. Whenever I murdered someone on the set, the fake blood would be cold, a sugary scent arising from it. The word *cut* would be yelled, and the person would get up, alive and well. With everything happening, a small part of me waits to hear the word again, so that the scene can be reset.

But I'm not on the set anymore. That was a lifetime away.

"Before we send them we send them to the sea, will anyone like to share a few words?" Octavia asks, a small orb of white light glowing in her delicate fingers. "I, for one, am terribly sorry for everything. Their deaths were anything but in vain. They died for a greater cause, a greater purpose. Their legacy lives on, with us."

Aye's from the crew. I cross my arms, a small spark igniting in me. Sullivan's death was anything but fair. His destiny was altered, taken from him. I take a slow, forced breath. He didn't deserve to die. None of them did. The others didn't deserve to be captured. No one from *The Fury* deserves the pain they're experiencing. Especially James.

"May I speak?" James asks sheepishly. Octavia nods, gesturing for him to join her. He walks to her, hesitant. "I just want to say they'll be missed." He kneels by the bundle that belongs to Sullivan, the hat still in his hands. "Father. I'm sorry I did this to ye. I know I made yer life hell.. I know I was a menace, but I truly loved ye. Ye became my father and I'll be forever grateful for that."

James glances at Héctor, shaking his head. Héctor softens his gaze, yearning to embrace James. To comfort him. Instead, James' eyes darken, looking away. Héctor takes a deep breath, hugging himself. Reassuringly, I place my hand on Héctor's shoulder.

"From the day Héctor brought me onto this ship, ye took me in like yer own son," James continues. "I finally had the family I always wanted. All thanks to ye. Thank ye for giving that ten-year-old boy a chance to prove himself."

A tear falls down my cheek, my heart tugging at his words. I want nothing more than to bring Sullivan back to his child. To his baby. But Sullivan's gone, and he's never coming back. Pain shoots from my chest, followed by a sense of emptiness.

Avenge him... a little voice in the back of my head says.

Next to Octavia stands a cloaked figure facing me, its golden staff twinkling under the watery sunlight. It's *him*. The ominous man from my dreams. No one else sees him. Just me. I tense up, removing my hand from Héctor's shoulder. The man points his staff at me, then at the four bundles laying upon the wooden deck, as if to say, *you did this.*

I blink rapidly, and he's no longer there.

"I shall like to say a few words about the Captain," Héctor says, as James retreats to Pedro. The quartermaster puts his arm around the child, rubbing his shoulder reassuringly. "I know at the moment I may not be liked, but I want to say this. It is rare to find someone who commands such immense respect from all who cross their path. Sullivan Edwards possessed a spirit that radiated wisdom and compassion, leaving an indelible mark on the lives he touched. He was a beacon of light in this darkness-filled world. He illuminated the way for me, for my brother. For many others. I know his impact will be felt for generations to come. Like The Seer said, *his legacy will carry on.* With us. With what we do. His death was not in vain." He glances at James. Aye's from the crew. James looks at the ground, trying his hardest not to cry. "And I am truly sorry for all the pain I caused. Especially to you, James."

I stand there, surrounded by mourners, the weight of grief pressing down on my chest, constricting my every breath. The air hangs heavy with sorrow and regret. Héctor and James' beautiful yet heart-wrenching words have brought waves of anguish over every single one of us. It was like a dagger shattered my already broken heart.

As tears stream down my flushed cheeks, Octavia releases the glowing white orb that lays in her hands into the sky. Once it reaches a few feet, it divides into four, all of them slowly floating up into the heavens. The pirates watch mesmerized as they ascend, dancing around each other.

"May those lights symbolize their souls reaching their resting place. Now, the four pass to the hands of The Collector," Octavia explains. "Now, they become a part of the balance that should be kept in the world. May they rest in peace, sailing the seas forever."

My breath catches. Did she make them? Is that her power?

Octavia reaches over to James, kissing his forehead. I hug Héctor, and he relaxes in my embrace, his breathing shallow and strong.

Lydia and Pedro, as the two highest of rank, approach the bundles, sending each into the depths of the sea with care. With Sullivan's body, they both hesitate, but ultimately, it's thrown overboard as well, James clinging to Octavia. She grabs the Captain's hat, placing it atop his head. They both smile weakly, sorrow in their eyes.

Pain weighs me down like an anchor in turbulent waters. It wraps its icy fingers around my core, threatening to break me. As I find comfort in the man I once could not stand, energy simmers within me, slowly engulfing my mind with unsettling thoughts. The pain inside me transforms into something else, something sinister. How could life be as cruel as to snatch away those who fought for good?

Every generation has great people, amazing advocates… and they're all snatched from us, while those who are vile still stand, spewing their hate. Erasing our heritage, our culture, our voices, our history. They deny us, antagonize us, eliminate us. It's a never-ending story. Over and over. Until the end of time.

Anger bubbles in me like a dormant volcano, simmering beneath my surface. Suddenly, I crave revenge. I need it. I need the enemy's blood on my hands. Thunder roars in the calm sky, the gale stirring all around us. Adrenaline races through my body. I release Héctor just as the crew disperses.

"Wait!" I exclaim, standing in the middle of everything. "I want to say something, too."

The crew stops walking, curiosity flashing in their expressions. The need for revenge consumes my every thought, weaving a dangerous web of darkness around my very shattered heart. I yearn for retribution, to inflict upon others the pain I was forced to endure at their hands.

"I didn't know Nicholas, Tim, and Juan, but their deaths will not be in vain. They will come back in the next life, stronger than before," I say, twisting the ring on my finger. "I did know Sullivan. In my time, in the *future*, he was my hero. I admired him and what he stood for. Which means you're all right. His legacy *will* live on. It'll continue for centuries to come. What he built, it won't be for naught."

"If yer from the future, why couldn't ye see this coming?" a man asks, and a couple of men agree. I scan the crew, their expressions ranging from confusion, to anger, to astonishment.

I take a deep breath, a vengeful fire fueled by the memories of my torture.

"I didn't, because we rewrote history... *I* rewrote history." I look at the floor. "Now, nothing is set in stone. We have no control over who lives or dies. Everything I knew is changing. History has its eyes on us." I glance at Héctor, and he nods, urging me to keep going. "I was there when Sullivan died, as was James and Octavia. Sullivan died defending who he loves most. His son. His son will carry his legacy. *We* will carry it down."

Aye's. Nods.

"But not Nau's. His legacy of hatred, oppression, and violence will cease soon. I will stop it. In my time, men like him exist, hunting us, killing us, claiming themselves our God. Mark my words, Johann will stop at nothing until our blood is on his hands."

Lightning lights the sky, the rain turning to a storm. Power courses through my veins once more, just like it did on the cell. I find solace in the idea of revenge, as twisted as it may be.

I raise my voice, "I know we're mourning, I know we lost one battle. But we have not won the war yet. Like the sirens that haunt the seas, I call to you. I implore you. It's time we stand together. This is a call for action. This is our time to show Johann that he nor anyone owns us! An evil is said to rise in these seas... let it be us! We are the fire on this sea. We are the coals that refuse to burn out. Our call is loud, that is why he hunts us!"

The ship sways, as agreements and cheers fill the air.

The need to have Johann's blood on my hands channels my anguish into a purpose, no matter how dark and destructive. Instead of letting go of the vengeful whispers that have taken hold of my soul, I relish in it. I close my eyes, letting the thunderous rain fall over my skin. When I open them again, I encounter motivated expressions amongst the crew.

Ravenous seas sways the ship. Rain lashes against the deck, lightning illuminated the dark skies. The crackling thunder roars like an angry Kraken amidst the ongrowing tempest. This. This is who I want to be. This is something I want to feel daily. This power. This... corruption. I want it.

"Let us mourn today and tomorrow. But we will no longer be hunted," I shout, fueled by the fires that courses through my body. "I call upon the chaos inside my veins. This is our destiny. Johann Nau will fall. We will rise. We will be the most ruthless evil the world has ever seen. And I swear to you all once more, their deaths will not be in vain. History has its eyes on us, so I say we give it a show! I vow to burn it all down. Every last ship. Every last man. Not a single plank of wood will be left standing."

CHAPTER
FORTY-TWO

Preparations for battle begin.

Lydia has called me, Octavia, James, and the remaining officers for a quick gathering up on the quarterdeck.

The cloudy day has been a blur. Thoughts of despair have turned to ravenous rage. I need his blood on my hands and I need it now. Especially since he has four of our people captured, and one of them is my grandmother.

"We know Nau won't risk venturing too close to Tortuga after risking himself the first time," Lydia says, throwing her navigational charts on a barrel. These are drawn by Héctor. I glance at him, and he looks away. We haven't spoken since before James' attempt. "He'll stay down here, trying to catch *The Fury* while he can."

"He has to know we're en route to Port-Salut," Pedro says, rubbing his hands together, itching to get revenge for his son. "While he's the devil incarnate, he's skilled so he must know we've barely entered Portland Point."

"Based on our location, one can assume he is a day behind us, which puts him around here," Héctor says, pointing at a spot on the map. James bites his nails, his murderous gaze upon his brother. "Wreck Bay. We can use the Cays to our advantage. It will also mean that we will meet halfway."

"'Tis too risky," Art jumps in. "Fishermen and watchmen work in these areas. They're innocent, and if they see us, they might call for reinforcements. We aren't ready to fight an entire armada."

"When have they cared about us?" I snap, crossing my arms. Art furrows his brows together, taken aback. The others stand there, not saying anything. "Those people don't care about us, and we surely shouldn't give two shits about them. Let's fight the fucking armada."

"Luisa Karina. What words are those?" Octavia asks.

I scoff, rolling my eyes. Anger roams through my veins, murderous thoughts bounce in my head. "Truthful words. In the world, there's two types of people. Those who are on the right side of history, making the change they want to see... and those who sit idly by watching from the sidelines, letting us burn... well, I say we do the same to them."

Her purple eyes land on my collarbone. "Take it off."

My eyes widen. "What?"

"Your necklace. Take it off." She places her palm in front of me, her pierced eyebrow raised. "Now."

I step back, studying her. Surely she can't be serious. When I make no sigsign to move, she reaches out and I slide away from her. "Oh, you're *serious*?"

Octavia nods, crossing her hands. "Remember what Ria said. Too much power and you'll be beyond recognition. You're letting it control you."

My body becomes rigid. My gaze sweeps over the group, a rising surge of anger within me. James has stopped biting his nails, staring at me pensively. I grip my necklace with my fingers, to prevent anyone from taking it.

"Good," is all I tell her.

So what if the power is controlling me? I like how it feels. It feels exhilarating. A flickering flame ignites in me, my jaw clenching as I scan the officers. Lydia, Pedro, and Art look at me in confusion, as if they've never seen a scorned woman. Héctor remains silent, his head slightly tilted, his eyes calculating.

I turn on my heel and stomp down the stairs.

❧❧❧

Arriving at the crow's nest, I slump down, bringing my knees to my chest. As my squinted eyes fixate on the cloudy horizon ahead of me. Fury courses through my veins like a venomous poison, intoxicating my thoughts. Its intensity grips my heart and soul with an unrelenting grip.

Kill them all. Burn it all. Choose yourself...

Every fiber of my being resonates with this burning desire to bring death and chaos upon the seas. It consumes me, fueling a singular purpose that overshadows all reason and compassion that lies within my body.

I grab my necklace, inspecting it. It's glowing, the light pulsating slowly, the color like the blood I wish to spill upon the seas. The breeze blows my dark brown curls, whispers being carried through the wind. The longer I look at the glowing red ruby, the more my surroundings blur.

It's your destiny, Aycayia of Destruction... Become the queen of evil in the seas. Ravage everything in your path...

"Yes, I will..." I chuckle, caressing the jewel as Sullivan's head being disconnected from his body replays in my head. "I will make them regret everything."

More ethereal voices.

A sudden thud wakes me up.

My eyes slice to the side. It's Héctor.

I drop my necklace down to my neck, the murderous thoughts retreating.

"Hi," I say, hugging my knees.

He sits next to me. "Are you alright?"

"Never been better."

He raises his eyebrow, pursing his lips together. "You lie."

I groan, leaning against the mast. "Did you come here to preach to me? Because the ladder is right there, you can go down the same way you came."

Héctor studies me for the first time since being together in his bedroom. And I don't mean a glance. I mean, he truly *looks* at me. His eyes are swollen and bloodshot, as if he had been crying a few hours before our meeting. The wind blows his hair around, tangling it.

He shakes his head, scooting closer to me. I don't move, instead I want him to move even closer. "I came because I am worried for you. What you experienced... It could not have been easy," Héctor says. "If you ever need someone to talk to. I am here."

All the anger I had dissipates, replaced by a refreshing sense of calm. I fidget with my hands, noticing his ring. Carefully, I slip it off my finger, giving it back to him.

"Thank you for this," I admit. "It kept me sane during my days of torment."

Héctor grabs my hand, closing my palm, the ring remaining in my hand. "No. If it brought you comfort, you should keep it, d'nanichi."

I shake my head, forcing it back to him. "No. It belongs to you. You've had it for fifteen years. It has helped you cope. It was more than enough for me. It's time it returns to its owner."

He refuses it. "Keep it for now. Please?" Defeated, I nod, putting it back on my finger. "At least you do not hate me like James does."

I shrug. "No, but I am rather mad at you. An East India Company worker?"

He chuckles sheepishly. "I do not want to talk about it."

"No, no. Tell me."

"I do not think it would be wise for your mental state."

A bit of anger rises. "Not wise? I did not get tortured for 'not wise.' I did not watch Sullivan get fucking beheaded in front of me for 'not wise.'" Tears come to my eyes. "I didn't watch my grandmother get shot and captured for 'not wise!'" Here comes the waterworks. I don't need this right now. "They both risked their lives because of me! You don't get to tell me what's 'not wise!'"

I cry, both out of anger and despair, and Héctor pulls me closer to him, putting his arm around me. I embrace him back, letting everything out. He presses me to him, his body smelling of gunpowder and faint lavender.

"I did this, Héctor," I claim in between sobs. "Maybe I am truly the Aycayia of Destruction, with all the pain I've brought the crew."

"You have not brought me neither pain nor misery. Headaches perhaps, but never pain," he reassures. "Actually, yes, you brought me pain." I look up at him, tears in my eyes. He smiles, his own eyes watery. His hand goes to my cheek. "You brought me pain when I did not know if you were alive or dead. That was the worst pain I have ever felt. I yearned to be in your place every night, every minute. You became my only thought, d'nanichi."

I sit up abruptly, looking at him with my mouth wide open. This can't be the same man who told me he would have no problem throwing me overboard. The man who was only after my necklace.

He dries my tears with his thumbs, kissing my hands afterward. This is the rawest I've ever been with a person. Not even Oliver himself has seen me like this. I've had lows with him, but never like this.

"I knew I was a pain in the ass, but not to that extent," I say, smiling. More tears trail down my cheeks.

He chuckles, holding my face in his hands. "Why must you hide your misery behind laughter? You can be yourself with me."

I don't remember the last time I was myself. My *true* self.

"Is what Nau did so horrible that it makes you want to refuse my help?"

I look away, unable to answer that question. But my silence is enough for him.

"I wish I could take that pain away. Those untold horrors."

Looking at the horizon, a new emotion in me rises. It's not anger, sadness, or fear. It's peace. My heart doesn't flutter. Doesn't race. It stays calm, like the current beneath us. That is more powerful than the anger I felt earlier.

"May I ask something?" he asks.

"Sure, ask away. Just nothing related to, you know," I admit.

"You mentioned you were from the future. That first night... is that where you had arrived from?"

"Yes. I confused Johann with my ex-boyfriend, Oliver, and everything began."

His eyebrow raises. "The man from the witchcraft box. The one you believed paid us? I recall you mentioning his name."

I chuckle. "Héctor, that was a phone. It's not witchcraft."

"I beg your pardon, but it made noise and held souls. I do not know what the future holds, but it seems like you all have mastered demonic works."

"I didn't have anyone's soul in there. Just pictures."

"Ah." He smiles, unsure. "I do not know what that is, either."

As we speak, Héctor is convinced the future is composed of witchcraft and dark magic. The longer the conversation goes, the more he lets his guard down. While he's curious and genuinely interested, anything he can't comprehend, he calls it the work of demons.

"You know, you're left-handed, and in some cultures that's a sign of witchcraft, so technically, you're calling yourself *demonic*," I snicker.

He chuckles nervously, looking at his left hand. "Perhaps it is *not* all witchcraft..."

I laugh, looking at the horizon. "Hey, Héctor?"

"Yes, Luz?"

I turn to him. "Thank you."

He watches me with his eyebrows raised. "What for?"

"For not throwing me overboard." He laughs and I roll my eyes. "No, but for not giving up on me. You didn't have to do that. I know I can be a handful."

He smiles, putting his hand on the crevice between my shoulder and neck, pulling me closer to him. "Not to me." He looks at my lips, then at my eyes. "You are a light, Luz. A star, like your other name. Karina. You shine so brightly in this never-ending darkness. So bright, no one dares enter your proximity. I want nothing more than to stay at your side, only if you allow me to do so."

I look at his lips, my breath catching. He does the same. Do I want this? *Him*? Is this a genuine feeling? Or am I yearning for a sense of home and stability? For someone to take Oliver's place?

I lean in. He does too.

His warmth is so close. So near.

The ship rocks violently, startling us. I clear my throat. A bell rings from under us, followed by loud chatter and commands.

"What's going on?" I ask.

"I do not know," he replies, taking out his knife. "I should go investigate. You stay here; I do not want you getting injured."

"No. Don't you dare leave."

Octavia appears, pushing everyone out of the way. My heart beats quickly as she throws the rope ladder down to the ocean, disregarding Art's safety concerns. She urges everyone to step back.

"I'm going to need help!" Octavia yells, tying her hair back. Lydia barks a command at a few men, and they scramble to aid Octavia. Sudden silence. Only the wind blows through the stillness of the day.

A frail, wet woman climbs up over the rail, collapsing on the deck. A pool of blood underneath her.

CHAPTER
FORTY-THREE

"Luz, get down here now!" Octavia yells.

I'm already halfway down the futtock shrouds, my heart racing inside my chest. Héctor follows, silent. The crew gathers around the fainted woman who is now in Octavia's arms. A second woman climbs over the rail, coughing viciously, her onyx hair clinging to her face and skin.

I reach Octavia, who's holding an unconscious and bloody Mami Julia in her arms. Heaving on the deck next to her is Ria, her entire body trembling. This time, she's got legs, thick, strong, and bronze. She's covered by a beige tunic that hugs her curvy figure. James approaches her with a waterskin, and she takes it, sucking everything out of it.

I push everyone aside with force, my eyes never leaving Mami Julia's collapsed body. She's faintly breathing, her long salt-and-pepper hair tangled and stuck to her skin. I gasp at the blood on her tunic, not knowing if it's hers.

Her blue necklace is gone.

"What happened?" I ask, frantic.

"She escaped," Ria explains, taking deep breaths. "She was near death when I found her. She needs help."

"Octavia. That potion thing. Give it to her," I demand.

"Captain. It's in your room. Fetch me the vial with the elixir," Octavia orders.

Lydia runs off, and I sit on my knees, taking Mami Julia from Octavia's arms. My grandmother's face is flushed, pale compared to her usual bronze skin tone. Her lips are parted and cracked, blood dripping from them.

"Mami?" I ask, trembling. I clutch her limp, unconscious body in my shaking hands. My vision blurs from the tears, and my heart pounds wildly in my chest, its erratic beats echoing the turmoil within me. "Mami." I shake her gently. "You can't leave me! Please, not again."

Trembling, I struggle to hold her weight as relentless waves crash against the boat, mirroring the storm within. My fingers tighten their grip on her, desperate to bring life back to her fragile form.

The air is heavy with the scent of salt and moisture; the atmosphere charged with electricity.

Lydia reappears with Octavia's bag. "I couldn't find the vial. Ye have a thousand tiny bottles in my quarters."

Octavia pulls a green glass vial from the satchel. The crew murmurs around us. Pedro appears, assisting Ria with a gentle smile. She grimaces and pushes him away, earning a chuckle from James.

Octavia kneels before us, murmuring in Creole. She opens a vial, holding it to Mami Julia's nose, its strong citrus, herb, and cinnamon scent wafting in. My tears mingle with the droplets of rain that fall relentlessly from the sky.

"Damn. Damn!" Octavia yells, putting the vial away.

She closes her eyes and her fingertips glow. She chants a few words in Creole, placing her palm on my grandmother's chest. I watch, paralyzed, my breathing labored as my grandmother's life hangs on a thread. Is this Octavia's power? She said her power came from the light. Is she healing Mami Julia?

Mami Julia shudders, her eyes still shut. Octavia opens hers, removing her hand.

"Wait. What happened?" I ask, thunder booming overhead, echoing the torment within me.

"She needs rest. She'll live," Octavia reassures.

"That man did this. The *blond* one," Ria hisses.

"Johann did this?" I ask, wrath writhing in my body. Ria nods. The water beneath me responds, rippling and churning in response to my inner turmoil.

"Luz?" Héctor asks.

"Casiguaya needs rest. I've done all I could. Now we wait for her to wake," Octavia says, her voice fading as my cloud of vengeance rises.

"Use my quarters," Lydia says, her voice a mile away too. Johann *will* pay for this.

A sudden touch brings me out of my stupor, startling me.

"Give her to me," Héctor says, gently.

He picks Mami Julia up, carrying her toward Lydia's room. The rest of the crew dissipates, giving us privacy. Octavia asks Ria if she needs aid, but Ria brushes her off, declining anything.

"Where is her necklace?" I ask, standing.

"The blond one stole it," Ria explains. "Just like he stole everything that belongs to us."

"Are there any plans to take it back?"

"He increased his defenses. Last I saw, he was exiting Port Royal. No one can approach him without being shot on sight by his new officers." She exhales loudly. "We can try getting close, but our people are in mourning for our losses."

My mind races with a torrent of thoughts, none of them coherent. Fury gnaws at me, tearing away at any semblance of composure I once possessed.

"No, that's fine," I say, forcing myself to look as unaffected as possible. "You go recuperate. What do you know of the captured?"

Pedro stands at my side at the mention of them. *Lucas.* Lucas is one of them.

Ria blows air through her pursed lips, crossing her arms. "In retaliation, he killed the white one. I think the drunk one and the younger one remain. But not for long."

Pedro presses his fist against the wooden rail. "Fuck him and his entire fucking bloodline!" he yells, turning to me. "Ye better destroy him! Yer the siren of ruin, coño! *Ruin* him!" He stomps off, cursing in Spanish.

I walk away, but I'm pulled into place. Ria. She studies me, my necklace. Her hair is disheveled, her pointy ears sticking out between the wet strands.

"It has begun," she whispers. She releases me, her breath shivering. "You are being corrupted."

"So?" I ask, rubbing my arm. "It feels good, Ria. You, of all people, should understand."

"Too much power—"

"First, you all wanted me to have a lot of power and defeat Johann against my will. Now, I have unmeasurable power, and you all want me to rein it in."

"Listen to her, Luz," Octavia warns. "We don't want anyone you love to get hurt." She places her hand in front of me, raising her eyebrow. "Give me the necklace, please."

"They won't. If you're all afraid I'll turn into Nau, don't worry..." I adjust my vest, watching a silent James out of the corner of my eyes. My screams as Johann cuts into me bounce around in my mind. James' sobs as he gripped his father's headless body will haunt me forevermore. "... I'll be worse." I throw her the necklace, marching away.

Arriving at the crow's nest, I slump, bringing my knees to my chest. The moon is high in the sky, basking us in its beautiful, gentle light. On the deck, Octavia approaches James, her hand on his shoulder. He nods, hugging her. She caresses his cheek and turns on her heel, placing my necklace into her pocket as she walks away.

As soon as I gave her the jewel, all the anger I had evaporated away. I watch as Ria sits on a barrel, Pedro next to her, trying to seduce her. She flips her long hair in his face and marches off to the officer's quarters. Héctor stands at the helm with a compass on his hand.

I sigh, looking up at the bright, shining stars as I twist Héctor's ring around my finger. It's been so long since I've seen the stars. In the future, I never sat down and looked at the sky or slowed down to enjoy life. Always go, go, go. Not once did I take a chance to breathe. Now, while I know I have to kill Johann and the need for revenge is the only thing driving me, I actually feel rather calm.

Maybe I can build a life here if I kill Johann.

Not in Port Royal, but in the past. Maybe live in a secluded swamp like Octavia does, where I'm not provoked. I could go to Puerto Rico and live in the center of the island. Jayuya, Lares, Barranquitas, Cayey. Areas untouched by the Spanish, Portuguese, and English. Areas where escapees and survivors of colonization have thrived.

It would mean being away from the sea, though.

And I want to be near the sea or even on it.

I no longer see myself on land.

I want to feel the wind on my skin and hair. I want the water to take me to worlds unknown. I want to see the various horizons the world offers. I want to live my life under the elements. I wouldn't have it any other way.

I close my eyes, sighing, but the memory of what Johann did to me replays in vivid detail. Every sensation, every sound is resurrected, as if time has folded back upon itself. My heartbeat quickens, the air feels thick and suffocating, squeezing the breath from my lungs.

Everything comes back in a matter of seconds.

I knew I shouldn't have given my necklace to Octavia earlier. I don't like how I feel without it. I miss the anger.

I climb down the ladder, my breathing labored. I take out the new daggers Lydia gifted me and toss them into the wooden walls, channeling my anger and frustration into the blades.

My mind goes to Sullivan. Beheaded in front of his son.

For the first time in my life, I let my emotions take over. I let them guide me.

I choose myself. I choose to fight.

I choose to eliminate that son of a bitch who reduced me to nothing.

He will die. And I will rise.

A knife isn't enough for what I'm feeling. I need something bigger, more lethal. I grab a cutlass from a stack where the spare weapons are kept.

This is where you will stay. I hit an empty barrel.

One fucker down, three more to go. Its hinges loosen.

The blond one did this. I scream.

We're the same, you and I. We're both monsters. I must destroy this barrel in the way Johann will be.

I scream as I break it down with the cutlass, tears escaping my eyes. My whole body shakes as I picture Johann with his devilish grin, etching my skin with the slur. He did this to me. Ruined me beyond repair. Fucked me up so I can't even close my eyes for five seconds or be alone with my thoughts.

"D'nanichi, what are you doing!" Héctor screams, his voice far.

I ignore him, breaking it down until it disintegrates. I have to make it disappear. I have to hurt Johann like he hurt me.

The cutlass slips from my hands, slicing my palm. The area stings and I drop the weapon on the deck, falling to my knees. The word *halfbreed* mocks me. Screams of anguish escape my body. He did this.

"I am here," Héctor says, kneeling in front of me. He pushes the cutlass away and holds my bleeding hand. "Breathe. He cannot hurt you. It is okay."

"Johann..." I sob, my body trembling. He embraces me, rubbing my shoulders.

"He cannot hurt you here. You are safe here. I will protect you."

"I'm not safe here. I'm not safe anywhere. I never will be."

"I assure you that as long as I may live, I will protect you from the likes of Nau. No one shall ever touch you again."

I cry some more in his arms, the horrors I experienced for the past week refusing to leave my mind. Footsteps approach as rain falls over us at once. I bury my face deeper into his shirt, not wanting to be seen. But it's pretty hard to miss the bloody sword, the pulverized barrel, and the bawling girl on the deck.

"What did ye do to her?" James shrieks. "Get yer hands off her!"

"James. You're not helping," Octavia warns.

"She is not a spectacle for either of your viewings," Héctor hisses. "Send for Art. Have him take over my duties for the night. I do not care if he is tired. He is to do what I say."

Someone runs off. Héctor releases the embrace he has me in, standing me up. My knees buckle, but he holds me steady. The rain pierces our skin. Octavia watches us, her hedgehog in her hands.

"I'm here," Art exclaims, out of breath. He glances at me, James standing next to him, clutching his chest. "Are ye–"

"You *will* take over tonight, Bartholomew. You are first mate for the night," Héctor snarls. "Do not bother us, do not send for me. She is my top priority and no one will impede on that."

He leads me away from the growing commotion. After entering his bedroom, he slams the door shut and locks it, separating us from the outside world.

Héctor approaches me with some gauze and a clean rag. Sitting next to me, he takes my bleeding left hand, softly wiping away the blood. I wipe my tears away with my other arm. His fingers are soft on my skin.

"What did Nau do to you?" he asks, not looking at me.

"It would be easier to ask what he didn't do, truthfully," I say.

"Luz…" He ties the gauze around my palm with care.

Shaking, I recount what Johann did to me. Every little detail. The rat in the crawlspace, the forced marriage, the decaying body in my cell. He listens, his fingers never leaving my hand. My voice breaks as I tell him about the carving of the slur into my skin, but I'm determined to tell him how I felt. How the laughter will never leave me.

Héctor never interrupts.

Instead, he stays quiet, guilt gnawing at his soul in his darkened eyes. While his body is tense and his breathing turns labored, his fingers stay gentle on mine, refusing his anger to even touch me.

When there is nothing more to tell and my heart is numb from all the tears, a sudden loss of energy overcomes me. As if retelling everything drained me.

"I am going to kill him," Héctor finally says.

"No. He's mine to deal with. You won't intervene," I say, wiping my face. "This is between me and him. One evil will fall. *Him.*" I stare into his eyes. "This is *my* destiny, Héctor... Not yours."

"Frankly, I do not care if it is your destiny. He hurt the woman I— he hurt you. He hurt James. He will not get away with it." He stands, outraged, blowing air out of his lips. "Fine, those men aboard *The Glory* will pay for contributing to your pain. *You* may be the one that kills Johann, but I will hunt the others. Every last one of them. Even if it takes me the rest of my days. I will find them and kill them all for what they did to you."

Héctor's words hang in the air, a fragile bridge between uncertainty and hope. Would he do that? Kill for me? I study him, wondering if he's lying to me, but realization washes over me like a gentle wave. As his brown eyes meet mine, a sense of wonder and gratitude fills me, making my heart flutter just a tad. His vow is one that ignites a flame of reassurance within me, dispelling any lingering fears of vulnerability, enveloping me in a warmth not even Oliver gave me before.

I clear my throat, breaking eye contact as my face grows hot. "Thank you for mending my hand," I whisper. "Perhaps you should go back—"

"I am not going anywhere. After what you told me, you are not getting rid of me that easily. I am staying right here, with you," he declares. "You need rest, d'nanichi."

"I don't know how I'll sleep. The darkness reminds me of him."

"Wo-would it be better if I sat near you? I want you to feel as safe as possible."

"Why not climb in with me?"

"You do not mind?"

"I prefer it, actually."

"Well, if at any moment you feel uncomfortable, please inform me."

With that, he climbs next to me. I scoot to the edge, and then we both lay down at the same time. Being so close to him, this is the first I've felt at ease while in the past. A real sense of home.

We look into each other's eyes, his gaze softening. He pushes some of my dark brown frizzy curls out of the way, leaving his hand on my freckled cheek.

"What are you thinking about?" I ask.

"I am thinking about many things. Murder, revenge. James," he confesses. "But my main thought is you. You are always on my mind. There is not a second of the day you are not in it."

I can feel my face going red. "I bet you say that to all the girls you have waiting for you on land, like Pedro does."

He brings my hand to his mouth, planting a soft kiss on it. "Contrary to popular belief, I have no one waiting for me on land." I laugh. "But fine. Let us say I tell that to every girl. Let us say there is someone I wish to court. The only woman I want is dealing with plenty. She does not need my burden, nor my past that haunts me. Whenever she is ready, I will show her the world. I will give her the life she deserves."

My eyelids grow heavy. "She's very lucky to have you. She'd be blind to not see that."

"No. I am very lucky to even be in her presence and be around her. I am the one who is lucky to have found someone I am willing to die for." He smiles. "Go to sleep, d'nanichi. I am right here, and I will never leave."

"Promise?"

"I promise. Sleep now."

I take a deep breath and let my exhaustion take over.

For the first time in a while, I feel safe.

Julia

CHAPTER
FORTY-FOUR

I open my eyes slowly, the haze of sleep dissipating as consciousness returns. I didn't have any nightmares.

This is the first night I've slept peacefully since Johann took me.

The soft morning light casts a gentle glow upon the room and it hits me. I'm still in Héctor's quarters. His arm is around my waist, his face burrowed into my neck. Even though I'm taller, my body aligns with his. When did we end up in this position?

Confusion washes over me. There's something about this moment I can't quite comprehend. I gaze at him, trying to decipher the emotions swirling within me. His gentle breathing lulls me into a sense of tranquility, comfort, and familiarity. I feel drawn to him, a magnetic pull that defies all reason and logic.

Why am I feeling like this when I never felt it for Oliver?

I try to sit up carefully so I don't wake him. I need to get back to Lydia's quarters to monitor my grandmother. I can't slip like this again. I can't be in his arms searching for safety. I must find my sense of safety until I fulfill this prophecy. That is my top priority at the moment.

Putting on my boots and standing, he rustles, but doesn't wake, instead mumbling and taking a deep breath. I sigh, relieved. I watch him in his peaceful form, his hair tousled and his face serene. I grab his vinegar rinse, an open journal next to the vial catching my curious eye.

I pick the notebook up, seeing how it's mostly filled with sketches and fancy penmanship. A few of James, a couple flores de maga from Puerto Rico, constellations, the tattoo on his neck, and an older woman. In all the drawings, her skin is wrinkled, her straight hair up in a bun. I recognize one word near her sketch. Bakutu. Grandmother. This must be her.

Knowing I've invaded his privacy, I place the journal back down, and the pages flip to a few sketches of another woman. Smiling, angry, pensive, snarky. I take a minute, but I realize it's *me*.

I blush as a tinge of self-consciousness washes over me. No one has *ever* drawn me before. My lips part with a shaky breath as I lower the notebook. My eyes land on him, then at the journal in my fingers. A smile creeps on my lips.

He *drew* me.

I quickly rinse my mouth and head to Lydia's quarters, where Mami Julia rests unconscious on the plush green bed.

A beige cotton blanket covers her bloody tunicA beige cotton blanket covers her bloody tunic. Her skin has regained some of its color, but it's still rather pale. I approach the bedside, sitting on my knees. Her loose hair is tangled and damp, so I untangle it with my fingers, just like she did to me when I was a child. When she fixed my hair, she'd sing in a language I couldn't recognize, but now I realize she was singing in Arawak. The language of my ancestors.

She'd do her best to teach me, to get me to speak it, but I always gave up when I got the pronunciation wrong. I knew some words, but not enough. She'd refuse to tell me what language she was teaching me, telling me to trust in what was being recited.

I sing the lullaby she taught me, my voice not as smooth or strong as hers. Time passes by as I continue weaving my fingers into her hair, praying for her safety and recovery. The door opens behind me just as I finish adjusting her long hair. The song ends, my chest constricting. She resembles her physical appearance at her funeral, when she was inside that godforsaken box.

"How is she?" Héctor asks quietly behind me.

"She's stable for now. Her skin regained color," I say, standing.

"That is good to hear." He fidgets with his fingers, his gaze soft. His black hair falls down to his chest. "That song. Did she pass it onto you?"

I nod, twisting his ring on my finger. He catches me and softens his gaze even more. "She used to sing a few when I was younger, and since she raised me, they stuck. She would reiterate it was the language of love, of togetherness. I didn't realize it was the language of my ancestors until I heard you and the sirens, actually."

"Really? So, my people, my traditions, my language. It is a part of you. That is why your anger at the treatment of us was so genuine."

I sit on my hammock, pushing my hair back. "The blood that courses through my veins is the mix of the enslaved, the slaughtered, and the colonizers."

He crosses his arm, leaning against the doorframe. "Slaughtered. Will my people continue dying?"

"Unfortunately, yes. But some will hide, others survive and persevere. Your people are strong people. They don't die so easily at the hands of the Spanish, English, or Portuguese. Not even the French. You're one of many who has beat the odds and will continue doing so."

"How is the future for those who survived?"

I glance at Mami Julia. "There's the good and bad, just like in every generation."

Mami Julia rustles on the bed, groaning.

"Mami?" I ask, heading to her.

"Mi Luz en la oscuridad," she whispers. I cry, pulling her in for a hug. Her arms embrace me back. "Mija, I missed you so much."

"You had me so worried!" I release her, grabbing her face in my hands. "Why would you do that? Why sacrifice yourself?"

"I had to ensure you lived, mi amor." She gasps, sitting up. "James. ¿Cómo está el muchacho?"

"He's in mourning." I help her stand and she winces. "As we all have been."

She notices Héctor, and he freezes. "You didn't stick to the plan."

"I know," is all he says, uncrossing his arms.

"You got Sullivan killed. James and my granddaughter nearly perished." She drags herself toward him. He holds his breath. "Regardless, you saved her. She was the priority, and I heard you nearly died yourself."

Huh?

Héctor's shoulders relax and he exhales. "I am fine. My focus is on her." He catches my eyes and looks away again. "And my brother. Not myself."

"You nearly died?" I ask, Mami Julia sitting back down on the bed.

The door swings open, and in comes Octavia with her arms crossed. James stands behind her but once he sees Héctor, he walks away, seething.

"Yeah, didn't you hear?" Octavia asks. "Also, have any of you seen my hedgehog?"

"No!" I shriek.

"Anyway, did you hear she plans to kill Johann?" Héctor asks my grandmother, taking the attention off him. "But, no Seer, I have not seen your pet."

"No, no. What do you mean *almost died?*"

"He nearly slipped off a roof trying to kill Johann with his crossbow after we left. When he didn't succeed, he threw a grenade into the crowd, which is when Lucas was out of the quartermaster's sight and got taken," Octavia explains.

"Héctor, why—"

"I got desperate!" he exclaims, sighing. "Can we move on, please? I do not want to talk about my failures."

"Very well," Mami Julia says. "Mi amor, is it true you plan to kill Johann? I assume you've controlled your power then, so it doesn't harm those you don't mean to." This time it's me who stops breathing.

"No, no she has not," Octavia announces, taking my necklace out from her satchel. "It's about time she learns to not let it corrupt her."

Mami Julia nods. "Find my general. Let's teach mi Luz how to harness her chaos."

"And if I can't?" I ask, crossing my arms.

"Then God save us all," Octavia remarks, shrugging.

"It is beautiful that you have shown a power unimaginable, and I, for one, am ecstatic," Ria explains, pacing back and forth. Her hair blows in the gentle breeze, her tunic hitting just below on her ankles. "However, with it out of sorts, it can hurt the ones you do not mean to hurt."

"But what if I like how it feels?" I ask, tightening my fingers around the jewel.

The midday sun hangs high in the sky, its warm rays cascading down onto the ocean's shimmering surface. The air is filled with a gentle sea breeze, carrying the faint scent of salt, seaweed, and sweat with it. The rhythmic sound of waves breaks against the ship. The crew continues preparing for the battle, and our ship has turned around in order to meet Johann in the islands Héctor mentioned. James and Pedro stand off to the side, watching the four of us. Pedro keeps his calculating blue eyes on Ria. She glances at him and scoffs, muttering in Arawak.

Héctor helps Lydia and Art with the preparations, but glances at me every once in a while, causing my cheeks to flush.

"We're not saying it's wrong to revel in it," Mami Julia says. "You're meant to destroy, but you have to control *what* you destroy."

"And mostly, you've been using anger, which is an emotion that corrupts a person. Remember, your necklace amplifies your emotions, especially those that make you crave death and despair," Octavia reminds.

"Try to control it with your song," Ria suggests.

"I don't have a siren song," I say.

"Bah. Yes, you do. The one you sang to me an hour ago," Mami Julia interjects. "That is your siren song. It won't work in English or Spanish, it has to be in our language."

"But I barely know it."

"Your Majesty, you did not teach her?" Ria asks, crossing her arms. Then she speaks in Arawak, glancing at Pedro.

"First, no, you can't kill the Spaniard, Curiama. No matter how irritating he may be," Mami warns. "Second, I did. But I could only teach her so much without her mother intervening."

My mouth drops open. "What did you say?"

Mami sighs, rubbing her forehead. "Adelaida knew, mija. She knew everything. She figured it out. That was the secret I meant to tell you before my death. She knew and forbade me from doing so, threatening to rip you away from me."

Mom knew?

My chest constricts, anger and anguish intertwining in my heart like a turbulent current. Realization sinks in. A flicker of rage ignites in me, a tempest readying itself to be unleashed.

Let it go...

"Control it," Mami Julia urges, stepping back. Her hands are in front of her protectively. "Do not let it control you."

"She *knew*?" I yell, my voice trembling with the weight of my emotions.

The air becomes heavy with moisture and the sky darkens. Malevolent tendrils snake their way through my being, tainting every fiber of my existence.

"Luz, your anger should not be directed—"

"Don't tell me how to feel!" I scream at Octavia. I grab my temples, my chest falling and rising rapidly. "She betrayed me like you two betrayed me!"

"Querida, would it be easier if we put ye in danger? That seems to always do the trick," Pedro mocks.

I fix my gaze on him, and with one quick glance at me, he pushes James behind him. My fingertips tingle like they did in the cell and I extend my hand in front of me, wanting to drown Pedro for interrupting me.

Kill him like he tried killing you...

The ship sways with force, a powerful water current rising behind me.

I speak in Arawak. Telling the water to go after him. It's like I'm fluent in the language and not a beginner from the twenty-first century. The water obeys, mixing with a mysterious red mist, both encasing him and throwing him overboard. Pedro's hands grip the rail as the wave chokes him, attempting to pull him under.

The necklace must be amplifying the darkness that consumes my body, clouding my mind and distorting the world around me. Many scream at me, but their voices are faint compared to the ones in my head telling me to end him. I revel in the whispers, remembering how he tried killing me all those nights ago.

Someone yells my name. I simply tilt my head, my lips quirking upward.

I'm tackled and fall to my side on the deck. The murderous thoughts retreat, as does the water. The ship sways once more as the ocean I borrowed returns to its home. I blink away the cloudy judgment, seeing Pedro cough as James and Art help him back over the rail. He grips the wooden rail, his chest falling and rising rapidly. His hair and clothes are plastered to his skin, his blue, bloodshot eyes widened in alert.

The taste of power sours in my mouth as I witness Pedro, one of the strongest men here, quiver and suffocate from the lack of air. I see the betrayal in his eyes, the pain reflected at me, and it strikes me with a searing intensity.

I *am* the evil in the seas.

I run to him, coming out of my ecstatic power. "Ped—"

"Do *not* do that shit to me again!" Pedro snarls, taking deep breaths.

"I'm so sorry," I say.

"Are ye? Ye seem pretty *ecstatic* to drown me!"

"This is who she is, *Spaniard*," Ria snaps. "If you cannot handle a strong inaru, then maybe you are not as strong as you think!"

Pedro glares at Ria, then at me. He walks off, water dripping from his clothes onto the deck. A few of the crew members disperse, fearful whispers surrounding us. They're afraid of me. James and Héctor remain, as far away as possible from each other.

Ria and Mami Julia talk in Arawak. In the heat of the moment of utter chaos, I lost myself in my sea of overwhelming emotions, nearly drowning the quartermaster.

"Sea la madre," I say, closing my eyes.

I know exactly what this entails now. If he doesn't trust me, he won't fight with us. He'll get his son back and as soon as he has him, he'll shoot me down himself.

I look at my hands, my thoughts a jumbled mess. How can I find control when all I want is to let the evil consume me?

"You let it control you again," Ria says, exasperated. "While that was satisfying, you cannot go around letting it affect the first person you lock eyes with. Have anHave an intention. Purpose."

"Purpose," I repeat. The power wants to take over me. And I want to let it.

Ria nods. "Yes. How about..." She glances at Héctor. "Perfect. He is the one you slept with last night. Try it on him."

Héctor chuckles. "We did not... I did not... That was—"

"You two did *what*? On *my* deathbed?" Mami Julia shrieks.

"Seems like their priorities are all out of sorts, ma'am," James states, smirking as he reads his book. Octavia laughs.

"You. Child," Ria calls him. "Join us."

"I get to drown too? And next to a *traitor*? How fun!" James says sarcastically, closing his book. "Red, if ye drown me, I'm comin' back and haunting ye for eternity."

Héctor pushes his black hair back. "James, I am not a traitor," Héctor assures.

James scoffs, throwing the book in his satchel. "Traitors get loved ones murdered. If ye had stuck to the plan..."

"Please, let me explain."

"No. I have nothing to say to ye." James crosses his arms, turning away from Héctor, his head held high.

"The time to argue shall come later," Ria says. "Now, it is time to drown you both." Ria faces me. "I want you to pick one. Focus on the one you pick. Control your power."

My heart pounds inside my chest. "Ria, I can't do this. Take James out of the equation, please," I beg. "I don't want to injure him."

"I ain't afraid of ye, Red," James says. "Besides, what more can ye do to me? I'm broken on the inside."

I gulp, my heart shattering. He smiles at me, and Héctor stands there, taking deep breaths. "I pick Héctor."

"Good. Focus on him. Aim your power at *him*."

"Wait!" James exclaims, taking his book out. "Let's make this entertaining. Do *not* get my readin' material wet, if ye do, ye ain't seeing tomorrow."

I laugh, rolling my eyes. His jokes relax me.

I inhale, looking right at Héctor. He clasps his hands behind his back; the breeze blows his hair back. As I gaze into his eyes, a surge of emotions rushes through me, the intensity of my powers pulsating within me. I place my shaky hands in front of me, squinting. He looks at me, an air of trust in him.

I throw my hands down to my thighs.

"Nothing's happening," I complain, "I really think I should just let it loose."

"No," Ria says. "No one learns in a few minutes. This takes time. Pick an emotion. A memory. Most of us resort to our hatred, but we just witnessed a taste of your anger."

"Let's see what happens if you use happy memories instead," Octavia remarks.

"I just don't want to—"

"D'nanichi," Héctor intervenes. Mami Julia and Ria glance at each other, their eyes wide. "Just do it."

I nod, bringing my hands up again, closing my eyes. I take deep breaths, searching for any happy memories I have. My emotions, like the currents of the ocean, can be rather unpredictable and overwhelming, so if it's a happy memory they want, a happy memory I'll drag out. If I allow myself to lose control, the water may cause unintended harm to Héctor.

The thoughts from last night resurface, and my chest tightens. I can't do this. My brows furrow together, my hands fall a bit.

"Breathe," Héctor encourages. "I will be fine. You cannot hurt me."

I search my mind for happy memories. Soledad, dancing in a daisy field, her brown curls swaying. My cousin Nico and I dancing bomba with Papi Gustavo. Mami Julia detangling my curls, humming our lullaby as her gentle fingers grazed my skin. Mami Julia and Papi Gustavo dancing under the rain. My dad taking me along to landscape a big house.

My fingertips tingle, the current of the ocean picking up. The quiet chatter of the crew surrounds me. My powers respond to my emotions, mirroring the calm I feel. I need more memories.

Octavia and I stealing food from the dining hall, running from the monitor. Gentle rain falls over us, caressing our skin. Me at the beach with Soledad and Oliver, watching as they built sandcastles. Hugging Mami Julia.

James playing the fiddle. Gasps erupt, power surges through my veins. Me waking up this morning, watching Héctor, seeing his amazing sketches.

I open my eyes, a gentle current swirling around me, encasing me. It's not hurting anyone. Instead, it's protecting me. A wide grin spreads across my face, my eyes sparkling with a newfound confidence. While the swirling water current is weak, I did it. I controlled my power.

Now I know what not to do when I unleash my hell on Johann.

CHAPTER
FORTY-FIVE

The weak current holds up and I force it to approach Héctor, who's standing in front of me proud. James is chuckling, reaching out to the water. He passes his hand through it, taking it out after.

Inside, my power surges, wanting nothing more than to be released. I focus on the happy memories, preventing them from letting my inner monster take over.

"Good job, you did great," Ria compliments, smiling. "Still a lot to learn, but for it to be the first time you control it, it is not bad."

The group congregates around me. Behind Héctor stands the cloaked figure, pointing his golden staff at me, then at Héctor.

Time ticks, queen of ruin. His ominous voice echoes in my head.

I gasp, the water dropping onto the deck with a splash. The air rushes in and out of my lungs in a frenzied cadence. Panic courses through my veins.

Who is that? Why does he keep coming back? How come no one can see him?

"Are you alright?" Héctor asks.

"I'm fine," I lie. I stand, doing breathing exercises.

The figure cackles, engulfed by his own shadows. Once gone, Héctor winces and grabs his temples, stumbling onto the deck.

"Héctor!" I call out, running to him. James reaches out but holds back, his brows furrowed and face muscles tightened. My heartbeat quickens, a steady thumping that reverberates within my chest.

"What happened?" I ask. "I remember you were disoriented a few weeks back. I thought you'd get better."

He sits up, his gaze unfocused. "It has gotten worse," he admits.

"It must be the—"

"Hush, Octavia," Mami Julia interrupts. "Don't."

"Don't what?" I ask, helping Héctor stand, and he stumbles again, squinting.

Octavia glances at me, turning on the ball of her heel and leaves.

No. She knows.

Mami Julia whispers to Ria. James hangs off to the side, wondering if he should help his brother or if he should remain angry. Ultimately, he approaches us.

"I'll take him," James sighs. "He ain't deserve my help, but he's helped me countless times."

"Thank you," I say, "James is going to take you now, okay?"

Héctor nods, his eyes closed, and James leads him away to his quarters. A restlessness stirs within me as I pace back and forth. I twist his ring around my finger, my body searching for an outlet. The zephyr picks up with my growing anxiety.

I face Mami Julia, who eyes me with pity. "You don't get to hide anything more from me," I state, departing to find Octavia.

She's up on the quarterdeck, watching me as I ascend the staircase. Her purple eyes don't leave mine, her ginger locs tied up in a bun. Lydia stands at the helm with a damp Pedro, both speaking of how, with the help of my grandmother, the battle would take place the day after tomorrow.

"Octavia."

She raises her eyebrow, clasping her hands in front of her. "Luz."

"Finish the sentence from earlier."

She sighs, leading me to the rail that overlooks the ocean. "I said it must be the symptoms."

I make a face. "What symptoms?"

"I'm not supposed to tell you this, Luz. But we agreed to keep no secrets between us."

She reaches over to my temples. A sudden rush of wind overpowers me. Flashes of light.

"You'll pay for that!" I scream, gripping a golden trident.

"And you should've stayed out of my way, queen of ruin," a strange yet mesmerizing Black man in black and golden clothes taunts, unsheathing a golden sword. "I warned you all those years ago."

Behind him, Héctor appears, holding a knife against his neck. His hair is shorter, and he wears black jeans with silver chains, along with a bloody gray t-shirt.

"You are going to regret coming after me... after us," Héctor seethes. The Black man laughs.

"Do it, Nau," the Black man says. *A disheveled Johann circles Oliver and stabs him, sending him to his knees. My chest constricts.* "Two down. Two to go."

Another flash of light.

Héctor placing some coins atop a table, nodding. Him exiting the building, encountering Johann. A shoot-off. Blood. Pain. Groans.

Octavia's face comes into focus.

"Héctor is supposed to be dead," she whispers.

Glass shatters somewhere inside me.

Pain swells up in my chest, causing me to stumble even though I'm not moving.

What just happened?

Héctor is supposed to be dead. Six words. One deadly sentence.

It can't be.

"When?" I ask, my breath trembling.

"The day you arrived," she says. "Listen to me. This is dangerous. Skipping a death date brings serious consequences. He's showing symptoms. The Collector is furious they made his job they made his job a mockery. By you, by Héctor, by me." She chuckles, rubbing her neck. "We're all in huge trouble, Luz. Everything shifted. The balance of the universe hangs on a thread."

"But you're The Seer. You *See* things. You didn't See this?"

"Oh,, I did." She sighs, placing her hands on the rail. I twist his ring on my finger. "Originally, Héctor was meant to die that same day you arrived. You were going to encounter Johann, and he was going to take you. To you, it was all going to be Oliver. That same night, you two were supposed to encounter the second mate and because you were going to be confused, Johann was going to torture him in front of you. It was going to trigger your powers." She fidgets with her dainty rings. "You were going to end up alone, afraid, and tortured at Johann's hands. That is not the end I wanted for you. Either of you. So, I did what was forbidden of me. I intervened. I saved you both. You both saved each other. But now history has been rewritten because of my actions, and you have to pay the price, Luz."

My heart pounds in my chest, a rapid and erratic beat that echoes the frantic thoughts racing through my mind. He was meant to die. Panic rises like a tumultuous wave. My hands clench into fists, nails digging into my palms. I pace back and forth in the quarterdeck, unable to find solace in stillness.

"How did you intervene?" I ask, pacing.

"By sending him to you. I was adamant it had to be *him*. It could've been any of the pirates, but out of all of them, his fate was the worst. And when I saw how horrible your fate was meant to be... I took it upon my hands to redeem both of you."

"You're not lying to me, right?"

"No, I promised I wouldn't lie anymore. Besides, would I make up a lie where *I* am in trouble? Where I have to face a trial with The Greats and possibly *lose* my abilities? I don't think so." She walks to me, gripping my shoulders. "Just know this. Two souls intertwined. Two hearts beat as one. You may be blind to see it, but I'm not. You and him were meant to find each other. You were meant to be each other's salvation. I Saw and felt it."

"When is he meant to die now?"

Octavia shrugs. "I can't say. I haven't gotten a vision regarding his death yet, but darkness is involved."

Darkness. At night? Or could she be referring to Johann? What if it's *me*?

"Love is a curious thing, is it not?" she asks, smiling at me. "Destinies aligned, fates intertwined. I will admit though, who wouldn't look at him that way? He's quite attractive."

"I don't have time to look at him in any way."

"Luz. I See things. Glorious things. Despicable things. I even See details you wish to ignore for your own convenience."

I suck in my breath. "Wow, calling me out." I smile, and she smiles back at me, a hint of playfulness in her eyes. "I don't see him looking at me in any way. Maybe his annoyance at me is gone, but besides that, I don't see anything else."

She laughs. A snarky laugh. "You cannot be serious right now! Are you kidding me?"

She playfully bonks me in the head and I laugh at her. We walk and sit in the bow's bow's section, watching the sea and the crew. Everyone does their duties diligently. Quiet chatter fills the air.

I turn to watch Octavia. Even in the past, her skin is gorgeous. It must be a perk to being immortal. Unblemished skin. Her aura, however, is different. Her energy. Her presence. In the future, she has always had a regal air to her. Luxurious. Delicate. Like a snowflake. Strong, but also feminine. Here, she's a bit of everything. Delicate. Flirty. Feminine. Badass. Headstrong. Wise.

Here she is The Seer.

"Why did you hide who you were from me?" I ask tenderly.

She turns to me, her gaze softening. "The life of a Seer is lonely. To know that everyone you meet will eventually die. To stay young while your loved ones grow old," she says, her voice breaking. "I prefer not to burden others. I See things. But at what cost? Across the lifetimes I've loved and lost. So, I dropped the act for a couple of years. Begin to enjoy and pretend I'm one of you. Besides, what was I going to say? *Hey girl, I'm immortal?*"

"To be fair, that's exactly what you said to me at your shack, and you're still not forgiven for that," I tease, and she smiles, shaking her head. "It must be horrible, though, isn't it? To see everything. To feel death."

"I've seen the good and bad of life. But the bad often overpowers the good. So, for your lifetime, I just kind of gave up. It was actually the first lifetime I tried making friends after… after the love of my life died." She wipes a tear away, bringing her knees to her chest as she watches Lydia on the deck. "What good is living a thousand lifetimes when the person you love lives only one?"

A stinging pain grows in my chest.

My mind goes to Héctor. Him and I. Lifetimes apart. Never to be.

I put my arm around her, pulling her close to me. She's warm and smells faintly of rum. Her words echo in my mind.

What good is living a thousand lifetimes when the person you love only lives one?

That must be so painful. I couldn't imagine having to go through that. To love someone with all your heart, all your soul, then they die of old age. And you continue living after them. Alone. Broken. Without purpose.

"I'm sorry. You must have so much pressure on you," I say and she leans her head on my shoulder, staring at the ocean.

"You get used to it." She takes a labored breath. "I'm sorry I betrayed you. I didn't mean to lie to you."

"It's okay. I forgive you."

As the day passes and we silently enjoy each other's company, everything she told me replays in my head. Even as I head to sleep.

I understand everything now. Mami Julia and Ria. Octavia and her powers.

I understand it all.

CHAPTER FORTY-SIX

After a night of restless sleep with nightmares of Pedro and Johann both attempting to gut me open, I've come to a conclusion.

If I'm to fight, I have to get the quartermaster on my side. I have to win him over again.

I get up from my hammock, my body trembling. The dark is no longer welcoming and calming, but a bringer of horrors untold. Pushing my hair away from my face, I encounter Héctor sketching in a journal.

When did he get in?

"Good morning, why are you not sleeping in your own room?" I ask, my voice groggy.

He looks up, unfazed by my question. "I was making sure you woke up alright," he whispers, closing the journal. "Lydia said you were thrashing around, mumbling to yourself while you slept. So, she let me in."

"Oh, I didn't mean to interrupt your sleep."

"You did not." He watches me. "Once again, I am ensuring you are okay."

"Was it that bad?" I grab my vest, putting it on.

"Very much so."

He gets up, approaching me. His sketchbook slips from his hands, and we get down at the same time to grab it. My hands reach it first, and it opens, revealing a small, messy sketch. Of me. This one is new. I blush. His face darkens, and he rips the sketchbook from my hands, throwing it into his satchel.

"Was that—"

"No. You are seeing things," he interrupts.

I take a deep breath, forcing myself to look at him. "Héctor—"

"I said it was nothing."

I nod, and he mutters to himself.

I step into my boots and walk toward the shelf space Lydia provided for me. I grab the bottle of spiced vinegar I had stolen from him. I swish some of the vinegar around in my mouth, spitting it out into the ocean from Lydia's window.

"Are you feeling better?" I ask.

"Yes," he says, pushing his hair back.

"Have you seen Pedro?"

This takes him aback. "The quartermaster?"

"I need to talk to him."

"Should be below decks." His voice is tense with a tinge of envy.

The bedroom door swings open, slamming against the wall. "Ay, Villanueva, don't you have anything else to do?" Mami Julia grumbles. Ria stands next to her, two inches taller than my grandmother. "First, Ria tells me you two slep—"

"We *didn't*," I snap.

"Well, that's what I heard... *d'nanichi*," Mami Julia teases, and Héctor looks down at his boots, mumbling to himself. Has he been *mocking me* all this time?

"Wait, what does it mean?" I ask, my heart fluttering. "Is it an insult?"

"No. I think it's best if he tells you himself."

I raise my eyebrow, glancing at him. "Well?"

He chuckles awkwardly and leaves, excusing himself. Ria bursts out laughing, snorting. She walks after him, calling him by my nickname.

"Mija, he's so awkward," Mami Julia says. "I'm surprised que te gusta."

I roll my eyes, my face growing hot. "Ay por Dios, Mami," I groan. "I don't like him. And why won't you tell me what it means?"

She giggles, adjusting the clothes Lydia loaned her. "He'll tell you when the time is right." Mami Julia gestures for me to leave. "¿Qué no tenías que hablar con el Pedro?"

I sigh dramatically, tying my detangled hair into a low braid. Afterward, I leave, shutting the door behind me.

❧❧❧

The deck bustles with activity. Crew members with their worn leather boots and ragged clothing move with purpose, their weathered faces etched with determination. The clatter of their boots against the wooden planks resonates in harmony with the ocean's waves.

The Fury's cannons, sleek and deadly, are positioned strategically along the sides, ready to unleash their destructive force whenever we face Johann and his crew. A few pirates stare at me, some with respect, others with fear.

"Ah, Luz," Lydia says. From below, we can hear Pedro yelling. "Don't strain yerself today. The battle is tomorrow. Yer grandmother agreed last night to help us. Just thought ye should know."

I smile, nodding. "Thank you, Captain," I say, and she tips her hat. "Lydia?"

"Aye?"

"You've been an inspiration all my life. I'm proud to call you my Captain."

She tears up, grinning. Sniffling, she embraces me. "Fight good, aye? We shall toast in victory when he's dead." She leaves, heading into Sullivan's quarters. "Wake up, sunshine! Time to sweep the deck!" James' voice groans from the inside, begging for more time, along with a thud. She shuts the door, heading back to the deck.

Now. To find the quartermaster.

I go below decks, quietinging my steps. The last thing I want to do is announce I'm coming. Thankfully, Lydia's orders drown out my noise. I glance around, searching for him. A couple crew members sweep and mop the area, others sort ammunition such as pistols, gunpowder, cannonballs, and even barrels of rum.

Doors are slamming, the echo of steel clashing together filling below decks.

I bump into Art, who's stacking some cannonballs together inside a fishing net. I nearly trample him and he stands. His tired, brown eyes with circles underneath show how little he has slept.

"Hey, Art," I say, and he nods. His eyes are unfocused. "How are you holding up?"

"I'm fine, Narváez," Art hesitates.

A loud Spanish curse from afar makes my heartbeat quicken. It's Pedro... and he's in one of his moods.

"I know you and Cyrus were really close. I promise we'll get him back."

He gives me a sad smile. "He's probably dead already, lass." He waves me away, placing a cigar in his mouth. "I ain't wanna talk about it."

"Narváez, stop pestering my crew," a voice booms behind me. I turn around, encountering Pedro, his arms crossed. "Unless ye plan on helping, I suggest ye leave."

"Wait, I have to talk to you," I admit, scrambling to get over to him. I run a bit out of breath. The lack of energy and sleep makes an appearance.

"Oh? What requires such importance, yer highness?" He walks off muttering, heading to a different area. I chase him.

"It's about Nau."

He grabs a couple of bundled up ropes, walking away. Once again, I follow.

"It's about Lucas," I say, catching up to him.

Pedro raises his eyebrow at me, stopping. "Proceed."

"I met Lucas. He's a wonderful young man."

"I'm aware." *Sarcasm.* He throws the ropes inside a barrel. "So, get to the point, querida."

"What I wanted to say was, I know how much he means to you. But if it's any consolation, Nau had a soft spot for him."

He scoffs, grabbing a sack of potatoes. "How's that consolation?"

"He won't die. Not yet at least."

Pedro rolls his eyes and walks away. "I know, Narváez. Tell me something I don't know." I go after him, and he throws the sack down. "Escúchame—"

"Lucas will be a great Spanish captain. His name goes down in history, where he will be studied and revered for centuries to come." I stand in front of him, looking into his eyes with determination. "He inspired a movement like no other, carrying Sullivan's legacy in the seas. His line will continue, and he's going to have five children in a happy marriage."

His lips tighten into a thin line. "The Seer confirmed my son lives and has... children. I know he has *descendants*." He rubs his nose. "Irritating ones that *taint* his legacy."

"What?" I take a deep breath, thinking of my next words. "Lucas Gabriel de Córdova Fuentes and his legacy will live on. No one will taint it. It is a great legacy. Everyone who studies Caribbean history knows of him."

Pedro crosses his arms and stays quiet. Watching me. Deciphering if I'm saying the truth. I've been under his scrutiny before, but never to this level. I can only hope my words got through to him.

"The Seer never told me of his death. Does he die by Nau's hand?" Pedro asks gruffly.

I shake my head. "No. Nau is not involved in his death."

He sighs, clicking his tongue. "Thank ye."

"Of course."

I make to leave, but he calls out to me. "Vos were the one with James when..."

"Yes. I saw everything."

His gaze softens ever so slightly, though he attempts to conceal it. "I'm not known for heart-to-heart talks, but... gracias."

"What for?"

"For being there with James when it all went down. He's like my second son." He places his strong hands on my shoulders. "Y gracias por decidme lo de Lucas. He and James are all I have left."

I nod, tears welling up in my eyes. I throw my arms around him, feeling the warmth of his embrace. "De nada."

He hugs me back, chuckling. "Ye and I have to talk about something else... but it can wait."

"What's it about?"

"Nothing important, querida." His arms tighten around me. "Nothing important." He releases me, clearing his throat. "Now, go. Fuera. Get that power under control so ye don't drown my ass again."

CHAPTER FORTY-SEVEN

The sun dips below the horizon, painting the sky with hues of orange and purple. The atmosphere on *The Fury* is alive with a mix of excitement and melancholy, for the battle with Nau is tomorrow. The battle that will seal our fates.

Lydia, as Captain, let them party one last time, helping them set aside their worries and revel in the present moment.

The deck is adorned with lanterns that cast a warm glow over the gathering. Pedro rolled out the barrels of rum, disappearing after. The sweet scene of the rum mingles with the salty sea breeze, encapsulating both the joy and defiance found in the crew.

I watch from the quarterdeck while a trio play tunes into a flute, drums and a fiddle, their melodies soaring into the night sky. James sat out of this one, reading up on the crow's nest. The pirates dance with wild abandon, while others sit in groups, sharing tales of past conquests. Their laughter is infectious, but like James, I decide to sit this one out as well.

I twist my necklace, scanning the deck for Héctor, but I don't see him.

"You're not going to join the death party?" Octavia asks, coming up the stairs with Ria and Mami Julia.

I shake my head. "I'm not in a celebratory mood."

"Mi amor, you can't be alone," Mami Julia says, caressing the ends of my hair. "We need to do something about this hair, too."

Art scoffs from the helm. "Excuse me, ma'am, she ain't alone, *I'm here.*"

"So, she's alone," Octavia teases.

"Don't push it, Guillebeaux."

"Oh, my dear Art, if I wasn't married, I'd push *you* in all the ways."

"Anyways, that was inappropriate," I say, rolling my eyes. "And yes, Mami, I agree." I sigh. "Actually, could you cut it? Right now? If you're not busy, of course."

She smiles, intertwining her arm with mine. "I'm never busy for you, mi amor. Come on."

"Octavia, find something to do for us that doesn't involve you being horny."

"Spin the bottle?" Octavia suggests.

"Girl, I am *not* kissing random men."

"Aye, she is not kissin' random men," Pedro says, coming up the stairs. "I ain't tryna watch ye all get action while I get *none.*" His sleeves are rolled up to his elbows, showing his tattoos.

"What if we use each other as target practice instead of exchanging our personal fluids?" Ria asks, running a hand through her black hair.

"Ria, please never say *exchanging our fluids* again," I say and she snorts.

"Luz, vente," Mami Julia says, pulling me. "You all figure it out, we'll be back."

❧❧❧

In Lydia's quarters, she motions for me to take a seat on the stool. I oblige, taking deep breaths. I made a promise to myself long ago that I wouldn't cut my hair but now I have reasons to do so. One, it's matted. Two, it brings memories of what was done to me. The sooner I cut it, the sooner I can release that weight that keeps holding me down.

Mami tugs my hair gently, the pressure releasing when she slices that chunk off with her dagger. I close my eyes, saying goodbye to my hair.

"Ay, mi amor, this is so painful to do," she admits. "In my culture, hair connects us with my roots and ancestors. I understand why you're doing it, though, and I'm here for you, mi vida."

"I don't want to do it either, trust me," I say. "I love my long hair. I was proud of it, but every time I run my fingers through it now, I remember how the officers in the Glory tried taking advantage of me. How someone stopped them and in retaliation they cut off one side of my hair and dragged me through the cell."

Another segment of my hair falls, and my heart aches.

A part of me and my identity... gone.

"Yo se," Mami Julia sighs. Misshapen, cut curls roll down my upper body. "Just relax, close your eyes. Focus on something else, mi amor."

I do as she suggests, feeling the movement of my grandmother's hands on my hair and scalp. With each tug, my chest constricts and the memories of what I am leaving behind pull at me. Cutting my hair is a sense of renewal and transformation. I leave beautiful memories, but also terrible ones. Hopefully, what comes next isn't as bad as what I experienced at the hands of Johann.

450

"Done, mi amor," Mami Julia says.

"Thank you for this. It feels much better. A new beginning," I say, standing. My neck feels lighter, my hair hitting right above my shoulders.

She smiles, hugging me. "May this beginning be kind to us all." She releases me.

A knock on the door and Art pops his head in. "Everyone is waiting for ye both," he says and eyes my hair. "Lookin' good, Narváez."

❧❧❧

Ascending the steps to the quarterdeck, we encounter a barrage of arguments between the officers, Ria and Octavia.

"Listen, General, ye may be as beautiful as can be, but for the last time, I ain't telling ye my weaknesses," Pedro states.

"Aye, 'cause if he lists them, he ain't never ending," Lydia remarks with a smirk on her face.

I choke on my laugh as Pedro glares at her. Mami Julia, Art and I arrive at the quarterdeck, and the party continues behind. James and Héctor have joined this argument, with James looking into an empty glass bottle next to Octavia. Héctor's back is facing me as he mocks Pedro, who's staring at me.

"Ah, she lives," Pedro comments, tilting his head to the side.

Héctor turns around and immediately stops in his tracks. My face grows hot under his gaze. I look away, clearing my throat.

"Did you all decide what we're doing?" I ask, walking toward Octavia. I can still feel his eyes on me.

451

Octavia smiles. "Spin the bottle. I explained to them what it was, how it's played, and we agreed to tell secrets instead," she says, eyeing Pedro and Héctor. "No exceptions."

"That is not a game, that is psychological *torture*," Héctor retorts, finally looking away.

"It'll be fun, first mate, live a little."

I grab Héctor's arm and his eyes soften. "Come on, it's a once in a lifetime opportunity to play a game from my time. Plus..." I lean into his ear. "We get to spend some time together."

He smiles. "Alright."

"Excuse me, we have a *child* aboard," Pedro snaps, pointing at James. "I ain't know what ye told him, but we ain't need to witness some baby-makin'."

"It is settled then!" Octavia claps, drawing attention to her over the background laughter that fills the sea. "Everyone sit in a circle." She turns to Art, who has moved back to the helm. " Join us."

"I ain't think it's wise—"

"Sit down and shut up, Zhào," Lydia orders.

I bring Mami Julia to the circle. She might not be interested in *esos juegos raros de ustedes*, but I want to spend as much time as possible with her.

We arrange ourselves on the quarterdeck in a spread out circle. Mami Julia, James, Octavia and I sit in the same way—with our legs crossed—while Ria lowers herself in a side saddle form. Music echoes in our ears, not as precise as James' melodies. Héctor comes to sit to the right of me, but just as he's lowering himself, Pedro plops down between the two of us, separating him and I.

"Just tryin' to keep this child-appropriate, don't mind me," Pedro says, rubbing his arms together. He brings one leg up, leaning his elbow on it.

"Córdova. You could not sit over there?" Héctor hisses, pointing to the point farthest from us.

"No. I quite like this spot."

I groan, rolling my eyes. "You are so—"

"Charming? I know, querida."

"Okay! Before this turns into an ego fest," Octavia says, taking the bottle from James and placing it in the middle. "Let me remind you of the rules. Whoever the bottle picks, they must tell a secret. No exceptions, no backing out." She smiles, glancing at us. "Ready?"

"Sure, let's get this over with," Mami Julia says, intertwining my arm with hers.

Everyone settles in their spots. Ria sits to the left of my grandmother, braiding a section of her hair. James sits next to her, moving his weight from one side of his body to another. As Octavia spins the bottle next to him, Lydia holds on to her. Art sits relaxed between the Captain and the first mate, smoking his cigar.

Octavia sits back down, the bottle pointing at her. "Well, fuck."

I cackle. "You unlucky bitch!"

Mami Julia taps my hand. "Language, Luisa."

"Yes, *Luisa*, listen to yer grandmother," Pedro teases, tapping my hand too.

"Okay," Octavia begins. "A secret of mine." She tucks in a loc behind her ear. "I am deathly afraid of heights. Which sucks because when I get my visions, they take me down a loophole, so I fall every time I See something."

"That's horrible," Art says. "Ye just keep fallin' over and over?"

She nods. "Yep, can't do nothing about it."

"That actually explains so much," I say, tilting my head. "I knew you had a phobia of heights, but I didn't know how deep it went."

"Believe me, it's hell on earth, but let's see who's next!" She spins the bottle, landing on Ria. "Curiama. Your turn."

Ria flips her hair, blowing air from her lips. "I once fell in love."

"How's that a secret?" Pedro asks.

"Because, *Spaniard*, when sirens fall in love, they give their whole heart. The person is immune to their song." She sighs, bringing her knees up to her chest. "He was beautiful. Mysterious. But he betrayed me and took my heart. Now, I have nothing left to give. He will forevermore remain immune to me, while I remain heartless."

"Oh, Ria..." I lament.

She looks away. "I do not want pity."

"So... I have *no* opportunity?" Pedro asks.

Héctor groans, tilting his head toward Pedro. "Have some respect for her."

"She doesn't want ye, quartermaster," James says. "I'm sure she got *taste*."

"Watch it, Edwards," Pedro scolds, suppressing a smile. James sticks out his tongue at him.

Octavia grabs Ria's hand. "Thank you for sharing. He didn't deserve your heart. What he deserves is a good smack to the head."

"Oh, you know him?" I ask.

"Well... I'd say I know him pretty well."

"It's her brother, mija," Mami says. *The Collector*?

Ria crosses her arms. "I do not want to talk about it anymore." *Ria fell in love with The Collector?*

The Fury's wooden deck buzzes with lively energy as the vibrant lanterns light up the pitch-black sky. The string music reverberates through the air as laughter creates a festive atmosphere, instead of a somber one.

Octavia spins the bottle again.

It lands on Lydia.

Lydia chuckles nervously. "I know how to play four instruments."

"What! Miss Lydia!" James exclaims. "How dare ye keep this from me?"

She pulls his hat down. "Well, ye didn't ask."

James clutches his chest after fixing his headwear. "We could've played together!"

"Spin the vial, Seer."

The salty breeze carries the scent of roasting fish and rum, mingling with the musky aroma of sweat. The fiddle player messes up repeatedly, causing James to cringe from the quarterdeck, but still he stays here.

The whirling bottle stops at Ria once more, so Octavia spins it again, halting at Art. Immediately, he blushes.

"I, uh," he begins. "I once loved ye, Captain."

Lydia stares at him, her mouth wide open. Octavia giggles, James grabs Art's shoulders, shaking him. *A love confession.* Art loved Lydia once.

I bring my hand to my chest. "Since *when?*"

"Well, I'll be damned," Pedro says, his eyebrows raised.

"I cannot believe he finally said it," Héctor remarks.

"Bartholomew, I ain't know ye felt that way," Lydia says.

Art looks away, his face red. "I was young and immediately fancied ye. I grew out of it... but I thought ye should know. Had to tell ye eventually, aye?"

Lydia grabs his hand, nodding. "If things had gone differently, perhaps I would've seen ye in the same manner."

He bows his head. "There. That's my secret. Spin the goddamn thing away from me."

"No, no. I want to know more," Ria says, smiling. "Tell us everything. What made you fall for—"

"Curiama, stop instigating," Mami Julia warns. "¿Tú sabes cómo se le dice a la gente así? Chismosa."

Ria rolls her eyes. "Moving on."

A sudden gunshot followed by laughter causes us all to jump. Lydia barks an order to the deck and the crew below quiets down. The music slows, giving the ocean an eerie feeling.

Silently, Octavia twirls the bottle. It points to my grandmother.

"My secret is I nearly killed Luz's mother once," Mami Julia admits, shrugging. "But I didn't."

My neck jerks, and I blink rapidly. "What the fuck?"

"It was an accident."

"I don't think that makes it better..."

"To be fair, she was planning on sending you to a fat camp for the school year."

My chest tightens. "What?"

"What does that mean?" James asks.

"Luz's mother was going to send Luz to a camp so her body could get thinner," Octavia explains, leaning her head on Lydia's shoulder, interlacing their fingers together.

"Why?" Héctor asks. "Who would willingly submit their child to physical torture simply to please others?"

I sigh. "My mother." I rub my face. "She has never liked how I look."

"Well, she should. It is your temple. She should respect it." Héctor looks at me, not breaking eye contact. "You are perfect as you are and she needs to accept it."

Our eyes connect for a few seconds too long, so we avert our gazes, blushing.

"Sickening," Pedro groans. "Ye hearin' this, grandmother?"

"I am," Mami Julia says. "First the sleeping together—"

"We didn't sleep together," I remind them, my face flushing. I place my hands on the nape of my neck, reminding myself that my hair is short now.

"Then the name he calls her," Ria giggles.

"I swear to God, if it's an insult..."

"If it is, ye should fight him," James interjects, looking at his nails.

"It is not!" Héctor declares. "It is a term for... admiration."

"Gone soft, have we, Villanueva?" Pedro asks, elbowing a blushing Héctor.

"Let me spin it before I throw up," Octavia says, sitting upright.

Octavia twists it with force and the bottle spins. With each turn, Pedro and Héctor visibly tense up, since their chances of being picked have increased. Finally, it lands between me and a tensed up Pedro. He holds his breath and hits the floor with his fist, causing the bottle to point at *me* instead.

"That's not fair!" I exclaim.

"The Seer ain't specify that couldn't be done," he shrugs.

Octavia cackles. "You dumb bitch!"

I sigh, trying to summon a secret, but none of them would make sense given the current time period. Nothing comes to mind, so I look up at the beautiful night sky.

The Fury's tattered flags flutter overhead, a reminder that this is my new life now. The music's tempo slows, the crew's energetic veneer diminishes by the second. The soft waves crash against the hull, lulling me.

"I think mine are inexplicable since they all have to do with my time," I confess. "Um... the only one that makes sense is that my ex-suitor is Johann Nau's descendant, but that's not really a secret."

"Tell us this then," Lydia suggests. "Ye said yer from the future. Do we go down in history?"

I glance around, thinking of how to answer this question without giving too much away. "I can't really say since it might change the course of events, but your legacies will carry on. Your descendants will carry your names and histories." I push a short curl behind my ear. "You will be as great as you hope to be. History will shine a spotlight on you." My eyes find Héctor's. "All of you." I take a deep breath. "Greatness lies within every one of you here. From here on in, history will be rewritten. It's just a matter of rewriting it for the better."

They all study me quietly. I avert my eyes, fidgeting with my hands. The slowed tune continues from the deck, filling the silence between us.

"I'll, uh, spin the thing now," I announce, rotating the bottle.

This time, it lands on Héctor.

"I do not want to—"

"No exceptions," Octavia interrupts him.

Héctor sighs. "Fine." He rubs his temples, running a hand through his hair. The sleeves of his beige shirt are rolled up to his elbows. "Even though I am both mesmerized and terrified by the sea's wonders and beauty," he glances at me and just as quickly looks away, "I am deathly afraid of drowning."

"Octavia, didn't you *drown* him?" I ask, whirling my head to her.

"I mean, it got him to do my bidding, didn't it?" she asks, chuckling nervously.

"*Octavia...*"

"What!" She crosses her arms. "I already apologized to him for doing so!"

"You do not have to be afraid of it, *first mate*," Ria reassures, the side of her lips curled upward. "It seems you could be immune to the sea's terrifying wonders."

"What does that—"

"Ria, my beloved, please do *not* answer that," I warn, blushing.

She raises her hands defensively. "I shall stay out of it."

Octavia whirls the glass bottle again, smiling.

It points to Mami Julia but since she went already we spin it again. Only two more people remain.

Fatigue sets in the air as the crew members from the deck disperse. The musicians announce they'll play three more tunes and that's it. The ship seems to exhale, settling into the rhythmic creaking of timbers as the night slowly reclaims its stillness.

The bottle stops and the next person is...

Pedro.

"Nah, can't it move to—"

"NO EXCEPTIONS!" Octavia yells.

Pedro tenses up, crossing his arms. "Uh... I hate all of ye, there, that's my *secret.*"

"Tell us somethin' we don't already know," James says, rolling his eyes.

Pedro exhales loudly. "I've always been afraid of lettin' people in. Ever since my brother died." He turns to Héctor. "Ye remind me of him."

"I did not know you had a brother," Héctor admits.

"It ain't something I blurt out, Villanueva."

I grab Pedro's hand. "Thank you for trusting us."

He smiles. "Don't get used to it."

"My turn!" James exclaims. "My secret is that I stole this," he removes a bracelet from his satchel, "and this," he takes out a leather bag, "and this," a deck of cards.

"Is that mine?" Octavia, Ria, and Art ask at the same time.

"Aye."

"Well, thank goodness this godforsaken game is over," Pedro says, standing up.

Héctor gets up, as does Lydia.

"Wait, before ye all leave," James giggles. "I also stole this."

He digs into the satchel and his hands release a hedgehog.

Octavia sits on her knees, glancing from James to the animal to James again. "IS THAT MY HEDGEHOG?"

"I need to know how you took it from the person who sees everything," I chuckle.

"It was easy. She left him layin' around," James confesses. "With her focus elsewhere, I took it and made sure she was always distracted."

"However did ye keep it alive?" Lydia asks.

"I got my tricks, Captain."

"Well, you have the qualities of someone I could use," Octavia contemplates. "If you ever want to stop being a pirate... you know where to find me, mini Edwards."

He tips his hat, pushing the hedgehog to her. "Thank ye."

Everyone continues talking to Octavia and James.

The distant sounds of rolling waves and a hesitant fiddle serenade us under the stars. My eyes land on the Orion constellation, which reminds me of what Héctor shared with me once. Of him using the North Star to navigate himself in his new home—the sea.

Lydia, Pedro and Héctor stand, trying to leave, but Octavia scolds them.

"I didn't dismiss y'all," Octavia says, shuffling her cards.

"I'm a captain, I dismiss myself," Lydia snaps jokingly.

"At least let me do a reading for what is to come."

Lydia nods, and the three of them stay standing. We all watch eagerly as Octavia mixes her deck with ease, mumbling over the cards. She removes a card with her delicate fingers, flipping it.

"The devil reversed," she breathes. "We are entering a dark phase, whether we want to or not, and we will do it with strength and power. Some need to release what is holding them back. Accept yourselves, forgive yourselves, or I fear you'll live a life in the shadows." She grabs a dice from her pocket, throwing it. The number *three* pops up. "A trio. This trio will affect and trigger dark times."

"How?" Lydia asks. "Who?"

"I can't say." Octavia removes a card from the deck, but two come out instead. She flips them both over, wincing. "The high priestess reversed. Secrets shall come to light. All will withdraw from the warmth. A silence that lasts two winters. The next is the tower upright. Sudden change will come. Chaos, upheaval, a dark awakening." She rolls the dice again. The number two comes. "Two dark paths, two creators of chaos." Octavia finds my eyes, then subtly looks at Héctor.

Two dark paths. Two creators of chaos.

The wind picks up, and I hug myself.

"Finally," Octavia flips a fourth card. "Death."

"Death?" I shriek.

"It may sound bad, but death is actually rather positive, Red," James explains.

"You're quite right, James," Octavia says. "A door will close but another will open. Transformation is a huge theme here. You all need to put the past behind and embrace new opportunities. It may be difficult, but it is important for this particular ending. Emotional and physical pain will be experienced, but it is necessary. A touch of destiny is involved here." She closes her eyes and shudders. "But yes, ultimately real death will come. Death will catch up. Death will replace. Death cannot be ignored." She looks right at me. "And there is nothing you will be able to do, Luz. Against the tide. Beyond the horizon. Death will win. Now and forevermore."

CHAPTER FORTY-EIGHT

The rats nibble on my exposed body. Johann's laughter roars as I'm eaten alive. The smell of blood and sea salt mixed.

I thrash around one final time, pushing the imaginary rats off of me. Once more, sleep will not be anywhere near me tonight. It has been replaced by nightmares, prophecies of death, and Johann.

I sit up from my hammock, sighing; it must be well after midnight. The eerie quiet unsettles me, especially after the rambunctious evening. I push my curls out of the way, stepping into my boots. After Octavia read her cards, I decided to sleep it off, her words repeating in my head like a mantra.

I rub my eyes and I find Octavia and Lydia sleeping on the bed, their breathing synchronized. James and Mami Julia have opted for Sullivan's room, wanting to be near him one last time.

Exiting the room, I enter Héctor's quarters to rummage through his sack of clothes. I fish out a poet blouse in a deep scarlet color. It matches the exact shade of my necklace.

Changing mine and putting this one on, I'm now the color of my source of power.

As deep as blood, as fiery as revenge.

Near the sack lies Héctor's journal, opened to a page with a sketch of me. My relaxed gaze fixed to the side, my hair blowing in the wind. He's written something, but this time, it's in Arawakan, so I can't understand it.

I catch myself smiling and close it shut.

I grab my dagger and vest, then head out, the sketch buried in the back of my mind.

I walk toward the deck. I can't be constrained inside four walls. Not anymore at least. I can't believe I used to prefer being cooped up inside. Now, I can't be inside for too long without wanting to break down.

The night watch is out and about, practicing a bit with their swords, daggers, and pistols after the party. Pedro is laying on the deck, looking up at the stars as he smokes his cigar. His words from the game repeat in my mind.

I've always been afraid of lettin' people in...

I turn to the quarterdeck, and Héctor is there with a compass in hand. I join him. There are things I need answered. Plus, I'd like to spend as much time as I can with him. Uninterrupted.

Especially if he or I could die tomorrow.

"Hey, you," I say, approaching him.

He looks up from his compass and smiles. That smile. I could watch it all day. The sketches he made of me comes to mind.

"Hello," he says. "Could you not sleep again?" I shake my head. "I am sorry. I tried to join you, but Art said no to the night watch tonight. Wants to enjoy his last minutes alive by himself, he said." He clears his throat, his eyes never leaving my hair.

"You are beautiful with your hair in that manner. You were beautiful before, but even more breathtaking now."

I blush. "Thank you." I fidget with my fingers, not looking at him for my next words. "Maybe we can both do what we did two nights ago. Have one last peaceful bit of sleep before everything."

"I would love that."

"I wish it didn't have to be this way. I wish we could be alone, you know? Just you, me." I catch myself. "A-and the crew of course. Sailing away from everyone."

He raises an eyebrow. "Do you want it to be you and me?"

This takes me off guard. "D-do you?"

He smiles, leaning against the helm. He's wearing the all-black ensemble I like so much. Shirt, pants, vest, boots. A strong desire to connect with him overcomes me.

"I would give everything to make it just me and you, and James of course," he replies. "If he ever forgives me."

"He hasn't come around?" I ask, approaching him.

He eyes my face and hair with urgency. As if he wanted to touch all of me at once. His presence gives me a sense of vulnerability I never felt with Oliver. With Oliver, I had to keep my guard up, but with Héctor I wish to be my true self, to show him my mind and soul. I also want him to trust me enough to do the same.

Héctor shakes his head.

"He will. He just needs time," I say. "And no crew?"

"You would be my crew." His voice softens as he gets closer to me, putting his hand on my back. "I do not need a crew. I just need you. I would take care of you until the end of time itself. I would sail across the seas to ensure your safety, and travel through centuries to be near you."

My face goes hot and I look away, but force myself to look back. My breathing staggers. "Well, I already traveled through centuries, remember?"

He chuckles, biting his lip. "Would you do it again? If given the chance?"

I lean in. "For you? I would."

You've a job to do, Luz.

He pulls away slightly, sadness on his face. "You would do that? For a man with no honor, no money, no land?"

I try to put up a wall to distance myself from him, but my heart betrays me, speaking before my mind does. "Yes. I like myself the most when I'm with you. I can be who I want to be. Who I truly am. I don't have to hide or worry about not being enough, because you'll accept me as I am. All my flaws, my mistakes. I don't have to be perfect. I can just be *me*."

Oh.

Oh, no.

Octavia was right.

I want him. His soul. His mind. His heart.

Embarrassed, I avert my gaze, stepping away.

"D'nanichi," he says, grabbing my hands, making me look into his eyes. "You are perfect. Just as you are. Do not be embarrassed of your feelings."

"How can I not be when I just told you all that?"

"You should not be ashamed because from that first second I saw you, I knew it was going to be you. It will always be you. You are my weakness, as well as my strength, my reason for living. Without you, I would be lost." He leads me to the side of the quarterdeck, overlooking the dark ocean. Not once letting go of my hands. "You make me a better person, a better man. I may not have riches, but I will help you live a life of comfort and acceptance. If we survive this, I offer you my entire heart. It has always been yours."

No one, not even Oliver, has said this to me before. I've never felt more accepted and wanted before. And that's what I've longed for. Acceptance. Comfort. Being myself with someone else. Safety.

"Do you mean this?" I ask.

"Very much so," he replies, kissing my hand. "Meant every word. The day I lie to you is the day Nau cuts off my head. Which he will never get to do."

"I meant everything I said as well." I put my hair behind my ear, nervousness arising in me. "Speaking of Nau, there's matters we have to discuss. No bullshit. No lies. Just you, me, and the truth."

"No bullshit?" he asks, raising his eyebrow. He's getting defensive.

"I want full honesty, okay?" I say. "I won't judge you. I want to understand some things, just in case the worst happens tomorrow."

He relaxes. Not much, but a little. "Of course, d'nanichi. I would never lie to you."

I take a deep breath, wiping my hands against my pants. "How do you and Nau know each other? What exactly did you do for the East India Company?"

He looks at me, gripping the helm, not saying a word. I stand there, awkward, not knowing if I truly want the answer. What if he led the Trade expeditions? What if he was in charge of something truly horrible? How deep does the story between Johann Nau and Héctor Villanueva go?

I stare back at him, a couple of minutes of tense silence having passed by. I'm not even sure he'll answer my questions. I wouldn't blame him. I wouldn't answer either.

"You don't have to tell me," I say. "I should've just not—"

"No, it is okay," he finally says. "Please sit."

He gestures to a nearby barrel, and I obey. He's nervous, fidgeting with his fingers, eyeing the ring on my finger, but he refuses it when I offer it.

"I do not have a Spanish father, contrary to what Córdova and the others have led you to believe," he begins. "My baba was Lucayan, my bibi native to Borikén. My father had sailed to Borikén from Guanahani, San Salvador for Europeans, and was killed at the hands of the Spanish before I was born. My mother was a pregnant indigenous widow, near a Spanish colony. That did not sit well with the Catholics."

He slowly moves towards me, hands on his belt now. "My adoptive father, Fernando, a Spaniard, fell in love with my mother. He agreed to give her and my bakutu security and shelter for a child that would be baptized and given a Spanish name. I was born and baptized as Héctor Villanueva." He does a quick bow and flourish, rolling his eyes. "His legitimate child even though he and my mother had nono children."

Héctor Villanueva.

The adoptive son of acclaimed and respected Spaniard Fernando Villanueva.

The man who brought thousands of slaves to the Caribbean islands.

I did not see this coming. It never occurred to me.

He moves his hair away from his neck, showing me his small tribal tattoo. A circle outline with six petal-like semi circles around it, two eyes inside and a mouth. "Secretly, my mother gave me another name. Mautiatibuel, or Tibuel for short. Like Chief Mautiatibuel, the son of dawn. I was born at dawn, so she named me. When I was of age, I gave myself skin ink. The symbol that signifies my name." Tibuel. It fits him.

He leans against the wood next to me, looking up at the stars. "I have never been accepted by either people, though. My people reject me and my mother for baptizing me, giving into the pressure of the new world. The Europeans reject me for my skin color and background. Everything I know about my culture, wa hebeyo'no is thanks to my bakutu and bibi." He sighs, clasping his hands together in front of him.

"That must've been so hard as a child, not fitting in anywhere. Being rejected and oppressed by all sides," I tell him, meeting his gaze. Taking his hand, he looks back at me with a sense of sadness.

"It was not as hard as when I turned sixteen," he shrugs. "My father had said, *ya es hora de que aprendáis un oficio honorable, venís de una familia honorable y vais a comportarte como tal.*"

I hadn't heard him speaking Spanish that wasn't directed at mocking or yelling at Pedro. While it's a sarcastic tone, his accent is nice. A mix of English, Spanish, and Arawakan. A mix of the blood that courses through my veins.

"I was a fisherman's apprentice, you see. I longed to be in the sea, to feel the ocean breeze on my skin, but a fisherman's trade was not honorable, per my father. It was for the poor," Héctor explains, rolling his eyes. "To him, honor meant working for the East India Company. He was a commander for it. As a commander, he worked with a recently pardoned Nau. And so it began."

A nineteen-year-old psychopath.

"After Nau's hasty trial to be granted leniency for pirate secrets, my father agreed to oversee him. Train him, teach him. Everything Nau knows is my father's. Once I came of age, I enlisted for the Company as a navigator. I was to work with Johann Nau, so he oversaw me, teaching me what he knew. My time as a fisherman taught me navigational skills, my father taught me the rest. I became valuable to them. They did not like me, but I had more knowledge than all of them combined, so they kept me."

"Valuable?" I ask. "It brought the honor your father wanted?"

He nods. "That and more. My father had said that if I could make it in the Company until age twenty, I was to be granted a higher socioeconomic status that allowed me honor, money, and stability. However, I did not want that. I wanted nothing to do with the Company, but I could not go against the man who had given me an education, the man who provided my bibi and bakutu with security. I tried everything to get a dishonorable discharge, but my father threatened them, making sure I was not to be punished."

"So, what then?"

"I quickly rose through the ranks and led smaller ships for commerce in the Caribbean two years later. Sugarcane, potatoes, tobacco, gold, animals, silks. I wanted no part in the commerce that Nau was in charge of." I take a breath of relief. "One day, my ship was ambushed by pirates, and I was taken prisoner. The others they killed. The pirates wanted the cargo, they had kept tabs on me since my route was nearly the same all the time. They were going to kill me too until I overheard them say that I did not carry the cargo they were looking for, that I was one of the useless ones. It hit me. They were aiming at the bigger ships. Nau's ships."

"The slave trade ships."

He wasn't doing what I imagined. He was working there against his will. Doing it to please his Spanish father. Doing it to ensure his family kept that security from being murdered.

From being dragged to the tobacco fields, working with illness and disease.

He was doing it to make his savior happy.

Johann was wrong.

Héctor is *not* the monster he was portrayed to be.

"Correct. I made a deal. I would help them interfere, giving them the locations and approximations. We had a common goal, a common enemy. The Company. They hurt my people. They were hurting countless others. If I was to be involved in the Company, I decided, *to hell with it.* I will do my best to dismantle it from the inside. They agreed. I was to be their informant. Once a month, I joined the Marauders in their secret meetings, where I met Captain Sullivan after a couple of gatherings. I provided them with charts, information, and money. No one from the Company was aware. No one pays much attention to the brown boy unless it is for wrongdoings."

Héctor leans against the rail, gazing at the sky.

"I killed my father when I was eighteen. I did not mean to. But, he raised his hand to my bakutu. In a fit of rage, I got blinded and stabbed him. He was my first kill. I do not regret it." He rubs his face, as if he was reliving the memory. "I lied to everyone, of course. Told them that a thief had broken in and killed him. This allowed me to keep working in the Company, thus, working with the Marauders for three more years. Pirates and fugitive sailors who would dismantle ships from the East India Company, recovering the stolen gold and people. Giving them freedom, a second chance at life. Countless ships were dismantled thanks to my help. Nau was furious. He knew someone must have been working from the inside, but did not know who. Eventually, one of my own mistakes was my end. I left one of my old crewmates alive, but he told Johann. I did not know that he would blab after we threatened him."

"That's why he hates you so much. You caused the slow commerce of the cargo disappearance. His most trusted worker. It was all you."

"Very much so. All hell broke loose. People claiming I was staining my father's name, ruining his legacy and what he had worked so hard to establish in Española. At least his wish of me staying until I was one and twenty became a reality." He chuckles, rolls up his sleeve, and shows me his scar. The logo of the East India Company. "They gave me this the day I was to be tried, marking me as a traitor for the Company. That same day, I cheated my death. I escaped. I had arranged safe passage with Captain Sullivan beforehand. He offered me a position aboard his ship. Many wanted me for my navigational skills. I am one of the few aboard this ship who can read and do arithmetic. Ultimately, I went with him, becoming a fugitive of the law. The Company's and the West Indies' most wanted criminal. The son of a renowned Spanish leader. With no honor, no prospects, no title. Shamed forever."

I take in everything.

I don't even know where to begin. I want to both hate and thank Fernando Villanueva. If it wasn't for that man, Héctor would've been killed at birth.

But eventually, his own savior complex bit him in the ass.

Then, there's the part with Johann. I can't imagine what he did when he found out that Héctor caused everything. The son of the man that trained him. If Johann tortured me and I did no harm to him, I can't even fathom what Héctor could've gone through. Was that scar, that branding mark, the least of the pain he endured?

What would've become of Héctor's life had his father let him do what he wanted? He'd be living a life of simplicity, of honesty. His life has already been filled with racism and oppression since the day he was born, but had he chosen his own future, would it be more bearable on him?

Would he have been able to live a long life?

"Héctor, I am so sorry I ever doubted you," I finally say, my voice cracking.

"I forgive you," he says. "You did not know, and I did not deny it." He looks at his hands. "People always spoke ill of me, so I went ahead, and became their worst nightmare. They already hate me. Why not give them a valid reason to do so?"

"Still, it wasn't fair of me."

"It is not something I tell people. No one stays around enough for me to trust them."

I smile sheepishly. "I'm glad you trust me and feel comfortable to tell me everything." I kiss his cheek and hug him, knowing how hard everything must've been. "And don't worry, I'm not going anywhere, second mate."

"*First* mate, actually. Terrible lack of respect you have for me." He smiles, releasing me from the hug. "I am not going anywhere either. I will never leave your side. I shall annoy you until the end of your days." He teases me, crossing his arms. "Making sure that you do not get into trouble."

"What? I'm not the one who brings trouble here. I'm not the West Indies' most wanted criminal. Trouble follows you. It sticks to you like that girl stuck to James' lap at the inn."

He chuckles, relieved. "Yeah, okay. Whatever you say." He puts his arm around my waist, leading me back to the helm. "D'nanichi?"

"Yes?"

"Thank you for not judging me. That was hard to tell."

You don't even exist at all in my time. "I'll never judge. We all have reputations and past histories that haunt us."

He smiles. "Well, I am glad my reputation is not scaring you away."

A laugh erupts from the stairs. "What reputation? That women fall at yer feet? Por favor. James gets more play than ye." Pedro. He chucks his cigar overboard. "Yer both makin' me seasick. I'll take over tonight."

"You are not a night watch member," Héctor says, not releasing the helm.

"Don't make me tell ye again. Go. Before I rid *The Fury* of its first mate," Pedro insists, pushing Héctor out of the way. "Enjoy yer youth for once, Villanueva. Spend time with the siren. Don't be like my brother."

Héctor's gaze softens slightly, and he nods. "Just do not steer us to oblivion."

"For that... I just might."

I smile. "If you could do that, it would be appreciated."

"Ye and yer death wishes," Pedro smirks. "Ye sound just like Lucas." He clears his throat. "Now, go. Goodbye."

CHAPTER FORTY-NINE

"I shall sleep on the hammock, and you can—"

"Fuck that hammock, Héctor," I interrupt as he guides me to his quarters. "I need you next to me. Not a few feet away. *Next to me.*"

He smiles, opening the door to his room. "Alright, then. Let me help you so we can get some rest."

✹✹✹

This will be the last time I ever fall asleep.

And it'll be next to the person who brings me comfort.

Both of us lie down on his bed, facing each other. The absolute stillness creates an almost deafening silence. Héctor gently takes my hand and kisses it, while I marvel at his beauty—his hair, his eyes, his skin, and his heart. Yes, he's taken lives, and so have I. If we survive, maybe we can embrace our darker sides together.

The evil in the sea.

Two dark paths. Two creators of chaos.

Just like Octavia hinted.

"Is that mine?" he asks, pointing at the fiery red shirt I stole from him. It fits like a glove and I forgot I even took it from his pile.

"Maybe it is, maybe it isn't," I tease. "You should hide things better."

"Maybe so. But I shall let it slide, because you took my breath away when you came to the quarterdeck earlier." *Héctor's supposed to be dead.* "You should try getting some sleep."

"I'm afraid to fall asleep." *I don't want him to die.* "Héctor. I need you to stay away from Nau during the battle."

He stirs, tensing up. "Luz, what are you—"

"Listen to me. He is mine to deal with. This is my destiny. Your destiny shall come."

"But—"

"And you have to promise me no matter what happens, you must not, will not intervene or go after him." He looks away, but I grab his face, forcing him in my direction. "Promise me, Héctor. You must promise me."

He leans his head toward my right hand. "I promise." He rolls up the sleeve of the arm where Johann carved the slur. His fingers caress my scars. I pull away. "I simply cannot bear to sit by and let him get away with what he has done to you."

"Well, you must."

Héctor stays quiet, but nods. "Fine."

I prop myself up on one arm, thinking of another topic. "Did The Seer really tell you the one you'd seek would wear a code only *you* would understand?"

"Yes, I thought she meant jewels."

"I'm sorry I wasn't what you expected."

He smiles, propping himself up. "No." He pulls me in, his forehead on mine. "It was better. You are worth far more than a thousand jewels to me. Far more than treasure. You are what I was seeking. She told me I would look upon you and see a queen."

"Are you convinced that who she spoke about is me? I mean, what—"

"Your name lights up the darkness, Luz. Your voice has united our crew to fight against our biggest enemy. When I look at you, I do see a queen. You are the queen amongst queens. I would let you rule me without hesitation."

I blush, heat creeping to my neck. "You have a way with words. Have you thought of being a poet? I know you're an artist."

He covers his face as he lies down. "Please, do not bring that up. How shameful."

"I didn't think it was embarrassing."

He sighs, not removing his hands from his face. "You were not meant to see it."

"Well, no one has ever drawn me before, you know."

He takes away his hands, looking at me. "No? They should. I have never seen such beauty before. Makes me wonder if your siren powers are enchanting me."

"I don't have those powers... *yet.*"

"Even so, without powers, you managed to enthrall me."

I take out his ring, blushing. He stares at me, softening up. "Here, it's time you have it back. It once brought me comfort." He shakes his head, but I place it into his hand. "But no ring compares to you."

He blushes this time, putting on the ring. "You know, it is really hard to keep people out when you continue bringing my walls down." He pushes some curls behind my ear. "You should go to sleep. Rest. I am not going anywhere."

"You promise?"

"You have my word, Luz. I will not abandon you. I never will."

Drawing nearer to him, he enfolds me in his arms, holding me close. "And I promise I won't leave you, Héctor. I'm staying right here. I'm not going anywhere."

CHAPTER
FIFTY

The ship cuts through the choppy waters, a mixture of anticipation roaming the deck. Shivers shoot down my spine, the weight of the impending doom crushing my soul. The somber crew gazes out into the vast fog, scanning the horizon for Johann. The wooden planks creak under their boots with mournful groans. The isles protect us.

Mami Julia controlled the waves at dawn, leading us to the cays and pushing them forward by half a day. Ria left shortly after, to command the siren army from underneath. Just as we had planned yesterday. Now, it's a matter of waiting.

I sit on the wooden staircase, counting down the seconds until I'm able to spill Johann's blood upon the ocean floor.

"Red," James greets me, plopping himself down next to me. "How are ye holdin' up?"

"I'm okay," I say, Arawakan voices echoing in my head. They chant death. "We haven't spoken much since—"

"Aye." He takes a shuddering breath. "I wanted to make sure yer fine."

I face him, his eyes bloodshot. "James, you don't have to pretend with me."

He laughs but it's forced. "Pretend? Who said I was pretending? I'm perfectly fine." His voice cracks and he clears his throat. "I'm fine." He looks at his hands. "Is it normal to want to die after somethin' that hurts?"

Oh, James.

"Yes. And all we can do is feel our feelings, mourn who we were. Try to learn to live with the horrors."

"I miss him so much."

James embraces me, weeping. He clings to my shirt and arms. Johann will pay for hurting him, for having The Ringmasters kill Sullivan.

"Just let it all out. Cry. I'm here for you and I'll never leave. I love you, okay?"

"Ye better not leave. I ain't got no one else I trust."

My heart tugs. "How about Héctor?"

James sniffles, grimacing. "He ain't deserve my trust."

"But you're brothers. He loves you, you love him. I know you're angry, but your bond is stronger than the nails holding this ship together. And after today, who knows who lives and dies. I know that if you don't talk to him and he dies, you'll regret it." I watch as he squirms with my words. "You don't have to forgive him, you know, but you will live a life of regret if something happens to either of you."

"Damn it, Red." He chuckles, wiping his tears. "Stop readin' my mind."

I smile. "No. I'm the voice of reason in that unhinged little head of yours."

I comfort him, the Arawakan voices in my head growing stronger.

Make him pay...

"D'atiao," Héctor says, approaching us. He hugs himself, his hair blowing in the cool wind. "I know you might not forgive me. But I apologize for everything. All the pain I have brought you. And I want you to know I will protect you with my life today." He turns to me. "I will protect you both."

James gets up. He's going to run off. Instead, he approaches his brother, embracing him hard. A sigh of relief escapes me.

"I'm sorry I blamed ye for Sullivan's death," James sobs. "I'm sorry."

Héctor's eyes water and he tightens his embrace. "No, it is okay, I deserve it."

"No. Ye don't. I'm sorry I called ye a traitor. I'm sorry I couldn't protect Sullivan. I was furious at ye and needed time to think."

"And that is alright." Héctor grabs James' face in his hands, his jaw clenching but gaze softening. "You are incredible, James Malachi Edwards. You are the toughest amongst us here. I am honored you picked me as your brother."

"Brothers 'til the end, Héctor."

They embrace and I wipe my tears, watching as the brothers reunite once more.

Inside me, however, fear awakens, unsure of what truly awaits us.

CHAPTER
FIFTY-ONE

"They approach," Octavia warns from the quarterdeck.

The crew rushes to the side, watching the outline of a ship heading toward us. The three of us stand, watching the fog. I stand up straight, my hands gripping the wooden seam. My heart pounds inside my chest. My knees lock, my breath shudders.

"Héctor…" I say, my voice cracks at the end of his name.

He grabs my left hand, interlocking his fingers with mine. "You are safe with me."

His words provide a warm embrace amidst the chaos, serving as a beacon of hope. As I look into his eyes, my anxiety subsides, a sense of calm replacing it. I'm still on edge and terrified of what's coming, his reassurance easeeases a significant portion of my worry. I'm not alone. I will never be alone again.

I cling to his arm. "Let's kill this white man, then."

The Glory comes into focus as they approach us.

Mami Julia stands at the other side of me, holding my other hand. With a flick of her wrist, the fog clears somewhat and the waves sway our ship. Fog. Water. Of course she controls it too.

A bell rings above us, signaling their arrival. The wind blows in my face, as the crew gets ready. Pedro is armed with two pistols, one sword, and a dagger. A few grenades hang from his waist belt, waiting to be lit and thrown. He catches me looking and raises his eyebrow. I nod.

Lucas will return to you.

James mumbles something and then does the symbol of the cross when done.

Pray for all of us, James.

"Art, hoist the colors," Lydia orders from the quarterdeck. "Crew, weapons at the ready."

I look down to make sure I have everything I need. My dagger. My pistol. My cutlass. The grenade hidden inside the small satchel across my body. Items that have become part of my daily life.

Anxiety rises the faster *The Glory* positions itself parallel to *The Fury*. Must be Mami Julia's doing.

"All arms at the ready!" Lydia orders, and we prepare ourselves for the worst.

The crew of *The Glory*, stands, watching us with their weapons drawn. I scan their ship, trying to find Cyrus and Lucas. They're nowhere to be seen.

"Sea rats of *The Fury*," a voice yells from *Glory*. It's coming from a man on the quarterdeck, but it's not Johann. In fact, I don't even *see* him. "Surrender the siren, or suffer the consequences."

I take a deep breath, but no one moves. No one says anything.

"Where's Nau?" I ask, making sure my voice carries over to *The Glory*. "Hiding?"

A laugh. A big hearty, mocking laugh. Johann emerges from the fog, hands stretched outwardly. "Here I am, my dear wife," he says. "Could not live without me?"

"Wife?" James mutters under his breath. *Not the time, James.*

Instantly, I catch on. Johann's putting on a performance. That's why he hid at first and only came out when I called him.

Well, two can play this game.

I, too, can give an excellent performance.

I'm an actress, after all, aren't I?

"Admiral, I've decided you were right," I say. "Pirates are the filth in this sea." I look at my nails as I stride across the wooden deck. "They do nothing but contaminate our perfect world, bringing *imperfection.*"

Grumbles from the crew, shouts of disbelief.

Think of happy memories, Luz.

You are worth far more than a thousand jewels to me.

Héctor turns to me, confused. "Luz, what are you doing?"

My fingertips tingle with my power. "I'm saying Johann was right. None of you deserve to live." I take out my dagger, giving Héctor a small cut on his cheek. He brings his hand up in disbelief. *I'm sorry.* "Especially you."

"What has gotten into you?"

"Ah, you've finally seen reason then!" Johann declares from *The Glory.* He looks proud, content. It's sickening.

Happy memories. *Soledad hugging me, her gorgeous brown eyes twinkling.*

"Yes." Weapons are being loaded, but Pedro barks an order to lower them. "You were right."

The sky darkens. Rain falls at once. This has to work.

I take out my cutlass, challenging Héctor to a fight. "Fight me, coward," I command, pushing him.

He stumbles, falling to his side. His mouth is slightly open, his breathing labored.

"No," he states, standing. "I will *not* fight you."

"FIGHT ME, VILLANUEVA!" I swing my cutlass but he intercepts it.

The air is thick with tension as we confront each other, our eyes fiercely engaged in a life-and-death battle. The creaking planks below mirror our every step, and the gusty wind heightens the drama. Despite my attempts to communicate that it's all a ruse and that I regret my actions, his attention remains solely on defending against my attacks. A snarl twists his lips, and the clash of our metal weapons reverberates around us. Swift and precise, we encircle each other, showcasing agile footwork.

The Fury's members rush at me, cutlasses raised, their shouts of betrayal echoing in the air. In response, I summon a feeble swirling vortex with a gesture of my hand, drawing rainwater to form a shield around me. The water strikes them, pushing them back. Héctor stands there, stunned, mouth agape. I direct the current at him, sending him stumbling. Meanwhile, Johann observes attentively from his ship, relishing the scene.

Héctor is on his knees, his hair disheveled and wet. His eyes have darkened, his chest falls and rises. He studies me, deciding if I mean it. The crew stands, drawing their weapons once more.

"If you're truly on my side, finish him," Johann says.

"I will," I say. A few people cry out. Octavia does nothing to hold them back, making my performance more genuine.

I sheathe my cutlass and place my hands in front of me, channeling happy memories. He's one of my happy memories. He brings me peace.

I'm sorry.

"Luz, do not do this," Héctor begs.

"Rest easy, Villanueva. Today you finally meet justice," I say, stone cold. Water surrounds us, separating him and I from them.

"I know this is not you." He takes a deep breath, never taking his beautiful eyes off mine. "Regardless, I trust you, Luz Narváez."

I smile. Happy memories. The water goes under my command, choking him.

Johann laughs and The Fury screams in outrage.

Kill him. Do it. Now!

I'm tackled and fall on my hip just as I send the ocean current straight to Johann. My concentration breaks, the water never reaching him. I groan, Pedro on top of me. A rain of bullets is fired at us. *The Fury* members get down. Héctor coughs, spitting out water. His breath is quick and shallow, his hands tremble, gripping his chest.

"What the fuck was that?" Pedro hisses, putting his hat on and moving away from me. "I ain't like Villanueva, but—"

"It was a performance," I breathe as we get up. "I had to take the chance."

The bullets end. "Wench!" Johann screams. "She tricked us! Bring the prisoners now!"

"It was a trick!" Lydia yells.

"Weapons ready to bring down Nau!" Pedro shouts. "The siren's on our side, lads."

I help Héctor stand. "I'm sorry," I say. "I had to see if I could kill him off like that. I'm so sorry about drowning you."

"Next time warn me so I can provide a much more believable performance," he admits smiling. He fixes his wet vest and heads to the crow's nest to shoot people down with arrows.

Cyrus and Lucas are pushed onto *The Glory's* deck by their tormentors, its members laughing. Pedro runs over, gripping the rail as smoke and woodchips descend over us.

Covered in a tapestry of blood, bruises, and cuts, Cyrus Khan and Lucas Córdova are unrecognizable. Every step they take resonates with agony, their bodies barely able to bear the torment. With brutal force, Cyrus is hauled onto the deck by one officer, his arms dragged heavily. Simultaneously, Lucas limps and is roughly pushed onto the wooden floor by another man, blood seeping from his mouth. My heart races as I rush to the rail, feeling power coursing through every fiber of my being. The insatiable craving for revenge gnaws at my very soul, growing stronger with each fleeting moment. The rain intensifies, transforming into a torrential monsoon.

Johann seizes a nearby officer's sword and swiftly strikes Cyrus, severing his left forearm. Cyrus writhes in pain and Johann advances toward Lucas as the crew of *The Fury* watches in horror. Clenching my fists, the thunder roars above, winds unleash chaos, and the sky darkens, signifying Johann's actions won't go unchallenged.

Johann *has* to die.

I'm seduced by the power that revenge promises, the sense of control it offers in a world that has shown me naught but cruelty. It becomes an intoxicating elixir, fueling my descent into darkness and numbing my conscience.

As the rage courses through my veins, an uncontrollable surge of power awakens within me. The turbulent emotions within my chest mirror the churning waters of the ocean surrounding me. The waves, once calm, now respond to the fury within, rising and crashing with an intensity that mirrors the storm raging within my heart.

A sudden wind knocks Johann off his feet, missing Lucas by mere inches. Lucas, while weak himself, drags himself to Cyrus and builds a tourniquet around his arm to contain the bleed. Still, Johann is relentless, trying to kill his young ex-officer.

I take deep, raging breaths, glaring daggers at Johann. He smirks, his head raised. I take out my pistol and shoot at him, screaming. The wind intervenes, making me miss. Out of anger, I throw my empty pistol into the sea, trying to control myself.

The sky roars above me. The clouds shine from the lightning. The wind is thunderous. Like a category four hurricane. My gaze doesn't leave Johann's.

I am the eye of the hurricane.

I am the daughter of the women they couldn't drown.

The daughter of the sea.

Of the sky.

Of the warriors.

Of the land.

I am the evil in these fucking seas.

My heart, once capable of love and compassion, now pumps hatred through my veins.

"Listen up, everyone," I yell, standing on the side of the ship, grabbing the rope. The rain is falling so hard it could cut our skin. "Do we cower like rats under the rain?"

"No!" The crew replies, drenched but giddy.

"Fire cannons then! We give them hell!"

"Fire cannons!" Pedro screams to the crew below decks and the war begins.

I turn to Nau, holding on, as the cannons get ready.

You will pay.

And you will die.

"Gentlemen, let's show these low-lives who we really are!" Nau yells and the men cheer, swords up.

"Crew of *The Fury*," I say. "We leave no survivors!"

This is war.

CHAPTER
FIFTY-TWO

The water beneath us roars, a primal scream of fury echoing across the expanse. It engulfs everything in its path, a ferocious manifestation of my anger and frustration. The ocean responds to the raw power emanating from my very being. I let it loose, not once controlling it.

The first cannon from *The Fury* goes off as a waterspout forms between the two ships, blocking the hit. I whirl my head around, the wind stopping, the rain thinning. Mami Julia controls the waterspout, her hair whipping behind her, a curtain of black and white waving as quickly as our flag.

"What are you doing?" I ask, approaching her, sword in hand. "¡Los teníamos allí mismo, Mami!"

"¡Están muy cerca!" She yells, struggling. "Lucas and Cyrus are still on that ship. They need to get off!"

I nod. "What can you do?"

She takes a deep breath, her hands shaking. "I can hold *The Fury* in place, but it has to be from underneath! Ria and a group will come and rid a few of the men from *The Glory*. Make sure James is far. His mental state is fragile and easily susceptible to our song."

She has to leave me again. This time, though, there's no certainty she's coming back. "No. Don't you dare leave me a second time."

"Mija, I don't want to leave you!" she cries, breaking the waterspout apart, both ships swaying unnaturallyly. There are screams and gasps on both. I lose my footing, but she holds me up. "But it has to be done. I'm no help from up here without my necklace. I've been on land for too long, I have to help as my true form. From underneath."

I throw myself on her, hugging her hard. The rain picks up again, thunder threatening to crack open the sky. She holds my face in her hands. Giving me a huge kiss on my forehead, she wipes away the shortened curls plastered on my face.

"I'm so proud of you, mija. Always have been. It's time you make yourself proud," she says and releases me. "Show them what we Narváez women are capable of and how deadly we can be. Aycayia, humana. Bring havoc."

"I will."

With a flick of her wrist, she causes *The Glory* to move with such force, it almost sinks. She will not will not give them a painless painless death. She, like me, wants them to suffer.

"Consigue a Lucas y Cyrus," she says. "Then, show el blanco who you truly are. Show him no mercy, mi amor."

The whirlpool grows larger and more powerful, drawing in the surrounding currents, as if the ocean itself is heeding my call. It becomes a maelstrom of chaotic energy;; the waves crashing and colliding in a mesmerizing display of nature's wrath.

The sea trembles under my command, responding to my tumultuous emotions. The water rises higher, towering like a titan, as if answering the call of my rage. It's a testament to the deep connection I share with this element, an extension of my very soul.

Mami Julia looks up at the rain and opens her arms, a huge stream of water falling directly from the sky. She falls back into it, swallowing her up into the ocean. Into her home.

Over the storm, a beautiful melody begins. A group of Aycayias sing, enchanting the men. Their hair is adorned in gold and seashells, the wind causing them to look as beautiful as the sea itself. In the middle? Ria. Fury in her face, blood running down her cheeks. Men from *The Glory* jump into the ocean, mesmerized by the tune. Ria receives them with her fangs and claws. But unfortunately, so are some of the Fury pirates. Including James.

He's in a trance. I pull him backward, shaking him roughly.

"Wake up, you'll die!" I shriek. He startles himself and panics, looking around. "Resist them. Your story is *not* over yet, Edwards!"

He nods, gasping for air. He's fighting it.

The song ends. The men from *The Glory* are screaming underneath, gargling water as they drown.

Those entranced, on the brink of leaping, awaken and regain their composure.

The fight ensues.

The storm and oceans bring our ships closer, encircling us in its deadly waters. Enough for us to get over to *The Glory* via a rope. The crew scrambles to get their footing under the rain. From the crow's nest, Héctor takes down men from *The Glory* with his crossbow one by one.

I need to find Pedro.

He's tying some ropes together, scowling and cursing under his breath.

"Quartermaster!" I yell, and he looks at me, knife in his mouth. "I can't swing to the other ship. That's not my area of expertise, but you can." He takes the knife away from his mouth and throws the ropes aside.

"Aye, get on with it, querida," he yells back, the rain feeling like pins and needles on our skin.

"Now's your chance to get Lucas. The ships are close enough for you to make the jump and get him."

He looks around, calculating the distance. "Aye!"

"Get your son, Córdova. I will get Nau's head."

He nods and releases the ropes he's holding on to. Lydia is screaming orders from the quarterdeck as she stabs two men next to her. They drop to the ground one by one, like flies.

Pedro grabs a rope, giving himself the momentum he needs to swing over. "Move!" he yells, and everyone clears a path for him.

He runs toward *The Glory* with the speed of a professional athlete, swinging over the ravenous sea beneath us. He lands with ease on *The Glory*, shooting a man down.

"Gentlemen!" Lydia calls out. "Give them hell!"

There's a scream in unison, and more pirates follow Pedro's lead.

Pedro takes the crew's surprise to his advantage and takes down at least two men with his sword. He throws Lucas over his shoulder, as if the boy was a rag doll. Lucas grabs on as Pedro shoots down another man. A second man grabs a panic-stricken Cyrus, tying extra ropes around them. Pedro swings back over to *The Fury* with his son, barely missing the side beam. He grabs on, yelling at Lucas to climb up.

Lucas crawls on board, with Pedro following.

The clash of swords and symphony of grunts fill the air. Two men from *The Fury* have boarded *The Glory*, fighting. Which means a couple of men from *The Glory* have boarded *The Fury* as well.

Woosh! An arrow passes me, piercing a man behind me. I glance at Héctor, nodding. He nods back, loading another arrow.

I take out my sword as a man approaches, yelling a battle cry. I intercept his sword, punching him in the face. This doesn't kill him, but it winds him down enough for me to catch Pedro and Lucas' conversation. To ensure he stays down, I make a cut on his thigh, causing him to cry out in pain.

"¡No te rescaté para nada!" Pedro yells, pushing Lucas toward the lower deck. Lucas stumbles, but never falls. It's amazing how alike they look standing next to the other.

"¡No, yo puedo pelear!" Lucas yells back. The rain washed away the blood on his body, showing the fresh cuts and bruises that Nau's crew gave him.

A second man comes near Lucas, ready to strike, but I stab his side with force. I push him back into the ocean, where he's engulfed by the fifteen foot waves. He screams as he descends, knowing the certain death awaiting him.

"Lucas, please. Stay safe or your father will have my head," I beg. He shakes his head, taking one of Pedro's swords instead. I sigh. "Just make sure you aim to kill."

He nods. "I will. Don't worry about me, preciosa."

Pedro pulls Lucas' arm. "Te dije que no, ¿no entiendes? ¿Acaso sos sordo?"

"Y yo dije que iba a estar bien. ¿No confía en mí?"

Pedro sighs, staring at his son. Ultimately, he nods. Lucas walks off, stabbing a Royal Navy officer. Pedro grabs my shoulder, taking a deep breath. "We still have a lot to do, querida. We shall toast in victory when Nau's dead, savvy?"

He runs off, shooting down a third man. Cyrus is carried onto *The Fury* by Art and Octavia takes over, tending to his arm.

Make him pay for it...

The vicious wind carries Arawakan whispers with it. I close my eyes, letting the rain prickle my skin. An insidious darkness grows within me, and my inner turmoil and need for revenge intensifies. Roiling turrets sway the creaking ships around the whirlpool, the voices screaming at me to avenge Sullivan.

"Nice to see you again, wench," a man taunts.

"Wish I could say the same," I say, and swing my sword hard toward him, my body seething, but he stops it, the iron clashing so hard my teeth chatter.

We fight, swiping our swords at each other, trying in any way or form to either kill or disarm the other. Even with all the rain and my rocky movements that are sure to be my downfall before the fight has even begun, I never let my grip go.

Rip-p-p.

The tip of a cutlass erodes from his abdomen and just as quickly, it's taken out.

The man suddenly drops his sword on the deck, a gurgly scream escaping his throat. Blood draws from his mouth and he coughs viciously, spitting blood on me. I wipe it away from my face with a grimace.

Finally, he falls to his knees and collapses on the deck.

Héctor stands behind with a bloody sword.

The Fury fires its cannons, the resounding boom echoing in my ears.

Smoke clouds form as tall as a skyscraper, engulfing us inside its bitter smell. The oceans burn, a ring of fire around both of our ships, entrapping us in this circle of hell.

Just like the prophecy hinted at.

Lydia is up at the helm, kicking off a man overboard, while another charges at her. Pedro is shooting everyone he encounters as Lucas stabs a man. James is on the stairs, fighting off a man with his own cutlass. Héctor is breaking another man's neck with his bare hands, the crossbow on his back.

More men from *The Glory* arrive, injured and beaten, but still determined to fight.

Countless people lay dead on both ships.

I'm determined to find Nau. Time to end this once and for all. I march off, but I'm grabbed from behind. I elbow the person in the face, an unpleasant sensation shooting down from my forearm to my fingers. I drop my cutlass.

The man that grabbed me is bleeding from his nose, his nostrils flaring, his fingers covered in his own blood. He charges at me empty-handed, and I let my power control me, engulfing him in the tumultuous current that forms from the rain. I tilt my head as he chokes, a murderous grin on my lips. *Oh, I've missed this.*

The raw Aycayia energy courses through my veins, and I relish in his gasps and squirms. The more I allow myself to be consumed by my power, the more I crave its destructive euphoria. Ria and Mami Julia were wrong. It's better if I let it rampage everything in front of me.

"My dear siren of ruin," a familiar voice calls out, my eyes slicing to him. The water bubble around the man's head breaks, and he flops dead on the deck. I face Johann, and he stands at the top of the stairs, holding James by his neck. "End this now, or this child pays for it."

A grunting, teeth-baring Lydia is held back by four men, all of them struggling to contain her. She's so strong that it took four men to overpower her.

James tries to get loose from Nau's grip, loud gasps causing everyone to quiet down.

"Your life for his," Johann bargains, loud enough for everyone to hear. With his free hand, he aims his pistol at James' head. My chest tightens. I push the whispers away, enough to concentrate on James.

I approach Nau, rain falling over us with such a force it could knock us from our feet. He's such a coward. Preying on the youngest. My eyes fall on Johann's neck. He wears my grandmother's necklace.

"Let. Him. Go." I enunciate, making sure my voice carries through the rain. "This is between you and me. He has no part in this."

He laughs. "This child became a part of this the day he was born a—"

I take out my dagger. "I dare you to finish that sentence, you absolute—"

"The more you speak, the less air reaches his lungs."

I drop my dagger to the side and stand directly in front of him, not taking my eyes off his. There's rage in them. Nau is out for blood and he won't stop until *mine* covers the oceans.

Well, I won't stop until his drips from my *hands*.

The rain continues falling at a steady, forceful pace. My anger rises inside my body. I want his blood spilled.

I need him dead.

The grenade...

Johann glares at me, spotting for hidden weapons. I raise my hands behind my head, as if I were getting arrested. Finally, he releases James. James falls to his knees, coughing viciously while holding his neck. I help him stand and hug him.

"When I say now, throw this grenade behind him," I whisper in James' ear, swiftly putting the grenade from my bag inside his shirt. He grabs it and crosses his arms, hiding it from everyone's view. "Throw it as far as you can. You've got good aim. Don't miss."

Lydia gets loose from the grip the four men have on her and punches two of them back-to-back. The third one's staggering shock brings his death as she buries her dagger into his neck. She runs up to Nau, taking out a pistol. She aims it right at Nau's head. The fourth one tackles her to the ground behind us just as she aims. She misses her shot, barely grazing his thigh.

The fourth man aims his pistol at her face and she snarls, not once lowering her gaze.

"Keep the bitch down!" Nau screams, grabbing my neck, pulling me close to his face. I bring my hands to his, trying to get loose from his grip. Mami Julia's necklace shines, a burst of light pulsating from within.

Cracks form in her necklace, blue filigree exiting the jewel.

"You will not conquer *my* seas," he whispers.

"Fuck you," I spit, trying to conserve my air.

"Nau!" Héctor calls out from behind us. *No.* "Let her go!"

"Héctor, don't get involved!" I yell between gasps, Johann's hands tightening around my neck.

"The whore has spoken." Johann licks his lips and glares at Héctor. "How about I make you watch as I kill her? Slowly. Intimately. Make her suffer a fate worse than death beforehand. Then, I'll kill you, Villanueva."

Rapid footsteps approach.

"James, NOW!" I yank my grandmother's necklace, ripping it from Johann's neck. I kick Johann's groin and fall to my knees.

"Fury, down!" James yells, lights up the rope and launches the grenade far behind us.

A blinding flash of light goes off just as it passes Lydia and the other man, throwing all of us across the deck.

CHAPTER
FIFTY-THREE

High-pitched ringing and the crackle of fire surrounds me as I open my eyes.

Groggily, I raise my head. I've landed on my back under a mast. Smoke billows and flames lick the air, splinters of wood and flecks of ash descending over us like rain. A few rigging ropes and canvas sails are scorched with singed marks. The rain has since stopped. I bring my hand to my pounding head and it comes away bloody. My other hand holds my grandmother's necklace, the jewel broken in half.

He stole it, then broke it.

Still, I take the split jewel.

I sit up, but pain overtakes my entire body. Ignoring it, I slowly stand, watching everyone else. Beaten up by the explosion. The man closest to the blast lies ahead of me, burnt beyond recognition. I have no idea where Johann landed, but part of me feels like he's still alive. James is facedown near me, and if it wasn't for everything going on around us, I truly would believe for him to be in a peaceful sleep.

I drag myself to him, shaking him. He groans softly. He's alive. Héctor stirs a few feet away, grabbing his side. His long, straight hair is disheveled, and he's got a cut on his forehead.

A bloodcurdling scream. It's Octavia.

I cough as I maneuver around the weakened bodies on the deck. Octavia herself seems physically fine, with no injuries. She holds an unconscious Lydia in her shaky arms, mumbling something in Creole. Blood trails from Lydia's nose to her lip, a fresh burn on her neck and shoulder. A wooden beam has impaled her still chest.

My eyes tear up.

Please. Not Lydia.

Memories of the Captain flash before my eyes, my chest constricting.

"She was closest to the blast along with that man who burned alive," Octavia cries, taking off Lydia's hat and cleaning the blood from her nose and face.

I fall to my knees. "No, no, no."

"All those things she said she wanted to do. The Royal Nightmare. Seeing her sister." Octavia chokes on a sob. "Why must history be so cruel?" She kisses Lydia's forehead, her lips quivering. "No, please. God, *please.*"

I sit here, frozen amidst the stirring chaos of the ships. Emotions surge within me, drowning me in sorrow. Lydia's lifeless body lies in Octavia's bloodied arms. Tears blur my vision, Lydia's absence feeling like a chasm in my soul. She was one of the first I trusted when I got here. She was my inspiration, my hero. She accepted me, became my mentor. She confided in me and I in her. All sounds fade away behind me, the sound of my heart breaking echoing in my ears.

Sullivan, Lydia. Two incredible human beings.

Gone.

I stand, determined to give Johann Nau the hell he deserves.

Octavia grips my arm, her nails digging into my forearm. There's tears in her eyes, urgency, pleading.

"Make him pay for it," Octavia pleads. "Burn him. Drown him. Do whatever you need to do."

I nod, taking out my sword and putting the remains of my grandma's necklace in my pocket.

"I will, I promise," I cry.

Octavia goes back to caressing Lydia's forehead while speaking softly in Creole. Her tears land on Lydia's bruised, burned face.

Goodbye, Lydia.

Two men are helping Johann up, but he pushes them off briskly, barking his insults at them. He catches me staring and his gaze turns murderous. I run toward the lower deck and Art gives instructions to man the ship.

"Art, fire all the cannons," I order. "Burn that infernal ship down."

"Aye!" Art says. "Fire all cannons! We leave not one sail standing!"

"Aye!"

I ascend the stairs, expecting to be hit or stabbed by Johann, but instead, I get nothing. Héctor passes me, dragging a semi-conscious James into their quarters.

Johann screams in frustration. He's scrambling across the destroyed deck, searching for something.

My grandmother's necklace.

The fight picks up again,, and the first few cannons from *The Fury* are fired at *The Glory*. Johann stops what he's doing to watch his ship get a few hits. A man lunges at me and I cut his leg, kicking his groin afterward.

"Johann!" I yell. He wipes away the blood from his mouth, taking out his sword. "This ends now."

"You destroy my ship? I'll destroy *you*," he spits at me, his gaze unwavering.

"Only one evil can survive here!" I strike him with my cutlass, and he blocks it. "And it'll be me!"

All the anger I've felt all this time rushes in my body, creating adrenaline. Torrential rain pours down, threatening to knock us both off our feet. *The Glory* burns, the wood loudly splitting in half from the heat. Those who aren't injured or unconscious from the blast are fighting, the clash of swords resuming.

"This is how you want to play, huh, my dear?" he asks, taking off the remains of his burnt wig. He throws it to the side, revealing his neck length blond hair.

"You began the problem!" I yell through the downpour. "This is me ending it."

He laughs, mocking me. "You think you're a Goddess? You're *not*. You're just like *me*. You're a *monster*."

I try another hit, which he also blocks with ease. One of the best swordsmen in the Caribbean indeed. I'll give him that.

I grin. "You're wrong. I'm not like you." He swings his sword and I intercept it. "I'm *worse*."

He screams and charges at me again.

We join the clash of irons that are battling for supremacy. I never lose my footing or give in to him. He strikes hard to stab my side, but I spin around away from him. He cuts my leg, slicing my pants as well. I wince, stumbling.

A cannon goes off, echoing inside my head.

A swift strike slices his cheek, drawing blood. He touches the wound with a smirk. His blows come relentlessly, one after another, preventing me from striking back. I can only shield myself, praying he spares any critical areas.

He's good. *Too good.*

My heart is racing inside my chest, my body giving out. All my energy is slowly being drained from me. Then, it hits me. *He's trying to tire me out.*

Well, two can play that game.

I throw my sword on the deck and barely escape his lethal hit. Instead, his sword ends up wedged in the mast behind me. He threw the hit with such force;; the sword doesn't want to budge. It's stuck there. A fair fight.

He turns to me and wipes the blood away from his face with his sleeve. I have no other weapons. He takes out a small dagger instead of his pistol. He must think I'm not worth one of his bullets. I evade his lunges at me, making him curse in French. I mock him, smiling. This only makes him angrier.

I throw a broken piece of wood and it hits his chest, bouncing down. He watches it with disgust, appalled at my audacity to even throw such a thing at him. So, I parkour toward the other side of the deck and he chases me, calling me a filthy pirate.

Pirate Luz Narváez.

I like the sound of that.

Boom! Destruction ensues for *The Glory.* The impact of the cannon explosion throws me off balance as I run, but I stick to it, determined to make it to the other side.

I evade the bodies between us, pushing people out of the way. Reaching the bow, I halt momentarily, allowing him to catch up, before abruptly retracing my steps towards the decimated staircase leading to the quarterdeck in ruins.

"You can't outrun me forever, whore!" he yells.

I ignore him. They set another blast off.

I slip and fall from the impact, landing on some rubble near the mast. My back aches. I groan, unable to move. I come face-to-face with a bloody figure. It's Lucas. He's underneath the rubble from the blast, unconscious. Pedro is frantically trying to take every piece of wood away from Lucas' body. Pedro prays in Spanish.

"You die now," Nau seethes, stomping toward me.

"No. She does not," Pedro enunciates and shoots Nau. Pedro never misses a shot, but for the first time, he misses Johann, shooting his left arm instead.

Unfortunately, Johann isn't left-handed.

He groans, gripping his arm. He drags himself away, being shielded by one of his officers as he ties a tourniquet around the wound. I'm so weak and disoriented, I don't dare risk taking a shot.

Héctor approaches me, helping me up. My body groans and screams for rest. Leaving my side, he moves on to help retrieve Lucas from the rubble. Nau screams at his officer.

"Is James okay?" I ask, catching my breath.

"Yes, I locked him inside our quarters," Héctor says. Pedro pushes him out of the way.

"Stop layin' around, get up and fight him, querida," Pedro commands, his voice trembling. "Villanueva, help me! Be useful!"

I get up, wrath coursing through my body like venom. Once again, the whispers surround me.

Kill him...

Become the queen of the seas...

The Aycayia of Destruction...

Another cannon.

Keeping my gaze on Nau, water swirls and writhes behind me with an unsettling intensity. I open my mouth, and I'm speaking Arawak fluently. The water grabs Johann and the officer, throwing them against the bow, then the quarterdeck staircase, and finally the mast. The officer is dead. Johann still lives, groaning, blood dripping from his nose. I march to him, an insatiable thirst for destruction growing inside me.

End him.

Rule the seas.

Become feared by everyone.

I take out my dagger, ready to slit his throat. Johann takes deep breaths, and the dagger slips from my hands. Oliver. It's *Oliver.* The water retreats, releasing him. He falls on his back on the deck, labored breaths escaping me.

No, no, no!

Boom. The impact makes me fall on my back, groaning against the broken staircase. My ears ring, my body aches all over.

Nau catches sight of me and charges at me, a stolen sword in hand. I try to control the rain but can't.

"Nau! Stop trying to fight her and fight me instead!" Héctor yells. I slowly get up, my trembling hands gripping to the rail. "I am the one you have been wanting for the past five years! I am the one who ruined your precious commerce!"

No.

You promised.

"Move, Villanueva. Or I shall kill you too," Nau snarls, wiping blood away from his mouth.

"Then do it. My life for hers."

The clash of their steel cutlasses reverberates in the environment. With a lightning-fast lunge, Johann narrowly misses his mark, his blade slicing through the air just millimeters from Héctor's chest. I attempt to stand straight but my knees buckle, my nails digging into the damp railing.

In their perilous dance of skill and precision, Johann twirls out of the way, Hector toppling onto the deck sideway. Hector grimaces, clutching his left elbow as his cutlass slides out of reach.

Johann stands above him, pulling his arm back, readying himself to stab a weaponless Héctor.

"Héctor!" I scream and he looks up at Johann, defiance in his eyes.

My eyes do not leave Héctor. Hastened footsteps approach as Johann grins.

A shadowy figure leaps into the action unexpectedly, intercepting Johann's lethal strike before it's too late.

Pedro falls to his knees, a sword lodged in his stomach. With his remaining strength, he pushes Johann with force, sending him back a couple feet.

I'm not like you... I'm worse.

CHAPTER
FIFTY-FOUR

"**G**et my son out of them scraps, Villanueva," Pedro orders, his voice softening by the second. Héctor holds Pedro, helping him lay down. Pedro grips Héctor's shirt, his breathing shallow. I run to him, pushing his wet hair away from his face. "Take care of them. Of Lucas, of James. Of Luz. Promise me."

"Córdova—" Héctor quivers.

Pedro coughs, spitting out blood. He takes out Nau's sword from his abdomen, wincing and groaning. It clatters on the deck. "Por favor, Héctor. Promise me."

Héctor cries. "I promise."

Johann stands from afar and Art comes out to fight him, screaming about Cyrus. The two fight.

"I'm sorry I stole yer pistols," Pedro jokes. "But yer a horrible shot."

"I am sorry I called you a whore," Héctor apologizes, a sympathetic smile on his lips. "Repeatedly."

"Ye weren't wrong." Pedro spits out blood, his eyes landing on mine. "Héctor, please do as I said... brother."

Héctor stifles a sob and nods. "Mi hermano." He stands and runs off to help Lucas.

Art and Johann continue fighting on the deck as Héctor arrives at Lucas' side.

Pedro takes a long breath and turns to me, gripping my hand. "I'm sorry I hurt ye, querida." He coughs, his eyes dimming with each word. The color from his face fades into a cool gray. "I wish I could turn back time and change things, but I cannot." His grip lessens. "S-show them what it means to be a Córdova."

I gasp, taken aback. "Wh—"

He nods, breathing rapidly. "That's what I wanted to tell ye." He coughs, blood splattering. "Sangre de mi sangre."

My heart quickens. No. This can't be. "I'll take care of Lucas. His destiny will be fulfilled."

Pedro takes a long gasping breath. Then, he's still.

His lifeless blue eyes stare at me, so I close them with my fingers, tears trailing down my cheeks.

Sangre de mi sangre.

She said it's from your grandfather.

Gustavo Narváez *Córdova.*

Pedro Córdova.

I'm Pedro's descendant.

Thunder grumbles above me. Johann punches Art in the face and Art hits his head as he stumbles, falling unconscious.

My eyes find Johann's.

"Fight me once and for all, Johann!" I yell, waterspouts forming on either side of *The Fury.* Johann charges at me and I swipe my cutlass at him. I take the fight up to the crumbling quarterdeck.

The wind picks up, whipping my shoulder-length hair behind me. The ocean that once flowed with grace and elegance becomes an instrument of destruction. It twists and contorts, doing what it wants. It's connected to my murderous emotions, forming powerful tendrils that snakes and ensnares every single member of The Glory, constricting and suffocating them with an icy grip. Dark clouds circle overhead, releasing torrential rain.

Another cannon.

We both fall. My cutlass slides away from me, Nau ending on top of me. Memories of when he carved the slur come back. My screams. His laughter. Thunder booms and lightning crackles. He stands on top of me, his legs on both sides of my arms. He takes out a golden dagger and leans down, pressing it against my throat.

"Just where I want you," he says, smirking. "Tell me. How does it feel knowing you've lost?"

"Oh, I'm not losing. I just gave you a head start to make this fight fair, *Little Shadow.*"

He grunts, pressing the tip of his blade deeper into my neck. Squirming, I make a swirling motion with my hand. The water refuses to listen to me. My breathing turns labored.

"Any last words?" he asks, smirking. He leans in as if going to kiss me. "Such a shame our marriage was never consummated."

A small current forms around us. He gasps, dropping the dagger.

"I hope you enjoy hell, monster," I taunt.

Johann gets dragged by the relentless water, screaming as he dangles from the air. The current takes him away from me. I get up, the rain washing away the blood on my face.

"D'nanichi!" Héctor's voice calls out, coming up the steps.

I strap Johann's dagger to my belt, then run up to Hector, hugging him hard. I shake my head at his actions. "Why must you be so reckless? I had it! You promised me! You could've died had you—"

A cannon goes off once again, breaking more of *The Glory*. More screams and commands are thrown out. The ship begins to break apart, disintegrating into the sea.

"I do not know what overcame me," he says, holding my face in his hands. "I did not. I could not bear to lose you a second time." The rain slows "If I had lost you, I do not know what would have become of me. You are my world. My life. My love... or d'nanichi."

The rain stops all at once. Is that... is that what it means?

D'nanichi. My Love.

"Now, you tell me?" I ask, chuckling and with tears in my eyes. "In the middle of a fucking *battle*?"

Boom! Héctor holds me up, his brown eyes twinkling.

He laughs, tearing up. "I had to tell you eventually, no?"

"I really hate you sometimes, second mate," I lean in, looking at him.

He holds my face in his hands. The world could break apart around us, but at this moment, it's just me and him.

Forever.

"Thank you for everything," I say, "and for showing me how to truly live."

"D'nanichi..." he whispers, his lips close to mine. "I choose you. You are the one my heart desires. You are the one I cannot live without."

"And I choose you. Always and forever. You."

He pulls me in for a kiss.

The water recedes around us. It's as if time stands still, the world fading into a blissful haze. The softness of his touch ignites a fire within me, spreading warmth and comfort to the very depths of my corrupted soul.

His breath intermingles with mine, creating a delicate dance amongst this chaotic venture. I open up to my emotions for once. He caresses my cheeks, my hair, each gentle brush giving me a sense of belonging. Time seems to stretch, encapsulating the sheer beauty of that fleeting moment, leaving an indelible imprint on my heart.

I pull away, breathless. We both smile, joining our foreheads together. Immediately, I crave him, wanting another kiss.

"I know you are meant to rule the seas," he whispers. "But you are already the queen of my heart."

I lean in for another kiss. *Boom!* We're taken off balance once more. I stumble, but Héctor grabs me, standing me up. A high pitch whistle goes off in my ears.

Boom! Boom! A faint ringing. Gunshots. My vision blurs. Noises that will never leave me. Héctor talks to me, but I'm not focusing on his words. I'm focusing on what's coming from behind him. It's Nau, climbing up the stairs with his hands outstretched.

"Villanueva!" Nau screams, grabbing Héctor's neck.

I lunge at Nau, jumping on his back and tightening my fingers around his neck. He releases Héctor, shoving him on the crumbling quarterdeck. We're both struggling, two macabre dancers flirting with death. Nau slips and loses his balance, causing us both to fall backward over the wooden rail.

Héctor holds out his hand on the side of the ship, trying to reach me. But he's too far.

I can't grab on.

"Luz!" Héctor yells, his voice getting fainter by the second.

Johann and I are screaming, dropping into our doom.

"Héctor!" I shout as my body hits the treacherous oceans of hell with force.

The color of blood surrounds me.

I descend slowly into darkness and madness. With only one thought in my mind.

I choose you, Héctor. Always and forever.

CHAPTER
FIFTY-FIVE

The sharp aroma of antiseptic, tinged with the scent of disinfectants and sterile cleanliness, hits my sinuses, making me nauseous. It pervades the air with force and intensity.

I groan, realizing I'm lying on something comfortable. Opening my eyes hurts, so I keep them closed, a pounding headache preventing me from doing much. Soft cotton brushes against my exposed skin, a chill running up my spine. My body is overcome with pricks and pain.

"She's awake," a voice says. "Send for them."

Bring them?

Bring who?

Where am I?

Footsteps leave. My chest tightens.

"Who goes there?" I try to ask, but a whimper comes out instead.

"Careful now, she's been missing for a year," the same voice warns. "We don't know what she's been through."

A set of footsteps enter my vicinity. I open my eyes, even with the pain. A surge of brightness floods my eyes, searing me like a burst of fire. My pupils fight for a desperate attempt to shield themselves from the intense light. I can't see very well. I cover my face as I blink, trying to clear my vision, but it doesn't help. Moving my hands away from my face, five shadows stand before me.

Three in white clothing, two in neutral.

"Luz?" a voice asks. Octavia. It's Octavia. I tear up, which helps with my vision a bit.

"Octavia?" I ask, panic rising in me. Rapid beeping startles me. *What the hell is that?*

My vision clears enough for me to see faces. And I cannot believe the one that's right in front of me.

Smirking.

Mocking me.

I scream and jump on him, my fingers circling his neck. Johann. Alive. He's *alive*. Without bruises or cuts. In pristine condition. We fall on the ground, people screaming all around us. I choke him, screaming at him. Others yell, trying to separate us.

"Where is he? Where are they?" I demand, my fingers digging further into his tender flesh, cutting the air from his trachea.

"Luz... Luz, please!" he struggles, his voice soft and pleading. He tries to touch me, but I squirm away from his touch, screaming.

"WHERE ARE THEY?"

Two sets of hands yank me away from Nau. I get lifted off the ground as I scream and kick my legs. Nau coughs, rubbing his neck. A person with a white coat runs up to him.

"Let me go!" I scream, flailing my arms around.

"Doctor! Should we sedate her?" a person grabbing me asks.

Doctor?

I study my surroundings.

The walls of the room are painted a soft seafoam green, reminiscent of the waters that engulfed me. Large windows overlooking the city and lush greenery offer ample natural light. Ferns and orchids sit next to my bed. My heart threatens to rip out of my chest. EKG machines beep next to me.

I find Octavia's down-turned brown eyes. Her complexion, usually warm and glimmering, has been drained of its natural vigor. Flickers of pain and horrific memories pass through her weary, pained expression. She fidgets with a bracelet, betraying her emotional turmoil. She wears a simple outfit of leggings and a t-shirt.

Bile comes up in my throat, and I heave acidic waste into a small trash bin, my throat burning. I stand afterward, encountering a mirror. A scream is lodged in my throat.

It's me.

Rabid looking. Covered in dirt, cuts, and bruises. My hair hits my shoulders. I've easily lost over fifteen pounds. My face is hollow. My body is less pronounced and round, my shoulders hunched. I wear a thin pristine hospital gown, covering my once plush figure. My arms are covered in scratchy, white bandages. They applied a salve to my face.

No.

It can't be.

Three IVs are connected to my right arm and I rip them all out with a swift move. The machines blare loudly in the room. The nurses and doctor try to catch me and put those back in me, but I bolt out past the door.

I need to leave this place.

The vinyl floor under my feet is freezing, the fluorescent lights from the hall blinding me. I wince, bringing my hands up protectively. People stare at me in awe.

"It's her," a patient acknowledges.

"The actress who was missing," a nurse says, covering her mouth.

My chest tightens, their words and gasps overwhelming me. I scream, covering my ears. My knees give out underneath.

It can't be.

I can't be.

"Luz? Breathe," Octavia calls out after me, standing in a protective stance. "Breathe."

"Octavia!" I cry. "Nau. He tried to kill me. In there!"

She shakes her head, offering me a hand. "Who's Nau? Luz... you attacked Oliver."

"Oliver?"

She helps me up, and I grip my chest with my left hand. She leads me back inside, soothing me with me. From the doorway, I watch as Nau is being tended to by the nurse, his hair hitting the nape of his neck. His face is clean shaven and hollow. His outfit consists of black pants and a blue hoodie.

It can't be.

"Oliver?" I ask, my voice cracking. He nods, turning to me.

His face etched with lines of exhaustion. His once vibrant eyes now reflect a mix of hope and guilt, glistening with unshed tears. Deep furrows trace his pallid face and forehead, evidence of sleepless nights and countless prayers.

No. That's not Oliver.

It *can't* be Oliver.

"Luz," he says, standing. "My Luz."

He reaches out to me, and I back away, not wanting to be touched by him.

No. It's not him.

It can't be him.

"Is it really you?" I whisper.

It's not Oliver. It's Johann Nau. It has to be. And if that's Nau, Héctor is somewhere nearby. Waiting for me. As is the crew.

Maybe I died and I'm trying to be revived. Maybe Héctor is holding my hand through it all, waiting for me to wake up, so we can live our life together with James.

"Yes, my love," he says. I tense up. Héctor. *My love.* "It's me. Oliver. *Your* Oliver."

If he's Oliver, then that means…

No.

I fall to my knees, Oliver rushing to me. The doctor and nurses stand back, giving me the space I require. My chest tightens, my vision blurs. Oliver embraces me, his touch sending shivers down my spine. Machines beep all around us, voices chatter in the front hall. A door slams, Octavia curses in Creole.

"I'm really back?" I ask.

"Yes, you're really back," Oliver assures, caressing my head. "It's been a year, but you're back. And you're safe now. No one will hurt you now."

My scream turns into a sob, my heart sinking into depths I never knew existed. The air feels heavy, and every breath I take requires an immense effort. The vibrant hospital is suffocatingly silent except for my anguish.

I push Oliver off, realization hitting me like a tidal wave. It crashes into my chest with an unbearable force. Someplace places their hand on my back as I mourn.

My destiny. My crew.

My love.

Gone.
Because I'm back where I began.

END OF BOOK 1

ACKNOWLEDGMENTS

Oh my God, y'all, I wrote a book. Like a full one. With a beginning, middle and end. All I'm going to say is... I'm *tired.*

I first came up with this idea in 2016 and it was drastically different from the product you just finished reading. I tore this up, gave up, fixed it, gave up again, scrapped it completely, researched, and cried until I finally found the story I wanted to tell. Now, I can't believe I'm sharing it with other people and I couldn't be more grateful for the opportunity to give you a piece of my heart, mind and soul.

There's so many people I want to thank, but I want to start off with my parents. They never knew at first that I was writing this book and I was really nervous to tell them. I finally mustered up the courage on my 22nd birthday and well, here I am. Your support means everything to me. You've made a lot of sacrifices so that I could achieve this dream and I'll never be able to repay you for it. I couldn't ask for better parents. Los quiero mucho.

My sisters. Thank you for letting me mess with you both (wink, wink). You're both some of the best people I know and even if I don't say it a lot, I'd be lost without you. Life would be so boring without you both and you make me work harder to give you guys a chance to follow your heart. I can only hope to be the big sister you both deserve and I can't wait to watch you both achieve your dreams. Also, thank you for providing me with plenty of inspiration for both James and Dominico. Love y'all!

Marie. Where do I even start, bestie? This book would not exist without you and your unhinged–yet helpful– comments. I can't begin thanking you enough for helping me. Your patience, kindness, and knowledge will never go underappreciated. I can't wait to see you succeed. I can't wait to own your book. I can't wait to fangirl over you and tell everyone I knew you before you rose to fame. You're one of the best people I've ever met. Thank you for everything.

Jeremmy. Because of you, my word count went up drastically (for a good cause), Cyrus got more scenes (for some weird reason), and a spin-off novella is in the works. You were an amazing beta reader (minus the death threat) and a much greater friend. I can't wait for you to sit down and actually write that book of yours so I can return the favor of threatening to burn your house down. Just because you got a paragraph doesn't mean I'm not mad at you. Please don't let the fact that you're mentioned here go to your head. Love you!

Lana. Girl. My inspiration. My bestie. My beautiful hypothetical wife. Thank you for hyping me up since day one of me coming public with this book. Thank you for all the support you've given me. You're the sunshine in my life and you're an amazing human being. I'd be nothing without you. Love you lots, wife.

My editors, Danielle and Shay. I love you both. Thank you both for yelling at me about the commas and holding me at gunpoint to add them. You're both so talented and your skills made me grow so much. I honestly would be lost without your guidance, advice and threats.

My mentor/editor, Ashlynn. Besides your never-ending thirst for Pedro (I mean... same), I really appreciate your insight, knowledge and sessions. You're amazing and I can't wait to see you be the successful woman I know you can be.

My beta readers. I love you all so much. Your feedback was so hilarious and helpful. I really appreciate each and every single one of you.

My besties. I would be nothing without your support and encouragement.

Kira and Omar. The two of you deserve the world. I'd die for the two of you.

To my illustrator, Clara. Girl. Your artwork is amazing. I bow down to you and your skills.

My cover designer, Kristin. You brought that messy vision in my head to life. Your talent is unmatched and I can't wait to continue working with you.

I also want to thank everyone who took their time to read A Touch of Destiny. I hope you guys enjoyed it and cried as much as I did. I love each and every single one of you who took a chance on this Puerto Rican author. Feel free to DM me on my social media or email me! I'd love to hear what you all think!

Mami y Papi. Gracias por todo. No sería nadie sin ustedes. Ustedes son mi razón de vivir y espero que los esté haciendo orgullosos. No puedo esperar a verlos otra vez. Los dos fueron inspiración para dos personajes. Los quiero demasiado. Gracias por creer en mí y darme todo. Me enorgullece ser su nieta.

AUTHOR BIO

Nicole Velazquez is a Puerto Rican author who writes fantasy, sci-fi, and dystopian stories filled with so many cliffhangers, it will make you want to fight her. She earned her undergraduate degree in Elementary Education from Indiana University, with concentrations on science and cultural education. She has a passion for storytelling, Caribbean history, and bringing awareness about matters that affect BIPOC communities. When she's not reading, writing or learning useless historical facts, she's a STEM teacher, and a menace to her family (and society). She currently resides in Indiana with her family and two dogs.

To connect with Nicole, you can sign up to her newsletter at www.authornicolevelazquez.com, and follow her on social media where she goes by @bookish.puertorican everywhere!

www.ingramcontent.com/pod-product-compliance
Lightning Source LLC
Chambersburg PA
CBHW022011300726
48970CB00003B/840